D1233016

His uncle disappeared down the hallway, a concerned look on his face. Alric sat back, resting his head against the wall, willing the ale to remain undisturbed in his stomach. He heard a door open, and then the familiar voice of his oldest brother, Alstan.

"He left early this morning, Father. I doubt he'll show his face around here anymore. There's nothing left for him in Weldwyn."

His father's voice, deeper but similar to his son's, boomed out, "About time. I can't stand people who work against their sovereign; it's the worse crime imaginable, in my opinion. You must remember that Alstan, for one day you'll be king."

"Yes, Father," the elder brother replied. "Do you think he'll cause any further problems?"

"I've made it quite plain in the capital that no one is to support his plan to rebel against the King of Merceria. We can't afford a war right now."

"Should we be taking precautions?" Alstan asked.

"I've sent word to the cities on the border. They'll keep an eye out for him. Hopefully, he'll skulk back under whatever rock he crawled out from and never be heard from again."

"So," muttered Alric, "the usurper has left. I suppose it'll be back to boring again. Pity, I was looking forward to a little excitement, not much happens around here these days."

He thought back to the joust and saw himself mounted on a large black horse. He was Alric the jouster, champion of all the cavaliers! A hand shook him awake, and he opened his eyes to see the face of his father looming over him.

"Alric? Are you all right?"

"Yes, Father," he stammered out, surprised at the interruption.

"Then get yourself to bed, boy. The last thing we need is a drunken prince passed out in the hallway."

Alric slowly rose to his feet and stood, wobbling, as he straightened his tunic. "Yes, Father," he said and staggered down the hall.

"And there," remarked Alstan, "goes the future of Weldwyn."

~

Also by Paul J Bennett

SERVANT OF THE CROWN, HEIR TO THE CROWN: BOOK ONE

After tragedy changes the course of his life, Gerald serves as a soldier for years until a single act of self-sacrifice thrusts his future into the world of politics.

Banished with little more than the clothes on his back, he seeks a new purpose, for what is a warrior who has nothing left to fight for?

A fateful meeting with another lost soul unmasks a shocking secret, compelling him to take up the mantle of guardian. Bandits, the Black Hand, and even the king, he battles them all for the future of the realm.

SWORD OF THE CROWN, HEIR TO THE CROWN: BOOK TWO

When an invading army crosses the Mercerian border, the only thing standing between victory and defeat is an heir to the crown with no battle experience.

Enter Dame Beverly Fitzwilliam, who has trained for this moment since she first held a sword. From her relentless pursuit of knighthood to the day she single-handedly saves the king's life and earns her spurs, she has searched for someone worthy of her fealty.

Her destiny will be determined in a monumental clash of forces where success can save the kingdom, but failure can only mean certain death.

MERCERIAN TALES: STORIES OF THE PAST, HEIR TO THE CROWN: BOOK 2.5

In a land where true heroism is more likely to be rewarded with accusations of treason, comes a recounting of past adventures by the unsung heroes of the realm.

From meeting a witch willing to sacrifice all in defense of her companions, to the discovery of hereunto unknown creature preying on the hapless villagers of Mattingly, to the act of simply falling off a horse changing the future of the realm, their accounts are spellbinding.

More than just a collection of short stories, it falls chronologically between books two and three of the Heir to the Crown series and can be read at any time.

HEART OF THE CROWN

Heir to the Crown: Book Three

PAUL J BENNETT

Copyright © 2018 Paul J Bennett
Cover Illustration Copyright © 2018 Christie Kramberger
Portrait Copyright © 2018 Amaleigh Photography

All rights reserved. No part of this book may be reproduced, stored in a retrieval system, or transmitted in any form, or by any means, electronic, mechanical, photocopying, recording or otherwise, without prior permission of the author.

First Edition: August 2018

Print ISBN: 978-1-7753355-6-6

This book is a work of fiction. Any similarity to any person, living or dead is entirely coincidental.

Dedication

To my team of Beta Readers, who allowed me to take this simple story and make it into an epic tale.

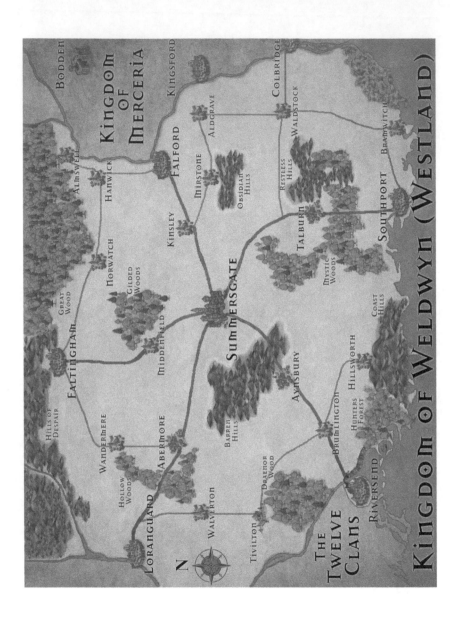

Kingdom of Weldwyn (Westland)

ONE

Alric

SPRING 960 MC* (MERCERIAN CALENDAR)

The dancers moved in harmony across the floor, their slow, measured steps carried out in perfect unison. They were ablaze with colour, for the noble lords and ladies of the Kingdom of Weldwyn vied to outdo each other with their finery.

Alric was not impressed. He sat, watching their movements, bored with the majesty of it, his young mind filled rather with thoughts of combat and glory. His musings were rudely interrupted.

"Alric, did you hear me?"

He glanced up to see the face of his mother, Queen Igraine, looming down on him in disapproval.

"Sorry, Mother," he answered.

"Don't sorry me, we have guests to attend to. I know you're young, but you're still a prince, and you have responsibilities."

"To do what? Dance with the young ladies?"

His mother's frown grew increasingly intense, and he knew he had overstepped. "Sorry, Mother, it's just that they're all so..."

"So what?" she pressed.

"Sycophantic?"

"Well, what do you expect? You're fifteen, Alric. Your brothers were both engaged by your age."

"That's not fair, Mother. Alstan is the heir, he had no choice, and you picked out Cuthbert's wife when he was only six." He watched her face soften but knew what was about to come.

"I'm sorry, Alric," she said. "I know it's a burden, but we are royals, we have responsibilities."

"And what, exactly, are my responsibilities?"

"We will have to see," she said, avoiding the answer, as always. "Now, let's get you onto the dance floor, shall we? You have an impression to make."

He knew he was defeated, as always, but he could never stay upset with his mother for long. Rising to his feet, he straightened his tunic and was about to step onto the dance floor when the music stopped, the melody complete. He glanced about desperately, anything to avoid the attention of Lady Julianne, who was now walking toward him. His eyes rested on his oldest brother, and he moved toward the eldest prince with purpose. Lady Julianne tried to talk to him, but he pretended not to hear and strode past, ignoring her entirely.

"Alstan," he called out.

Prince Alstan was standing in a small knot of people and turned upon hearing his name. His face lit up. "Alric? What is it?"

The young prince had kept walking until he was directly in front of his brother, but now words failed him. He had been so eager to avoid the attention of the young lady that he had stumbled into what perhaps might be an even more embarrassing moment. He glanced back over his shoulder to see Julianne bearing down on him, and he felt a moment of panic.

"Court," he blurted out, "something about the court."

Alstan knit his brows, "I'm surprised you heard about that. I didn't think you had an interest in such things."

Now that Alric was part of the conversation, he dove in, desperate to avoid the unpleasant encounter he had run from. "I was quite fascinated," he said, trying to sound like he knew what he was talking about. "Tell me more."

Alstan pursed his lips, and Alric knew he recognized his bluff. Luckily, his brother also knew not to embarrass his family in a public place, but that didn't mean he wouldn't have fun with it.

"He's coming back tomorrow," Alstan said at last. "You should come by and see how Father deals with him."

Alric had no clue what his brother was talking about but felt trapped. "What was the fellow's name again?" he asked.

Alstan smiled, "Lord Garig of Eastwood."

"From Mercenaria?"

Alstan leaned in close to whisper, "I've told you before, Alric, they call themselves Merceria now, have done for centuries. If you had spent as much time with your books as your sword, you'd know that."

Alric blushed. "Of course," he said, "but why would a Mercerian noble come to our court?"

"He wants to raise a rebellion against his king."

Alric snorted, "Father won't go for that."

"True," said Alstan, "but Father is wise enough not to dismiss him out of hand. He told him to come back tomorrow. He wants to hear his story in private."

"And by private, you mean..."

"With his advisors, of course, the usual bunch."

"So you, as his heir, will be there."

"Precisely," said Alstan, a smile crossing his face, "but I think you should be there too. It'll do you good."

Alric was not sure it would be a positive experience, but he had buried himself in his rush to avoid the young lady, and now he was committed.

"Besides," said Alstan, interrupting his thoughts, "Lord Weldridge will be there."

Alric's eyes lit up, "Uncle Edwin?"

"Yes, and I believe he just might have a seat for you at the tourney."

Alric smiled; a day at the jousts was just what he needed. He heard soft footsteps approaching from behind, but now his mood was joyous at the thought of tomorrow's activities. He wheeled about suddenly to face a startled Lady Julianne.

"Lady Julianne," he said, bowing deeply, "what a pleasant surprise. May I have the honour of this dance?"

He took her hand as she looked on in surprise, and led her to the dance floor; Uncle Edwin always said it was best to take the bull by the horns.

King Leofric of Weldwyn sat on a chair at the head of the table as Alric and Alstan entered. The king's eyebrows rose when he saw his youngest son.

"Alric? Are you ill?"

It was Alstan who spoke up, "No, Father, I thought he might benefit by coming. Shall I send him away?"

"No," responded the king, "it's good he's here. He'll give me another perspective. Come and sit beside me," he said, indicating the seats to his left. "Lord Weldridge will be here shortly, and then we'll let our visitor in."

They sat down and waited while the servants brought wine. Before they could pour, the king interrupted them, "I'll do that. Leave us."

After the servants left, Leofric turned to his sons, "Listen, but don't interrupt. You may ask questions if you like, but don't accuse and don't comment. We'll feel him out, see what he really wants."

Alric thought the whole affair was probably going to be a waste of time but nodded his head dutifully. The door opened to admit Lord Weldridge.

"Edwin," said the king, "good of you to come."

"Thank you, Sire, it was gracious of you to invite me. And what do we have here, do my eyes deceive me? Two Princes of the Realm?"

Alric blushed. It was all an act, he knew, and yet he was always glad to see his lordship. Lord Edwin Weldridge was not related by blood, but he may as well have been. He was the lifetime friend of the king, and to the rest of the family, he was simply Uncle Edwin, except, of course, at official functions.

"To what," Edwin said, glancing at the two young men, "do I owe the pleasure of such grand company?"

King Leofric spoke, "Alstan thought it might do Alric some good, learning the ways of court and such."

"Hmm," said Lord Weldridge, "I suspect it's a bit more than that, but perhaps that's a discussion for another day." He looked to the king, "What do we know of this fellow we're about to see?"

Other than his mother, Alric had only ever seen Uncle Edwin talk so informally to the king.

"The fellow who's coming to see us is a noble from Merceria."

"Merceria, you say? Anyone I might have heard of?"

"I doubt it; a man named Lord Garig. He's a minor noble, but he comes representing the Earl of Eastwood. What do you know of this earl?"

Weldridge pursed his lips as he often did when thinking. "I believe he's a very powerful man, Leofric, perhaps one of the most powerful men in their kingdom. We'd best listen carefully to what his representative has to say rather than dismiss him out of turn. Are we sure this isn't some type of trick?"

The king smiled, "I knew you'd say something like that. I've had the Steward of the Heralds check his documents. The seals are legitimate, as far as we can tell."

"Well then," said Weldridge, "let's get the man in here and see what he has to say."

King Leofric called out the order, and the door swung open, revealing a middle-aged man with a plump belly and a shortage of hair atop of his head. He stepped forward, bending his knee as he bowed.

"Your Majesty," he said, "I bring you greetings from the Earl of Eastwood."

"Please, Lord Garig, arise. Come, sit down, have some wine. We have plenty of time to discuss matters."

The man took a seat at the end of the table while servants rushed in to provide him with wine. Alric noticed that the maid, Lerna, was serving; the Royal Family had trusted her for years. She would remain during the discussion to look after them, and her excellent memory could be counted on for an accurate account of the dealings.

"Now, Lord, tell us what has brought you to our court," encouraged Lord Weldridge.

The Mercerian took a small sip of wine. "Thank you, Lord. I have the esteemed pleasure to offer you the chance to deal with a... let's say, problem, that has been plaguing your border for years." The man looked at the faces around him as he spoke, trying to draw them into his speech.

"What problem might that be?" asked Alric.

"Yes, please," said the king, "do explain, my youngest son is not familiar with the politics of Merceria."

Lord Garig smiled and nodded at Alric. To Alric's mind, the man looked like a serpent preparing to strike, but he sat still and listened, heeding his father's earlier words.

"There has oft been trouble between Merceria and Westland," the man started.

"Westland?" asked Alric.

Alstan leaned close to him and whispered, "That's what they call Weldwyn."

"Why Westland?" asked Alric, still confused.

"Think about it for a moment, Alric. Honestly, sometimes you can be as thick as a post."

The king's glare quieted the elder brother. Alric, finally understanding the name, nodded to himself, pleased with his conclusion.

Lord Garig, who had waited while the two brothers were whispering, now continued, "As I was saying, there has oft been trouble between our two kingdoms and it is known that the court of... Weldwyn would prefer to have a friendly neighbour. The Earl of Eastwood is proposing just such an arrangement."

"I see," contemplated the king, "and what would the earl want in return for this friendship?"

The man took a sip of his wine. Alric watched him closely, realizing he was trying to build courage for his next statement.

"His Lordship would wish you to support his claim to the throne."

There was silence at the table as the words sank in.

"I was not aware," said the king at last, "that the position of King of Merceria was available."

"Strictly speaking, it is not," agreed Lord Garig, "but King Andred is unpopular, and the people demand someone more... reasonable."

King Leofric nodded in understanding, "I see. Please tell me Lord Garig, what sort of support would the earl require?"

"Troops, Your Majesty, to ensure a... smooth transition of power."

Alric observed the neck muscles tightening on his father's throat; this suddenly had become very interesting.

"Let me get this straight," King Leofric clarified, "you would like us to send soldiers into Merceria to support the earl's bid for power. Is that correct?"

Lord Garig sat back, and Alric recognized an obvious look of triumph on the man's face. Little did he know what was about to happen.

"Precisely," the visitor agreed.

King Leofric looked to Lord Weldridge and raised his eyebrows. Uncle Edwin looked back, and as their eyes met, the king simply nodded, ever so slightly.

"Tell me," said Lord Weldridge, "what do you think would happen if a foreign army invaded Merceria?"

"Why, the people would flock to their side, my lord," said the Mercerian.

"I doubt it. Instead, they would unite in defense against a foreign invasion, and then both Merceria and Weldwyn would be embroiled in a war."

Alric watched his father as he stood, looking squarely at the man.

"I will not support this endeavour," he stated. "Weldwyn and Merceria have never been friends, but to act against your lawful king is treason, and I will have no part of it. You will leave our kingdom immediately."

The man opened his mouth to speak, but Lord Weldridge stood alongside King Leofric, "I think it's time you left. Alstan? Alric? Perhaps you would escort his lordship from the chambers?"

Alric sprang from his seat at the unexpected mention of his name. So taken by surprise was he that he banged his knee on the table as he stood. He tried to be stoic and ignore the pain, following his brother, only to limp as he went.

Lord Garig, for his part, kept calm, leaving the chamber to meet his own retinue outside.

Alric and Alstan watched the man depart; no doubt he would cause trouble elsewhere, but his time in Weldwyn was done.

TWO

News from Court

SPRING 960 MC

The brisk wind blowing in from the east cooled the day as Alric joined his uncle Edwin in the Royal Box. Below, the sight of the men armouring up was quite riveting.

"I hope I haven't missed anything, Uncle," said Alric, peering down at the contestants.

"No, Alric. They're still preparing. It looks to be a good turnout today."

"Who do we favour?" asked the young prince.

"Keep an eye on young Jack, Alric. I think he might surprise you."

"Why is that, Uncle?"

"Take a look," he said, pointing. "See that older man down there, the one with the neatly trimmed grey beard? Do you know who that is?"

Alric stood to get a better view. "Can't say that I do. Is he someone important?"

Edwin smiled, "That's Ned Hathaway. He was the champion of Weldwyn years ago. He's come out of retirement to help Jack Marlowe."

"Marlowe, I know that name," pondered Alric.

"So you should, he's the son of the Viscount of Aynsbury.

"Aynsbury, that's where Father purchased my horse."

"Yes, the Viscount is quite proud of his stables. His breeding stock is said to be the best in the kingdom."

"I'm surprised," said Alric, "that the viscount allows his son to joust. Isn't it dangerous?"

Edwin chuckled, "Young Jack has always been headstrong. He'll do whatever he wants, and his father will simply have to put up with it; he's the only son, you see. Besides, I think secretly, the viscount is proud of his boy."

"They're mounting," interrupted Alric, the excitement raising his voice.

Lord Jack Marlowe hoisted himself into the saddle with ease, then held out his hand, waiting, while a servant rushed up with his helm. The young cavalier looked around the assembled crowd, spotting a group of women sitting near the lists. Jack was a good looking man, and he knew it. The cocky warrior smiled at the ladies as he placed his helm upon his head, the crowd cheering him on. Seizing his lance, he expertly guided his horse to one end of the lists.

His opponent, an imposing man, clad in a red surcoat, waited restlessly at the other end, his horse pawing at the ground. The two combatants nodded at each other, and then the man in red lowered his visor and set his lance. With a yell from the official, the horses began their trot toward the inevitable clash of steel. They quickly picked up speed, the trotting soon replaced by the thunder of galloping, and the crowd's yells grew in intensity as they approached each other.

There was a collective holding of breath at the moment of impact. The younger cavalier had placed his lance to perfection, catching his rival squarely on the chest. His opponent flew backwards, hurtling from his saddle, crashing into the ground below. Jack galloped on, only slowing his horse's pace as he arrived at the opposite end. He manoeuvred his mount into the turn, then looked back at his foe, removing his helmet to gain a better view. The red cavalier lay still, a group of men rushing towards him. Alric, noticing the local Life Mage running to assist, wondered how it felt, being struck from a horse. A moment later the mage began incanting and, much to everyone's relief, the man in red waved his arm to indicate he was fine.

"Outstanding," exclaimed Edwin. "Did you see how Jack twisted in the saddle, just before impact?"

Alric had been too excited to notice, but feigned acknowledgement, "Yes. Is that rare?"

"Rare?" uttered his uncle. "I'll say it's rare. I've never seen its like. If his timing had been off, he'd have been skewered."

"How did that help?" asked Alric, eager to learn.

"Well, you see, Alric, by twisting as he did, he angled his shield to deflect his opponent's blow."

"Couldn't he have just moved his shield?"

"Shifting his body put more weight into the deflection. It was a master-stroke! The man must be a lunatic to try that. Let's go down and meet him, shall we?"

"Now? What about the next joust?"

"Oh, we have plenty of time. When they call the healer in, there's always a break. They'll want to make sure he's all right before they continue."

"Very well, Uncle, lead on."

The two of them made their way out from the box, which was slightly raised at the centre of the tournament field. Edwin led them onto the grass, and as they strolled toward Lord Jack, Alric spotted the man waving to the young women. He had ridden over to the seats and was leaning from his saddle as a lady gave him her kerchief.

"I see he has supporters," remarked Edwin.

"Supporters?"

"Yes, people who admire him. It's half the reason they joust, I think."

As they drew closer, Edwin called out, "Lord Jack?"

The young cavalier turned from the ladies to see his approaching visitors. A smile of recognition erupted on his face, and he bowed in respect.

"Your Highness, Lord Edwin."

"An impressive display," remarked Edwin. "I take it you've been keeping that in reserve?"

"Indeed," Jack replied. "I have a few tricks I'm saving."

"A risky tactic, I should say," Edwin stated.

"The rewards make the risk worthwhile," Jack replied, casting his eyes at the beauties nearby. "Tell me, Your Highness, what did you think?" he asked, now looking towards Alric.

"I think you're mad, Jack. You could have been killed."

The cavalier smiled at the comment, "Mad Jack, I like it. Suits me, don't you think?" Once again he glanced at the young ladies, who smiled in delight.

"Well," continued Edwin, "I shouldn't like to keep you from your duties, Jack."

"That's awfully kind of you, Lord Edwin," Jack replied. "I would hate to disappoint my supporters."

"Come along, Alric," Edwin prompted, "the other competitors are lining up. We need to get back to our seats."

They began making their way back to the Royal Box. "What do you make of it, Alric," his uncle asked.

"I've always wanted to joust," he replied. "I'd be a cavalier myself, if I could."

Edwin laughed, "Your father would never allow it. You're a royal, how would it look to have you speared in a tournament?"

"I know, I know, but I can dream, can't I?"

Edwin tussled his hair, "That's the spirit, Alric, never say die."

"Never say what?"

"Die, Alric. Never say die. It's an old expression, your father used to say it a lot when we were young. It means never give up, keep the hope alive."

"Of course, I knew that."

They sat back down in their box, waiting for the next round to begin.

"You seem distracted lately, Alric. Is something bothering you?"

Alric kept staring at the cavaliers gathering below as he answered, "Just the usual. I don't know my place. I'm not the heir, and I'm not the spare. I'm just... well, I don't know what I am."

"You're still young Alric, give it some time. You'll figure it out."

"I suppose so, Uncle."

"Tell you what," Edwin continued, "after the tourney, I'll take you down to the stables. We can talk to the competitors, maybe invite them back to the Palace for a drink."

"We can do that?"

"Of course we can, you're a prince, aren't you? Might as well have some fun with it."

Alric smiled, it was true. He might not have any real responsibilities, but he damn well had coins, so he might as well take advantage of it.

It turned out that cavaliers can't resist free ale, and so a number of them had taken the young prince up on his invitation. Alric was enthralled by their stories, though he suspected many of them were made up; there were far too many battles mentioned, at least to his mind. If all the stories were true, the kingdom would still be at war, even now! Once the alcohol was flowing freely, the conversation turned to another type of conquest; that of women and Alric felt out of his depth. It was his uncle who finally came to his rescue.

Alric sat on a chair, nursing a tankard of ale as the cavaliers regaled each other with tales of their accomplishments, ignoring the young prince. Each boast was louder and more ribald, in a quest to outdo their peers. Edwin rose from his chair, coming to stand over Alric, his shadow blocking what was left of the late afternoon sun which peered through the window.

"Heard enough?" he asked.

Alric looked up, his uncle appearing to his mind like some overpowering ancient hero. "I think so, Uncle," he replied, his voice slurring slightly.

"I think you've had enough of this," Edwin said, removing the tankard from the young prince's hand. "We should get you out of here."

"What about the cavaliers?" asked Alric.

"Let them be, they've earned it. I'll have them chased out later." Alric made to stand and found his legs were having difficulty working. "Easy there, now," urged Edwin, "take your time. There's no hurry."

His uncle, taking his arm to steady him, led Alric from the room, the noise of the champions of Weldwyn dying in the background as they made their way through the Palace.

"I think," said Alric, stopping suddenly, "that I might have to be sick."

Edwin's eyes opened wide, "Let's get you seated, and I'll arrange a bowl of some sort. We can't have you vomiting all over the Palace now, can we? What would your mother say?"

He sat down rather heavily onto a bench seat that was in the hallway.

"I'll be fine," he said, "I just need some water."

His uncle disappeared down the hallway, a concerned look on his face. Alric sat back, resting his head against the wall, willing the ale to remain undisturbed in his stomach. He heard a door open, and then the familiar voice of his oldest brother, Alstan.

"He left early this morning, Father. I doubt he'll show his face around here anymore. There's nothing left for him in Weldwyn."

His father's voice, deeper but similar to his son's, boomed out, "About time. I can't stand people who work against their sovereign; it's the worse crime imaginable, in my opinion. You must remember that Alstan, for one day you'll be king."

"Yes, Father," the elder brother replied. "Do you think he'll cause any further problems?"

"I've made it quite plain in the capital that no one is to support his plan to rebel against the King of Merceria. We can't afford a war right now."

"Should we be taking precautions?" Alstan asked.

"I've sent word to the cities on the border. They'll keep an eye out for him. Hopefully, he'll skulk back under whatever rock he crawled out from and never be heard from again."

"So," muttered Alric, "the usurper has left. I suppose it'll be back to boring again. Pity, I was looking forward to a little excitement, not much happens around here these days."

He thought back to the joust and saw himself mounted on a large black horse. He was Alric the jouster, champion of all the cavaliers! A hand shook him awake, and he opened his eyes to see the face of his father looming over him.

"Alric? Are you all right?"

"Yes, Father," he stammered out, surprised at the interruption.

"Then get yourself to bed, boy. The last thing we need is a drunken prince passed out in the hallway."

Alric slowly rose to his feet and stood, wobbling, as he straightened his tunic. "Yes, Father," he said and staggered down the hall.

"And there," remarked Alstan, "goes the future of Weldwyn."

THREE

The Traitor

SPRING 960 MC

Alric's cavaliers, as they soon came to be known, had been a welcome diversion for the young prince, but now he had grown bored of them. It became apparent that they had little respect for him, but a great deal of respect for his coins, and so he simply stopped hosting them. This had the secondary effect of allowing him to awake each morning refreshed, rather than hung over.

It was a dreary morning this day, with dark clouds threatening rain. A portend, perhaps? He shrugged off the thought; the Gods didn't send portends, they merely watched things unfold. Mankind was far too fickle by itself to demand the direct attention of the Gods. He had decided to wander downstairs and get something to eat, but as he began descending the staircase, he heard rapid footsteps and turned to see Alstan hurrying behind him. His elder brother rushed past, ignoring him, his face decorated with a look of concern.

"Alstan?" he called out, but his brother kept going.

This must be something exciting, he thought, and so he followed along behind. Down the hallway Alstan ran, his younger brother desperately trying to catch up, his stride not quite up to that of his taller brother. Alric rounded the corner to see him enter their father's study, and rushed forward, grabbing the door before it could fully shut. He opened the door slightly, peering inside to see his brother, along with his mother, father, and uncle Edwin. Alstan was talking in a rush while everyone listened to him intently. Alric slipped into the room, closing the door quietly behind him.

"We've just received news, Father. I'm afraid it's bad," Alstan began.

"Spit it out, son," the king urged.

"I have just received word from Falford. Lord Garig has convinced the baron to support his plan."

There was a collective gasp in the room, and the king looked to the queen. "This is bad," Queen Igraine said, "if troops from Weldwyn cross into Merceria, it will be war."

"We must put a stop to it as quickly as possible," said Edwin. "We have to act before it's too late."

The king absorbed the details. "It's likely already too late. By the time we send troops to Falford, they'll have crossed the border."

"What shall we do?" asked the queen.

"We must do what we can," announced the king. "What are our options, Edwin?"

The slightly younger man pursed his lips in thought before speaking, "We must arrest the baron immediately, of course. We have to take action to show we don't support this."

"What if he's crossed the border with his troops?" asked Alstan. "Do we go after him?"

"No!" decreed the king. "Under no circumstances do you cross the border."

"I agree," said the queen, "it would only make the matter worse. If we cross the border to follow, it might be construed as a full-scale invasion."

"Send me," implored Alstan. "I can leave within the hour. I'll arrest the baron. Perhaps, if we're fast enough, we can get there before they march; it takes time to assemble an army."

"Very well," the king agreed, "leave as quickly as you can. Take a company of horse. I'll issue a warrant for his arrest immediately."

"Let me go with him," piped up Alric. "I can help."

The king turned in surprise at the sound of his youngest son's voice but recovered quickly. "Very well, Alric, go with your brother, but remember my words, gentlemen; under no circumstances are you to cross the border."

Alstan turned and quickly left, with Alric following along behind.

The door closed and the queen looked to her husband, her face full of understanding. "You think it's too late, don't you?"

"I do," he replied. "We received word today, but the message likely took five or six days to get to us. It'll take just as long for Alstan to get there. The army has marched, I am sure of it."

"Then Malin help us," the queen avowed, "for the future of the kingdom is now in jeopardy."

~

The ride to Falford was long and arduous, and by the time the rooftops of the city came into view, Alric was sore. He considered himself an excellent horseman, but five full days in the saddle had left him with aching legs, and a backside that begged for release from the saddle.

The city looked so peaceful from this point of view as the contingent rode down the hill toward the river valley wherein lay the town. No guards accosted them, and Alric's fear that the city had risen in revolt were soon put to rest. They entered the cobblestone streets, making their way to the baron's estate; a large house set back from the river. To their amazement, they were welcomed; a groom taking their horses, seemingly unaware of any impending emergency. Could they have been wrong? They were escorted inside, where a servant offered them food and drink. The baron, they were told, was indisposed but would be with them shortly.

"What do you make of it, Alstan?"

His elder brother looked about the finely appointed room, before speaking, "It looks pretty normal here."

"Could the reports have been wrong?"

"No," Alstan said defensively, "it's from a trusted source."

"So what do we do?"

"Don't offer any information. We'll talk to him first, then arrest him once we confirm some details. Just follow my lead."

"Very well," Alric agreed.

Shortly after the door opened, the Baron of Falford stepped through. Lord Hartly Babbington was a middle-aged fellow, with a rosy complexion and a healthy appetite. His robust frame was tightly squeezed into a well-made surcoat, while jewels adorned his fingers.

"Your Highnesses," he began, "I'm sorry I wasn't here to welcome you, but your visit was most unexpected, and I was otherwise engaged. I trust you've been looked after?"

"We have," replied Alstan. "Thank you. Your servants have been most gracious."

"Excellent," their host said, moving toward a chair. "Pray sit, and tell me the purpose of your visit."

"We have heard," said Alstan, taking a seat on a comfortable looking armchair, "that an army was raised to invade Merceria."

If they were hoping to see surprise on the baron's face, they were very disappointed. "That's true," he said, simply. "What of it?"

"Only the king can order troops across the border. It's an act of war!"

"My dear prince," the baron replied, "calm yourself. I assure you that no Weldwyn troops have entered Merceria."

"But troops did march?"

"Yes, certainly," the baron said, smiling.

To Alric's mind, the nobleman was playing a devious game of some sort.

"Can you explain how that can be true?" Alstan said at last. "Did troops enter Merceria from Weldwyn or not?"

The baron paused to take a sip of wine. "Yes, Your Highness, troops did cross the border, but they were not from Weldwyn. They were mercenaries."

"Mercenaries?" Alric blurted out. "Where would mercenaries come from?"

"Perhaps the term 'mercenaries' gives the wrong idea," stated the baron. "Let's instead call them volunteers."

Now it was Alstan's turn to speak out, "You let troops cross into Merceria without royal approval. You've committed treason!"

"Have I, Your Highness? I think not. The rebellion against the King of Merceria will succeed, and then there will be a friendly monarch on the throne. Surely that outcome is worth the gamble?"

"You're a fool, Baron," spat out Alstan. "Do you have any idea what the Mercerian army is like?"

"They're a bunch of barbarians," the baron stated. "A few hundred volunteers should easily be able to defeat them."

"I've studied Merceria," Alstan continued, calming himself. "I've learned all I can about them. They have a massive army, much bigger than ours, easily twice the size. Do you know why?"

The baron, caught off guard by this tidbit of information, simply shook his head.

"The entire kingdom was founded by mercenaries. They even call it the warrior's crown. To them, fighting is everything. They've been fighting for their survival since they first formed the kingdom, been in almost a constant state of warfare. You've just given them an excuse to invade Weldwyn."

Alric was taken aback. He had always thought of Merceria as the enemy, but he had no idea what they were really like. To hear they had such numbers troubled him deeply.

"In the name of the Crown, I place you under arrest on the charge of treason," Alstan announced, the rage gone from his voice, to be replaced by resignation. "We will be escorting you back to the capital to face judgement."

"I'm sure the king will understand-"

"The penalty for treason is death," Alstan interrupted. "The king issued the warrant for your arrest." He produced the warrant, handing it to the baron, whose face grew pale as he read it.

"Guards!" called Alstan and four of the king's men entered the room. "Take this man into custody. We'll ride out as soon as the horses have been watered."

The soldiers escorted the prisoner out, while the baron blubbered. "It's all a misunderstanding!" he shouted, but Alstan ignored him.

The room fell silent as the elder prince paced.

"Is it as bad as it sounds?" Alric asked.

"Yes," Alstan replied. "War is looming, and I fear a Mercerian reprisal. They're a bloodthirsty kingdom and no friend to Weldwyn. We're in no shape to face them."

"Surely the army-" protested Alric.

"No," interrupted Alstan. "The bulk of the army is west. The Twelve Clans have been restless of late, and there have been signs we might have to repel an invasion. This comes at the worst possible time."

"The Clans have always been restless. What makes this any different?" Alric enquired.

"In the past, they were always distracted by infighting, but now they seem united in their determination to expand their borders. Word is they even elected a High King, something that has never happened before, as far as we know."

"A High King?"

"Yes, each of the twelve clans have always had their own chieftain, but never have all the clans spoken with a single voice. Now it seems they've buried their differences."

Alric fell silent. Events were rapidly building, but to what end he didn't understand.

FOUR

Treason!

SPRING 960 MC

King Leofric of Weldwyn sat upon his throne, staring at the man in front of him. Lord Hartly Babbington, the Baron of Falford stood before him in chains, his face staring at the floor, ready to face the king's justice. The members of the Earls' Council were nearby, waiting to hear the proclamation. Everyone in the room knew there could be but one outcome; death, for the baron's actions had placed the security of the entire kingdom in peril.

The king spoke only two words, "Explain yourself."

"Your Majesty," Lord Babbington pleaded, "I have only acted in the best interests of the Crown. Long have we feared our neighbours to the east. For almost a thousand years we have lived under the threat of attack from Merceria. It was only a matter of time before they once again tried to conquer us."

The king was not a man easily moved. "And so," he said, "you thought you'd accelerate the process and convince them to invade us sooner?"

The baron's face paled, "That was never my intention, Your Majesty. I was assured the uprising had an excellent chance of succeeding. It would have placed a sympathetic king on the throne of our nemesis."

"Tell me, Lord Babbington," the king continued, unswayed by the man's arguments, "what do you know of Lord Garig?"

The baron straightened his back and raised his face to look directly at the king.

"He is a most trustworthy man," he said. "He represents powerful nobles in the realm of Merceria."

"And how, precisely, do you know this?"

Lord Babbington was suddenly at a loss for words.

The king continued, "Did he mention, by name, the nobles who support him, by any chance? Did he indicate how many troops they had raised on their own? Perhaps he gave you an outline of how their military campaign might progress?"

The baron stared dully at the king.

"I thought not," said the king. "It appears, Lord Babbington that you have failed us completely. This Lord Garig came to our court with empty promises. Since that time, I have had people look into him. There is no record of a lord by that name in Merceria, as far as we can tell. You have been lied to, and the result is that your actions have placed the entire kingdom in jeopardy."

"Surely not, Your Majesty. We have the mightiest army-"

"Our army is woefully unprepared to fight off an invasion from the east. The bulk of them have been sent west to stave off incursions by the Twelve Clans. We cannot fight on two borders; we haven't the numbers."

"Then perhaps, Your Majesty, we need a stronger leader!"

The entire room sat in silence, stunned at the words.

King Leofric rose to his feet, stepping toward the condemned man. "If you were unhappy with my leadership, you should have brought it to the attention of the Earls' Council. As it is, you have violated the law. I have no choice but to pass judgement on you." He looked around to see the nods of approval from the assembled nobles. "It is my judgement that you be stripped of your title and condemned to death. The execution will take place within the week." He cast his eyes around the room. "What say you, my lords?"

Almost as one, the nobles agreed. The king waited for the noise to die down. "Very well," he continued, "the earls have spoken. You shall be taken from this place to the dungeons. Your execution shall be carried out in public as soon as arrangements can be made. Take him away!"

The guards came forward, grabbing the prisoner by his arms. The former Baron of Falford was dragged, screaming, from the room.

"Now, my lords," continued the king, as the sounds died in the distance, "we must make plans. We have to decide how we will respond to this emergency. Let us adjourn to more comfortable quarters."

The earls followed the king from the throne room.

Alric had just returned from a ride and was walking past the throne room

when the door opened. A guard held the door as his father entered the hallway. "Ah, Alric, go and fetch Alstan and meet me in the reading room."

"Father?"

"We're meeting with the Earls' Council, I want you both there."

"What about Cuthbert?"

"I've sent him west with the army. We'll send word to keep him
informed. Now hurry along, we've no time to waste."

It didn't take long for Alric to locate his oldest brother; he was sitting
outside with his wife, Lady Elswith. Alstan's marriage had been arranged
years ago; his wife's father was a powerful earl. The two princes took their
leave of the Lady, making their way to the reading room, their father's
favourite place to hold meetings. It was a large room, full of bookshelves,
boasting a long table, around which sat almost the entire Earls' Council.
King Leofric preferred the more relaxed atmosphere of the room to the
official council chambers, and the earls tended to agree.

"Ah, Alstan, Alric, come and have a seat," their father invited.

They dutifully took their places, while a servant brought them
some wine.

"I have asked my sons here," continued the king, "so that if something
should happen to me, the plans may be continued." King Leofric raised his
hands to still any objections. "Let me assure you, gentlemen, I am in perfect
health, but sometimes decisions must be made by local commanders, and
since my sons could command our military forces, it is imperative that they
understand what is happening."

Alric scanned the faces of the earls. They seemed calmed by the
statement.

"Now, let us continue," the king said. "I've asked the Earl of Faltingham
to go over the salient points. If you would, Edwin?"

Lord Weldridge stood, the better to command the earls' attention. "We
find ourselves in a prickly situation, gentlemen. Due to the actions of the
traitor, we are faced with the prospect of an invasion."

There were nods from the earls; they had all born witness to Lord
Babbington's sentence.

"How dire is it?" asked Lord Warford.

"If it had happened last year, we'd be in a relatively good place, but with
the recent developments in the west, we've been forced to move the bulk of
our army. Our eastern border is now woefully unprepared."

"Can't we recall the army?" asked Lord Mainbridge.

"And leave the western border to the mercy of the Clans?" someone said.

"I'm afraid," continued Lord Weldridge, "that Lord Canning is correct. We cannot move troops off the western border without exposing us to more danger."

Once again, Lord Mainbridge raised a concern, "Is it possible that Merceria has incited the Twelve Clans for this very reason, to strip away our defenses in the east?"

"We cannot eliminate the possibility," continued Lord Weldridge, "though I think it unlikely. Coordinating such a move would prove difficult."

"Yes," agreed Alstan, "we know the Clansmen to the west seldom work with each other, let alone allies that live hundreds of miles away."

"So," continued Lord Mainbridge, "we can't get more troops eastward. What do you propose, that we just offer them the Crown of Weldwyn?"

There were objections all round, and Lord Weldridge let them die down before speaking. "King Leofric has suggested we send a delegate to the court of Merceria and try to reason with them."

Once again objections arose, but the king stood, quieting the room. "I know you think of Merceria as the enemy, and in some ways, they have been. Since the founding of our kingdom, they have been an ever-present threat to our east. Despite our prejudices, they are people, much like us; I have to believe that. I believe they can be reasoned with."

"Your Majesty," objected Lord Canning, "are you suggesting we subjugate ourselves?"

"No, Aelford. I'm suggesting that diplomacy might work where arms have failed in the past. It will, at least, buy us some time. If we stabilize our western border, we can move troops east to mitigate the threat."

"And who shall we send?" asked Lord Mainbridge. "Surely not the Crown Prince?"

"No," interjected Lord Weldridge, "I have volunteered to go."

The room grew quiet as each person thought it through. It would be a dangerous mission, they all knew it. It was just as likely that the King of Merceria would execute an envoy from Weldwyn instead of welcoming him.

"I admire your courage," Lord Mainbridge spoke up, "and we send our prayers that you might be successful."

"Thank you, gentlemen," Lord Weldridge returned. "I shall pray to Malin for guidance."

As the conversation devolved into details, Alric soon lost interest. His uncle was going to Merceria! He wondered what this might portend. Such a mission had never before been attempted; surely they were on the cusp of great events!

FIVE

The Court of Wincaster

SPRING 960 MC

I t was late spring as Lord Edwin Weldridge, Earl of Faltingham, approached the gates to Wincaster. The trip to the Mercerian capital had been blessedly peaceful and without incidence. He wondered if anyone in the kingdom was even aware that Westlanders were riding their roads.

They had learned from fellow travellers that the rebellion had been put down. The king had lost his second son in the fight, but the unexpected assistance from another army had saved them. The Earl of Faltingham wanted to know more, but his priority must be to meet with King Andred IV of Merceria.

The guards at the gate were oblivious to the origin of the travellers, easily accepting the Weldwyn coins that were offered. It appeared that everywhere they went, the western currency was an accepted form of payment; the merchants far more concerned with coin weight than where it was minted. He suspected there was more trade between kingdoms than his king knew, for merchants are often quick to look for profit.

The city of Wincaster was similar to their own capital, full of people, but it seemed more constrictive here as if the narrow streets echoed the close eye that the Mercerian King was said to keep on his subjects.

They soon found lodging at a well-to-do inn and settled in. There was no advance warning of their arrival, therefore no messages awaited them. Lord Weldridge knew that they must make contacts if they were to obtain a private audience with King Andred. He was eager to learn as much about the uprising as possible; was Weldwyn implicated in it? He sent his people out looking for more information.

Some time later, there was a knock on his door, and he bid them enter. His sergeant opened the door to admit a short, thin individual with a balding head.

"This man says he has information for you, my lord," the sergeant said.

"Very well, Phipps, show him in." His eyes met the stranger's. "Please have a seat."

The thin man sat, and the Earl of Faltingham noticed the nervousness in the visitor's actions.

"How do you do?" the earl began.

"Very well, Your Grace," the man answered. His accent was Mercerian, and the earl detected some lower class mannerisms.

"Please," the earl continued, "tell me about yourself."

"I work at the Royal Court, Your Grace, as the master of the stable."

"I take it that's a very important position?" the earl asked.

"Oh yes, the king does so love his horses."

"My sergeant said you have some information for me. Would you be so kind as to share it?" The stable master hesitated, so he added, "I'd be more than willing to compensate you for your time."

The visitor visibly relaxed at these words. "That's awfully kind of you, Your Grace. I heard you were asking questions about the recent rebellion."

"Yes, please, go on."

"Well, there were three armies, you see. The Earl of Eastwood planned the whole thing. He hired men to strike in the west to pull the army away, then attacks from the northeast."

The earl nodded, "Very clever of him, but why didn't it work?"

"Well," the visitor smiled, "they didn't reckon on the princess, you see."

"The princess?"

"Aye, Princess Anna. She raised an army, defeated both the western forces, and then marched back to Wincaster to help the king defeat the usurper."

The Earl of Faltingham was startled, "Princess Anna? I thought the king's daughter was named Margaret?"

"Oh, aye, she is. But this is his other daughter, the younger one."

"Younger? I thought Margaret was still young. Are you saying a child stopped the invasion?"

"Well, she had help, of course. Some powerful men advised her, and a woman too."

"A woman?"

"Yes, Dame Beverly, a Knight of the Sword. She led the cavalry that smashed the invaders at Kingsford, the whole city's talking about her."

"Curious," the earl reflected. "I hadn't heard that. Tell me more about the rebellion. You say she defeated the armies to the west, what about the army that descended on the capital?"

"Well, the king sent an army under Marshal-General Valmar to chase down the usurper. They met outside of the city of Eastwood. There was a big battle, and the enemy was defeated. Even beat off an attack by Orcs."

"You say the king sent an army, he didn't command it himself?"

"No, my lord, he was still overcome by the death of Prince Alfred."

"Did they capture the usurper?" pressed the earl.

"Oh yes, had him executed in Wincaster, it was quite the spectacle."

"Very interesting. What happened then?"

"The king ordered a celebration in honour of their victory. There's to be a huge gathering at the Palace this evening. Everyone's invited."

"Everyone?"

"Well, everyone of any import. All the nobles of the land will be present."

"And how would one gain an invitation to this event?"

The master of the stable smiled, "Anyone can get an invitation if they have enough coins, Your Grace."

The Earl of Faltingham chuckled, it appeared Mercerians were not so different after all.

That evening the Palace was packed. The Earl of Faltingham's carriage rolled up to the gates, joining the long line of elegant nobles preparing to disembark. He waited patiently, it would not be seemly to complain and risk alienating these people.

King Leofric had been adamant that the mission needed to be successful and had given the earl enough funds to grease whatever palms needed it. As the carriage rolled up, a servant rushed forward to open the door. Lord Weldridge stepped down, observing the others around him. It appeared the majority of people were already in the Palace. He had purposefully arrived late, the better to make an entrance worthy of a king's emissary. Followed by his small entourage, he made his way through the Palace, guided by a servant. He heard music drifting toward him as they approached the great hall. Arriving at the entranceway, he announced himself to the finely dressed man stationed there, and then waited.

A moment later, the music stopped, and the buzz of talk died down as the delegation entered the room. King Andred was at the far end of the court, easy to recognize as he wore the Warrior's Crown; a simple, steel crown, devoid of gold or jewels, which denoted the ruler of this country of soldiers. As if on cue, the crowd parted, allowing them to move toward the king. Walking forward, he noticed the guards stationed just behind His Majesty, along with a dark-haired woman off to the side, which he assumed to be the queen.

"Your Majesty," he proclaimed when he felt he was close enough, "allow me to introduce myself."

King Andred nodded, and Lord Weldridge continued, "I am Lord Edwin Weldridge, the Earl of Faltingham, and I have come from Westland bearing greetings from King Leofric." He took a breath. He had remembered to call it Westland as was the custom here, but now he must touch on a stickier subject.

"He apologizes for the troops that entered your kingdom from our borders," he continued, "and hastens to assure you that he had no part in the attack. The troops were sent without his knowledge and the man responsible has been punished." He held his breath, waiting for the king's response.

The Mercerian King scrutinized his visitor before finally replying, "And what does King Leofric offer in recompense?"

The earl drew a silent breath of relief; King Andred was willing to talk, and that was a major victory.

"King Leofric wishes to make amends and gifts you this," he said, waving his hand to beckon two of his men forward to drop a large chest before the warrior sovereign. The Earl of Faltingham waited as the lid was opened to reveal a king's ransom in gold and jewels. The immediate look of desire in the Mercerian ruler's eyes told him all he needed to know; the gift was acceptable.

Lord Edwin continued, "He invites you to send a delegation to our kingdom that we might better understand the bonds between our two realms. We, in turn, shall send an ambassador of our own."

Without warning, King Andred stepped forward. Faltingham resisted the urge to flinch as the king's hand shot out.

"I accept your hand as the hand of friendship," King Andred said unexpectedly, "let it be thus between our two kingdoms."

Lord Weldridge took the king's hand and shook it. King Andred had a firm grip and locked eyes with the earl. He waved his hand, and the music resumed.

"Come now," said the king, "we should speak, there are matters to discuss."

He guided the earl to the side of the room while servants brought food and drink. The dark-haired woman followed them, though she wasn't introduced.

"Tell me," said the king, "how are things in Westland."

"We are doing well, Majesty, though King Leofric is eager to establish relations with Merceria. For too long we have been at odds with one another. Surely it is time for us to reconcile?"

"I think that a wonderful idea," the king replied. "Tell me more about this proposal."

"It is King Leofric's desire that we send delegates to each other's court, the better to represent our causes. I'm sure our kingdoms have much in common."

"No doubt," the king agreed. "I suppose it would have to be someone important, I can't just send anyone." He scanned the room, his eyes surveying his nobles.

The earl watched him, observing his disapproving scowl as his eyes fell on his courtiers. No doubt, he was considering much, for a noble had just been executed for treason. He would likely balk at sending his closest allies as he would need their support. His eyes finally rested on a young, expensively dressed woman amongst the throng of people. She was obviously enjoying herself, surrounded by many young knights.

"What about a member of my family?" he asked, indicating the young lady with his goblet of wine. "Would she be suitable?"

"Sending a member of the Royal Family would indeed be an honour. I'm sure King Leofric would be most pleased with your choice, Majesty."

"I think it's a wonderful opportunity," Andred said. "I can have my daughter, Margaret, ready to travel by the month's end. Would that suit your king?"

"Most certainly," replied the Earl of Faltingham. "I think he will be delighted to host her. I shall send word immediately so that arrangements can be made. He will wish to show her every courtesy. Of course, you will send an honour guard?"

"Naturally, some Knights of the Sword to protect her, along with a suitable amount of servants. I should send an advisor as well."

The earl was elated, "I should think that would be perfect," he agreed.

"Now," continued the king, "let me show you some of our finest wines."

He led them toward a long table where servants were generous with the drinks. The dark-haired woman remained where she was, but he recognized that she was upset about something. He put it from his mind to concentrate on the king.

In the end, they agreed that the princess would leave for Westland in the early summer. The visit would last a year, during which a representative from the Weldwyn court would remain in Merceria. The Earl of Faltingham could now return home to deliver the good news to King Leofric.

SIX

Plans

King Andred sat at his desk, staring down at the list before him. The names of the nobles of the realm were there; all sworn to his service and yet he knew that some of them must have been complicit in the rebellion. The Earl of Eastwood had raised an army in an effort to take the throne, but he wouldn't have attempted the task without the tacit approval of at least some of the nobles. The fighting was now over, the earl dead and buried, but still, the question lingered; who could he trust?

There was a knock at the door, and he called out absently, "Enter."

Lady Penelope Cromwell, the king's mistress, peered in to see what he was up to. He stared blankly at her, upset by the interruption but a smile from her softened his mood.

"Come in, my love. I need a distraction."

She glided into the room, "Why, whatever vexes you so, Andred. Surely the affairs of the kingdom can be handled by lesser men."

"If only," he groused, "but since the recent uprising, who can I trust? The earl couldn't have acted alone, he must have had help, but who?"

"A valid question," she agreed. "But he is defeated now, surely it is no longer an issue?"

"Ah, I wish it were so. I have to send Margaret to Westland to keep them occupied while I root out the rot in my court."

"And why is that a problem, Andred? Do you think her unsuitable for the task?"

"It is not the sending that has me so worked up, it is the guarding."

"Please explain, I'm afraid such matters are beyond me."

"I must send knights to protect her, she is a royal, after all."

"Then send knights, where is the problem?"

"I need all my knights here, Penelope, don't you see? There's bound to be more to this rebellion than just one earl. We must root out those responsible. I need men I trust to carry out my will and yet I cannot send untrustworthy men to guard my daughter."

"Perhaps there is another solution," she offered.

"You have me intrigued," he said. "What are you suggesting?"

"Tell me, is it imperative that Margaret, herself, be the one who visits?"

"I have committed to a royal, I see no other choice."

"What about Princess Anna?" she suggested.

"She is too young," he replied. "They would see it as an insult."

"Was she too young to lead the defense of the realm? She did win two battles, did she not?"

King Andred sat for a moment, absorbing her words. "I suppose she did," he admitted at last.

"So she is more than capable of looking after herself."

"Still, she would be representing the kingdom to our enemy," he persisted, "and she has little experience in such things."

"Send advisors," she countered. "She's already gathered a few of her own. We can make sure we have agents in their midst to report back on her progress if you're worried about it."

"And if they take offense?" he asked.

"Then let them. She is a Royal of the House of Merceria. Surely that is enough to guarantee her safety."

"And if they don't?"

"Tell me, my love. If such a thing were to come to pass, who would you rather lose, the daughter of your own blood or Princess Anna?"

Andred smiled, "A perfectly valid point."

"So there you have it," said Penelope, "you have come to your own conclusion."

"I still have the same problem," he growled. "Who do I send to guard her."

"Didn't you let her raise some knights?" she asked.

"I did," he admitted.

"Then she is already guarded. You must insist that she fills out her roster of knights before she leaves."

She walked closer to him, placing her hands upon his shoulders as he sat. "All the arrangements can be made by her people, freeing you up for more pleasurable pursuits."

"And if she is placed in danger?"

"For goodness sake, Andred. Send the Life Mage if you must, he certainly would be small loss around here."

"The Life Mage? Surely not!"

"Your Majesty," she purred, "he has shown himself to be quite lacking in skill. You, yourself, have said as much. With the rebellion crushed you are quite safe. When was the last time you needed healing?"

"Many years ago," he replied.

"You see? He is quite unnecessary. Do what you know is right and send young Anna to Westland."

She moved to his side and held out her hand. He took it, rising from his seat. She pressed her body close to his, bringing their faces together in an intimate embrace. "Now," she cooed, "let us concentrate on more pleasurable pursuits."

Gerald's armour jingled as he walked through the Palace, the sound echoing down the long halls.

"Are you sure about this?" he asked.

"Absolutely," replied Anna. "I've made up my mind. Just think about it, a chance to see a foreign country."

"I don't think he'll send you. He seems to have made up his mind to send Margaret."

"Nonsense, Gerald. I intend to convince him that I am the better candidate."

"But it could be dangerous, Anna," he said.

"You mean like the battles we fought in?" she reminded him. "I doubt it would get more dangerous than twisting an ankle dancing. We have a chance to make history; bring about a lasting peace between our kingdoms."

"We don't know much about Westland and its people."

"Precisely," she retorted. "I can't do this without you, Gerald."

"Well," he said, "if you can convince the king to send you, I'll be by your side. Just how, exactly, do you intend to do that?"

"Simple, I'll draw on my recent success in the rebellion and remind him how we saved the kingdom. He knows I've assembled an outstanding group of friends."

"You should refer to us as followers, Anna."

"But you're my friends," she objected.

"Yes, however, your father would be more impressed if you refer to us as followers. He's a king, remember?"

"I could hardly forget, now, could I?"

"What if he says no?"

"Then we're no worse off than we are now."

"You want this badly, don't you?" he asked.

"Of course," she replied, "it's the chance of a lifetime."

They arrived at their destination; a blue door that led into the king's private chambers. Two knights stood guard, their breastplates bright and unblemished.

"I'm here to see the king," announced Anna.

The guards looked down, towering over her small frame. Gerald was about to say something when the door suddenly opened, revealing Lady Penelope Cromwell.

"Princess Anna!" she exclaimed. "What a pleasant surprise. Is there something I can help you with?"

"I've come to talk to the king," the princess replied.

"A happy coincidence," said Penelope. "I was just talking to him, myself. Come along, Highness, I'll take you to him. I'm sure he'll be happy to see you."

Gerald took a step forward to be met by Penelope's palm, held in front of him. "You can leave your bodyguard here," she said, "you won't be needing him."

"I'll wait here, Highness," he mumbled, bowing his head slightly.

Anna stepped through the doorway with the king's mistress, while Gerald watched as the door snapped shut.

He paced back and forth in the hallway, trying to kill time, but his mind was whirling with worry. What would the king say? Would he let them go to Westland? Would her arguments convince him? He heard the shuffling of feet and turned to see the two knights watching him as he paced. He arrested his movement, turning to face them. Distracted by their attention, he wondered if they had fought at Eastwood. Of course, he could just ask them, but he sensed an air of contempt for him and felt slighted. He wanted to lash out, but realized they had done nothing; he was simply imagining things.

The door opened unexpectedly, and Anna reappeared.

"That was quick," he said, surprised.

Anna marched back down the hallway and Gerald struggled to keep up with her pace. He was beginning to wonder what had upset her so. Had the king refused her offer? They exited the Palace by the back, into the elegant gardens, and then Anna finally slowed.

"Anna," he begged, "what happened?"

She turned to him, breaking out into a big grin. "We're going to Westland!" she yelled.

"What?" he responded. "You were only in there for a moment. I thought he'd refused you."

"On the contrary," she replied, "he quite agreed with my reasoning."

"That quickly?"

"Yes, it took me completely by surprise."

"When do we leave?" he asked.

"Soon," she said. "We have a few things to see to first. We need to get everyone together and start making plans."

"You've already been making plans, Anna. I know you."

"Of course, Gerald, but now we need to start moving forward on them."

"Who should I gather?"

"Let's start with Beverly, Arnim, Revi, and, of course, Lily. I would also like Baron Fitzwilliam to be present."

"What about Lord Greycloak?" he asked. "The Elves were quite helpful to us."

"I know they were," said Anna, "but I'm sure the king would not want Elves going on the trip with us. He's never been comfortable with them, but I will send a letter thanking Lord Greycloak for their help."

"And Dame Hayley?" he asked. "She is a Knight of the Hound, after all."

"I don't really know her yet. I think it best I stick to those I'm more familiar with."

"And where would you like them to gather? No doubt you've got somewhere in mind already?"

She smiled, "Why Sergeant Matheson, you know me all too well. I thought we might impose on the baron. He has a house in the city, does he not?"

"He does, though he doesn't use it much. I'm sure he'd be more than willing to host a get-together."

"Find Beverly first and have her arrange things. I'll want you to escort me there when you're done."

"What will you be doing in the meantime?" he asked.

"Changing out of this very stiff and formal dress," she said, tugging at her waist bindings.

"All right," he agreed. "I won't be long."

"You'll have to find Beverly first; it's a large Palace."

"It's just after mid-day," he remarked, "she'll be in the practice yard."

"I should have known," said Anna.

"That's what I'm here for," replied Gerald.

The food was cleared away from the table, leaving the baron with a glass of wine. He waited as servants brought forth drinks for his guests and smiled as he saw Gerald marvel at the tankard of ale placed before him.

"You see," he said, "I remembered. You don't like wine."

Gerald blushed, "It's not that I don't like wine, my lord, it's just that I prefer ale."

"After all these years, surely you can call me Fitz."

"Of course, my lord," replied Gerald to the amusement of all around him.

"Perhaps, Father, we should get to the business at hand?" suggested Beverly.

"Of course," agreed the baron. "If you would be so kind, Highness?"

"Thank you, Baron," said Anna. "As you know, the king has selected me to travel to Westland on a diplomatic mission."

"What type of diplomatic mission?" asked Arnim. "Are we to become permanent ambassadors?"

"No," she replied. "We are to visit their kingdom, learn more about them, and show them we're not the ruthless mercenaries they think we are."

"I thought," offered Beverly, "that your sister, Princess Margaret was supposed to go?"

"And so she was," said Anna, "but I managed to convince the king to send me instead."

"And he agreed to that?" asked Fitz. "I find that surprising."

"He did," she responded. "In fact, he thought it was an excellent idea. I was quite surprised at how easy he was to convince. Not only that, but he insisted that I take Master Bloom with us."

The mage, who had been picking at some leftover food on a small plate, looked up in surprise. "He did? I find that quite strange. I would have thought he'd want the Royal Life Mage kept close."

"He was quite adamant about it. He said he didn't trust the physicians in Westland to look after me."

"Much as I am flattered by the opportunity," said Revi, "I am on the cusp of understanding a matter of great import." He looked around the room; save for the baron, they all knew he was referring to the Saurian Temple they had found at Uxley. "I should like to return to Uxley to study it in more detail. Perhaps, with Lily's help, I might be able to decipher the rest of the writings."

Lily chirped something in the Saurian tongue.

"What did she say?" asked Beverly.

"She said she'd be happy to," remarked Anna.

The entire room looked at her in surprise.

"I don't remember the mage casting the spell of tongues," said Arnim.

"He didn't," said Anna. "I've started learning some of her words."

Gerald cleared his throat to get their attention. "What if Revi and Lily were to go to Uxley and then catch up to us in Westland?"

"Good idea," said Anna, turning back to the mage. "How long would you need?"

"I would hope no more than a month or two," he replied.

"Could you join us in the Westland capital in the autumn?" she asked.

"Definitely," he agreed, "and I shall be sure to bring Lily with me."

"Excellent," said Anna, "then let us make it so."

"What about a detachment of knights," said Fitz. "You'll need some guards."

"Sir Arnim oversees my foot guards," she replied, "and my father has authorized the raising of ten knights. How is that going, Beverly?"

"Quite well, Highness," replied the redheaded knight. "Dame Hayley is interviewing two potential candidates even as we speak. If they're suitable, that will bring us up to five."

"We'll take them with us to Bodden," said Anna. "I should like to escort the baron home. From there, we'll head south to Kingsford where we'll take a ship to Westland. I would like to have the rest of the knights sorted by that time. Can we do that?"

"It'll be difficult," said Beverly. "There's not likely to be many candidates on the way to Bodden. No offense, Father."

"None taken, my dear," remarked the baron.

"I can see to the rest," offered Arnim. "I'll travel directly to Kingsford, and put the word out that interested parties should assemble there. I'll have them all interviewed before you arrive."

"Very well," agreed Anna, "though we will miss your presence, Sir Arnim."

"What about the baggage train?" asked Revi. "It's bound to be large, there'll be servants and supplies to sustain us, not to mention the coin."

"I'll look after the baggage train," announced Gerald, "with some help from Beverly. We managed quite well during the rebellion. I daresay a nice peaceful trip like this won't be much work. Might I ask how we're to pay for all of this?"

"The king has authorized a substantial purse. I have a letter in his hand allowing its release. I was hoping we might convince the baron to hold onto it for us while we're here in Wincaster. I can't say I fully trust the Royal Treasurer not to skim coins, but it would be convenient to have it close at hand."

"I would be honoured," agreed Fitz.

"There will be lots to do in the next few days," continued Anna. "I suggest you all get a good night's sleep."

As one, they rose from their chairs, bidding each other good night.

"A moment if you will, Master Revi," called out Anna.

They waited for the others to leave; only Gerald, Anna and Revi remaining.

"Yes, Highness?" said the mage.

"I want to know what you hope to find at Uxley," said Anna.

"I've had some time to pore over the books in Andronicus' library," explained Revi, "and I'm convinced that I can make sense of what we found. I need to return to the temple and study the runes again so that I can unlock them."

"Unlock them?" asked Gerald.

"We discovered new glyphs," continued Revi. "In order to use them, we must determine how to pronounce them; how to control their power."

"Do you think they are powerful, these new runes?" asked Anna.

"Yes, Highness. I'm convinced the magical flame represents a far greater power than we initially suspected, and unlocking the glyphs will allow us to control it."

"Meaning?" asked Gerald.

Revi looked from Gerald, back to the princess. "I'd rather not say at this time, Your Highness, but it is imperative that I be allowed to complete my studies. A discovery of this nature could have far-reaching consequences, and Lily's mastery of the Saurian tongue is of inestimable value."

"I shall ensure we leave you sufficient funds to continue your investigation, Master Bloom, but I expect you and Lily to join us in Westland in the autumn."

"Thank you, Highness," replied the mage, bowing deeply.

SEVEN

Bodden

SUMMER 960 MC

Dame Beverly Fitzwilliam stood on the top of Bodden Keep surveying the countryside. It was good to be home, but she knew she wouldn't be staying long. She heard a noise behind her and turned to see Celia Blackburn, one of the newest Knights of the Hound, approaching.

"You're wanted, Dame Beverly, we're to meet in-"

"The map room," the knight completed.

The blond knight looked at her quizzically, "How did you know that?"

"My father loves the map room. It's the only place he holds meetings."

Celia moved up beside her, looking down over the walls of Bodden. "I see your father has catapults," she said.

"Yes, after the last siege he decided he'd had enough of being on the receiving end. We added two of them to the gatehouse defenses."

"Does he really expect another siege?"

"We've had more than our fair share over the last few years, so yes, it's a very real possibility."

"Let's hope it doesn't come to that," said Celia.

They stood for a moment in companionable silence while Beverly took in the view.

"Do you mind if I ask you a question?" enquired Celia.

"By all means," replied Beverly.

"I'm grateful to be a member of the Knights of the Hound, but I was wondering how many of us there are? I've only met four."

Beverly couldn't help but laugh, "That's because we're brand new. At the moment there's only five of us, though that is about to change. I was the first, I swore myself to the princess's service months ago. The next was Dame Hayley, she used to be a King's Ranger. Sir Arnim Caster was knighted just before the Battle of Eastwood; you'll meet him in Kingsford. Then, of course, there's you and Levina, you both joined us just before we travelled for Bodden."

"Shouldn't there be more?" she asked. "It seems like a very small order."

"It is," Beverly agreed. "The king authorized the princess to recruit ten knights. Sir Arnim will be bringing the rest with him. They'll join us just before we leave for Westland." She gazed out at the village below. How long would it be before she came home again, she wondered. "I suppose we should get going, the meeting won't wait forever. Who's present?"

"The princess, your father, Gerald and the rest of the Knights of the Hound, at least the few we have here."

"All right, we don't want to keep them waiting."

She left the ramparts, leading the way, with Celia following. Upon entering the room, she noticed that a large map was spread out on the table, taking her back to her youth. She could almost imagine herself on a chair, pulled up to the table, fascinated by the little wooden soldiers.

Princess Anna was standing, examining the map that was spread out before her, but instead of the region around Bodden, it showed a map of the two kingdoms. Behind her, stood two of her knights, Dames Hayley Chambers and Levina Charleston. Beverly had been in correspondence with Dame Levina for some years and had arranged for her to join them as they passed through Tewsbury on the way to Bodden.

Beverly's father was standing to one side of the princess, while Gerald stood on the other. They were pointing to markings on the map, her father looking up as she and Celia entered.

"Ah, my dear, so good to have you here."

Beverly smiled, always pleased to see her father. "So what planning have you been up to?"

The baron smiled and looked to the princess, "Her Highness was about to let us know."

"As you know, we're headed to Kingsford, where we'll meet up with Arnim and the rest of the knights. From there, we'll sail upriver to Falford, where a delegation from Westland will meet us and escort us to their capital."

"I do wish you'd let some of my knights accompany you, Your Highness," offered Fitz.

"Thank you, Baron, but your troops are needed here. The north is still a dangerous area, and I'll feel safer knowing that the border is secure in your hands."

"Any news from Revi?" asked Hayley.

It was Gerald who spoke up, "He's still in Uxley with Lily, as far as we know. I'd feel better if there was a healer with us, but the princess did grant him permission to investigate."

"When do we leave?" asked Beverly.

"Soon," said Anna. "I would like to be in Kingsford by the end of the month."

"Shouldn't be a problem, Your Highness," offered Gerald. "We can be underway whenever you wish. We don't have a large supply train to move, merely some carriages and a couple of wagons."

"What can we expect in Westland, Highness?" asked Beverly.

"I've been giving it some thought. I know they don't call themselves Westland, they refer to their own kingdom as Weldwyn."

"That's a strange name, isn't it?" remarked Hayley.

"It's named after a mage, actually," Anna answered. "Mages are much more common in their land. I suspect we shall meet quite a few of them. King Leofric is the ruler, with three sons and two daughters, but we know little else about them. I'm told the king is not the absolute ruler there, he is assisted by an Earls' Council."

"So he's a weak king," implied Beverly.

"No, not weak, he has strong support from his nobles. I expect he will be a generous host as this visit is important to their realm. He wants to secure the borders; we've been adversaries for years. I imagine we'll travel to the capital and then spend the year attending parties and getting to know them better."

"That doesn't sound too bad," offered the baron.

"If everything goes as planned, I daresay it will be quite enjoyable," suggested Celia.

"Yes, but things seldom go as planned," said Gerald.

Beverly looked to her mentor, "Is that you, Gerald? For a moment I thought it was Sir Arnim. It's not like you to be all doom and gloom."

"Never mind him," explained Anna. "He's just not happy about having to take a boat."

"I've had a bad experience with the river," grumbled Gerald.

"How many people are going?" asked Beverly.

Anna looked to Gerald, who consulted some papers. "Let's see," he began, "there's the princess, me, Beverly, Hayley, Celia and Levina, along with Sophie and a number of other servants. That's not including those we pick up in Kingsford, which will include Arnim and the rest of the knights, along with servants sent from Wincaster by the king. All told, we should number about three dozen."

"What about the guards?" reminded Beverly.

"Oh yes, I forgot about them. We'll have to add another dozen or so to the tally as they'll be joining us in Kingsford along with Arnim."

"Sir Arnim," corrected Hayley.

"Yes," agreed Gerald, "Sir Arnim. Thank you for correcting me, Dame Hayley."

"Really? You can just call me Hayley, you know."

"Of course, Dame Hayley," Gerald repeated, winking at Anna, who coughed to cover her smile.

"Well," continued the princess, "there's little more we can do today. I suggest everyone relax this evening. It could be some time before we have the opportunity again."

EIGHT

Revi

R evi Bloom stared into the green fire that made strange shadows dance around the chamber. Beside him, the Saurian, Lily, held a lantern so that he could see the ancient runes.

"*A little closer, Lily,*" he spoke, though if anyone else had been present, they wouldn't have understood.

He had cast the spell of tongues, and now, as he spoke, the chittering sound of the Saurian race fell from his tongue. Lily brought the lantern closer, careful not to upset the book that the mage had propped open on the pedestal.

"Hmmm," Revi muttered, more to himself than to Lily. "*This is most interesting. Some of these runes I can understand, but there are at least two here I can't name.*" He lifted the book, holding it beside the runes. Was that a faint glow he spied? "*Douse the light, Lily.*"

"*What? That will make it dark?*"

"*Don't worry, I can make light with magic if needs be, though I suspect I won't have to.*"

The petite Saurian doused the flame using a snuffer, and the room went dark save for the eerie green glow coming from the eternal flame. Soon, their eyes adjusted and Revi watched as the runes in the stone began to glow. Within moments it was as if the room was brightly lit.

"*Aha!*" he cried. "*It's as I suspected! The runes react with light. When the light is extinguished, the magic shines through. This is most wondrous news, most wondrous indeed.*"

"So you have found the secret of the flame?" asked Lily.

"Not quite, but I'm on the right track. It seems your ancestors were highly advanced, magically. They have a larger alphabet."

"Ee-pok-chula," replied Lily.

Revi swore. Just as things were getting interesting, his spell had expired. "One moment my friend," he said and quickly repeated the incantation.

A moment later Lily spoke again, *"What was that? I didn't quite hear."*

"I said, your ancestors had more magic letters."

"What does that mean?" asked the diminutive lizard.

"It means...well quite frankly I don't know what it means. Magic is based on a universal alphabet, a magical alphabet, if you like. Every race has its own alphabet, but the magical letters are the same, regardless of the language; the same symbols, the same sounds. It's the combination of these letters that allows us to channel spells."

"And this means new spells?"

"Oh yes, my friend. This is a most astounding discovery. I must make copies of these runes." He reached into a bag he had left lying on the floor, withdrawing a set of bound papers. Next, he dug through the pockets of his robe, pulling forth some charcoal, but now a fresh obstacle presented itself.

"Too dark to draw," said Lily.

"Hmmm," muttered the mage. *"We shall have to relight the lantern."*

Lily began opening up the door to the lantern, but Revi stopped her with his hand.

"No wait, I have a better idea." He called forth a spell, drawing from the power within him and soon a small globe of light floated just above his hand. He concentrated on it, raising it into the air, some three feet above the floor. *"That's it. Now I can draw these runes."*

He spent the next little while sketching the runes as best he could. The images reminded him of some of the existing letters, and he wondered if they were related. Somehow he must decipher their pronunciation, or they would be useless.

His task completed, he placed the paper back in the bag, returning the charcoal to his pocket. *"I think it is time we leave, Lily. We still have much work to do."*

Lily picked up the lantern, but it remained unlit as they made their way out of the temple. By the time they came out of the well, it was dark, and Revi was surprised with how much time it had taken to carry out the research. They hurried back to Uxley Hall to retrieve their horses. They must now hasten to Wincaster to the library of Andronicus, where he hoped he might find the answers he sought.

The trip back to the capital had been uneventful, though more than one of the folk hereabouts had wondered at the strange being riding on the back of Revi's horse. Most people assumed it was a creature created by magic and gave the Royal Mage a wide birth; the rest likely didn't care one way or another.

They had no sooner arrived at the ramshackle home of Revi Bloom than he rushed to his master's library. No, he corrected himself, it was his library now, the Library of the Court Mage. He left Lily to her own devices and started pulling out tomes left and right, searching throughout the next few days for any indication of how his studies might proceed.

He had been working for Saxnor knows how long when Lily chirped. He quickly cast the spell of tongues; he must remember to enchant a ring at some time. Of course, he must learn how to enchant a ring first.

"What is it, Lily?" he asked.

"You need help, this is too much." She pointed to the vast number of tomes spread across the floor and furniture.

"You're right, but I don't know anyone, and I know you don't read Human. Even with my spell, you wouldn't be able to understand most of this. What I really need is a helper."

"An apprentice?" offered Lily.

"Wait, what did you say?"

"An apprentice, a helper you train to be a master."

Revi leaped to his feet. "That's it. I need an apprentice. I remember something about that, now what was it?" He struggled to pull the image from his mind. He was riding somewhere, and someone was talking to him. The female knight, "Dame Beverly," he said out loud. "What was it she said to me, something about a cousin." He moved to the bookshelf, digging through more tomes. "Here it is, the book of nobility. Let's see if Dame Beverly's family tree can remind me of the name." He flipped through the pages, finally stopping to examine the writing. "Ah, here it is. Hmmm, no brothers or sisters. No, wait, she said cousin. I must check her father. I see here an uncle of hers with three children. Here it is, Aubrey, Aubrey Brandon. That was the name."

Lily was getting excited just by watching his discovery. "Will she help unlock the runes?"

"Probably not, but she can help search through these books. We'll take the lot with us."

"On horse?"

"No, we'll need a wagon. I need to make arrangements. You grab us something to eat, and no raw fish this time. There should be something in the pantry." He pointed to the kitchen, "Whatever you like."

Lily left the room in search of food while Revi started piling the books he thought he should take.

Two weeks later the wagon trundled up the laneway leading to the estate of Baron Robert Brandon, the master of Hawksburg. The estate servants had seen their approach, and now one of them neared their wagon as they stopped in the laneway.

"How may I be of assistance, sir?" the man asked, before noticing the presence of Lily. He was unable to hide his astonishment when he took in the Saurian's visage.

"Yes, I am Magi Revi Bloom, the Royal Life Mage. I'm here to see Lady Aubrey Brandon."

"I beg your pardon, sir?" the servant stammered out.

"I'm here to see Lady Aubrey. Are you deaf, man?"

"No sir, one moment sir, and I'll see to it."

The servant ran off back into the house. Everyone around here seems to be in a hurry, Revi noticed. Lily remained sitting in the back of the wagon, leafing through a book. The door opened again, and a mature woman came out.

"You must be Lady Aubrey," he said.

"No, I am Lady Mary Brandon, wife to the baron and Aubrey's mother. Might I ask the nature of this visit, Master Bloom?"

"Revi will do. I'm here to consult with her on a matter of some importance."

"Indeed? And what matter might that be? Are you proposing a union of some sort? Is this to be a proposal?"

Revi was flabbergasted, "Proposal? No, of course not, I just want your daughter."

"I beg your pardon!" she responded. "She's a proper young lady, and I will not tolerate such behaviour."

Revi suddenly understood her meaning and blushed. "No, Lady Mary, you misunderstand. I am here to consult with her on matters pertaining to the arcane arts."

It was now her turn to be surprised, "Pardon?"

"Magic. I was told she might have the capacity to learn it. I am in need of an apprentice."

"And who told you of such things?"

"Dame Beverly Fitzwilliam."

Her face softened, "Well, I suppose you'd best come in then. You may bring your friend, too," she said, pointing at Lily.

"Thank you, Baroness," Revi replied. "You are most gracious."

They hopped off the wagon and made their way to the doorway where Lady Mary led them into an inviting sitting room. "Please have a seat. I'll have servants bring some wine. Does your friend drink wine?"

Revi looked to Lily, "No, but cider would do."

Lady Mary gave the orders and then sat down, examining Revi Bloom in some detail. "You look a little young for a mage," she commented.

"Well, yes. I should have been an apprentice for longer, but Andronicus, my master, died prematurely. Now I find myself in need of an assistant."

The servants returned with drinks, and while they sat, Lady Mary sent one to fetch Aubrey. Revi was complimenting the baroness on the wine as Aubrey entered. She was shorter than he had expected. Her long brown hair hung loosely from her shoulders, and while she was impeccably dressed in fine clothing, he was struck more by the manner in which she carried herself. This woman, who looked quite young to his eyes, carried herself with grace and elegance.

"I'm here, Mother," she said, as she entered.

"Aubrey, dear, this is Magister Revi Bloom, the Royal Life Mage."

"Pleased to meet you, Master Bloom," she said.

"He's come to see you, Aubrey."

"Me? How can that be?"

"I was told," said Revi, "that you already have some knowledge of magic?"

"Who told you that?" she asked.

"Does it matter? Is it true?"

"I know a little, though I'm sure my education pales in comparison to yours."

"Dame Beverly told me," he finally revealed.

"Cousin Beverly? How fares she?"

"Quite well." Revi continued. "She is sworn to the service of Princess Anna. But what I'd really like to do is ascertain your knowledge. Would that be all right?" he requested, looking to Lady Mary, who simply nodded.

"How would we do that?" she asked.

"I'll show you some symbols, and you tell me what they are. How's that for starters?"

"All right. When would you like to begin?"

"As soon as possible. I do have to get some books from my wagon, and then we can start."

"Are you staying in town?" asked Lady Mary.

Revi looked to the baroness, suddenly aware of his lack of planning. "I haven't made those arrangements yet, my primary objective was to meet Lady Aubrey, here."

"Well, we must put you in a guest room. Might I enquire as to your friend here?"

"This is Lily, she's a Saurian."

"A Saurian!" exclaimed Aubrey. "I've heard of those. I thought they were extinct?"

"So did we, till we found Lily, here."

"Are you able to communicate with her?" Aubrey asked.

"Yes, by using a spell. I'll cast it on you later so you can see how it works, but right now we have more important matters to attend to."

The baroness interrupted the exchange, "I shall have your horses and wagon seen to. Would you like the cargo brought indoors as well?"

"Yes, please, though I need to pick out a book or two before that happens. If you'll excuse me a moment, I shall just fetch my notes."

He rushed out the door to retrieve several books while Lily looked around the room. Her chair was tall for her short legs, and she dangled them, swinging them back and forth while she surveyed the furnishings. Soon, Revi returned with two books.

"I have a one here which is designed as a primary trainer," he explained. "It goes over the magical alphabet. Let's see how you make out." He laid the book on the arm of her chair and opened it to a page. "This is the letter Mu," he said.

"Yes, I recognize it," Aubrey replied, "but isn't in pronounced more like moo?"

Revi was taken by surprise, "Yes it is. How did you know that?"

"I've read everything I can about magic. My mother thinks there might have been mages in our family generations ago."

"Astounding," said Revi. "Flip through the pages and see if you recognize any other letters."

She began going through the book, page by page, naming all the runes. Revi was impressed, it had taken months of hard work for him to master the basics, and Andronicus had told him it was difficult for a mage to find someone with magical potential. By his reckoning, he had just struck gold.

He opened the second book and withdrew a loose paper, handing it to her. "What do you make of this?" he asked.

She scrutinized it before answering, "I don't know this one, though it has similarities to both Sep and Mar. Is this some type of hybrid?"

"No," he replied. "This is a new rune."

"New? I thought the magical runes had all been discovered years ago."

"So did I, but a recent discovery has told me otherwise. How would you like to help me decipher this?"

"I would love to. Would it involve travel?"

Revi considered the question before answering, "Not immediately, no. We'd study it here, though not in this room?"

"What's wrong with this room?" asked Lady Mary.

"We don't want to damage any of your fine furniture, Baroness," replied Revi.

"Is there danger involved?" the baroness asked, a look of fear on her face.

"No," he replied, "but when playing with runes, sometimes minor magical tremors can erupt. They usually shake things a little, more like a vibration. I wouldn't want you to be worrying all the time. We would just require a room with a couple of chairs and a table, and maybe a window for light, that's all."

"Is this an offer to make her your apprentice?" asked the baroness.

"Yes, I suppose it is. Though I daresay it won't be a traditional apprenticeship, I have little experience in training others. Would that be acceptable?" He looked to Lady Mary for acceptance.

She visibly composed herself before replying, "Lady Aubrey is a young lady of only sixteen years. I must have assurances you will treat her with the respect due her station. She would be your apprentice only, nothing more."

"Of course, I can assure you I will treat her properly. Besides, I'm sure if I didn't I'd be sliced in half by your niece, she seems to think highly of Lady Aubrey."

"Will we be seeing Beverly?" Aubrey asked.

"Eventually, but not right away, we must unlock the secret of the runes."

"There's more than one?" she asked.

"Oh yes, didn't I mention? There are two new runes."

"Does that mean two new spells?" asked the younger Brandon.

"No, runes are combined to form magical spells. These two new runes could potentially combine with others to form many new spells."

"So how do we unlock them," she asked, her excitement at the prospect obvious to all in the room.

"First, we find out how to pronounce them, and then we start combining them and watching for effects. It's a long and tedious process, but it should work."

"Well then," said Aubrey, "we best get started."

NINE

Kingsford

SUMMER 960 MC

S ir Barnsley Granville looked across the cobblestone courtyard, shaking his head at what he saw. "What a strange assemblage of knights."

His companion, a middle-aged man with a thick beard, wiped down his sword as he responded, "Whatever do you mean?"

"Well," the younger man continued, "it's rather an unusual mix, don't you think?"

"It's rather an unusual situation," interjected Dame Aelwyth, running her hand through her long, brown hair.

"Why would you say that?" asked the bearded man.

"It's simple," responded Aelwyth. "We're going into a potentially hostile foreign kingdom in the service of a young girl.

"The king must have a sense of humour," observed Sir Barnsley.

"Why," objected Aelwyth, "because most of us are women?"

"No," he replied, "because none of us appear to be nobles. Are any of us from well-to-do families? How about you, Sir Howard?"

"Not I," replied the bearded man, "though I've been a knight for nigh on ten years, I was born a commoner. What of you, Aelwyth?"

"I'm from Wickfield," she replied. "I earned my spurs on the Norland border."

"What's your family name?" asked Sir Howard.

"Our family uses no name. We trace our ancestors back to the time of old."

"What, pray tell," said Sir Barnsley, "does that mean?"

"It means," offered Sir Howard, "that she can trace her ancestors back to the original mercenaries who came to this land."

"So," mused Sir Barnsley, "an old family."

"Old? Yes, but not a noble one," explained Dame Aelwyth. "We have no land holdings to speak of and no influence at court."

"But you can fight," offered Sir Howard.

"How do you know that?" she replied.

"Simple," he responded, "if you couldn't fight, you wouldn't have been knighted."

"What do either of you know about our other two companions?" interrupted Sir Barnsley.

It was Aelwyth who responded, "The shorter one, Dame Abigail, is from the south, near Shrewesdale. Not sure of her family, but she talks like a commoner."

"And the other?" asked Sir Howard.

"That's Dame Juliet, but I just met her, so I don't know anything else about her."

"Another from an old line, perhaps?" pondered the older knight.

"She's very comely," observed Sir Barnsley, "like a newborn butterfly on the wind, she doth make my heart yearn for spring to return."

"You're a poet," observed Sir Howard.

"Among other things," he admitted.

Drawn by the conversation, their new companions wandered over. The taller of the two, Dame Juliet, had long, sandy coloured hair which was braided into two tails.

"I hear we are to work together," she remarked.

"Be still my heart," said Sir Barnsley.

Dame Abigail laughed at the remark.

"You doth wound my heart with your merriment," Sir Barnsley announced.

Dame Abigail grew quiet suddenly, the smile disappearing from her face. "I'm sorry, I thought you were jesting."

The young man held his face in its sorrowful expression for the briefest of moments and then he broke into a grin. "I was," he admitted, "though I pray it caused no offense."

"Why are we all here?" asked Dame Juliet.

"We are here," said Sir Howard, "because we have been recruited by Sir Arnim Caster. Did he not recruit you also?"

"Of course," remarked the sandy-haired knight, "but I meant what are we doing here, in Kingsford."

"Good question," remarked Sir Barnsley. "I'd never heard of Sir Arnim before. Had any of you?"

They each shook their head, save for Sir Howard. "It doesn't matter," the older knight said, "he's not our new commander."

The others all looked at him, surprised by this nugget of information.

"Then who is?" asked Barnsley.

"Dame Beverly Fitzwilliam," he replied.

"Now that's a name I recognize," said Dame Abigail.

"Didn't she run into some sort of problem in Shrewesdale?" asked Sir Barnsley.

"That was just an excuse to get rid of her," defended Dame Abigail. "The Earl of Shrewesdale doesn't like lady knights."

"Well, I must say it's his loss," announced Sir Howard. "She proved her mettle well enough during the rebellion."

Hearing a door open, they looked across the courtyard to see their recruiter approaching.

"Here comes Sir Arnim," said Sir Howard. "Doubtless he'll let us know what's going on now that we're all assembled."

~

Sir Arnim Caster, Knight of the Hound, walked across the stone courtyard. He saw the knights standing about, chatting with each other and lamented the fact that they were not common soldiers used to a more disciplined approach. He was about to yell at them, but thought better of it, these were knights, after all. He didn't offer any sign of greeting, merely grumbled as he approached.

"Line up," he commanded. "The royal party will be arriving soon. Smartly now, like proper soldiers."

"We're not soldiers," objected Sir Barnsley, "we're knights."

Arnim's face grew red, and he looked like he would explode in a rage, but then he took a deep breath, letting it out slowly.

"Then line up like knights," he responded. "The princess will be arriving shortly and the head of our order would like to have a few words."

They wandered into a rough line, each looking expectantly at the gate that was open to the road. Sir Arnim took up a position at the end of the line, closest to the gate and waited.

The sound of horseshoes striking stone soon echoed toward them and then a rider turned up the road, coming into view. She was a redheaded woman, wearing very expensive looking armour, riding a Mercerian

Charger. She pulled up a short distance from the line and looked toward Sir Arnim.

"What have we here?" she asked.

"I have the rest of your knights here, Dame Beverly. Would you care to inspect them?"

"I would," she said, dismounting in one smooth motion, dropping the reins of her horse; the great beast obediently remained stationary. She made her way to the first knight in line, Sir Arnim falling in beside her.

"And who do we have here?" she asked.

"This is Sir Barnsley Granville," answered Arnim. "He hails from Colbridge."

"You're close to home, Sir Barnsley," commented Beverly.

"Indeed I am, Ma'am," replied the poet.

Beverly turned her attention to the next in line.

"This," offered Arnim, "is Dame Aelwyth."

"Ah, I heard your name years ago," remarked Beverly, "but had no way of finding you. I see you carry an axe, do you use any other weapons?"

"I do," the woman replied, "though I favour the axe over the sword."

"I'm trained in the axe myself," said Beverly. "It will be interesting to face someone skilled in its use."

"You use the axe?" replied Aelwyth. "Your reputation says you favour the sword or hammer."

"I'm proficient in many weapons," explained Beverly, "I've learned them all. If you survive long enough, you might get to meet the man who trained me."

"Are we expecting danger?" asked Aelwyth.

"Expecting? No, but we must always be prepared," Beverly said as she moved to the next in line.

"And you are?"

"Sir Howard Elsworth," he replied.

"I know that name," she mused. "You earned some renown in the north, didn't you?"

"I did, though that was some time ago. Kind of you to remember."

"I'm surprised you weren't already sworn to service," remarked Beverly.

"Alas, I was, but my previous lord dismissed me as a cost-cutting measure."

"Surely not!" exclaimed Beverly.

"I'm afraid the Earl of Tewsbury has seen tough times. He dismissed a number of people from his service."

"His loss is our gain," offered Beverly, moving to the next knight to find herself towering over the recruit before her.

"Dame?" she asked.

"Abigail," the diminutive knight replied.

"Abigail Thompson?"

"Yes, but we've not met before, have we?"

"No, but a dear friend once told me about a few female knights and your name came up, among others." Beverly paused to clear her throat before continuing, "I see you use a mace, an interesting choice of weapon. It looks like it's seen a lot of use."

"It has, I've been fighting Orcs near the Artisan Hills for years."

"You were in service to the Earl of Eastwood?" asked Beverly.

"Only until he rebelled," she replied. "I left his service when he made a deal with the Orcs."

Beverly stared at her for a moment, deep in thought. "I trust that you don't hold any old loyalties to his family?"

"Of course not," Dame Abigail replied. "I'm fully committed to the service of the princess."

"Excellent, then we'll have no trouble."

"And this," offered up Sir Arnim, "is Dame Juliet."

"Dame Juliet...?" asked Beverly.

"I prefer not to use my last name," the woman replied.

"I trust you're not in trouble?"

"Not at all, but I wish to make my own way, not rely on my family's reputation."

"I respect that," said Beverly, turning back to Arnim.

"They seem adequate to the task, Arnim. Have them report to the Earl of Kingsford's estate, they will meet the rest of the hounds there."

"I'll see to it," responded Arnim.

Beverly turned her attention back to the line of knights, "Are there any questions?"

It was Sir Barnsley who spoke up first, "Might I enquire how we are to address you? You are our commander, are you not?"

"I am," she responded, "but this is a small detachment. Only ten knights, once you include myself and the others. You may address me as Dame Beverly or Lady Beverly if you wish. My father is the Baron of Bodden, and my mother died many years ago so I may also be addressed as Lady Fitzwilliam, if that suits your fancy. When we're not in the presence of her highness, you may simply address me as Beverly. I'm not a stickler for protocol, though I am very strict about training."

"What can you tell us about the princess?" asked Aelwyth.

"Despite her young age, she is highly intelligent and battle tested. She led us to victory on the battlefield during the recent rebellion. You will treat her at all times with the respect due her station. While we are abroad, she will always be accompanied by a bodyguard. This will usually be either myself or Gerald Matheson, but on occasion it might be one of you."

"Who's Gerald Matheson?" asked Sir Barnsley. "I've never heard of the man."

Beverly stared at the young man for a moment before replying, "He's the princess's closest friend and the man that taught me everything I know about fighting, so don't annoy him."

She waited for further questions but none were forthcoming.

"Oh yes," she pondered, "is anyone here afraid of dogs?"

Sir Howard looked up and down the line and then offered a reply, "No, why?"

"Because you're going to meet the largest hound you've ever seen."

"Meaning?" asked Sir Barnsley.

Beverly smiled, "You'll see, you'll see."

TEN

Across the Border

T he river current gently swayed the boat as it made its way upstream. Dame Celia strode across the deck toward Lady Beverly, careful to avoid the crew members as she went. At the sound of her footfalls, the redheaded knight turned.

"Celia," she said, "how are the other knights doing?"

The blond-haired knight stared out over the railing before answering, "Other than Sir Barnsley, they're fine."

"Why, what's wrong with him?"

"His stomach doesn't like the water. Dame Levina's looking after him."

Beverly smiled, Levina was the oldest of the knights, and had quickly become the mother figure. "Are they settling in? I haven't had time to really get to know them yet. What are your first impressions?"

Celia appeared to think for a moment before replying, "They're an interesting group, but I'm not sure where Arnim found them."

"The princess wanted them to all be women, but there's not enough in the kingdom to fill in all the spots. Still, we ended up with seven women and three men, including Arnim. All-in-all, not a bad mix. Have you had a chance to talk to them yet?"

"Yes," Celia replied. "Sir Barnsley is quite a poet when he isn't being seasick. He's rather refined."

"And what of the other man, Sir Howard?"

"Seems solid enough for an old soldier. It'll be interesting to see if he can keep up with the rest of us."

"Don't let age cloud your judgement, Celia. With age comes experience, just look at Gerald. What about the women?"

"Well, Dame Abigail looks competent enough, but I can't understand why she insists on using a mace, it's such a unrefined weapon.

"A mace is a decent weapon, very useful for caving in heads, though I prefer a hammer," provided Beverly.

Celia paused, surprised at Beverly's choice of weapons, then continued, "Dame Juliet tends to be on the quiet side. She's just a little older than you, though not high born."

"Interesting," mused Beverly, "I would have said the opposite. What do you make of Aelwyth?"

"A little rustic for my tastes, but she does have battle experience, even if it's only against Orcs."

"Trust me, I've fought Orc's, they're not easy to kill. It appears that you and Arnim have a lot in common."

"How so?"

"You both see the worst in people, not the possibilities. You have the makings of an outstanding knight, don't let your prejudices ruin that."

Beverly turned away, thinking back to her time in Bodden. She supposed she would have to break them in. Her father, the baron, had always complained about the lack of discipline in knights. Beverly would have to find time to drill them while they were in Westland. No, she corrected herself, she must remember to call it Weldwyn now. She didn't want to insult their hosts.

"Something I might help with?" offered Celia.

Beverly was broken out of her reverie, "Pardon?"

"You appeared deep in thought. I thought it might be something I could assist with."

"I was just thinking that we should arrange some time for training once we disembark. I should like to ensure the knights can work well together; some of them have probably never fought in a group."

"Do you really think that'll be necessary? I'm sure our hosts will be concerned with our safety. After all, the whole reason we are here is to stop a war with Merceria."

Beverly supposed Celia was right, but she remembered the dire warnings that the druid, Albreda, had shared with her; there was a dark presence, a shadow across the land. If the princess were threatened, she would need all the protection they could muster. Realizing she was, again, remaining quiet, she turned back once again to Dame Celia.

"It's our duty to fulfill our obligation to the princess," she stated, "and that means being prepared at all times. I'll work up some drills for us to practice. It'll also be good to establish some discipline and meld the knights into a cohesive unit."

Celia raised her eyebrows, "I think you're being overly cautious, but I'll let the others know." She left Dame Beverly to her thoughts.

～

Gerald clutched the railing with a vice-like grip. The ship rolled with alarming regularity, and he prayed to Saxnor that the voyage would end quickly. Water was for bathing, not for sailing, he thought; better to be back on dry land. He felt a hand touch his arm and looked to see Princess Anna beside him.

"Are you all right, Gerald? You look very pale."

"I'm fine," he snapped, then thought of Anna. "Sorry, I'm not comfortable over water, and the damn boat is pitching too much."

Anna smiled, "The boat's hardly moving, Gerald, it's a very smooth sailer. You need to relax a little. What is it about deep water that troubles you so much?"

Gerald gripped the railing even tighter, "I had that bad experience, years ago. It was not at all pleasant."

"The water in the grotto didn't bother you, why does it now?"

"This is different," he said. "In the grotto I could touch the bottom, and there were no currents that could carry me away."

They stood in companionable silence for a few moments as the boat made its progress, and then they rounded a bend in the river, revealing the city of Falford on the distant shore.

"There, you see? We're almost here." She looked to Gerald's face, but his eyes were locked on the distant docks.

"There's our welcoming committee," he said. "I see a Royal Standard, it looks as if they've sent a royal to welcome us."

"King Leofric?" asked Anna.

"I doubt it, there'd be more soldiers. Probably one of his sons."

"I suppose we should put on a good show, then. I'll get Beverly to organize the knights."

Gerald, snapped from his fear, turned to examine the deck of the boat. Beverly was already moving, and even Tempus had awoken from his slumber to trot up to Anna's side.

"How do you want to do this?" he asked.

"Have the knights disembark first. We'll be up against the dock so they can cross as soon as the boarding plank is down. Beverly will form the honour guard on the docks. You and I will disembark together, and then Arnim can bring the rest behind."

"What about Tempus? He didn't like the boarding plank."

"I've thought of that," offered Anna. "I'm going to have Hayley entice him across with some food."

Gerald smiled, "You seem to have thought of everything. What about once we're on the dock?"

"That largely depends on what they have planned for us. King Andred arranged for horses to be waiting for us, and a Royal Carriage was shipped ahead of time. We only have to unload the knight's horses, and we'll be ready to move on, though I suspect we'll be hosted here for a day or two. They'll want to get the measure of us before taking us to the capital."

With the boat tied to the dock, Gerald released his grip on the handrail and started to return to his normal self. His mind was working quickly now that the colour was returning to his face.

"I'm a little nervous about this, Anna. We know very little about these people."

Anna grabbed his hand in hers. "We're on an important mission here, Gerald, but I can't do this without you. You're my father, in everything but name. I need your strength to sustain me."

He looked down at the young woman before him and still saw the young girl he met so long ago. "I'm there for you, Anna, you know that. No matter what happens, I'll make sure you're safe."

She squeezed his hand gently, "I know. Now let's get moving, we have work to do."

～

Alric shifted his feet. It was an uncomfortably hot afternoon, and he didn't like waiting. Far better to be in a tavern with a cool glass of ale.

"They're almost ready," said Alstan. "They're tying off the ship now."

It was true, the Mercerian vessel had just sailed up, and even as he spoke, the crew was leaping onto the dock to secure the vessel with ropes.

"How long, do you think, before they come ashore?" asked Alric.

"I don't suppose it'll be long," observed Alstan. Then added, "Now that's a surprise."

Alric tried to follow his elder brother's gaze but failed to discover his observation. "What is?" he said, with some irritation.

"It seems the envoy is of Royal Blood after all."

"How can you tell?"

"Their Royal Standard is flying, see, on the mainmast?"

Alric followed his brothers pointing finger. "I thought they decided against sending Princess Margaret?" he pondered.

"So did I. I suppose we shall have to wait and see who's arrived

"Perhaps their king has sent one of his sons," suggested Alric

Alstan frowned, "He's only got one son left, remember. He's not likely to send the Crown Prince."

"Perhaps a cousin, then, like we did?"

"I really have no idea. I suppose we will know soon enough."

They watched in silence as the boarding ramp was lowered, and then a group of warriors began making their way to the dock.

"Here come the knights," observed Alstan.

"Knights? I've heard of them. Aren't they considered minor nobility?"

"Yes, so we treat them as we would a baronet. Most of their attitudes towards nobility should mirror ours. I don't suppose it'll be much of an adjustment."

Alric stared at the warriors, rubbing his eyes to make sure they didn't betray him. "Am I seeing things or is that a woman wearing armour?"

Alstan chuckled, "Oh yes, didn't I mention it? They have women warriors in Merceria."

"These foreigners are full of surprises. Anything else I should know about?"

"Ever seen a Mercerian Charger?"

"No, but I've heard of them, why do you ask?"

"I heard their knights would be bringing them. They're the largest breed of horses in the land."

"I doubt they'd stack up well to ours. We have some of the finest steeds in the three kingdoms."

Alstan looked at his younger brother. "You need to get out more, Alric. The Mercerian Chargers are bred to carry heavily armoured knights while wearing barding themselves. They wear much more armour than our cavalry. It would take a beast of a creature to carry the weight."

"I don't see anything all that exciting so far," Alric stated, "apart from female warriors, that is."

"They'll doubtless unload the horses later. It'll be interesting to see them, I've heard the stories."

They observed a commotion on the boat. The Mercerian warriors stood on the dock in line with a redheaded knight drawing her sword. With a yell of command, the visiting knights drew their weapons, holding them in front with both hands. A small golden-haired female began walking across the ramp, with an older man in a chainmail shirt holding her hand.

"What's this?" asked Alric. "Are we to nursemaid a child?"

"It appears that King Andred of Merceria has sent his youngest daughter to us."

"I thought Princess Margaret was the youngest child?"

"You need to pay more attention to the goings-on at court, Alric. The king has a second daughter; her," he said, pointing at the dock. "And now it's up to us to make sure she's kept safe."

"I suppose," grumbled Alric, "that'll mean endless dances and social events."

Alstan lightly punched his brother on the shoulder. "Aren't you lucky, your favourite things!"

The girl finished crossing the ramp, and the knights scabbarded their weapons, all save the redheaded woman, who turned to face the princes with their welcoming committee. She marched up to them, stopping some five paces from them, safely out of weapon reach.

"I am Dame Beverly Fitzwilliam," she said, "daughter to the Baron of Bodden, and I have the honour to present to you the Princess Anna of Merceria. Long may she live."

Alstan nodded his head in reply, then nudged Alric to follow suit. "I am Crown Prince Alstan of Weldwyn," he announced, "and this is my brother, Prince Alric. On behalf of our father, King Leofric, we welcome Her Highness to our kingdom."

The lady knight bowed, and then turned, walking back to the princess. After exchanging some brief words, she scabbarded her sword, taking up a position behind. The princess advanced, the old man beside her. Alric noted the young girl's demeanour and almost laughed. It was as if one of his younger sisters was play-acting; it was such a ludicrous sight.

Princess Anna strode forward till she was standing only a pace or two away from them.

"It is my pleasure to be received by such distinguished hosts," she said. The man beside her was looking directly at Alric, and it made him feel uncomfortable. Could this man read minds?

Alstan interrupted his thoughts with his next words, "If Your Highness permits, we have arranged a feast in your honour. We would be delighted to escort you there."

"By all means, Your Highness," she replied, "though I suspect between the three of us, all this 'Highness' nonsense will get a little tedious. Since we are all royals, perhaps we should just use our given names."

"Very well, Anna, if you'd come this way?"

Alstan held out his arm for her to hold but Alric noticed a look of confusion on the girl's face. It appeared this was likely not the custom in Merceria. The princess merely stood beside him, indicating with a sweep of her arm to proceed. The small group departed the wharf, heading toward the banquet that awaited them. The old man and the redheaded woman fell in behind the royals. Alric felt as though he was being watched the whole time.

Alstan and the princess were chatting as they walked, but Alric paid them no mind. He wondered about the woman in armour. She had said she was the daughter of a baron; did nobles in Merceria send their women to fight? It seemed barbaric. He would have to learn more.

They soon entered the hall, decorated for the occasion with the flags of Weldwyn and Merceria. They were led to a large table set up at one end of the hall where seats had been arranged. A servant dutifully pulled out a chair for the princess, while Alstan and Alric took their seats.

"I shall require another chair," she stated.

"Is this one not suitable, Your Highness?" asked the servant.

"This chair is fine," she replied, "but I shall require a second."

Alric, stunned by the exchange, could only stare, open-mouthed. He suddenly realized this and closed it. Was this girl completely untrained in etiquette?

"Might I enquire for what purpose?" asked Alstan.

"For Gerald, here," she said, indicating the old man. "He is to sit to my right."

The servant looked to Alstan for confirmation, who nodded. "Of course, Princess, we'll see to it immediately."

To Alric's mind, this was ridiculous. They had gone to considerable lengths to arrange the tables, and now she was throwing things into disarray. Was this a deliberate tactic or the whims of a spoilt child? It took only a moment to bring a chair, and the seating was soon settled. Alstan, as the king's representative, sat in the centre of the table with Anna beside him, to his right. Alric, on his brother's advice, was shifted over one place, now sitting beside the old man instead.

They were all seated, along with their guests when the servants began bringing in the food and wine. Alstan engaged the princess in light conversation as Alric looked around at the newcomers. One of the lady knights had taken up a position behind the princess and stood alert, though what she was looking for was beyond Alric's comprehension. Now that he was closer, he saw she was armoured in chainmail but with metal plates on top, a type of armour not seen in Weldwyn before. It was quite remarkable, and he resolved to find out more. He was, perhaps, staring at her a little too long when her eyes met his. He blushed, changing his focus to the old man beside him. The warrior's armour looked old, with patches where links had been replaced over the years. This man had seen combat, Alric thought, and likely lots of it.

"Gerald, isn't it?" he said, not sure what title he should use.

"Yes, Gerald Matheson, Your Highness," his dinner guest replied.

Alric had expected a more eloquent reply and found himself at a momentary loss for words. "And what, if I may ask," he finally said, "is your precise relationship to the princess?" He tried to sound polite, but the irritation in his voice must have been obvious for the man turned to face him.

"I'm her friend," he said. "I've known her for years."

Alric found himself intimidated by the man's stare. He abruptly turned to the food placed in front of him. "I see." He quickly added, "Hope you like the food." He dug into his meal, hoping that his seating companion would find distraction elsewhere.

A moment later there was a bark from the far end of the hall. A brunette woman in armour had entered, though rather than the chainmail worn by the other warriors, she was wearing a leather jerkin. Her hand was on the back of a gigantic dog, and Alric suddenly stood, reaching for his sword. A Kurathian Mastiff! It must be a trap!

He heard the rasp of steel throughout the room as guards also drew their blades. Dame Beverly drew her sword, glaring at the guards.

"Please," begged the princess, "put your blades down. It's just my dog."

"'Tis a Kurathian hound," yelled one of the guards. "The weapon of our enemy!"

Alric was looking around nervously, but his elder brother appeared calm.

"Put the weapons away," commanded Alstan. "It means us no harm."

Weapons were scabbarded as the woman led the mighty beast to the head of the table. The creature ignored all those around him save for the princess. He trundled up to her, squeezing between her and Gerald to take up a position underneath the table. Alric was amazed the creature could even fit under the table and peered beneath to see the creature lying on his side, the princess's feet rubbing his belly. The old man beside him seemed unfazed by the commotion around him.

Alric decided the best way to handle the situation was to ignore it and retain his composure. Things soon settled down, and the eating resumed.

Sometime later the meal was cleared and servants came to take away the tables. In Weldwyn this was a common tradition, the better to let the nobles mingle and converse, but the visitors appeared surprised by the move. Everyone wanted to meet the princess, of course, but the presence of the hound constantly at her side meant that only the bravest of them actually approached.

Alric was bored, this was turning into another intolerable social affair, and he wanted to leave, but he knew his absence would be noted. He glanced around the room, taking it all in. The Knights of Merceria caught his attention again. There were almost a dozen of them, most of which were women. He saw Lady Beverly and decided to engage her in conversation. At least, as a noble, she could be counted on to carry on a decent discussion. She was standing to the side of the room constantly on the lookout. He approached her slowly, nodding slightly when their eyes met.

"Lady Beverly," he said, trying to sound as polite as possible, "I hope you're enjoying the festivities."

She nodded slightly, "Yes, Your Highness, they are most agreeable."

"Have you sampled the wine? We have a number of fine vintages."

"I regret I have not, Highness. I drink very little."

"I must say, I was surprised to see women in armour. Is this common in Merceria?"

Lady Beverly smiled, "It is rare, but not unheard of. The princess insisted we recruit as many as we could for the order."

"The order?" asked Alric.

"Yes, Highness. Knights are sworn to an order, a type of brotherhood, or sisterhood, if I may be so bold. It binds them together. Have you something similar in Weldwyn?"

"Well, we have cavaliers. I suppose they would be the closest thing. Tell me more about this order of yours, I find the topic fascinating."

The redheaded knight warmed to the conversation. "In Merceria, knights are sworn to the service of the crown. The king's order is the Order of the Sword. The king, on occasion, allows knights to follow other nobles. These knights are usually assigned to these orders on a temporary basis, but we are different."

"How so?"

"We are sworn to the service of the princess. We are the Knights of the Hound."

"Fascinating," mused Alric. "And so, knights would be Knights of the Sword as well as the Hound? Can a knight belong to more than one order?"

He watched a look cross the woman's face before she answered.

"In most cases," she continued, "every knight would be a member of the Order of the Sword, but I am only a Knight of the Hound."

Alric felt there was more to this story but could sense the unease in the woman. Was she disgraced somehow? He decided to change the subject.

"I must say the armour you wear is quite fascinating. I see your smiths have managed to fashion steel plates over your chainmail. We have no such armour in Weldwyn. The chest plate you wear seems quite ornate. If you don't mind me asking, how much did it cost you?"

Beverly smiled, "Nothing, Highness. My father's smith made it."

"Surely the man must command a fortune for such work?"

"He is in service to my father, it is his duty and passion."

"I'm sorry," said Alric, "I'm afraid I don't understand. Is the man not a craftsman?"

"Indeed he is. However, my father looks after him, provides the smithy, feeds him, pays him his wages. In exchange he makes armour and weapons for the Keep, is it not so in Weldwyn?

"No, here smiths are independent professionals. Hired by the crown in many cases, but every weapon is paid for."

"So you are saying even an earl has to pay for each and every weapon?"

"Yes," Alric answered.

"An interesting situation," mused Beverly. "I wonder how Aldwin would fare under these conditions?"

"If your armour is any indication, he would do quite well for himself. Tell me, is such armour common in Merceria?"

"Only amongst knights and the nobility. The cost to make such armour is very high."

"But I thought you said the smith was not paid for his work?" prompted Alric.

"There is still the cost of the iron. It requires a high grade of metal for this sort of work. Most armour is not of this quality."

"Perhaps I shall entice this smith of yours to come to Weldwyn and serve my father. I'm sure he would be well paid."

Beverly smiled again. "I doubt he would be interested," she said.

Alric thought he detected a slight blushing on her part but put it down to the warmth of the room. "So tell me," he continued, "how long have you known the princess?"

"Only a few months, Highness. I met her this last spring, though I must admit it seems like such a long time ago, now that I think about it."

"How well do you know this Gerald Matheson fellow?"

"Quite well," she announced. "Why do you ask?"

"I'm not sure what he does," Alric stated.

"What he does? What do you mean?"

"Well, I understand the knights, their purpose is obviously to protect the princess. Then there's the woman who brought the dog, she's obviously the beast's handler-"

"That was Dame Hayley," she interrupted. "And she's not a handler, she was a King's Ranger, and now she's a Knight of the Hound."

"Oh," said Alric, "I meant no disrespect. Tell me, who actually handles the beast?"

She stared back at him for a moment before answering. "Tempus? No one handles Tempus. He'll listen to the princess and Gerald. He seems to like Hayley, and I suppose he'd listen to Sophie, but no one really handles him."

"Tell me you're kidding. Kurathian Mastiffs are trained to bring down war horses. Aren't you afraid he'll kill somebody?"

"Tempus? He's very gentle when he likes you, though I've been told he can rip out a throat with very little effort." She smiled, and Alric felt uncomfortable.

"But I digress," stated the prince. "You were going to tell me about this Gerald person. What is this hold he has over the princess?"

Lady Beverly laughed, "Gerald Matheson was my father's Sergeant-at-Arms. A more worthy man you won't find this side of the Afterlife."

"So you know him?" he asked again.

"I've known him all my life. He was my mentor. It was he who taught me how to fight."

"So he's a knight, then?"

"No, though he's more than worthy. He was born a commoner. Nobles don't like that in a knight."

"So where does he fit into the princess's entourage?"

"He's Gerald, that's all that matters. I suppose you'd see him as the princess's right-hand man. He's her advisor but also her friend."

"So how do I treat him? Do I treat him as a commoner?" This was all so confusing.

"You treat him as you would any other Human being. He is a man, just like you."

Alric bristled. "I'm a prince," he replied, somewhat insulted by the comparison.

"True, Highness, and I meant no disrespect. But it's men like Gerald who keep the kingdom safe, isn't it? The man has seen more battles in his day than likely the rest of us combined. His experience makes him especially valuable."

"So he is a military advisor?" Alric pressed.

Beverly sighed, "No, Highness, as I mentioned, he is her friend. You have friends, don't you?"

Alric was taken aback. "Of course I have friends, I'm a Prince of the Realm."

No sooner had he said the words than he was shocked into a realization. Did he have friends? Certainly, people paid him attention, but did he truly have what he would consider a friend? He thought of Uncle Edwin. He was the closest friend of his father, wasn't really an uncle, and yet he could say anything in his father's presence. He was accepted by the whole family. Did he have anyone in his life with such a relationship? He had to admit to himself that he didn't and it suddenly left him feeling somehow alone, despite the busy room.

"I thank you for the enlightenment, Lady Beverly," he said finally.

"I'm typically addressed as Dame Beverly, Highness," she replied, "though Lady Beverly is perfectly acceptable."

"Dame Beverly it is, then," Alric agreed. "Now, if you will excuse me, I have many people to talk to."

"Of course, Your Highness," she replied.

It was in the wee hours of the morning that Alric returned to his room. He was about to enter when his brother hailed him as he walked down the hallway.

"Alric, what did you think of our guests?"

"Confusing," he replied. "I think I have a better understanding of their knights but this Gerald person still baffles me."

"How so?" prompted Alstan.

"He's a commoner. It sets a dangerous precedent to have a commoner advising a royal."

"Have you seen the man's armour? He's seen battle, and I daresay many times. I'd love to know what he could do against our cavaliers. I bet he'd give them a run for their coins."

Alric perked up, "You think so? I think he's just an old man. Likely he served the king, and this cushy job is his reward for past service. I don't have anything against the man, I'm just not sure how to treat him. How do I address him?"

"You've put far too much effort into this," teased Alstan. "Just treat him like one of our mages, they're all commoners."

"I suppose that would work. So I call him Master Matheson?"

"Everyone in the Mercerian delegation simply calls him, 'Gerald'. I suppose Master Gerald would be more appropriate, but I wouldn't keep worrying about it. You should get to sleep, Brother, we have to move out tomorrow, and we need to be on the road by noon."

Alstan left him to his thoughts. He soon fell into bed thinking about his day. One thing was certain, the coming months were likely to be anything but boring.

ELEVEN

Ambush

SUMMER 960 MC

T he sun was high in the sky by the time the entourage was ready to move. Anna sat in her carriage along with her maid, Sophie and Tempus, while outside, the soldiers were forming up. King Leofric had provided a Royal Guard for the visitors, and these troops made up two detachments; one to the front and the other to the rear of the column. In between marched the knights, with Hayley leading, the princess's bodyguard under the command of Sir Arnim, and the servants, who followed behind the Royal Carriage. Gerald rode to one side, while Beverly rode her horse, Lightning, to the other.

Alric had watched them mount up and was stunned by the sheer size of the Mercerian Chargers. He had been raised around horseflesh, even considered himself a master rider, but the great Mercerian mounts were astounding to see. Not all the knights rode them, Dame Hayley, in particular, preferred a more nimble beast; a surefooted breed. He wondered if some of these mounts might be purchased and bred in Weldwyn? He would have to suggest this to his father.

The plan was for Alstan and Alric to ride just ahead of the Knights of the Hound. Alric noticed his brother chatting with the guard captain. He rode past Lady Beverly, nodding at her as he did so and was surprised to hear a call from the carriage.

"Prince Alric?" came the princess's voice.

"Yes, Princess?"

"Are we leaving soon?"

"We should be marching in a few moments. Captain Brown informs me that his men are ready, we're just waiting for some of the supply wagons to pull into line."

Getting a line going with this many people was a difficult task, he thought; the princess likely has no idea how much work is involved.

~

Anna leaned out the window to call to Gerald, "Any sign of when we're going to move?"

Gerald looked toward the back of the column before answering, "'Fraid not. I don't think these people have a clue how to organize this thing."

"It's a good thing we didn't have this problem when we marched to Eastwood."

"I might remind you we had precisely this problem, Anna. It took a lot of effort to correct that mistake."

"Should we speed things up a bit, do you think?" she asked.

"I wouldn't suggest it. We might upset them. We're not really in a hurry, I think it best we let them have their moment. Perhaps the princes are just inexperienced."

~

Alric rode up to his brother near the front of the column. "Are we ready to go yet?" he asked.

"Shouldn't be long now."

"What's the holdup?" asked Alric, eager to be on the way. "I don't want to put up with the whining from the princess."

"Yes, about that..." said Alstan.

"What about it?"

"I've been thinking about our guest. I've decided to have you ride in her carriage, if she has no objection."

"What? You can't do that to me! I don't want to be stuck in a carriage with the girl."

"Oh come on now, Alric, she can't be worse than Althea, and she's almost the same age."

Althea was the eldest of Alric's two younger sisters. She was a constant pest, and Alric could well imagine what she would be like if she were here. "Can't you send someone else?" he whined.

"As a matter of fact, I can't. Come on, Alric, she's a Princess of Merceria, we can't ignore that. We need to make a favourable impression."

"Then you ride with her," he pleaded.

"I can't. I've too much to do here. Besides, you're whining, you two should get along well," he said, laughing at his brother's obvious discomfort.

"Fine, I'll do it, but you owe me big time."

Alstan smiled, "Of course, Brother, anything for you."

~

The column finally started moving down the road. The carriage lurched forward and then had to stop. The whole column moved and stopped like a large accordion until the rhythm of the march finally took hold and their speed stabilized. Alric sat across from the princess, absently gazing out the window at the passing countryside. It was Anna who broke the silence.

"So tell me, Alric," she said, "do you really think all these guards are necessary?"

Alric, startled out of his daydreaming, looked at the girl sitting facing him. "Of course. You're a Royal Princess, anything less would be impolite. We place great importance on your protection."

"No offense, but I'm pretty sure my knights are more than capable of defending me."

"Yes, but our troops lend an air of respectability to the march."

"Are you saying," asked the princess, "that my knights aren't respectable?"

Alric stammered, "No, that's not what I meant. It's just that you're in Weldwyn now, it's only proper you be guarded by our troops."

"I suppose that's acceptable," responded the princess. "So tell me, is your brother the heir to the crown?"

"Yes, Alstan is the heir, as the oldest son. Were my father to die, he would be crowned after his approval from the council."

"Approval? What do you mean by approval?"

"Well," Alric continued, "the Earls' Council has to approve him."

"So the earls control who becomes the next king?"

"Not really, it's just a formality."

"Interesting," mused Anna, "but what if they didn't agree?"

"I beg your pardon?"

"What if they didn't agree to making him the next king? What would happen?"

"The king's wishes are never questioned, it's just a formality," stated Alric again, beginning to get agitated.

"But what if they objected?" she pressed.

"The question is irrelevant," Alric responded, perhaps a little too vehemently, "they've never disagreed."

Anna smiled, "There's a first time for everything. It would be interesting, I think, to see what would happen. Is your father an absolute ruler or a constitutional leader?"

Her questions were starting to infuriate Alric, but he told himself she was just a girl. Perhaps if he imagined his sister across from him, he might be able to avoid this problem. "My father, you see, is the king. He is the ruler of the land. People do what he says because he's the king."

"I'm not ten years old," exploded Anna, "you don't have to treat me like a little girl. I'm asking you if there are other limits to your father's power. You already mentioned the Earls' Council."

Alric knew his tactic had failed and tried to start again. "Sorry, I'm used to dealing with my sisters. My father has a lot of power, but there are limits," he offered.

"Such as?"

"He can't declare war without the support of a majority of the council. Other than that, he pretty much has free rein to do as he pleases."

"So, if I understand correctly, the earls here have a lot of power."

"Well, yes. Isn't it the same in Merceria?"

"Yes, and no. Titles don't necessarily imply power, but certainly, some have more influence than others."

"But isn't your father an absolute monarch?" he asked.

"King Andred has absolute power, but it wasn't always that way. For years the nobles held the balance of power, but after the Farmer's Rebellion, years ago, the crown started taking it back, slowly but surely."

"And that," offered Alric, "led to a happier kingdom?"

Anna took a moment to digest the question before answering, "I wouldn't say that exactly. Merceria, like any kingdom, has its detractors."

Alric smiled, "You can't say that about Weldwyn. We have the happiest people in the land."

"I doubt that," muttered Anna.

The conversation stuttered to a halt after that, and they rode in silence for some time, Alric eventually falling asleep in the carriage.

The journey to the capital was estimated to take two weeks. The plan was to rise early each day to start on their way, only to halt just after noon. The remainder of the day would be spent setting up camp and cooking the meals. Tents would be set up and guards posted while the rest of the day would be spent in relative peace.

The first time they stopped, Anna walked the camp, watching the soldiers setting up shelter for the guests. She came across Alric, observing some Weldwyn guards putting up a tent.

"I see you're working hard," she commented.

Alric turned to see her approach. "I don't understand," he said.

"Don't you consider yourself a warrior?"

"Of course," answered the young prince. "Both Alstan and I have been trained extensively in war-craft."

"Gerald says that warriors should be able to look after themselves."

"I'm a royal," said Alric. "I don't have to. I have men to put up my tent for me."

"Is that how you inspire your men?" she teased.

"I don't see you putting up a tent," he retorted, perhaps with more venom in his voice than he intended.

"I'm too young," she replied, "they won't let me."

"The advantage of your gender," he announced.

A look of fury crossed the young princess's face before she turned to stomp off in the direction of the Mercerian tents.

Gerald pulled back on the rope, keeping it taut while someone pegged it down. "That's it," he encouraged, "nice and tight, we don't want it collapsing in a fair wind."

The soldier tapped down the peg with a mallet and then moved to the other end of the tent. Gerald stretched his back, arching it and placing his hands on his hips. He straightened in time to see Tempus, who was watching him, start wagging his tail. It could only mean one thing, and he looked in the direction of the dog's gaze to see Anna approaching, followed closely by Beverly and Celia. He smiled as she drew close.

"What brings you down here, Highness?"

"Give me something to do, Gerald, I'm bored, and I want to help."

"All right, grab that peg over there, and I'll pull this rope taut."

Anna smiled, happy to be included. She picked up the peg and brought it over, looking to her bodyguards. Beverly grabbed a mallet, but Celia simply watched.

"Is this work beneath you, Celia?" asked Beverly.

"I'm a princess, and I'm doing this," added Anna.

Celia grabbed another peg, bringing it over while Beverly smiled. "Welcome to the real world, Dame Celia."

∽

The progress toward the capital seemed slow, and it began to look to Alric like it would be winter by the time they arrived. They had been on the road a week, and he was chafing at the bit. He was tired of spending his days in the carriage and longed to ride away, avoiding her incessant attempts to talk to him. He had to admit she was much smarter than he had assumed, but her constant questions about everything were driving him to distraction. The sooner they could get to the capital, the sooner he would be shrift of her.

~

Beverly woke in the middle of the night to the sound of distant fighting. She instinctively grabbed her sword, making her way toward the princess's tent. The two guards on the tent flap were alert, their weapons drawn as she stepped past them. She entered the tent to see the princess with her faithful dog pacing the space nervously.

"What is it, Beverly?" she asked. "Tempus woke me, something's happening."

"We are under attack, Highness. We must get you to safety, whoever is attacking is likely looking for you."

"Where do we go?" she asked.

"The command tent, it'll be the most heavily defended, but we must go quickly."

They exited the tent with Anna's maid, Sophie dutifully following behind. Tempus stayed close, his nose sniffing the air as they went. The command tent was the main meeting place each night. As a larger, more ornate structure, it was used to house meals for the honoured guest. They entered to see Prince Alric along with Captain Brown and some of his men.

"Highness, good to see you're safe," commented Alric. "We have the guards forming up around the tent."

"Do we know who's attacking?" asked Anna.

"We're not sure. It's still dark and very confusing at the moment," offered the captain.

"Where's Gerald?" the princess enquired.

"I'm here," he said, as he entered the tent, Sir Arnim in tow. "Fighting has erupted in the camp, it's all chaos at the moment."

"Where, precisely, is the fighting?" asked Anna.

"It seems to be coming from the paddock. I've sent Hayley and four knights to secure the mounts."

"I'll dispatch more soldiers," offered Captain Brown. He gave the orders, and his men left, their swords drawn. The tent grew silent as the occupants strained to listen. The sounds drew closer, and everyone turned to face the tent flap, waiting to see what would happen.

Beverly stood stiffly, expecting someone to burst through the entrance, but to her surprise a scream erupted beside her. She turned with horror to see Anna collapse to the ground as Captain Brown thrust a dagger into the princess's stomach. Beverly's instincts kicked in, and she drove the point of her blade into the man's chest. The blade pierced his heart, protruding out his back. She let go of the weapon, instantly dropping to her knees beside the fallen princess, quickly examining her wound. Blood was pouring over the ground, and she placed her hands around the wound trying to stem the flow of blood. She felt hands on top of hers and looked to see Gerald, his face as pale as Anna's.

"We have to get the blade out," he said, a look of determination on his face. "Get ready to cover the wound."

She nodded her assent and Gerald pulled the blade free, absently tossing the weapon to the side. Beverly moved her hands in an attempt to prevent Anna's lifeblood from leaving her. Now Sophie was there, offering a kerchief to help. Beverly grabbed it, tried desperately to cover the hole, but her hands were now slick with blood as the pool on the ground grew larger.

Alric watched in horror the scene before him. The princess would likely die, he thought, and it would mean war. The King of Merceria had sent his own child, and they had allowed her to be killed. He paled at the very thought and suddenly realized he was being selfish. This young girl, through no fault of her own, lay dying before him, and he had failed in his duty. Someone was screaming his name, and he broke his gaze to see the old man, Gerald, yelling at him.

"Is there a healer nearby?" he was shouting.

He was about to retort that he had not been called Highness but couldn't speak. He watched as Sir Arnim tore at the dead captain's cloak, passing a fragment to the lady knight who desperately tried to plug the wound.

"No," he finally stammered, "the nearest Life Mage is in the capital."

"Then go and get him!" ordered Gerald.

Alric balked, "Who do you think you're addressing?" he retorted.

"You, you little shit. Do you want to explain to the king how a Princess of Merceria died on your watch? For Saxnor's sake, go and get help!"

Alric fled the tent, stunned and shamed by the man's words.

Arnim applied a compress to the wound, but even so, the blood still flowed freely through his fingers, and he looked at Gerald, shaking his head.

"It hurts so much," Anna said, through gritted teeth. "Gerald!"

Gerald held her hand tightly as her body shuddered in pain. He recognized the voice of the ranger yelling outside just before she entered the tent, where she immediately absorbed the scene before her.

"Hayley, check the dagger on the floor," Gerald commanded.

The brunette stepped carefully past the group huddled around the princess, stooping to cautiously lift the weapon by the handle. She took it to a nearby lamp, examining the blade.

"It doesn't look poisoned, as far as I can tell."

"Thank Saxnor for small miracles," uttered Beverly. Tears were running freely down her face, and she struggled to get the words out.

"It's bad," said Arnim. "If we can't stem the bleeding, we'll lose her. Without Revi here there's nothing we can do."

"You're wrong," announced Gerald. "I've lost two families, I'll not lose Anna, too." He looked to Beverly, "Take her hand, Beverly, look after her, I'll be back soon."

Beverly took the princess's hand, feeling the weak grip.

He grabbed a lantern and paused at the door, "Hayley, with me, I'll need your help," then left, the ranger following.

"Where's he going?" asked Arnim.

"I don't know," confessed Beverly, "but if I know Gerald, he's got something up his sleeve."

Alric ran from the tent, feeling real fear for the first time in his life. Struggling to suppress his terror, he stopped running and tried to get his bearings. The sound of fighting had subsided, and he recognized his brother, among a group of Weldwyn soldiers. He made his way toward him, trying to will himself into calmness. Alstan looked up at the approach of his brother, a look of shock on his face.

"They were Royal Guards," he stammered out. "How could we be betrayed like this!"

"It's worse," added Alric. "The princess has been attacked."

Alstan stared back at him. "How bad?" he asked.

"She was stabbed in the stomach, she likely won't see daybreak."

"Who attacked her?"

"Captain Brown. He's dead, killed by the bodyguard."

The Crown Prince paled, "This is bad, Alric, if she dies, it could well ignite a war. By the Gods, even if she survives it could mean war."

"What do we do?" asked Alric. He suddenly felt alone, as if the world was falling apart around him.

It took only a moment for Alstan to make up his mind. "You're the fastest rider," he said. "Take five men, ride for the capital with all speed. You must get to the Dome and get help."

"The Arcane Council Chambers?"

"Yes." Alstan continued, "You have to find Arcanus Roxanne Fortuna, she's the most powerful healer in the realm. You must get her back here as fast as possible."

"Will it be enough?" asked Alric. "It'll be days before we can get back."

"It will have to be," said Alstan, "we have little choice. Now go, and may Malin's speed go with you."

The dawn's early light began bleeding through the trees. They had managed to make the princess more comfortable, but she was dangerously pale. The blood still leaked from her wound but had slowed considerably. Gerald entered the tent, Hayley following behind. Prince Alstan was now in attendance though no other Westlanders were present. Gerald dropped to Anna's side.

"Anna, stay with me. It's Gerald, I've brought warriors moss."

He began packing the moss around the wound, Arnim moving his hands as it was applied.

"Moss?" asked Prince Alstan. "Are you sure that's wise? It could kill her."

"It's warriors moss," offered Hayley as she began to help apply the remedy. "It will absorb some of the blood and draw out any infection."

"Will it heal her?" Alstan enquired.

"No," the ranger replied, "but it'll buy us some time. How long before we get a healer, Highness?"

"Likely a week or more. I've sent Alric with extra horses and men. They'll make good time, but I fear the distance is too great."

The moss was carefully packed into the wound. Sophie had been cutting the dead captain's shirt up, and now she was using the material to bind the wound, keeping the moss in place. Tempus was lying with her, his massive head beside hers, a look of utter distress upon his face.

"We can't move her till she stops bleeding," Gerald announced. "And even then, it'll likely be a few days before she can be moved any distance. Are we close to a small town or village?"

"Kinsley is nearby," offered Alstan. "The baron has a manor house there, would that suffice?"

"I should think so," replied Gerald, "but she needs to stabilize first."

"Then it's in Malin's hands now," offered the prince.

"Malin?" asked Hayley.

"God of Wisdom," said Anna, through gritted teeth. "He's their primary God here in Westland."

"Weldwyn," corrected Alstan.

"Sorry, Weldwyn. I'm a little distracted here."

Alstan looked to Beverly, "Why is it you call us Westland, anyway?"

"It's a sign of contempt, really. You beat us hundreds of years ago. You've simply been the land to the west, not worthy of a proper name. It's the way of Saxnor."

"The God of strength?" replied the prince. "He's one of our Gods too, but he's a minor God."

"Now is not the time to debate our beliefs," stated Beverly. "The princess needs rest. With all due respect, Your Highness, I'm kicking you all out of here save for Gerald, Sophie and Tempus. Now go and pray to whatever God you like. Right now we need all the help we can muster."

TWELVE

Ride like the Wind

SUMMER 960 MC

The road had been long and tiring, but finally, the walls of Summersgate, the capital of Weldwyn came into view. Alric's horse was spent, the poor beast having given its all, and now, after two very long days, he rode through the gate. He had switched horses at countryside inns; ridden hard and worn out a slew of mounts, leaving his escort far behind. He halted at the gate entrance, dropping to the ground.

"Secure this mount," he said, "and call me another horse. I must get to the Dome as quickly as possible!"

The guards sprang into action, and within moments a fresh horse was brought. Alric took a swig from a proffered wineskin and then climbed back into the saddle, ready to ride across the city and finally finish his mission. Quickly he rode, ignoring the hails as he passed. It was strange for a Prince of the Realm to be in such a hurry through the streets of the city, and the dust and dirt that covered him must have had the bystanders wondering what had happened.

The Grand Edifice of the Arcane Wizards Council, more popularly known as 'The Dome', was an ancient structure, one of the first built when the great city was founded almost a thousand years ago. The architects had designed a towering structure in which the masters of the arcane practiced their craft. The great dome was encased in copper, proof against the ravages of wind and time. The wizards of the day had cast spells of enchantment to protect the copper, such that, unlike its contemporaries that had turned green with age, it shone as bright today as it did so long ago.

He pulled back on the reins and halted at the great steps that led to its entrance. Taking them two at a time, he rushed upward. News of his arrival had somehow made it here ahead of him, and he saw a robed individual exit the building, heading toward him. As he drew closer, he recognized Arcanus Tyrell Caracticus, Grand Mage of the council.

"Arcanus," stammered Alric, "there's been an attack on the Princess Anna of Merceria. We need a healer immediately."

"Come with me," he said, without preamble. "We must go and find Roxanne as quickly as possible."

Up the stairs they hurried, past the gilded doors into the building proper. Apprentices stared in disbelief as the young prince was guided through the marble-floored structure; never before had a royal entered the grand edifice.

"I believe she's in the main council chamber," said the mage, "we'll look for her there."

They ascended a staircase, and as they passed a robed man the mage spoke again, "Malson, have them saddle up two horses. We'll need them immediately."

Not waiting to hear the quick reply in the affirmative, the wizard kept moving, Alric struggling to keep up. They came to a set of doors without handles or knobs of any sort, only runes were emblazoned upon them. The mage simply put his hand to the door, and the runes lit up with magical energy while the door opened to reveal the top floor directly beneath the great dome.

To Alric's eyes, it appeared to be an immense library with shelves lining the walls and tables arranged alongside, many with open books upon them. In the middle of the room was a great circular table, directly beneath the centre of the Dome, and here he saw the Life Mage, picking gingerly at a plate of food while she flipped through the pages of a tome of some sort.

"Roxanne," uttered the mage, "Prince Alric brings dire news, I'm afraid your skills will be needed."

The woman looked up, her grey hair glowing in the light which streamed in through the windows. "What is it, Tyrell? What has happened?"

It was Alric who spoke next. "Princess Anna, Arcanus. She was wounded two days ago. We need you."

She immediately rose, forgetting her studies for the moment. "The Princess of Merceria? Where is she?"

"Some distance, I'm afraid," Alric replied. "We must hurry, we may already be too late."

"Horses are already being readied," offered the Grand Mage.

"We shall leave immediately," she said. "I will just need to gather some things. Is Aegryth about?" This last question was directed to the Grand Mage.

"Yes, I saw her in the chamber of magic. Shall I fetch her?"

"Yes, we'll need her to enchant the horses to increase their stamina. We must make haste."

Alric wasn't sure what exactly just happened, but both mages began giving orders to servants that appeared from every nook and cranny. Arcanus Roxanne left while Tyrell escorted Alric to a small table, along with a servant, who placed quill and ink before him.

"You must pen a quick note to your father, the king, to let him know what has transpired."

"Of course," agreed Alric, his mind whirling with the sudden activity.

"The king will likely send a larger escort, but we haven't time to wait for it. You should be out of the city before the next bell tolls."

Alric scribbled hastily, passing the note to a servant.

"We shall see it's delivered, Highness," offered the mage. "Now, I'm afraid we must get you to the stables, you have more work to do today."

The Grand Mage escorted Alric through the building toward the stables at the back, where the mages kept their mounts. A servant was already standing by with two horses, holding them by the reins. A rather non-descript woman was standing nearby and as they approached she began an incantation.

"Don't be alarmed, Highness," said the mage, "Aegryth is about to banish your fatigue."

"She can do that?" queried Alric.

"Of course, Highness, she's an enchanter. But the spell will only work for a few hours. You will feel especially tired by the time it wears off. Roxanne will be able to help with that, through healing, but every spell has its price. You may find by the time you're done that you need to sleep for several days."

"I'll bear that in mind, Grand Arcanus," said Alric, remembering to use the proper title. He had never really dealt much with mages before; they were a class unto themselves. By their own rules, they were banished from the politics of court, offering only advice or counsel when requested. They were a powerful force but kept entirely apart from the world of the Royal Court.

Alric felt a strange sensation over his entire body, like there was a vibration in the air and then, as it subsided, he felt refreshed as if he'd just woken up.

"That's incredible," he muttered, more to himself.

"Remember, the effects will force you to pay a price later. Don't get too used to it," warned Aegryth. "Now, you must be on your way."

"But the healer," uttered Alric.

"Is right here, Highness," said Roxanne as she entered the stables. "Now, we must ride like the wind."

~

Anna shifted slightly in her sleep. Tempus raised his head, looking longingly at his sleeping mistress, and then put his head back down. He was lying on the end of the bed, and it shifted slightly. Sophie wrung out the cloth, dipped it back in the cool water, then laid it gently on the brow of the princess.

The door opened quietly, and Gerald peered in, "How's she doing?"

"She's no better," the maid returned, "though no worse. She spends the time asleep."

"Perhaps it's better this way, at least she's not fidgeting. I was afraid she'd reopen the wound."

It had taken two days before they had decided to move her and then another day to get her to the village of Kinsley. The baron had immediately made his manor house available. Anna had been carefully placed in the great bed, and now there was little they could do but wait and see. Gerald hoped the young princeling had managed to get help. Prince Alstan had posted a guard, but Gerald had insisted that only Mercerians be allowed in the building. Now the Knights of the Hound vigilantly stood guard.

"Gerald," uttered Sophie, "she's awake!"

Gerald moved to the side of the bed as the maid gave way. He grasped Anna's hand, "Anna, can you hear me?"

She squeezed his hand lightly. "I'm here," she said.

Gerald breathed a sigh of relief. "You had us worried, Anna. How are you feeling?"

Her other hand reached out, and Tempus crawled forward, placing his head beneath it. "Weak, it feels strange. I almost imagine myself floating."

"Resist it, Anna," begged Gerald, "it's the Afterlife calling you."

"Well, it'll have to wait a while," she said, managing a slight smile. "I'm not ready to leave yet, you still need me."

"I'll always need you, Anna," said Gerald, choking on the words.

"Typical, isn't it?" she mused.

"What is?"

"That I need a healer the one time Revi isn't around. All those months travelling together and I didn't need him once. Now, here I am, lying in agony."

Gerald was at a loss for words. By Saxnor's beard, he would make sure the mage was around in the future. "I've sent a messenger back to Merceria, Anna, though it'll likely be some time before we get a reply."

"What happened to the man who attacked me?" she asked.

"Beverly killed him. Prince Alstan has promised to look into the matter, but I can't say that fills me with confidence. There's the very real possibility that they're behind the attack."

"I doubt that," responded Anna. "My death would likely cause a war. I don't imagine our king would be too pleased."

A rumbling noise interrupted her, and she looked down at her body, covered by the blankets. "It appears my stomach is hungry."

"Sophie, here, will feed you some soup, only broth though, we don't know how badly you're wounded."

A yell from outside brought Gerald to his feet, and he made his way to the window, opening the shutters to let in some fresh air. He spied a small group of riders approaching down the roadway and yelled out, "Hayley, can you make out the riders?"

"Yes," the ranger replied, "it looks like the prince has returned. There's a woman with him and a couple of guards."

"It must be the healer," Gerald yelled. "Bring her up straight away."

"Of course," she replied.

Gerald turned back to Anna, "It seems the Life Mage has arrived.

"Revi?" asked Anna.

"No, one from the capital. We'll have you up and about in no time."

"Don't exaggerate, Gerald. Remember when you were injured in that bandit attack? You still had to rest for days afterwards."

"Well, yes. But at least I was able to move."

A commotion below interrupted their conversation as the door was thrown open and then footfalls rushed up the stairs. Hayley stepped into the room, holding the door for their visitors.

An elderly woman, perhaps a little younger than Gerald, made her way into the room. "You must be Anna," she said in a pleasant voice. "How are you feeling?"

"Much better now that you're here," she replied. "Are you the Life Mage?"

"Yes, Highness. I'm Roxanne Fortuna, a Life Mage. I'm going to cast a spell, and you'll feel a little strange, but the feeling will pass. Are you prepared?"

"Yes, I've seen healing before."

"Excellent. Now hold still and try to relax."

She raised her hands in the air and began to chant. Gerald had no idea what the words meant, but soon the air around him began to buzz, and he felt the hairs on his arms stand straight up. He had seen Revi use spells in the past, but this time the effect was more pronounced. The mage's hands began to glow and then she placed them on Anna's stomach. Even through the covers, he saw the light leave her hands, penetrate the blanket, and for a brief time, he saw Anna's entire body enveloped by the glow. It lingered for only a moment and then dissipated as Anna let out a breath of air.

"How do you feel?" asked Roxanne.

"It doesn't hurt anymore," stated Anna. "I feel quite well, just tired."

"That's to be expected, you've lost a lot of blood. It will take several days before you'll be on your feet again."

The mage peeled back the blankets to examine the wound, untying the bandages that were present. "Ah," she uttered, "I see you've used warriors moss." She looked up to Gerald, "Was that your doing?"

"Yes," he replied. "I hope that didn't cause any problems."

"Problems? No, you saved her life. You kept her alive long enough for me to heal her, you should be proud. Have you slept?"

"A little," Gerald lied.

"Very little," added Hayley.

"Then I suggest you get some rest. I will remain here until she can move, then I'll travel with you back to the capital."

"I'm not leaving Anna," he declared.

The princess beckoned him over, then had him lean over to whisper to him, "Go and rest, Gerald. I will need your counsel later, and I need you healthy."

Her friend straightened himself. "It appears I need rest," he said, defeated. "Where's Beverly?" he asked next.

"She's downstairs," offered Hayley. "Why?"

"There are arrangements to be made," he said. "We can't leave the princess unguarded."

"And who do you think's been looking after her while you slept?" asked Hayley.

The blank look on Gerald's face said everything. "Beverly?"

"Of course," added the ranger, softening her tone. "Now get ye to bed, young man." She pointed at the door.

"I suggest," said Roxanne, "that we let the princess rest. Her maid will stay, along with her dog, but everyone else: out!"

"I have to guard her," protested Hayley.

"Very well, but do it quietly, near the door. She needs her sleep."

Alric had sat down in a chair in the entranceway, having found himself too tired to stand. He saw Gerald coming down the stairs and wanted to say something, but his mind was fogged with fatigue, so he mutely watched as the old man approached him.

"Your Highness," Gerald began, "I very much wanted to apologize for the harsh words I used after the attack. I should have used proper manners and addressed you accordingly. I will accept any punishment you deem necessary."

Alric could hardly believe his ears and struggled to answer. "Nonsense, Gerald, you were acting in the best interest of the princess. There's nothing to forgive."

A look of relief crossed the old man's face, and, for the first time, Alric truly recognized the look of concern that had been present. Was this the effect that his Royal Personage had on people? Were they afraid of him? He thought back to Beverly's words; he had no real friends, and yet he saw these strangers holding together like a family. He resolved then and there, to make a concerted effort to truly care about these visitors.

"Your Highness is most gracious," said Gerald, who then turned to leave.

"Wait, Gerald," called out Alric, struggling to stand.

"Your Highness?"

"I know I haven't been the most...gracious of hosts, but I want to tell you I'll be more attentive in future. Your visit here is important, to both our kingdoms, and I'll make every effort to ensure you are kept safe. You can rest assured that we'll get to the heart of this assassination attempt. My father will not stop until this conspiracy is uncovered, I give you my word."

"Thank you, Highness, I'm sure the princess will appreciate it."

Dame Beverly strode down the path toward the gate; the metal structure was the only entry point to the estate. She had issued orders for two knights to be stationed here at all times to watch for intruders and keep the princess secure. Now, as she approached, she saw Dames Juliet and Celia in their assigned positions, talking between themselves. As she came within earshot, Beverly could hear their discussion.

"It's a good thing the prince got here in time," Dame Celia was saying. "If she'd died we'd be stuck here in hostile territory, miles from home."

"Do you think it would have been war?" asked Juliet.

"Don't you? Imagine if, say, Prince Alric were visiting Merceria, and he was attacked and killed. Don't you think King Leofric would be furious?"

"Of course, but enough to start a war? I think cooler heads would prevail. War is to be avoided at all costs."

"Nonsense," retorted Celia. "War is the natural state of Humans. Our kingdom's been at war for almost its entire existence; it allows the strong to rise to the top."

Juliet was about to refute this statement when Beverly intervened, "If you two have finished arguing, I need to speak with Dame Juliet for a few moments."

"We're not arguing," stated Celia, "just musing. I'll wander back down the road and give you some privacy, shall I?"

"That would be appreciated," responded Beverly. She waited until Dame Celia was out of earshot before continuing, "Dame Juliet, when we met, you told me you didn't want to reveal your family name."

"Yes," Juliet confessed, "but I sense that is no longer possible."

"Considering the attack on the princess, I think it would be best if you were to confide in me. We can't afford to have any more secrets."

Juliet nodded her head in agreement. "I suppose I should have known I couldn't keep it hidden forever. My father is the Earl of Tewsbury."

Beverly's eyes revealed her shock, "You're full of surprises, I didn't see that coming. I take it the countess was not your mother?"

"No," she agreed, "my mother was a servant. The earl carried on a relationship with her for years, until she died."

"I'm sorry," said Beverly, "I know how difficult it can be, not having a mother. Were you close before she passed?"

"Yes," said Juliet, "though as I grew older, I grew more rebellious."

"How did you take up the life of a knight?"

"With the death of my mother, there was no place for me at the estate. The earl suggested it would be better if I left, and then settled a yearly remittance on me to stay away; he's been very generous in that regard. Since I couldn't live in Tewsbury any longer, I headed west and settled down in Kingsford. I was rather lost, not really knowing what to do with my life. When I heard the Duke of Kingsford was sending troops to Wickfield, I volunteered to go."

"Didn't they object to your sex or lack of training?"

"They did, but there was such a shortage of volunteers they agreed to take me. Women fighters might be rare, but they're not unheard of."

"True enough," continued Beverly, "but being a soldier is not the same thing as being a knight. How did that come about?"

"The duke was travelling with us to the east, intending to continue on to

Wincaster when we headed north. One night there was a commotion in his tent while I was on guard, a clang of swords, and I rushed in to find someone trying to kill the duke. His Grace was prone on the ground with his attacker ready to strike the final blow. I took down the assassin, stabbing him through the back. The duke was so thankful he recommended I be knighted.

"It seems there are two nobles with an interest in your future," mused Beverly.

Juliet shrugged her shoulders, "I should have refused the honour. As a knight, I was an outcast. The Duke of Kingsford had no use for me, and I couldn't go to Wincaster for fear of running into the Earl of Tewsbury."

"How were you inducted into the Order of the Sword?" asked Beverly.

"By Royal Proclamation, there was no ceremony. I still have a copy of it, if you'd like to see."

"That's not necessary. Does the Earl of Tewsbury know about all of this?"

"No," said Juliet, "I've always been careful not to reveal his name. As far as anyone knows, my father was a soldier who died in the border wars. If the Earl of Tewsbury found out about my position, he might cut off my remittance."

"I can imagine," offered Beverly. "He has a son, doesn't he?"

"Yes, though I've always managed to steer clear of him. I've kept myself away from the capital for that very reason."

"Well, you've certainly given me something to think about."

"Will you tell everyone about me?" asked Juliet.

"No," Beverly replied. "The only people that will be informed are the princess and Gerald. None of the other knights needs know of this, at least for now."

"Thank you for your discretion," said Juliet, "it means a lot to me."

"Just make sure you continue to loyally serve the princess, and there won't be a need for another private conversation between us."

THIRTEEN

The Capital

AUTUMN 960 MC

A nna's health recovered quickly, and a week later they resumed their journey to the capital, Summersgate. Autumn weather had decided to make itself known and the cooler evenings were seen as a blessing. As the Grand Mage had predicted, King Leofric had sent more troops to escort them, and now the column that entered the city's gates numbered more than three hundred. Anna, however, kept her guards even closer and had taken to wearing her Dwarven sword at all times. Gerald was ever present, and even Beverly and Hayley seemed to spend more time in the princess's company.

As the carriage rumbled through the gatehouse, a deafening roar burst forth, and Gerald looked out the window. "It seems the people of Summersgate have decided to turn out to welcome you."

Anna looked out the carriage window. Prince Alric was riding nearby, so she beckoned him over, "What's going on?"

"My father has arranged a welcome for you, Highness. All you have to do is follow my men, we'll lead you to the Palace where my father and mother will meet us."

Anna looked at Gerald, "I don't like this."

Gerald shrugged, "We'll keep you safe, Anna. We won't let anyone get close to you. Do we really have much of a choice? We came here to help with relations between our two kingdoms; we can't just ignore their hospitality."

Anna pursed her lips, "Any word on Revi? I'd feel much more comfortable with him here."

"No reply as of yet, but if he were coming, he'd likely not get here for another month or two."

She looked out the windows to either side; the ever-present proximity of Beverly and Hayley reassured her, and she visibly relaxed, falling back into the soft cushioning of her seat.

"How much further do you think?"

As if on cue, Beverly leaned over in the saddle and knocked on the window. Gerald lowered it to hear her. "We're almost there. I can see the Palace just up ahead."

Anna sat up again, instantly alert. Even Tempus, at her feet, suddenly raised his head in expectation.

"You know the drill?" asked Gerald.

"Don't worry, Gerald," Beverly responded, "I've got it. We'll all be in position."

The carriage rolled up to Summersgate Palace. Unlike Wincaster, this Palace wasn't fortified but formed a large estate, with lush gardens. The carriage halted, and they waited while the Knights of the Hound dismounted. Commands were issued, and then Beverly opened the carriage door. Her knights were formed to either side, presenting a safe corridor for the princess to walk.

Anna stepped from the carriage, with Gerald just behind her. She waited until he had completed his egress and then held onto his arm while Tempus took up a position to her left. Now, safely between her two best friends, she made her way forward, the knights walking in step with her, forming a protective wall to either side.

Ahead, was King Leofric along with Queen Igraine. Beside them were Alric and Alstan, along with two young girls, one roughly Anna's age.

The Knights of the Hound halted while Anna and her small party continued making their way forward, foregoing the protective cocoon. The nearby crowd gasped as they did so, and it took a moment for Gerald to realize it was Tempus who was causing the stir.

"They seem to like your dog," he remarked.

"That's cause he's such a good dog, aren't you boy," she said, stopping to pat his head. The great dog seemed to smile back at her.

King Leofric stepped forward, a breach of etiquette that made his guards nervous. He walked towards them with purpose, ignoring the complaints from his officers and held out his arms.

"Welcome to Weldwyn," he said, his voice loud and clear.

A welcoming cheer broke out from the assembled crowd, and while he waited for it to subside, he looked back to his queen who stepped forward, coming quite close before she spoke in a low tone.

"Let us get you away from here, my dear, you've had quite an ordeal, and I doubt this is helping." She glanced at her husband and Gerald watched as the king absorbed her meaning.

"Yes, by all means," said King Leofric. "We've arranged a banquet in your honour, but perhaps it's best if we spent some time visiting first, away from the crowds."

Anna smiled, "That would be nice, Your Majesty."

"Come along, then," he urged. "We'll go through the main door here and turn left, into the private wing."

He offered his arm, and as Anna placed her hand upon it, he covered it with his own. They walked toward the building, King Leofric on one side, Gerald on the other. Tempus followed closely behind along with Dame Beverly.

The guards had obviously not been informed of the king's decision, for when they entered the Palace, guards were formed up on the right, expecting them to enter the grand hall. The king stopped and waved forward a well-dressed servant, whispering in his ear. The man nodded and moved to the left, opening the door for them. They walked through a large room that was sparsely furnished, save for some chairs against the wall.

"This," the king said, "is where people usually wait when they're coming for a private audience. We'll go through those doors at the far end, and then we can relax. There's a comfortable living area just beyond."

Weldwyn guards were scrambling to take up new positions at the end of the entourage, and Tempus growled as one stepped too close. Beverly turned to eye the intruder, and he fell back a few paces.

The king halted at the inner door and turned to his guards, "We won't be needing you, gentlemen. You may wait out here."

There were looks of shock on the soldier's faces, but they did as they were told. King Leofric released Anna's hand to open the door, beckoning Anna to enter. The room was large, furnished with comfortable looking furniture, overshadowed by a enormous fireplace to the right. The ceiling here was high, two stories tall, and along the far wall was a massive stack of shelves that ran from floor to ceiling. Some sort of strange contraption held Gerald's attention, and he had to stare at it for a moment before realizing it was a wheeled ladder that could be moved about to reach the highest books. Anna had stopped just after entering, taking it all in while the Royal Family filed in behind her, entering the room proper.

"Do have a seat, Highness," suggested the queen. "Make yourself comfortable."

Unbidden, one of the shelves moved to reveal a door behind it, where the well-dressed servant entered, and the king ordered some refreshments. If the man was surprised with the change in locale, he didn't show it, merely bowing slightly before turning and leaving the same way he had entered.

Anna chose to sit down on a large, wide chesterfield, and when Gerald balked, she looked to him, patting the chair beside her. He dutifully sat, looking uncomfortable in the fine surroundings. The king reclined upon an armchair to her right, while the rest of the Royal Family took various places around the room.

"I should properly introduce you to the rest of the family, Highness," he began. "You already know my oldest, Alstan, and of course, Alric here. They have a brother, Cuthbert, who is my second son but I'm afraid he's up in Loranguard. Hopefully, you'll have a chance to meet him before you return to Merceria. These are my two daughters, Althea," he pointed to the oldest, "and Edwina. Althea is close to your age, but Edwina is four years younger. And of course this lovely lady," he indicated the queen, "is my wife, Igraine."

"Pleased to meet you," Anna replied. "This is Gerald, my friend and advisor and this is Tempus." She pet her dog's head. "Lady Beverly here is my bodyguard and Commander of the Knights of the Hound."

"We are so pleased that King Andred decided to send you, Anna," said the queen warmly. "And we look forward to spending some time with you. Tell us, have you had a nice journey?"

"Aside from the assassination attempt? Yes," she replied.

"I apologize for that," said the king. "Alstan has informed me of the situation. I must stress that we had no part in it. I gave orders for Alstan to investigate, and he's already been digging into the traitor captain's background. I understand you have your own guards?"

"Yes, ten knights and twenty-four foot soldiers. We also have our own servants."

"Our troops are at your disposal, of course, but considering what you've been through I suspect you would be more comfortable with your own people guarding you?"

Anna nodded, and Gerald was impressed by her calm demeanour. The conversation was halted when a group of servants came in bearing drinks. Once everyone was served, and they were once again unattended, the discussion resumed.

"Have you any idea who might be behind the attack?" asked the king. "Anything at all might help us in our investigation."

"I'm not sure," offered Anna. "There was a recent uprising in Merceria, perhaps a survivor wants to punish our king? Or it could be Norland behind the attack, they've always been a thorn in our side. There's also bound to be people in Westland, pardon me, Weldwyn, who desire war. It could even be The Black Hand."

"The Black Hand?" queried the queen.

It was Gerald that spoke up, "Yes, a group of criminals intent on killing members of the Royal Family. They tried to kill the Crown Prince and Princess Anna a couple of years ago."

Queen Igraine's face visibly paled, "Oh, you poor child, that sounds terrible. We must guard you more closely. We can't have your visit here suffer as a result. We will do our utmost to protect you, you can be assured."

"Where did you get your dog?" piped in Edwina.

"Not now, Edwina," said Alric.

"No, it's all right," said Anna, turning slightly to face the young girl. "He was living at my estate. He saved me from The Black Hand when I was a little girl."

"Is he friendly?" she enquired.

Anna had to pause a moment before answering. "He can be very affectionate," she responded, "but he takes his duty seriously."

"His duty?"

"Yes, protecting me."

"So he's your guard?"

"Yes, and also my oldest friend."

"He's older than Master Gerald?" Edwina persisted.

Anna smiled, "Older, no, but I've known him longer. Gerald is older in years."

The young girl was enthralled by the large creature at Anna's feet. "May I pet him?"

"Certainly," offered Anna.

Edwina rose from her chair and timidly approached the large beast, gingerly reaching out with her hands to rub his head. Tempus laid down on the floor and then rolled onto his side.

"He likes me!" she exclaimed.

"He's a good judge of character," added Gerald, who then blushed when he realized he had spoken out of turn.

"Gerald, here, is an experienced soldier," said Alric. "The princess tells me he's fought in numerous battles."

"Indeed?" commented the king. "You must tell us about it sometime when things have calmed down a bit. I suspect the next few days will be hectic for you."

"How so?" queried Anna.

"Well, there's today's banquet, plus there's a large number of nobles that would like to have meetings with you, at your discretion, of course."

"Might I ask where we will be billeted?"

"Billeted?" responded the queen. "You make it sound like you're all soldiers."

"We are a warrior culture," replied Anna. "Is that not the term you would use?"

"It will do well enough," offered the king, "though we would say you are being hosted, but let us not quibble over minor variances in language. We have a large mansion in town that has been made available for your exclusive use. I assume you will want your own staff, but there will be a small contingent waiting to familiarize your people with the place. Royal Guards will be stationed outside of the estate for your protection."

"Would those be the same Royal Guards who attacked me?" asked Anna, her voice a little more bitter. "I must insist that my own guards take up that duty. I'm sure you have other tasks that will keep your men busy. With whom shall I liaison?"

"I have a trusted minister," said the king, "whom I believe you've met, the Earl of Faltingham. He is the man who visited your father's court."

"I'd feel more comfortable with someone I'm familiar with. Perhaps Prince Alstan?"

"I'm afraid his investigation into the attack will keep him quite busy. May I suggest Prince Alric?"

"That is acceptable, Your Majesty," Anna replied, though not with much enthusiasm.

"Now," continued the king, "if you're ready, perhaps we can make our way to the banquet, there's an army of nobles waiting to meet you."

"By all means," agreed Anna, rising.

Gerald offered his arm and was surprised by the iron grip that indicated her nervousness. Placing his other hand over hers, he squeezed it slightly to give her some reassurance while they followed the king to the banquet.

The banquet was an endless spectacle of speeches and welcomes. It was quite late by the time they approached the manor house that had been made available to them. Arnim and the Mercerian Bodyguards had searched through the estate while Anna was still at the banquet and so, by the time she arrived with her knights, the place was secured, and their belongings unpacked.

She was welcomed at the door by Captain Arnim himself, along with Sophie, who was waiting to whisk her off to bed. As they made their way from the hallway, Gerald turned to the captain, "All secure, Arnim?"

"Yes, we've displaced all the Westlanders. Our people are in control here."

"Where's Hayley? I didn't see her at the banquet."

"She's on special duty," offered Arnim.

"Special duty?"

"Yes, she's found a perch on the roof where she will keep watch with her bow."

"Do you really think that's necessary?"

"Someone's already tried to kill the princess on this trip and failed. Whoever is behind it is likely to try again. We must be extra vigilant."

"We're safe here for the time being," offered Beverly as she entered. "We're guests of the king."

"Guests," questioned Arnim, "or prisoners?"

FOURTEEN

Autumn

The cooler weather had come, and with it, boredom. Endless visitors begged an audience with the foreign princess, and her appearances at court had ensured the Palace was filled to capacity.

To Gerald, it was all a blur. He was constantly at Anna's side. He felt out of place; a commoner amongst the nobility but he did it for Anna. The late evenings were the most enjoyable for they would often sit in the mansion's library, reading through tomes as they regaled each other with interesting tidbits they found. Anna was a voracious reader and would read five books to every one that Gerald perused.

He was particularly pleased, one evening, to find a history of the army of Weldwyn, and it was with great interest that he discovered the events that led to the formation of their two kingdoms.

"Gerald?" prompted Anna.

He looked up from his book. She had set hers down and was sitting up, a look of excitement on her face.

"Yes?" he responded.

"I've got an idea!"

He recognized that she was bursting at the seams. "This wouldn't have anything to do with that map you were looking at earlier, would it?"

She grinned,"You know me all too well."

"Go on then, what's your idea?"

"I was thinking," she continued, "that instead of turning into hermits here, we could travel around Weldwyn meeting the people."

"Do I need to remind you that someone in Weldwyn tried to kill you?"

"Yes, but that's all politics. I mean the commoners. Remember when we went to Wincaster and watched the play?"

Gerald laughed, "Yes I do, but if you remember we almost got arrested. Besides, we can't really get away with disguising you as a commoner anymore, you're too well guarded."

"True, but at least we could get out and see some interesting sights. This city is too much like Wincaster."

"Summersgate is far nicer than Wincaster," he objected.

"Yes, but it's still a big city with lots of nobles with their superior attitudes."

"I suppose you've picked out the places you'd like to visit already," he said, good-naturedly.

"Of course! Come here and look."

She flipped through the book in front of her. The illuminated pages were filled with sketches and small maps. She was about to start talking when the door opened and Dame Beverly poked her head in.

"Your Highness, Prince Alric is here. Shall I show him in?"

"Yes," she replied, and then turned back to Gerald with a look of mischief in her eyes. "We'll save this for later, I'm already in planning mode."

Gerald struggled to hide his smile as Alric entered.

"Greetings, Highness," began the young prince.

"Alric, you bring news?" Anna countered.

"Nothing too exciting. I've brought you a schedule. There are dozens of nobles and wealthy merchants who want to meet you."

Anna held up her hand to forestall him, "I've had more than enough of those. I've already received investment offers, as well as three proposals of marriage."

"Really?" Alric stammered.

"No, I'm joking, but I've had no end of enquiries. Last week alone I had to send off over thirty letters back to Merceria."

"I'm sorry it's not more entertaining," Alric commiserated. "I know life at court can get very tedious at times."

"Tell me, Alric, what do you do for fun?"

"Fun? What do you mean, fun?"

"Do you have snowball fights? Do you build soldiers out of snow?" She looked to Gerald who covered his smile by faking a cough.

"Well," the young prince responded, "we have jugglers and troubadours-"

"No," she interrupted. "I don't mean what you do at court. I meant what do you, Alric, do for entertainment when you're not at court?"

"I like to go to the tourneys."

"Tell me more," she prompted. "I've heard about the tournaments, but I've never seen one. What are they like?"

"Well, cavaliers go at each other with weapons until only one man stands. It's quite exciting."

"Cavaliers? They're similar to knights, aren't they?"

"I suppose. Cavaliers are professional warriors who practice their craft in the tournaments. Before Weldwyn was a kingdom, it was populated by numerous tribes. They united to drive out the invaders."

"That was us," Anna said, turning to Gerald.

"Us?" asked Gerald.

"Yes," Anna continued, "the invaders were the mercenaries that landed on the south coast. The united tribes defeated the invaders and drove them east, leading to the founding of Merceria."

"Yes, that's correct," said Alric, "but after the unification, there had to be a way to settle disputes without going to war. King Loran and the Earls' Council set up the tournament system. If ever there were a dispute between earls, they would each send a champion and fight it out. Eventually, it became more symbolic. Now the tournaments are for entertainment rather than settling differences, though it does keep the warriors in training."

"So cavaliers are the earls' champions?"

"They were originally, but now they can be anyone. They do, however, have to prove themselves before they can enter a tournament."

"How do they do that?" Anna asked.

Alric smiled, warming to his favourite subject. "There are different ways. Sometimes a warrior will distinguish himself in battle, but usually, they have to go through a series of preliminary fights to prove they're worthy to enter the ring."

"Interesting," said Gerald. "Is it true they knock each other off of horses?"

"Some do, that's the jousting, probably the most exciting part of a tourney. Others will compete in the melee events. There's even an archery competition."

"And how often do these tourney's occur?" asked Anna.

"Smaller events take place throughout the year, all over the kingdom, but after harvest there'll be a grand tournament here in the capital. All the cavaliers flock here to become the Champion of Weldwyn."

Gerald noticed the excitement in Alric's voice. The young prince had passion, and this was the first time it had manifested itself in Anna's company.

"Don't you have tournaments in Merceria?" Alric asked.

"No, not anymore," said Anna. "They used fight in arenas, but that stopped generations ago."

"Then how do your soldiers stay ready to fight?"

Anna looked to Beverly who was still standing by the door. "What do you say to that, Beverly?"

"We kill the enemy," she replied. "We have enough that we're always in demand, at least on the frontier."

"There, you see," offered Anna. "We have enough enemies on the border. Is it not so in Weldwyn?"

"Well," Alric replied, "we've had our problems with Merceria in the past, but it's been quiet for years."

"You mean other than the army that invaded us from here?" prompted Gerald.

"That wasn't our fault," defended Alric. "The baron responsible was tried for treason. Anyway, that was an internal matter. Your own earl betrayed you."

"True enough," admitted Anna, "but what of your other borders?"

"The north is defended by the Great Wood. The Orcs there don't typically bother us much. To the west lie the wild lands of the Twelve Clans, they occasionally raid across the border. They're more of a nuisance than a real threat."

Beverly took an interest, "Orcs, you say?"

"Yes, savage creatures. Do you have them in Merceria?"

"We fought them at Eastwood," answered Anna. "I'm just surprised they're here in Weldwyn. Is there an Orc city in the Greatwood?"

Alric looked confused. "Orc city? Since when do Orcs have cities?"

"The Orcs had great cities before the coming of man," explained Anna. "They're rumoured to have been destroyed by the Elves. It would be exciting to see the ruins of one, even better to find one intact."

"I have no idea about Orc cities. The Orcs of the Greatwood live in small, scattered bands, little more than an annoyance.

"What of the south?" Anna continued.

"The sea lies to the south. The biggest issue there is with piracy; the Sea of Storms is a dangerous place. Occasionally the Kurathians will raid, but that hasn't happened in years."

"Kurathians?" said Gerald. "Tempus is a Kurathian Mastiff."

"Yes," acknowledged Alric. "They employ groups of them to bring down cavalry, that's why it was a shock to see him, but the Kurathians are mainly sea raiders. It's very rare that they would land an army. They've hit our coast many times over the years, the most recent was when I was a young child. The great ports of Weldwyn are fortified against such attacks these days. Don't you have the same problem in Merceria?"

"No," answered Anna. "Our access to the sea is cut off by the Great

Swamp. Mercerian ships haven't braved the river route to the sea for many years."

The room fell into silence, and Anna sipped her drink. "I should love to see the Greatwood," she stated.

Alric laughed, "It's far too dangerous, my father would never permit it."

"More dangerous," she countered, "than your guards? And what would you do if I decided to go anyway, lock me up? Keep me prisoner?"

Gerald smiled at the look of dismay on the young prince's face. Here we go, he thought.

"But you can't just go gallivanting off to the north," Alric sputtered. "Arrangements would have to be made, soldiers dispatched..."

Anna smiled, pleased with the result. "Excellent, it looks like you already know what needs to be done! Please inform His Majesty that I have decided to travel to the north. Lord Edwin has an estate up there, doesn't he?"

"Yes," said Alric, "in Faltingham."

"How long till the snow comes, do you think?" she asked.

"We don't get much snow in Weldwyn. Even in winter, the roads are generally clear."

"Perfect," Anna added, "then it's settled. We'll travel to Faltingham, and then go on to Loranguard on the western border. I understand there's a lot of shipping on the river."

"Uh, yes," said Alric, "but the king will insist on sending an escort."

"Then I suggest you go and speak to him with all haste, the better to be ready when the time comes."

Alric stood, a look of indecision on his face, "Then I shall leave you, Highness."

Anna smiled as Alric left the room. She waited till she heard the foot-steps recede before turning to Gerald.

"We're going on an adventure!" she burst out.

The Royal Court of Weldwyn was busy as Alric made his way into the great hall. His father was in deep discussion with several nobles and Alric was loath to interrupt him. He kept going over, in his head, how to break the news that the princess wished to travel north.

A voice interrupted his musings, "Alric, what news?"

He turned to see Alstan, striding across the room, drink in hand. "I've been coordinating things with our visitor," he said.

"And how's that going, Brother?"

Alric had to think a moment before continuing. He looked around conspiratorially to make sure no one else was in earshot. "It's infuriating," he said at last.

"How so?"

"She won't follow protocol. She wants to go tearing off on... a tour of the kingdom. I have to figure out how to tell Father."

"She'll need an escort," his brother offered.

"You do it," he half pleaded.

"No, I can't. I have pressing engagements elsewhere."

"What about Cuthbert?"

"He's not back from Loranguard. I'm afraid it has to be you, dear brother."

"That's not fair," sulked Alric.

"Life is seldom fair," his brother commiserated.

"I hate this. Chaperoning a spoilt little girl."

"That little girl is a Princess of Merceria. Need I remind you how important it is that we stay on friendly terms?"

"I know, but she seems to delight in tormenting me."

"She probably just likes you, Alric."

"Don't even go there, Alstan, it's not funny."

"On the contrary, I find it quite amusing."

Alric made a face and turned to stare in his father's direction, but the conversation still continued, and he dared not interrupt.

"Listen," offered Alstan, "what if you asked a cavalier to accompany you. You'd like that. You've been following Lord Marlowe's son, see if he'd be interested in commanding the guard."

Alric smiled, "Yes, and maybe he will teach me a thing or two about jousting."

"You know you can never joust, Alric. You're a royal."

Alric sighed, "I know. Mother has made that plain on a number of occasions. Still, having a cavalier along will likely keep the trip interesting."

Alstan chuckled, "I don't think it'll take a cavalier to keep things interesting. Trouble seems to follow the princess wherever she goes."

"What do you mean by that?"

"Nothing, Brother, nothing at all. Now you must excuse me, I have important matters to tend to."

Alric watched his brother leave. Was there something he wasn't telling him? Only time would tell.

∽

Princess Anna of Merceria began plotting the trip. It would take days before she was finished, but once she was in planning mode, there was little anyone could do to dissuade her. Gerald watched as she pored over maps of the realm, learning as much as she could about each possible destination before she finalized their itinerary.

He was sitting at the end of the table snacking on some chicken as she pored over yet another map at the other end. They were interrupted by Sophie, who brought news of a visitor.

Anna looked up, "Who is it, Sophie?"

"Prince Alstan, Highness," the maid replied.

The princess began carefully folding up the map, "Please send him in," she said, then turned to Gerald. "What do you think he wants?"

Gerald finished chewing before he spoke, "I have no idea. It's unusual, to say the least. Perhaps Alric can't make it, and he's taking his place?"

"We shall have to see," she mused.

The door opened to reveal the Crown Prince. "My apologies for coming unannounced, Highness, but I have a matter of some importance I must bring to your attention."

"That sounds very ominous, please have a seat. Sophie, would you bring some wine, please?"

"Yes, Your Highness," replied her maid, then left the room.

"So what is it that brings you here today?" Anna asked.

Prince Alstan flicked his eyes towards Gerald, and then back to the princess. "I'm afraid it is for your ears alone."

"Gerald stays." Her tone indicated there would be no argument. "Anything you say to me can be said in front of him."

Alstan looked uncomfortable, a mask of indecision etched on his face before he finally relented. "Very well, where shall I begin?" This last statement was said more to himself, but she quickly picked up on it.

"How about the beginning," she prompted.

"When Captain Brown attacked you, we were very concerned."

"As were we," added Anna.

Gerald watched the face of the prince redden. This was a difficult subject for Alstan to broach and he was curious where the conversation was going.

"I was tasked by my father to look into the affairs of the late captain to see if we could find any indication of why he might carry out such an attack."

Anna smiled, leaning forward in her chair to rest her elbows on the table. "And you've finally found something. Tell me more."

"I took only trusted soldiers, men I've known for years, and we searched his properties. We found a secret compartment beneath the floor in one of them. There were all kinds of papers."

"What was the nature of these papers?"

"They appear to be written in many hands and indicated troop positions and strengths across the realm."

"So," mused Anna, "he was collecting information from agents across the land?"

"Yes, precisely. We think he was forwarding messages on to someone else but haven't been able to discover the beneficiary of this information."

"I understand, but I don't see what this has to do with us. Someone spying on Weldwyn is your concern, but we are Mercerians. Surely you don't think he was communicating with us?"

"No, but amongst the cache of documents was this." He withdrew a folded paper from his pocket and passed it to the princess. Gerald rose, walking to stand behind her to examine the document as she read it.

"It describes," continued the prince, "the defenses of Bodden Keep in great detail."

Anna finished reading the note, and then passed it directly to Gerald. "What do you make of it, Gerald?"

He moved to the window for better light and held it up to look for any clues as to its origin. "I don't see any distinguishing marks, though the writing appears to be in a feminine hand."

"Yes," said Anna, "I noticed that as well. I must thank you, Highness, for bringing this to our attention."

"Certainly, Highness," said Alstan, rising to his feet. He began moving toward the door, but stopped, turning suddenly back towards the princess, "Might I enquire how you will proceed?"

"That depends. What actions are you taking?"

"I afraid that I am not at liberty to go into detail; it's an internal matter now."

"Internal?"

"Unfortunately, Princess, these are not subjects for discussion with foreign dignitaries, even if they are royalty. We will, however, keep you apprised if we discover anything else that might concern you."

"I see."

"Do you have any other questions, Highness?"

Anna rose from the table. "No, this is an internal matter, we shall look after it from here."

Gerald was about to speak but realized the princess was already considering options.

"Very well," said Alstan. "I will leave it in your capable hands. I shall ensure that no one else is informed of this."

"Thank you, Alstan, that is most appreciated. Before you go, might I ask how many people know of this already?"

"Myself, two guards, who have been sworn to secrecy, and the king."

Anna nodded, "Then please, thank King Leofric for his discretion."

The door opened, and Sophie entered bearing a tray with drinks. She looked in surprise at Alstan, who was just about to leave.

"It's all right, Sophie, the Crown Prince has to leave on important business. You may bring the wine over here, we'll serve it ourselves."

The young maid dutifully placed the tray on the table, withdrawing from the room immediately after Alstan.

Gerald sat back down, the letter still held in his hand. "This is bad news."

"Yes, it means we have a traitor to deal with."

Gerald was at a loss for words. After all the travel, the death of the assassin, the wounding of the princess, it was almost too much to take.

The look on his face must have told her much for when she spoke it was in a soft voice, "We'll get through this, Gerald. We'll figure out who the traitor is and who's behind this."

He looked at her, feeling his years. "How do we track down the spy, Anna? Whoever it is has been with us for some time."

Anna smiled and held out her hand for the letter. He passed it to her as if the very touch of the paper was distasteful.

"Tell me," she asked, "you've read it, how accurate is it?"

"It's quite detailed," he grumbled.

"So, whoever wrote this has some knowledge of fortifications and such."

"Yes, the average person wouldn't understand half of that."

"So, we can assume that the author has some military experience."

"I hadn't thought of that, but it's true."

"It also mentions the catapults. Those are new to the Keep."

"Yes," agreed Gerald, warming to the task, "that means the writer must have been with us at our last stop at Bodden, or have been in contact with someone who was."

"So at least we know a few things," she said, absently staring at the letter.

"Actually," Gerald offered, "we know more than that."

"What do you mean?"

"We are looking at a feminine hand with military experience or training. That limits our choices considerably."

"Are you suggesting it's one of my knights?"

"It has to be. Half the servants can't even write, and those who can wouldn't know a parapet from a gatehouse. A woman wrote the letter, and the only women who understand such things are the knights who came with us."

"That leaves a short list."

"Yes," agreed Gerald. "Beverly, Hayley, Celia, Levina, Aelwyn, Juliet, and Abigail. I think we can safely eliminate Beverly, it's not as if she'd betray her own father."

"We can't eliminate anyone, Gerald. Perhaps someone is controlling her."

"No, I'd know. I've known her since she was born. No, it's someone other than Beverly. The question now is what we do about it?"

"We don't do anything," said Anna.

"What? We can't just ignore this,"

"No, but we'll observe carefully and wait for the spy to slip up. We can't just arrest everyone concerned without proof."

"Can't we? You're the princess."

"Yes, but that would only sow distrust and make people nervous. Plus, if we're wrong, the spy might use the opportunity to get away. No, we must be sure."

"We'll have to be careful," he prompted. "We should at least inform Beverly, it's her father's Keep that could be in danger."

"Likely not," said Anna.

"Why do you say that?"

She smiled as she held up the letter, "Whoever wrote this doesn't know it was intercepted. The message never got through to its intended recipient, so Bodden is safe. Perhaps we can use this to our advantage later on, with a little subterfuge."

"You have a devious mind," observed Gerald.

"Now," she continued, "we shall have to plan this out carefully."

FIFTEEN

Unexpected Visitors

AUTUMN 960 MC

Anna stood, looking out the window at the courtyard below. It was a beehive of activity as servants exited the house, each bringing more goods to store on the wagons.

"I remember when it took very little for us to go on a trip," she commented.

Gerald was leaning from a chair, rubbing the belly of Tempus. He stopped as the princess spoke and Tempus, who was lying on his back, knocked his arm with his paw, begging for more attention.

"You didn't have such a large entourage back then," he said. "It was just you, me and Tempus, here."

She turned, smiling at her dog, "I miss those days. We were more carefree back then when we didn't have to worry about dealing with a traitor."

"True," he agreed, "but we can't change what's happened. You're a proper princess now, and you have important responsibilities, but Tempus and I are still here for you."

"I know," she said, turning back to watch the work proceeding below, "but I still miss the days of just the three of us. It seems like we can't even go for a stroll without a bevy of guards."

Gerald rose, coming to the window to gaze out, like Anna. "Saxnor's beard, it looks like they're taking everything from the house!"

"Good thing they don't know my background. I still remember stealing scones from cook back in Uxley."

"You know she put them out for you to take."

She looked at him in surprise, only to see him smiling. "I choose to believe I used my masterful sneaking ability to obtain said scones," she said, in her most regal voice.

"You can have all the scones you want now," he offered.

"You're right!" she exclaimed. "Let's ask for some scones right now, with jam, and we'll go out into the garden and have a picnic. Just the three of us."

"And the guards," he reminded her.

He watched her face fall, and it was heartbreaking. She was a girl on the cusp of womanhood who needed someone her own age, yet there was no possibility of it here, not with treachery at hand.

She turned silently to gaze back out the window, and then suddenly her face grew animated. "Someone's coming."

He gazed out the window and even Tempus, alerted by her tone of voice, stood up, coming over to stand with his front legs on the window sill.

"What do you make of it?" she asked.

"Looks like a common enough carriage," he offered. "The type that's easily available for the right price."

"It's certainly filthy. I can only surmise it's been travelling for some time."

"I don't see a coat of arms," offered Gerald. "It may be a merchant of some sort."

They watched as the horses halted. A guard had come from the house to investigate, with Dame Celia following. She walked over to the carriage and began talking, though they could make out no sound at this range. The knight then turned and headed back to the house.

"Who do you think it is?" Anna asked.

"I don't know. I suggest we go down and find out."

"I have a better idea," said Anna, and swung open the window. She leaned out and Gerald, fearful she might fall, grabbed her, holding onto her waist.

"You there," she yelled, getting the attention of the guard. "Who's in the carriage?"

The soldier looked up, answering, "A Master Revi Bloom and guests."

"Well, don't just stand there, invite them in for Saxnor's sake." She turned hurriedly, leaving the window wide open. "Come along, Gerald, we have guests to greet."

They made their way downstairs and emerged in the entranceway just as Revi, Lily and two unknown women were entering through the front door. The guard who had escorted them in appeared uncomfortable around the Saurian, but Anna ran forward to embrace her friend, uttering something unintelligible to Gerald's ears.

Revi looked surprised, "I thought you needed my spell to talk to Lily?" he asked.

"No," she replied, "I learned a fair bit on our trip to the Darkwood. Now that she's back, I can continue. It's good to see you, Master Revi. Please don't leave my side again."

The mage nodded quizzically. He was unaware of all that had transpired since he left them, for he had not crossed paths with the messenger on route.

Anna looked at the other two guests. They were both well-dressed women, one perhaps sixteen or so, the other somewhat older.

"And who do we have here?" she asked. "Did you get married during your absence?"

Revi blushed, and it made Gerald laugh.

"No, Highness. Permit me to introduce Lady Aubrey Brandon, daughter to Lord Richard Brandon, Baron of Hawksburg."

The younger woman bowed, "Pleased to meet Your Highness," she said.

"And this," he indicated the slightly older woman, "is Lady Nicole Arendale. She's been sent by your father to be your Lady-in-Waiting."

"My Lady-in-Waiting? I have Sophie," Anna sputtered.

"The king," continued Revi, "thought it best you have someone with breeding to advise you."

"You talked to the king?"

"No, but I have a letter with his seal here for you," he rummaged through his voluminous robes, withdrawing a small scroll case. He untied the top, withdrawing an ornately written parchment.

Anna took the paper, while Gerald looked at Lady Nicole. He sensed something out of place here, perhaps an agent sent to spy on them? He hated living this life of intrigue and deception, but held his tongue.

The princess handed him the paper while she continued, "Welcome, Lady Nicole. I've never had a proper Lady-in-Waiting before, so you'll pardon my manners if I don't utilize you to your full potential."

The woman curtsied, as was the new fashion. "Your Highness is free to use me as you see fit," she replied. "I am at your service."

"Lady Aubrey," Anna continued, "you are cousin to Lady Beverly, are you not?"

"I am, Highness," the young woman replied.

"Are you here to attend me as well?"

"No, Highness," she replied.

"I took Lady Beverly's advice," said Revi, interrupting the conversation.

"Which was?" asked the princess.

"Lady Aubrey is my new apprentice. I've already started training her."

"Congratulations, Lady Aubrey," offered Anna, "though perhaps I should say commiserations. I think Revi might be a handful."

"Very funny," said Revi, reddening. "I see Gerald's behaviour has started to rub off on you."

"Is my cousin here, Highness?" asked Aubrey. "I would love to see her."

"She's out training some of the knights," offered Gerald. "Shall I go and find her?"

"Let's all go," offered Anna. "I think I should like to see how they're doing."

They filed out of the hallway, heading toward the back of the house.

Dame Beverly struck, and the defender's shield flopped to the side. The brunette on the other end of the blow cursed, yet again.

"This is hopeless. Can't I just get back to using my bow?"

"No, Hayley, this is important, it could save your life someday."

"But I'm useless like this. I feel like I weigh twice as much as I should. This armour is weighing me down."

"You're a knight now and you need to get used to the weight. One day it'll likely save your life. Now lift the shield higher, this time grip the handle a little tighter and allow the blow to glance off."

She struck again, and the shield moved only slightly. "You see? The blow is deflected so it doesn't travel up the arm."

The ranger smiled, "You're right, let's try it again."

"For Saxnor's sake, Hayley," cursed Dame Celia, "just get on with it will you, or we'll be here all day."

Beverly turned on Celia, "You have something better to do?"

Duly chastised, the knight looked down at her feet, "No, Dame Beverly, sorry."

"Now," said Beverly, "let's try it one more time, then we'll work on your swordplay. The rest of you pair up and go through your drills."

Groaning was heard all round as the knights began to take up their positions.

"What of Sir Arnim?" asked Levina. "Is he not to join us?"

"He's busy seeing to the guards," explained Beverly, "so the rest of you should continue without him."

"But that makes an uneven number," objected Dame Abigail. "How do we do that?"

"Simple," replied Beverly, "Celia will defend while both you and Aelwyth attack."

"Two on one? That doesn't seem fair," complained Celia.

"Do you expect an enemy to play fair?" asked Beverly. "I once had to fight three men at the same time, but I didn't complain."

The grumbling grew quiet to be replaced with half-hearted sword strikes and blocks. Soon, they would get into it, Beverly thought, and then they would see the wisdom in it. It's not that they were a bad bunch, but few had seen combat in years. They had grown soft with peace and needed honing. Hayley, of course, had seen battle at Eastwood, and she was an excellent archer. Beverly thought it unlikely that the young ranger should accompany a cavalry charge, but she needed some basic skills to defend herself should the need arise.

She was taking up her stance again to strike Hayley when a voice rang out, "Cousin!"

Turning in surprise, she saw her cousin Aubrey Brandon, no longer the young girl she so remembered. "Aubrey? What are you doing here?" She strode over, scabbarding her blade.

"I'm the new apprentice," she exclaimed. "I'm learning magic!"

They embraced and Beverly, for the first time since leaving Bodden, felt a heartfelt hug. "It's so good to see you," she exclaimed. "How are things in Hawksburg?"

"The family is well, so much has happened. We'll talk about it later."

"I think," offered the princess, "that you've done enough for today. Why don't you go play catch up with Aubrey?"

"But what of the knights, Highness?" She protested.

"I can take care of them," offered Gerald, "if you think they could learn anything from me."

Beverly made an exaggerated bow at Gerald, "It would be my honour to allow you to train the knights," she said, straightening. "Train them hard, Gerald, like you used to train me."

Gerald smiled, "It will be my honour, Lady Beverly."

"Hayley needs some work with the shield and Celia weakens her guard. Sir Barnsley has an issue with-"

"I know how to train soldiers, Beverly. I can handle it."

"Of course you can," she responded. "With Your Highnesses, permission, I shall steal Aubrey away for a while."

"Of course," said Anna. "Why don't you take her into town?"

"Marvellous idea!" added Gerald. "There's a tavern nearby called the Old Goat."

"I shall give it a try," offered Beverly. "Is the food good?"

"Oh, yes," offered Gerald. "They have the most excellent cheese. Just like Hawksburg Gold!"

He laughed as she shook her head. It was nice to see Beverly in a good mood.

The expedition, as the princess liked to call it, was ready to move, and now they waited only for the arrival of their escort to begin the trip north. Anna had elected to ride for the first few hours, leaving her guests to travel in the Royal Carriage. Lily sat with Tempus, the dog now showing his age more than ever. With them rode Lady Nicole, displaying obvious discomfort with her two strange companions. Aubrey had elected to ride a horse as well, and now rode beside Beverly, the two chatting amiably as they prepared to follow just behind Anna and Gerald.

"Where in the Afterlife are they?" fumed the princess. "Don't they know we have a lot of ground to travel today?"

"I'm sure they'll be here soon, Anna," offered Gerald. "These are West-landers remember, they can't organize anything quickly."

Anna laughed. "I suppose so."

"And it's not like we're really in that much of a hurry," offered her old friend. "A few hours here or there won't really make much of a difference."

The clattering of hooves drew their attention; Dame Hayley was approaching.

"News?" asked Anna.

"Yes, Highness," the brunette responded, pushing a strand of hair from her face. "They're almost here. Prince Alric is riding with someone at the head of their column."

"How many, do you think?" Anna queried.

"I should say about a hundred men, plus wagons."

She looked at Gerald with a sour expression. "Do they mean to send an entire army with us?"

"They can't very well have a foreign force marching through their kingdom unaccompanied, can they?" advised Gerald.

"No, I suppose not." She turned to watch the road and soon saw the column coming into view. "Who's that with Alric?" she asked.

"I was told it's someone named Jack Marlowe," Dame Hayley supplied.

"Who's that, I wonder," muttered Gerald.

Hayley continued, taking Gerald's remarks as a question. "Not sure, but from the way he's dressed, he's likely a noble."

"Oh great, just what we need," he cursed.

"Now, now, Gerald," the princess said, trying to placate the frustrated warrior. "Let's not make rash conclusions. He's likely a friend of Alric's. Let's keep an open mind. Shall we go and meet them?"

They rode over to the column with Beverly, Hayley and Aubrey following. As they approached the Westlanders, the column halted, and Prince Alric rode forward with his companion.

"Princess Anna," he began, "may I introduce, Lord Jack Marlowe, son of the Viscount of Aynsbury."

The man bowed his head solemnly, "Please, call me Jack." He raised his head to reveal a large smile.

"Pleased to meet you, Lord Marlowe. This is Gerald, Dame's Beverly and Hayley, as well as Lady Aubrey Brandon." She pointed to each as she named them.

The man's eyes locked on Beverly for some time. "A lady warrior, I am enchanted," he said, once again bowing deeply, but before Beverly this time.

Beverly frowned, and Gerald could almost feel her sense of loathing for the man.

"Shall we begin moving, Your Highness," Gerald asked Prince Alric.

"By all means," he responded. "We have many miles to cover."

"I thought your men might bring up the rear since we're already formed up," offered Beverly.

"Certainly," responded Alric, "though perhaps Jack and I might join your company near the front?"

"Of course, Highness," responded Anna.

Gerald grumbled. It was beginning to look more and more like this nice country ride would be poisoned by the politics of court.

The weather was most pleasant as they rode out through the northern gate of the city to the green countryside beyond. The rich pastureland of Weldwyn reached to the horizon. Gerald was surprised to see that more of it was not under cultivation.

Alric rode to one side of Anna, with Gerald to the other. The young prince was pleasant enough and included them both in the conversation. Gerald hated to admit it, but he was growing fond of Alric. He had proven to be a capable organizer, the column notwithstanding, and the more he relaxed around the princess, the easier it was to get along with him. Jack had fallen back behind him and was now riding beside Lady Aubrey, while Beverly rode to the other side.

"Tell me, Alric," asked Anna, "how many mages are in Weldwyn?"

"That's hard to say, Anna," he replied, falling into the more familiar address now that they were on the road. "The Mages Council oversees all that. Why do you ask?"

"They're exceedingly rare in Merceria, but there used to be more. I was wondering if the same was true in your kingdom."

"We have a rich history of magic," he countered. "It dates back centuries. The mages were instrumental in helping defeat the invaders," he said, blushing slightly.

"You mean us, of course," offered Anna.

"Yes, sorry. The master of all magic at that time was the high mage, Weldwyn."

"I assume the kingdom is named after him?"

"Yes," he assured her. "He was instrumental in the war, but died at the final battle, sacrificing himself to win. He was King Loran's closest advisor."

"And so the mages helped form the kingdom?" she asked.

"Yes and no. It was Weldwyn's belief that magic be kept separate and distinct from the crown. Even before the final battle he and the king had made plans. Mages have their own rules. They may never sit upon the throne, it's enshrined in their pledge."

"Pledge? What's that?"

"Each potential mage must swear an oath to become an apprentice."

"So they can't sit on the throne. What else can't they do?" she asked.

"They advise the king, but they have no votes on the Earls' Council and must renounce any title to assume the role of a mage."

"Does everyone agree to that willingly?"

"Magic takes a lot of time to learn. A noble has duties that would preclude studying the arcane arts, or so I'm told."

"It seems to be a well thought out process," she offered.

"Yes, it was planned out centuries ago and has held sway over them for generations."

"Tell us about this Jack Marlow fellow," interrupted Gerald. "What do you know of him?"

"Mad Jack?" confirmed Alric. "He's a cavalier, perhaps one of the best."

"So he participates in the tournaments?" enquired Anna.

"Yes, he's the reigning champion. He took down all his opponents this year."

"He looks a bit young," commented Gerald.

Alric chuckled, "He is. He's the youngest cavalier to ever win the title."

"What's his background?" enquired Anna.

"As I mentioned earlier, his father's the Viscount of Aynsbury, famous for their horses. They say Jack's the finest horseman in the kingdom."

"Who says?" asked Gerald.

"Well, mostly Jack himself, if you ask him. He's certainly good. You should have seen him at the last tourney, the man's amazing."

"I'd put my coins on Beverly any day," offered Gerald.

Alric turned in his saddle to look behind him, "The redhead? Surely not."

"You'd be surprised at what she can do with that horse of hers," Anna responded.

"There's a big difference between riding a big horse and handling one," offered Alric.

"I think it's you that would be surprised," challenged Anna. "Perhaps we'll arrange a demonstration sometime in the future.

"I would enjoy that," said an eager Alric. "Perhaps a wager?"

"It wouldn't be seemly to place bets against a foreign prince. Perhaps a friendly challenge, no more. I wouldn't want to embarrass you."

Alric appeared pleased with this and Gerald observed how comfortable these two royals were becoming in each other's company.

Beverly kept her eyes to the front, trying to ignore Lord Jack but the man wouldn't, or couldn't stop talking.

"Tell me, dear sweet Aubrey, what has brought you here to so brightly enlighten us with your presence?"

Aubrey, riding a smaller horse, more fitting to her height, nodded at him in acknowledgement. "You have a way with words, Lord Marlowe."

"Please, call me Jack," he insisted.

"Very well, Jack. Tell me, do you compliment all the ladies with this silvered tongue of yours?"

"Only when the voice enraptures the heart like a warm summer's day," he responded.

"Oh, please," said Beverly, "enough of this drivel. Shouldn't you be riding with Prince Alric, Jack?"

"It wounds my heart to know that I have upset you, Dame Beverly. I shall vacate this position immediately." He spurred on his horse, catching up to the prince.

Aubrey and Beverly looked at each other and burst out laughing.

"Is he real?" asked Aubrey.

"I'm afraid so," countered Beverly. "Watch out for that one, he's bad news."

"Surely not," said Aubrey. "He's a bit flowery-"

"He's only interested in one thing, Aubrey, and I shouldn't have to tell you what that is. He'll likely be using the same line on the other knights later."

"You're just jealous," Aubrey teased, "because Aldwin isn't here." Beverly was about to retort when her cousin cut her off, "I'm just kidding, Cousin. I wouldn't tell anyone else about Aldwin. It's your secret to share."

Beverly relaxed in the saddle. "How's your training going? Is Revi treating you well or do I have to knock some sense into him."

"Master Revi is perfectly fine. I'm trying to learn my first spell, but it's proving difficult."

"Your first spell? I thought you'd have to be an apprentice for years before learning spells."

"Normally, yes. But Revi said I've mostly mastered the basics, and he's eager to get me casting."

"So what is he starting you with?"

"He let me pick, so I decided to go with healing. It's very tricky, you have to mentally focus on the letters while you perform these intricate manoeuvres with your hands. It's most challenging."

"Letters?"

"Yes, the magical letters, some call them runes. Each letter has a proper way to say it along with a physical movement. In addition to that, you have to form the correct mental images. It's the hardest part of casting, I'm told. It would be similar to what you do, riding, fighting and taking in all the surroundings at the same time."

"It took me years to master that," stated Beverly.

"Precisely. That's why it's so difficult, but I love it. The sense of manipulating things using these unseen forces is quite exhilarating."

"I understand that," Beverly replied. "I get the same feeling after battle, though I hope you never have to kill anyone."

"Not me, I want to be a healer. Imagine all the good I could do making people better."

"You seem to have found your calling."

"It's all thanks to you, Cousin. You're the one that gave my name to Revi."

"Did I? I thought I recommended you for a maid's position."

Aubrey laughed, and it reminded Beverly of that visit, all those years ago, when she first met her cousin. "Say, once we stop for the night, what say we go out on a little ride, just like old times?"

"I would like that," said Aubrey. "I'll tell you all about the family, and then we can talk about the loves of our lives."

Beverly looked to her cousin, "Are you in love, Aubrey?"

Aubrey laughed, "No, but you are. Now, I'll race you to the head of the column." She spurred her horse forward, and Beverly laughed; no one could outpace Lightning.

The course had been picked out when they set up camp for the afternoon. While the cooks started preparing the meal, the rest gathered near an empty field where the challenge would be duly carried out.

Alric, Anna and Gerald had settled upon a circuit that would take the riders past three main obstacles and then return to their starting location. Each rider was allowed to trot through the course to familiarize themselves with it. A burnt out tree stump formed the first leg of the race, where the riders would circle around behind it and then proceed to the great oak tree that was at the back of the field. They would pass toward the outside of the tree then head toward a broken wagon that lay rotting in the sun. From there they would race to the finish line, marked by two spears placed into the ground.

Mad Jack had chosen to wear his soft cotton shirt with ridiculously tight pants and high boots. He made a show of strutting around the audience, paying particular attention to the female knights in attendance. Beverly remained in her usual travelling attire, a leather jerkin and sturdy pants, only removing her armour. She was standing, stroking Lightning's nose, chatting to Aubrey while they waited for Jack to complete his display.

"He certainly puts on a show," commented Aubrey.

"He's a showman, I'll give you that," Beverly agreed.

"I suppose he would have to be. He's in tournaments all the time."

"Tournaments! These people are barbarians. Can you imagine fighting for fun? Someone could get killed."

"I'm told," offered Aubrey, "that they have healers standing by."

"Still, very dangerous. Even a healer can't fix you if you're dead."

"But you're playing his game, aren't you? Doing this race, I mean?"

"That's different," Beverly defended. "No one's going to die here."

"Not unless Jack upsets you again," chortled Aubrey.

Beverly laughed, releasing some of the pent-up anxiety. "It's good to have you here, Cousin. You make me unwind."

"Look, he's finally done his show," noted Aubrey.

It was true. After bowing outrageously before the crowd, Jack was moving toward his mount. He stopped beside it, put one hand on the saddle and then leaped onto the creature's back. The crowd, duly impressed, clapped and he waved at them, flashing his teeth. He trotted over to Beverly and bowed, waiting for her to mount.

Beverly had thought to jump into the saddle but changed her mind. She spoke to Lightning, and then the great horse went down on his front knees. She straddled the saddle and, without using her hands or a word of command, the great beast stood, making Jack's horse seem much smaller in comparison. Seeing Jack's look of surprise, she smiled.

"Take your positions," called out Prince Alric, and the two riders trotted over to the line formed by the two spears.

Gerald was standing on the line, holding out his hand. The riders brought their horses forward, aligned with each other. Gerald stood to one side, clear from any obstruction and raised his sword in the air. The crowd held its breath, and then he swept the sword down; the signal to begin.

The horses burst forward, clumps of grass and dirt flying up from their hooves. Jack's horse was nimble and gained an early lead. Down the side of the course he rode, yelling in triumph. Beverly paced Lightning for she knew he would need a burst of speed near the end. Round the burnt stump rode Jack, making a tight turn. Beverly saw him clear the marker and then leaned her mount into the turn. Lightning was moving well, not even exerting himself, waiting for the command to unleash his full potential.

Jack peered over his shoulder, and Beverly spied a flash of white as the man smiled. Could he be so cocky so early in the race? Silly question, she thought, of course he could.

The large oak tree drew nearer, and she slowed Lightning to make this second, and slightly tighter turn. She observed Jack ahead of her, but his horse was sweating heavily; he was pushing his mount and could make no more speed. Round the tree they flew and onto the next stretch. She spotted the broken cart in the distance and lined up the run. Lightning made a jump to clear a small stream, and then she let him have his freedom.

Jack was looking over his shoulder again, displaying his bravado when suddenly Lightning exploded into a frenzy of speed. Jack turned back to face forward, and dug in with his heels, pushing his horse to the limit. He made the last turn around the broken wagon, and then stood slightly in his stirrups, whipping his reins to drive his mount even faster. Above the sounds of his own horse, he heard the thundering of hooves, and looking to the side, he witnessed the massive Mercerian Charger passing him.

Beverly released her reins and let Lightning sail past the finish line, allowing him to slow down naturally. Once he was back to an easy trot, she wheeled him around with her legs, patting him on the neck. Jack crossed the finish line, looking on in appreciation. Not one to miss an opportunity, he stood on his horse's back and bowed to the audience as he trotted by, waving at the crowd.

Beverly rode over to Aubrey, who was standing by the finish line. She dismounted some distance from the line and let Lightning trail her without a lead. The great horse followed her obediently, stopping when she did. She bowed before the prince, and with a hand motion, bid her mount to do like-wise. The crowd roared with approval, and she noticed Jack out of the corner of her eye, his face a mask of annoyance; she had stolen his adoration.

"The winner is clearly Dame Beverly," announced Prince Alric. "Our congratulations to you both, for the fine show you have put on today."

Jack rode over, finally dismounting by leaping from the saddle. Was there no end to this man's showmanship?

"My most heartfelt congratulations," he said. "It was a race most fair, though I fear you have the finer mount." He was examining Lightning's lines in appreciation. "Perhaps I could arrange to purchase one of these fine steeds."

"Lightning is mine," Beverly stated. "A gift from my uncle, Lady Aubrey's father. It's he that raises the breed."

"Ah," said Jack, turning to face Aubrey, "I see that the Brandon's are well bred, along with their horses."

Aubrey blushed, not sure how to handle this remark. "I understand you raise horses yourself, Lord Jack."

"My father does, the finest horseflesh in the realm. Perhaps we'll travel there someday, and I will give you a tour."

"That would be delightful," she replied. "I'm sure my cousin and I would like that very much."

He glanced over to Beverly, and another look of irritation crossed his face. He covered it quickly with a smile. "I yield the riding to the finest equestrian," he said, "but at least I know I can still beat anyone in a fight."

Beverly was about to step forward, but Gerald put a hand on her forearm. "Let him have his moment, Beverly," he said. "It's just bluster."

She took a breath, holding it just a moment before letting it out slowly.

"Now," exclaimed Jack, "it's time to drink!"

SIXTEEN

Faltingham

AUTUMN 960 MC

The estate at Faltingham was large and sprawling. It sat at the northernmost border of Weldwyn, close to the very western end of the Greatwood and just south of the Hills of Despair. As such, it was in no danger of attack, for it was said that no army could penetrate the heavy brush of the Greatwood, and none would dare to attempt to pass through the hills, for there were spirits of the dead that lived there, ready to consume the souls of those who dare trespass.

The nearby city was a massive structure, with traditional walls and towers, yet Gerald observed that they were falling into disrepair. Likely the town had never seen a battle larger than a drunken brawl and the citizens sat behind their defenses, feeling secure.

They passed through the city without stopping, for Prince Alric was apparently eager to arrive at his destination. Lord Edwin Weldridge, the Earl of Faltingham, was the king's closest friend, so close, in fact, that Alric called him uncle. He was, of course, indispensable to the king and had remained in the capital, sending word to his wife to expect visitors. Now, as they rode up to the estate, Alric recognized his Aunt, Lady Alicia Weldridge, waiting to greet them.

Alric travelled in the carriage along with Anna and Tempus. Gerald and Beverly rode to either side while Lily was in a second carriage, along with Aubrey, Revi and Lady Nicole. The rest followed along on horseback, with an army of wagons and servants that made up the rest of the procession.

As the carriage rolled to a stop, the servants dutifully came forward to open the door. Alric invited Anna to exit the carriage first, and she descended the small step to greet Gerald, who, having dismounted, was waiting, his arm extended for her to hold. Alric came next, followed by Tempus, the great dog rocking the carriage as he jumped to the ground. Lady Alicia bowed deeply, then Alric stepped forward to hug her affectionately.

"It's so good to see you, Aunt Alicia. How have things been in Faltingham?"

"They have been well," she replied, "but look at you! You've grown so much. You're filling out nicely; I suppose all the fair maids in the capital are swooning over you."

He blushed at the compliment and then turned to introduce his guest, "This is Princess Anna of Merceria. She has decided to travel the kingdom to meet the people and has chosen Faltingham as the first stop."

Lady Alicia bowed again, "We are honoured by your visit, Highness. I hope you will find the accommodations to your satisfaction."

"Thank you, Countess," Anna responded.

"Countess?" Lady Alicia looked to Alric for an explanation, but the young prince had the same look of confusion.

"Is the wife of an earl not referred to as 'Countess'?" she asked. "It's the title we use in Merceria."

"No," explained Alric. "She's just addressed as Lady Alicia. The term 'Countess' would only apply if she were a widow."

"Why is that?" Anna asked.

"As a woman, the only way she can hold a title is if she is widowed."

Gerald detected a hint of annoyance in the prince's voice; Alric was tired of explaining things from the sound of it. Anna also reacted to the tone; he noticed her jaws clench.

"An interesting custom," offered Gerald, bowing. "Allow me to introduce myself, I'm Gerald Matheson."

"Yes," agreed Anna, "pardon my manners. Gerald here is my closest confidant and this," she held her hand out for her dog to move closer, "is Tempus."

"What a marvellous hound," said Lady Alicia, "and so large! I bet he has a healthy appetite. How about the rest of you? Are you hungry? We've laid out a spread. Come inside, we don't stand much on ceremony here."

"It's true," added Alric. "Aunt Alicia doesn't hold much love for court life. My parents often come up here just to relax."

"Our king hunts to relax," offered Anna. "Do they hunt around here?"

"No, it's too dangerous. Oh, the area's safe enough near the city or estate, but nasty things live in the woods and hills in these parts."

Gerald, at first, thought he might be spinning a tale, but the serious look on the prince's face told him otherwise.

"Is there anything we should know about?" he asked in concern.

"No," responded Alric. "You'd have to go miles before running into anything dangerous."

They made their way into the mansion, where a large room had been prepared. Chairs were scattered all around, with small tables nearby.

"It is our custom," offered Lady Alicia, "that we sit and chat while we pick at finger food."

"Finger food? Isn't all food eaten using fingers?" asked Gerald.

"This food is," offered Lady Alicia, "but more formal meals require forks."

"Oh yes, forks," replied Gerald. They had always fascinated him for some reason, and he suddenly wondered what the forks of Faltingham might look like? Were they the same as in Merceria? Certainly the ones in the capital were pretty normal looking. He was startled out of his reverie by Lady Beverly, who was tapping him on the shoulder.

"I'd like to see to the billeting of the column, with your permission, Gerald."

"Why do you need my permission?" he asked, dumbfounded by the question.

"The princess told us you were in charge of all her troops. Didn't she tell you?"

He looked across at Anna, who was sampling a pastry. As their eyes met, she smiled and nodded, perhaps with a mischievous glint to her eye.

"Oh, I see how it works," he muttered. "Very well, Dame Beverly, you may see to their billets. I'm sure there are servants here who can tell you where to put them."

Beverly turned to leave, but Gerald quickly grabbed her arm, "Hold a moment," he said, indicating with his finger that she should lean in close. "Make sure you have the room next to Anna," he whispered. "We don't know who we can trust."

"They're putting two to a room," she replied.

"Then share a room with your cousin, I'll talk to you about it later."

Beverly nodded, a slight look of confusion on her face. She bowed to the princess and then left the room.

Aubrey supervised the unpacking of Revi's carriage. There were chests with all manner of things inside, along with a copious number of books.

"I see you've become quite the librarian," said a voice from behind her. She turned to see Beverly approaching.

"Where have you been, Cousin?" said Beverly. "I was starting to worry that Mad Jack might show up."

"If you're looking for Revi, he's talking to Captain Caster. Sorry, I suppose I should say Sir Arnim, shouldn't I."

"We don't stand much on ceremony here, unless it's something official. I'm sure you can simply call him Arnim. Now, what do we have here?"

"These are my training books," she swept her arm over the pile.

"All these? It'll take months to get through that lot."

"Actually, I've already read most of them, but I need to check on a few things every now and again, so I have to have them close. That reminds me, do we know what rooms we've been assigned to? I'd like to get these indoors."

"As luck would have it," said Beverly, "that's precisely why I'm here. You and I will be sharing a room."

Aubrey looked pleased. "Just like back in Hawksburg," she exclaimed. "We can chat into the wee hours of the night."

"Yes, but I still have duties, so I have to get SOME sleep."

They both laughed and Beverly starting picking up books. "Come on, then, let's get this load of ancient knowledge up to our new room. I suspect we'll be here awhile."

They were housed on the second floor, with the princess being given a room in the northwest corner of the building. Beverly and Aubrey were right next door, to the east, while Gerald had an adjoining room to the west.

Beverly had thought to put guards on the floor, but something about Gerald's warning made her pause to think. Was there a threat to the princess here? She didn't think so, but her mind hearkened back to the warnings of the druid Albreda. She decided to post Hayley in the hallway, leaving Arnim's guards to patrol the rest of the estate.

It was late evening by the time everything was settled. Beverly and Aubrey were finally sitting in their room, enjoying some wine when they were interrupted by a quiet knock on the door.

"Come in," Beverly and Aubrey chimed in unison.

The door opened to reveal Gerald, his face a mask of worry.

"What is it, Gerald, is something wrong?"

"I must talk to you in private, Beverly. Something very important."

"Aubrey is completely trustworthy," she stated.

A look of indecision crossed his face, and then he nodded, moving into the room to sit on the end of one of the beds. He leaned forward to talk in a quiet voice, his audience mimicking his behaviour.

"We've recently learned there may be a traitor in our group," he said, pausing to let the words sink in.

"A traitor? What makes you say that?" asked Beverly.

"After the attack on Anna, Prince Alstan did some investigation. He discovered a letter hidden away in the late Captain Brown's house."

He withdrew the letter, passing it to Beverly. She perused the document, sharing it with Aubrey, as Gerald spoke. "This information was intended for someone, and it details the defenses of Bodden Keep. It has to be someone who was there. Even the catapults are mentioned, and they're recent additions."

"Who do you suspect?" asked Beverly. "Surely not me?"

"No, of course not. And Lady Aubrey here is family, plus she's never even been to Bodden. But you must keep this to yourselves."

"You discovered this some time ago, why bring it to our attention now?" asked Aubrey.

"I need your help," he continued. "We have to keep an eye on a number of people, but Anna and I can't do it alone. I'm starting with you two because I know you can be trusted."

"Who else knows?" asked Beverly.

"The princess and I are the only ones, here. We've discussed this at length. You and Aubrey will be the first two, and later I will have discussions with Arnim and Revi."

"Arnim was sent by the marshal-general. Can we trust him?"

"I know you're suspicious of him, but we have a shared past. There were...events that transpired at Uxley before you arrived. I think we can safely trust him. Whoever is behind this is not working for Valmar. This is the hand of someone else, likely a Norlander."

"So who are the suspects?" asked Aubrey, warming to the task.

"The letter was written in a feminine hand and indicates knowledge of military terms. We're going on the assumption that it's a knight, but they might not be working alone. I need you two to just keep your eyes open and your ears to the ground. Don't get carried away, simply note anything you see as out of the ordinary."

"Consider it done," said Beverly, with Aubrey nodding in agreement.

"And say nothing of this to anyone, save myself and the princess."

"Agreed," the two women chimed in.

"Now, enjoy the rest of your evening, for I fear we'll be busy for the next few days," Gerald said cryptically. He rose from his seat, to open the door, pausing as he did so, "Good night, ladies," he said, then left the room, closing the door behind him.

"Well, that was interesting," remarked Aubrey. "Is it always like this?"

"No," replied her cousin, "sometimes things get really strange!"

A few days later found Gerald and Anna sitting in her room, with a fire going against the increasingly chilly nights while Tempus lay, snoring on the floor.

Gerald was picking absently at a plate of cheese while Anna rifled through papers on a small table.

"I have a plan," she stated.

"All right, let's hear it," he responded.

"We're going to run away for a while."

"Come again? I thought we put that off the table a long time ago."

"I don't mean forever. I mean we're going to sneak off on a little expedition."

"And by 'we' you mean?"

"Just you, and I, and half a dozen guards or so."

He absently brushed his hands free of cheese. "And where, precisely, are we going to sneak off to?"

"Norwatch. It lies on the northern road that goes east from here," she stated.

"What's in Norwatch that's got you so interested?" he asked.

"The Greatwood. Alric said there were Orcs there. I'd like to meet them."

Gerald was shocked. Their last encounter with Orcs had them fighting each other at Eastwood.

"May I remind you," he countered, "that it was only this last spring that we were fighting Orcs?"

"That was politics. I've been reading up on them. They're an interesting race."

"The Elves tried to kill all of them," he reminded her.

"Yes, but the Elves also tried to kill Humans years ago, as well. I don't think the Orcs are evil. From my research, they appear to be a race of hunters. We know from Beverly's encounter that many of them speak the common tongue, and even if they don't, we've got Revi with his spell."

"Why is it, exactly, that you find them so fascinating," he asked, though he suspected he already knew.

"I want to know more about them. All the books are tainted. They're written by people who fear them or loathe them. History is like that, always written from only one point of view."

"And you want to make your own judgement," he offered.

"Yes, but I'm being cautious. I'm not saying we have to meet a chief or anything. Even just an Orc hunter or two would be most informative."

"I see you've already made your mind up about this," he said.

She smiled, "You know me all too well, but I've still some planning to do."

"Out of curiosity," he asked, "how do you intend to get away from your Royal Guard?"

"That's the least of my worries," she countered. "Once we start, Prince Alric will either have to leave right away with us, or catch up later."

"He won't like that," he exclaimed.

"No, but he won't really have a choice."

"You said it was the least of your worries. What else are you worried about?"

"We still have a traitor in our midst. I want to flush them out."

"How do we do that?"

"I was thinking we take a small group, including at least one of the suspects."

"Is that wise? They might be dangerous."

"In a smaller group, they might be more inclined to try something. No one's going to try anything with an army like we have here in Faltingham."

"I don't like it," he complained. "It puts your life in danger. We almost lost you this summer, I can't go through that again."

"You won't have to, Gerald. We won't let it go that far. There will only be one person to watch, and there are enough of us to be on guard at all times."

"And Revi will be with us this time," remembered Gerald.

"Yes, agreed. Revi will be with us at all times."

He thought about it for a moment. She had a good point. Any attempt on her life was unlikely to occur with so many soldiers around, but would they necessarily try something on a smaller expedition?

"I'm not sure it'll work, Anna. What if they don't make a move?"

"Then we're no worse off and we hopefully still get to meet some Orcs."

"All right, I don't like it, but I'll go along with it."

Anna stood to walk over and give him a hug. "Thank you, Gerald. I was hoping you'd agree."

"Now, who do we take on this little expedition of ours?"

"Who do you think we should take?" asked Anna.

"Beverly, of course, and Revi, for healing. I think we should leave Lily here, I don't want to put her in harm's way. Do you have anyone to add?"

He watched Anna stroking her chin, mimicking the actions of Baron Fitzwilliam. "I should like to take Hayley. I think her ranger skills might prove useful."

"What if she's our traitor?" asked Gerald.

"I think it unlikely," Anna replied. "To hear Beverly talk, our ranger friend doesn't seem to know much about fortifications."

"So if we strike Hayley off the list of suspects, that leaves us with only five," Gerald concluded.

Anna thought for a moment before continuing, "Who are your top two suspects?"

"Aelwyth is from an old family who has seen better times, and she's also from the northern border. Perhaps she harbours some resentment towards the crown?"

"Interesting, I hadn't considered that. Who else?" prompted Anna.

"Juliet. I have no idea of her background, and she keeps to herself. What do you think?"

"I agree with you about Aelwyth, but Beverly assures me that there is a reason for Juliet's secrecy. What about Celia, she was there with us in Bodden?"

"True, she was, but so was Levina," Gerald added.

"Yes, but Beverly has been in correspondence with her for years," Anna reminded him. "So, if we assume it's either Aelwyth or Celia, how do we choose which one to bring?"

Gerald shrugged his shoulders, "Does it matter?"

"I suppose not," agreed Anna. "We'll take Celia."

"What about Arnim, will he be coming along?" Gerald asked.

"I thought about that. We'll tell Arnim about the traitor, and then he and Aubrey can keep an eye on things here. I think we're better served by leaving them at Faltingham."

"He won't like being left out," Gerald warned.

"No, but he'll see the reasoning. I want him to look into a few things. With us out of the way, the guards will be less intrusive. He might be able to dig through some belongings looking for clues."

"If Prince Alric discovers this, he'll insist on coming."

"That's the beauty of my plan. It'll still work, even if he comes with us."

"You realize that he'll likely bring soldiers?"

"Not if he has no advance notice. We'll plan this in secret. He'll only know we're leaving when he sees us on the way. He'll have to hurry to catch up so he won't have time to assemble his men. We'll make sure we pack extra food for him; I shouldn't like for him to have to starve."

Gerald chuckled, "I can't imagine he'd like camping out in the wilderness without a tent."

"He'll like it even less when we get to Norwatch," she stated.

"Why is that?" he asked.

"We'll be travelling in disguise. He won't get to play the royal card."

"You're enjoying this far too much."

"I know," she agreed. "Now, what do we call this little operation?"

"A walk in the woods?"

"Excellent," said Anna. "It'll let us talk about it in plain hearing. We'll work out more details tomorrow."

"Agreed," said Gerald, "but it's time for bed. You have some visiting to do tomorrow, we don't want to slight our hostess." He rose, and started heading for the door.

"Wait," pleaded Anna. "You can't go yet."

He turned in surprise, "Why?"

"You haven't told me a bedtime story!"

"Aren't you getting a little old for that?"

"From you, Gerald? Never. One day you're going to be telling stories to your grandchildren, you need all the practice you can get."

"Grandchildren? I'm far too old to have a child, let alone a grandchild."

"Nonsense, Gerald. You're my father now, and you'll be grandfather to my children. That's your legacy. Now, how about that story?"

Gerald felt a tear forming in his eye and coughed to clear his throat. "All right, I'll tell you the story of how Beverly broke up a duel between two knights."

"Really? She did that?"

"Not that I know of, but it will make it a more interesting story if you know the characters."

SEVENTEEN

Norwatch

AUTUMN 960 MC

The plans were made and finally, a week after their arrival, they were ready to be executed. Anna had written a letter for Lady Aubrey to deliver to Lady Alicia once they had left. The plan was to return within the fortnight after they'd had a chance to investigate Norwatch. Beverly and Hayley had discretely arranged for two pack horses loaded with supplies to be ready in town. The ranger would pick them up in the early morning, rendezvousing with the rest on the road.

Anna and Gerald were the last to leave, for they were watched the closest. They made as if to take a light ride around the estate, the better to be prepared for travel. Aubrey had insisted the ruse be complete and had hidden away travelling clothes on the estate the night before so that they could change along the way. Strict instructions were left behind for Arnim. He would assume temporary command of all the knights in Beverly's absence and keep an eye on them, with Aubrey's help.

Tempus was loping along in front of them when they cleared the grounds of the estate. They hurriedly changed and were beginning to trot toward the rendezvous when they saw two riders; Alric and Jack. They had gone over the possibilities numerous times and so, rather than run, they slowed their pace, waiting for them to catch up.

"Out for an early morning ride, Highness?" asked Jack. "You should have let us know, we could have accompanied you."

Alric was a little more alert, noticing the clothing they were wearing. "What's this? Sneaking off somewhere are we?"

"We are," stated Anna. "Are you coming with us?"

Alric was taken aback by her stark honesty. "Where are we going?"

"'WE' are going nowhere, Highness, unless you want to lose that Royal Persona of yours."

"Meaning what, exactly?" Alric bristled.

"Meaning, we're travelling as commoners," stated Gerald. "We thought you might like to join us, so we have some extra clothes in the bag."

"Clever, Your Highness," commented Jack. "I never pictured you as someone who would go slumming."

"We're not slumming, Lord Jack," corrected Anna. "We're out to meet common folk in the countryside. Are you interested in accompanying us?"

"Of course," uttered the cavalier. "It'll be a story for the ages. I can just imagine sitting around the fireplace, a warm drink in one hand, a warm girl in the other-"

"We won't be sitting around a fireplace," interrupted Anna.

"No," agreed Gerald, "though a fire pit might be appropriate."

"What do you mean 'a fire pit'?" Jack exclaimed.

"We'll be camping out tonight," said Gerald.

"Camping out? That's barbaric. Why would you camp out when there's a nice set of beds waiting for you at the hall?"

"Because we'll be on the road to Norwatch," explained Anna.

"We'll need guards," commented Alric, his face difficult to read.

"We have them already arranged," explained Gerald. "We'll be rendezvousing with them shortly."

To Gerald's trained eye, the prince did not look happy, but he swallowed his pride. He doesn't want to lose face in front of Anna, Gerald thought.

"Very well, Highness," said Alric. "Lead on, and we shall follow."

Surprised by his easy capitulation, Anna urged her mount forward, Gerald pulling up beside her.

"That seemed a little too easy," remarked Anna.

"Yes," her friend agreed, "the prince is full of surprises."

They rode in silence for a little longer, and then Gerald laughed.

"What's so funny," asked Anna.

"I can't wait to see Jack's expression when he learns we're sleeping on the ground."

The laughter that erupted from Anna startled Jack and Alric.

"What's so funny," asked Alric.

"Nothing, Highness," replied Gerald. "I was just watching Tempus running ahead of us; he likes to chase flies." He grinned at Anna and the shared joke remained their secret.

They arrived at the rendezvous point to see the rest of the group ready to go. Hayley and Celia were riding with a pack horse behind each of them, while Revi sat on his mount, waiting for the princess to arrive. Beverly, surprisingly, was riding a regular horse, not her infamous charger, which Gerald immediately noticed.

"Where's Lightning?" he asked.

"I left him in Aubrey's care. He kind of sticks out in a crowd. I thought it best to leave him behind."

"Where's your armour?" asked Anna.

"Don't worry, Highness, it's packed up with the rest of the supplies. It would raise too many questions."

"I see you've still got your weapons," noted Gerald.

"Well, a girl can't be too careful these days."

Jack looked on in appreciation, "You clean up nicely, Dame Beverly. I never would have taken you for such a beauty."

Beverly flushed with anger, but Gerald recognized the look and quickly changed the conversation.

"If we're to travel as commoners, we'll have to avoid using titles," he stated.

"Quite right," proclaimed Anna. "That means no more 'Highnesses' and 'Dames'. Only first names will do."

"Agreed, Anna," said Alric.

"How interesting," stated Jack. "Perhaps we should adopt some sort of cover story. I suggest that I am travelling with my wife, Beverly and that the rest of you are our relatives."

"I don't think that's quite necessary," added Gerald quickly. "We'll just use our regular names. We shouldn't need to worry about anything else."

"Yes," said Anna, "the more we make up, the greater the chance to slip up. No one should be expecting a royal in Norwatch, so we'll just mind our manners."

"Hayley," ordered Anna, "you and Beverly take the lead. Gerald and I will follow with Jack and Alric behind. Celia and Revi will bring up the rear."

"What about the dog?" queried Jack.

"What about him?" said Anna.

"Where will he fit in?" the cavalier asked.

"Wherever he wants to," she replied and urged her horse forward.

The road to Norwatch was easy to follow, for it was used quite frequently by traders. They passed a number of these, some slowly meandering towards Norwatch, others returning to Faltingham. If they had feared discovery, they were reassured, for these people had little interest in their band.

They decided to forgo the roadside inns that dotted the roadway and instead stayed outdoors. Hayley had brought extra blankets, and these were gratefully accepted by the group. They camped around a fire each night, always leaving people on watch. There was some discussion about this, but eventually, they decided to divide the watch into three shifts. Anna and Gerald insisted on taking the first shift while Hayley and Revi took the second. They, in turn, would wake Celia and Beverly for the early morning watch. They decided to let Jack and Alric, neither of whom had camped out before, get a good night's sleep.

The second day of their journey Jack was overly quiet. Being the son of a viscount, he was used to a life of luxury, but he refused to complain, seeing it, perhaps, as a weakness. By the fourth day, he began to return to his normal, exuberant self as the town of Norwatch grew close. A traveller had told them they would arrive before noon. The thought of a nice meal or a drink of ale seemed to bring out the more social nature of Jack.

"Out of interest," he stated, "what's the plan when we get to Norwatch. Are we dropping in on the baron?"

"No," said Alric. "We're supposed to be commoners. Why would we be dropping in on the baron? Besides, he's down in the capital."

"So what, precisely, is the plan?" Jack reiterated his question.

"We make our way to a tavern," offered Gerald, "and start asking around for news."

"At least we'll be able to get some decent ale," muttered Jack. "That stuff you brought was foul."

"Hey," uttered Hayley, "I paid good coins for that ale."

"It's not your fault, oh glorious maiden of the wood. All the ale up this part of the country is raw."

"Raw?" noted Celia.

"Yes, it tastes like horse piss."

"Then why do you drink it?" the knight asked.

"Why, because it's in my nature," he said, flashing her a smile.

"All right, you two," said Gerald, "the village is coming into view, let's not create a scene."

As they approached the edge of the village, they saw a group of six mounted soldiers coming out. The armed men halted, their leader trotting over to them.

"Have you come from Faltingham?" he asked.

"Yes, why? Is there danger hereabouts?" asked Gerald.

"We've had some trouble lately with Orcs. They shouldn't bother a group of your size but keep your eyes open. I wouldn't suggest travelling at night."

"Have they entered the town?" Gerald asked.

"No, they tend to stay away from Norwatch, but we've heard they've hit some farms nearby. Have you seen anything unusual on the road?"

"Only a party of royals," muttered Jack, under his breath. Alric smacked him with his hand.

"What was that?" asked the soldier.

"Sorry, Sergeant," Alric replied, "my friend has had a little too much to drink. We haven't seen anything on the road, other than the odd traveller."

"Welcome to Norwatch," the man replied. "If you're looking for lodging, you might try the Fiddlers Bow, you can't miss it."

"Thank you, Sergeant," said Gerald, who then urged his mount to the side of the road to allow the soldiers to pass.

Anna waited for the patrol to disappear down the road before speaking, "What was that all about?"

"It seems the Orcs are not so friendly in these parts," offered Alric. "This might not have been the best time to visit."

"Nonsense," Anna proclaimed. "It's the best time to visit. Our chance of meeting an Orc has increased substantially."

"You can't be serious," said the prince.

"You don't know Anna," remarked Gerald. "Once she gets an idea into her head, there's no changing her mind."

"Oh, great," uttered Jack. "We're all going to die."

The Fiddlers Bow was a cozy little tavern, much like those found in Merceria. It was still early in the day, and the patrons were few as Gerald and Anna entered. They had decided to split the group up, giving them a better chance of hearing something. Revi, Celia and Beverly would guard the horses, along with Tempus, while Hayley had entered earlier, taking up a seat near the bar. They ignored her as they came in, making their way to a table in the corner, the better to observe the locals. They ordered a light meal and some ale and settled in, enjoying the welcoming atmosphere.

The food was soon laid out in front of them, and Gerald was pleased to see a large sausage, plump from cooking, its aroma making his mouth water. He bit into it, enjoying the flavour as the fat dripped down into his beard.

"You're enjoying that a little too much, Father," said Anna.

"You mean, Da," he said.

"What?"

"I notice that around here they like to call their father, 'Da'."

"Why is that?"

"I have no idea," he stated, "but if you want to blend in, you'd best use it."

"All right, Da," she said, trying to sound natural.

Gerald managed to demolish his food quickly, while Anna picked at hers. The ale was quite acceptable, but he drank sparingly, lest he dull his senses. Some time passed before Alric and Jack entered. The plan was for them to take a separate table and this they did, ordering a round of drinks. Jack did all the talking while Alric looked apprehensive.

The afternoon crowd began to arrive, and the cavalier made it his purpose to engage them in conversation. He was a natural at this type of behaviour, and soon he had a small group of admirers standing around as he told his tales. He bought round after round, engaging all within earshot with his stories. Gerald strained to hear details, but the cavalier was getting carried away, and instead of asking questions he was regaling the crowd.

It was Hayley that approached them in the end. She walked over to the table, followed by a local man.

"May we sit?" she asked.

"Of course," said Gerald. He used his hand to call for two more ales. "Who's this?"

"This," said Hayley, "is Simon Grayly. He's a local hunter. He has some information about the Orcs."

"Do tell," said Anna. "What can you tell us about them?"

"They're a peaceful race," he said, "driven from their hunting grounds by something."

"How do you know that?" asked Gerald.

The stranger looked around as if someone else might be listening. "I've traded with them," he explained. "They're moving south because they have to."

"What's driving them south?" asked Gerald.

"That I don't know, but I know someone who does." Once more, he looked around the room with a piercing glare.

"Are you willing to take us to this person?" asked Hayley.

"I am, provided you can prove you're not intent on killing them. That seems to be the overwhelming opinion these days."

"We're not from around here," offered Gerald, "and have no cause to fight Orcs. We would like to talk to them, nothing more."

"Perhaps," offered Anna, "we can help them?"

"How do I know I can trust you?" the stranger asked.

"You don't," stated Gerald, "nor do we know we can trust you. You could be leading us into a trap to kill us and take our coins."

"True enough," the man replied. He appeared to be thinking things over, for he stared at the table for some time before answering, "All right, I'll take you. You must meet me out front after dark. If I take you in daylight, we might be followed."

"Very well," agreed Gerald. "Hayley, here, will meet you and then we'll met up the street. If we all stand around, people might get suspicious."

Simon nodded his head and tilted back his ale to finish it off. "Agreed. I'll return at sunset," he said.

Darkness found them waiting at the edge of the village, behind the blacksmith's shop. They soon caught sight of Hayley leading the stranger, their lanterns held high.

"So," the man observed, "it appears you have a rather large group."

"Is that a problem?" asked Alric.

"No, not at all. Now come with me and watch your step, the woods can be treacherous in the dark."

"The woods? Surely not!" exclaimed Jack.

"Not the Greatwood, no, for it is some miles away. We go to Harken Wood, which lies nearby. There you'll meet a friend of mine who will tell you more."

As they stepped into the woods, the quiet night air was interrupted by the crackle of breaking branches and dead leaves as they made their way down a rough path.

"It's not much further," Simon indicated. Soon, they came into a clearing, and he stopped, placing his lantern on the fallen trunk of a tree. "Now we must wait," he explained.

Gerald took a seat next to the lantern. His legs were sore, and he knew it was his age working against him. He looked at Anna who was petting Tempus, the great dog lying in some leaves. She had said he would be grandfather to her children, but now he wondered if he would live that long. If he was feeling his years after this short walk, how long before age claimed him?

With the snap of a twig nearby, everyone froze, peering into the darkness, trying to see what made the sound. Soon, a large, dark shape came through the underbrush, pausing briefly to push a branch out of its way. The green skin left no confusion, for here stood an Orc, his massive green shoulders and chest bare to the cold autumn night.

"This is Grim," said their host. "He hails from the Wolf clan. Don't worry," he added, "he speaks the common tongue."

"Greetings, Humans," Grim rumbled, his voice a rich baritone.

It was Anna who spoke first, "Greetings, Grim, we are most honoured to meet you."

The great Orc walked through the group, examining each in turn. He stopped at Gerald, peering closely into his face. "You are a warrior," he announced, then held out his hand. "It is an honour to meet you."

Gerald held out his hand for the Orc, who gripped it with firmness.

"You have seen many battles," observed Grim. "I see it in your eyes."

"Too many, I'm afraid," offered Gerald.

Grim released his hand and turned to face Anna, "You speak for the others; you are more than just a youngling."

"My name is Anna," she said in reply. "Let me introduce the rest of our group." She pointed at each as she spoke. "This is Hayley Chambers, she's a...expert archer, and this is Beverly and Celia, they're both-"

"Warriors," completed the Orc.

"How did you know that?" asked Beverly.

"It is in your stance. You stand ready to attack, your hand is itching to grasp your sword. Do you fear the Orcs so much?"

"My apologies," offered Beverly, "if I've offered you insult."

"There is no insult," he replied, turning to Revi. "You look like a shaman," he announced.

"Revi Bloom. I'm a mage."

"Honour to you," said Grim.

"And this," continued Anna, "is Alric and Jack. They're accompanying us."

The broad-chested Orc nodded a greeting. "You may leave us now, Simon," he said.

Simon picked up his lantern, "Well, I said I'd take you to meet someone. My work here is done."

He hurried off back to the village, his lantern light dancing haphazardly as he rushed down the path.

"Why are you here?" asked Grim.

"We come seeking the Orcs," said Anna. "We wish to find out why they are encroaching on Human lands."

"You are hiding something," said Grim. "A party such as this is here to fight."

"Perhaps," replied Anna, "but not the Orcs."

"What d'you mean?" uttered Jack.

"I think something is driving you south, pushing you out of your lands. You've come here because you have no choice."

"You are very perceptive," said Grim. "I see why you are the leader."

Alric was about to object, but Jack stilled him by touching his arm.

"Do you know what is pushing you out of the Greatwood, Grim?"

"No, but I'll take you to someone who does. One of our Shamans will want to talk to you. Do you have horses?"

"Yes, but they're stabled in town," offered Gerald.

"Then get them and meet me back here. We will travel north, into the Greatwood. You will need to bring food and water unless you can hunt."

"We will bring what we need," announced Anna. "I shouldn't like to slow down the trip more than necessary."

The Orc smiled, his ivory teeth showing in the dim light of the lantern. "You are wise beyond your years." He looked like he was about to say more but suddenly paused, looking beyond the princess. "What is this noble creature?" he said, pushing past her. He walked up to Tempus, who had risen from his bed of leaves. The great beast wagged his tail slightly as Grim gently placed his hand on the top of the dog's head.

"That's Tempus," offered Anna. "He seems to like you."

Grim looked back to the rest of the group. "A most interesting find, indeed. The shaman will want to know more about you, but first, you must go and retrieve your mounts."

"I'll take Hayley and Celia," offered Beverly. "We will retrieve the horses and meet you back here."

"Very well," said Anna. "That will give us time to talk to Grim, here."

The three knights left the clearing leaving the rest to wait. Grim seemed fascinated by Tempus who simply sat, letting the Orc scratch his head.

"Your name surprises me," remarked Anna. "I thought Orc names were different."

Grim smiled, "It's the name Simon uses for me. It's not my real name."

"How long have your people been pushing south?" she asked.

"Since the summer solstice. The game was becoming scarce so we pushed south to find better hunting."

"You killed all the game?" asked Jack. "That seems a bit silly."

"No, something else is killing the game," the Orc explained.

"Then we shall have to find out what that something else is," said Anna.

"Well," announced Revi, "since we're going to be here awhile, we might as well make ourselves comfortable." He sat down on the tree trunk, beside Gerald. The older man shifted slightly, rubbing his leg. "Is your leg giving you trouble Gerald?"

"Just my body wearing down with age," he replied.

"You should have said something, I can help you with that. Hold still." The mage began chanting, and Gerald recognized a slight tingle in the air as if a swarm of flies had suddenly appeared. Where Revi placed his hands upon Gerald's leg, a warmth soaked into his sore limbs. A moment later, the ache disappeared.

"That was amazing, Master Bloom," he announced. "I thought that spell only worked on wounds?"

"So did I," the mage replied. "But I thought it worth a try. I suspect we'll have to repeat it in a month or two, but other than that, you should be fine."

Gerald stood up, bending his legs in a squat. "I feel years younger," he declared.

Anna was smiling, "You better," she said. "You're going to have my children to look after."

Alric, who was starting to nod off, suddenly sat up straight. "Princess, are you pregnant?"

Anna blushed at the thought. "No, Alric, I just meant eventually. Saxnor's balls, I'd have to get married first. I'm not quite ready to have children, give me a few years."

Alric began to relax but Gerald wondered if there might be more to his attitude. Was the young prince starting to warm to his charge? He made a mental note to talk to Beverly about it.

"You are a princess?" asked Grim.

"Yes," she admitted, "I am of the Royal House of Merceria."

"I don't know where that is," admitted the Orc, "but you will still be welcome in the tribe."

It took some time for the knights to return with the horses and then the group, led by Grim, started heading deeper into the woods. The Orc appeared to know the area well and set a brisk pace. Early morning they finally paused, and Grim suggested they get some sleep. He explained there was still a full day's travel ahead of them, much of it through thick brush, and they would need their energy.

Beverly and Hayley stood lookout while the rest tried to get some rest. Grim kept to himself, sitting by the fire, staring into its flames. It took some time for Beverly to realize the Orc was sleeping, though it looked more like a trance.

Sooner than Gerald would have liked, they were up and moving again, covering the distance rapidly as they travelled north. They were going in single file, each riding their mount. Grim was in the lead while Tempus delighted in rushing through the green plants to either side of the path. The further north they travelled, the thicker the woods became until Tempus could no longer make headway off the road. He settled on trotting behind his mistress, the pace comfortable for him.

It wasn't long before even the trail began to get congested with low hanging branches and plants. They resorted to walking their animals while

Gerald wondered how much longer this trip would take. The path, if it could still be called that, twisted and turned and he looked to the ranger to see if she had any idea where they were, but she just shrugged. It appeared they were at the mercy of their host.

The column was halted by Grim, who held his hand up in the air, signalling the stop. A moment later, there was some rustling in the woods just before two Orcs appeared, dressed in furs and carrying spears. As they talked to Grim in the Orcish tongue, Gerald noticed Revi gesticulating and came to the conclusion he was using his tongues spell.

"What do you make of it, Master Bloom?"

The mage waited until the Orcs finished their conversation before answering, "They're taking us to a camp that lies nearby. I suspect our journey is almost over."

Sure enough, Grim turned to the rest of the group, "We go now to meet Andurak, one of our Shamans."

He led them off the trail where they forced their way past the undergrowth, emerging into a small clearing. There were a number of structures here, little more than lean-to's, many of which were simply a few sticks supporting animal skins. The entire camp looked very makeshift, reminding Gerald of an army camp.

"Is this your village?" asked Alric.

"No," answered Grim. "Orcs do not live in villages, not since the days of our ancestors. This is a hunting camp. We roam the area, setting up camps like this until we move on."

He led them toward a larger shelter. The open side of the lean-to was toward them, and there sat an Orc at a fire, poking it with a gnarled stick. His head rose at their approach, and then he stood, the stick becoming a staff.

"Greetings, strangers," the Orc said. "I am Andurak, shaman of this family."

Anna bowed, "Greetings Andurak. We are humbled by your presence."

The shaman waved his hands indicating that they should sit around the fire. They spread out, forming a circle around the flames, then plopped down on the ground. Another Orc brought out a bowl containing a milky white liquid. He handed it to the shaman, bowing at the waist.

Andurak took the bowl, raising it to his lips. "Let us all celebrate our kinship by drinking of the milk of life," he said.

He took a sip from the edge of the bowl and passed it to Grim, who did likewise. It next went to Anna, then it was Gerald's turn. The liquid reminded him of milk, but with a thinner texture. He passed it to Beverly who sat beside him. No sooner had the bowl reached her hands than he felt a sudden light-headedness and he turned to Anna. She looked perfectly fine, but he struggled to maintain his focus. Her face began to blur while he tried to speak, but his tongue wouldn't work. The last thing he saw before sinking into darkness was a look of alarm on her face.

He was running through the woods, the trees rushing past him as he made his way to his destination. He looked at the ground and was astounded to see his four legs carrying him forward. He was a wolf, following a scent, he could almost see it. He stopped, perking up his ears. Something was close, so he crouched, pulling himself toward some nearby undergrowth to conceal his presence.

Soldiers came into view. There were dozens of them, carrying swords and axes. Some were armed in chainmail, while the rest wore rough padded armour. They looked Mercerian, but something told him otherwise. They were wearing the colours of the Royal House and yet, to his practiced eye, they were not equipped as such. On and on, they marched past, till he counted at least one hundred. Warriors were coming; he must warn Anna.

He opened his eyes to see two shapes hovering over him. Anna was there, tears freely flowing from her eyes while Revi Bloom was touching his forehead.

"Can you hear me, Gerald. Come back to me," she was pleading.

He tried to move but his body wouldn't respond, he could only look on, helpless, while she fretted above him. He heard a calm voice in the background.

"He awakens," the shaman was saying, "and will soon have a tale to tell."

He felt his limbs tingle and then moved his fingers. His whole body was afire with pins and needles as if his blood had suddenly rushed back into his veins.

"Anna," he cried out, and he felt her hands grasp his.

He sat up slowly, his surroundings still swirling. He closed his eyes, taking a deep breath, as he felt Anna hug him.

"I thought I'd lost you, Gerald," she said, through sobs of joy.

He held her tight, fighting a wave of nausea.

"What happened," asked Gerald.

"You passed out," said Revi, "just after you drank from the bowl."

"He has had a vision," announced the Shaman. "He bears the mark of the wolf."

"What does that mean?" asked Alric.

"It means our ancestors saw fit to give him a vision. Tell us, old warrior, what did you see?"

Gerald was reminded of the visions of Albreda. Is this what she experienced? If it was, he was more than willing to forgo them. "I was running through the forest, I was a wolf. I saw soldiers."

"What kind of soldiers," asked Alric.

"I'm not sure, they had a mix of weapons and armour."

"Could you tell whose soldiers they were?" pressed Alric.

"No," he lied.

Something screamed inside him to share what he had seen, but years of experience on the frontier made him disbelieve what he had observed. He needed time to think it over, but there was so much as stake. Beverly was still holding the bowl after taking a sip. She passed it to Jack, who politely declined the offer.

The shaman put his hand out, waiting for the bowl to be passed back to him. "The test is done," he announced.

"Test?" Anna turned suddenly. "You almost killed Gerald. What sort of welcome is that?"

"He was never in danger," replied Andurak. "He was on a spirit journey, guided by our ancestors. I have never seen it have this effect on a Human before, though I must admit few Humans have tasted of the milk of life. Now you must come with me." He rose to his feet, waiting while the others did likewise. He held his hand in the air to get their attention. "Only a few may go," he said, turning to Anna. "You must pick, no more than four."

"Gerald, Beverly, Hayley and Revi," she announced. "Does Tempus count?"

The shaman smiled, "You chose wisely, the beast may accompany us."

"Where are we going," asked Gerald.

"To a place not far from here, there is something you need to see."

"Why can't we all go?" asked Alric.

"There are some here," the shaman replied, "who are not yet ready to face what is to come. Bide your time, they shall return before daybreak."

"But it's not even dark yet," complained Jack. "Do you at least have wine here?"

They filed out of the clearing, following the Shaman in single file. He was walking with slow, measured steps and Gerald thought he might be counting paces. They stopped when they were out of range of the sounds of camp. The shaman turned to face them, raising his staff in his right hand.

"I shall invoke a spell," he said. "Be not afraid, for it will not hurt you."

"What spell?" asked Revi.

"Your spirits will be transported to another location. When the spell is done its course, you will be returned here."

"What will happen while we're in this spirit form?" asked Anna.

"You will be taken to another place. You will be able to see and hear all around you, but will not have physical substance. You will be able to observe, but not interact, and will appear ghostlike to each other."

"Master Revi," asked Anna, "have you heard of this?"

"Indeed I have, Highness," he remarked. "It's called spirit walk, though I've never seen it in actual use. It's mentioned in an ancient tome in my library. I believe it was developed by the Elves."

A harsh look crossed the shaman's face, "The spell is Orcish in origin, not the blasphemous magic of the Elves."

"I stand corrected," said the mage. "I meant no disrespect. I am at the mercy of those who wrote the tomes of which I speak."

"Understandable," said the Shaman. "Our traditions are oral, therefore we have no written works. It seems quite likely the Elves took our discovery as their own."

"Why do you hate the Elves so much?" asked Anna.

"Many generations ago they destroyed our cities in a war that lasted for years. We call it the time of the great parting. Our people were scattered to the ends of the land, to live out their lives in exile."

"How many cities were there?" she persisted.

"There were seven great cities," he replied. "But now is not the time for a history lesson. There is much for you to see. Are you ready?"

They nodded their assent and then the shaman began chanting. Gerald noticed some runes on the Orc's staff begin to light up as he spoke, and a feeling of warmth spread over him. He felt himself being pulled out of his body and suddenly he flew into the air in a rush, his physical form left below. The air seemed to distort, and then he was standing on a ledge, looking into a ravine. It appeared to be a box canyon, with only one way open. He glanced to his side and saw Anna standing beside him, her whole being lit like an angel. He became aware of others when moments later they appeared, as if from thin air, materializing slowly in their ghostly form.

"We are here," announced the shaman. "Look below and tell me what you see."

Gerald crouched at the edge of the ledge to look. There were dozens of dead deer carcasses, partially stripped of meat and rotting in the sunlight.

"This is horrible," remarked Anna. "These animals have been slaughtered.

"Yes," agreed Gerald. "Someone's killed them all, but why?"

"Food, most likely," offered Hayley. "I can see arrows in the bodies. Someone has stripped some meat but done a sloppy job of it."

"This was done by soldiers, not hunters," said Gerald.

"How do you know that?" asked Anna.

"They've only taken the easy cuts of meat."

"No Orc would allow this to happen," said the Shaman. "It unbalances nature."

"Can we go down and get a better look?" asked Hayley. "We might be able to get some idea of who did this."

The shaman nodded his head, leading them to a steep incline. Soon, they were walking through the carnage, the stench of death overpowering.

Hayley stooped near a body, trying to withdraw an arrow, but her ghostly fingers slipped through it. She walked among the dead until finally, she spotted what she was looking for; an arrow lying on the ground. Likely someone had missed the target, and it had come to rest here.

"The arrow looks Mercerian," she stated. "The arrows in Weldwyn have different fletchings."

Beverly walked over to take a look, crouching down, almost lying on the ground to examine the tip in detail.

"This is no Mercerian arrow," she stated.

"How do you know?" asked Hayley.

"The arrowhead is cheaper metal. No smith in Merceria would make such a weapon."

"What are you saying?" asked Gerald.

Beverly rose, blushing slightly, "I've spent quite a bit of time in a forge. Aldwin taught me all kinds of things about weapon craft. I think this is a Norland arrow."

Gerald considered this carefully as things began to fall into place in his mind. "What would happen," he mused, "if Mercerian troops attacked Norwatch."

"It would be war," said Beverly. "But we don't have an army here."

"But if soldiers attacked Norwatch dressed as Mercerians, wouldn't the effect be the same?" he persisted.

"How do you know they're after Norwatch?" asked Revi.

"It has to be," Gerald continued. "Don't you see? If they attacked further east, they'd have to come across the river, or no one would believe it. I don't know what my vision was, but I saw soldiers wearing the colours of the King of Merceria."

"Why didn't you say so sooner," asked Anna.

"Something was wrong. I've seen lots of soldiers back home, but their choice of weapons and armour felt out of place. They must have been Norlanders playing the part."

"We have to get back to Norwatch," chimed in Hayley, "before they attack."

"How many troops are in the village," Anna asked.

"I saw no more than a dozen," offered Beverly, "and half of them are likely out patrolling the road. They'd never be able to stop the troops who did this. Judging by the arrows, there must have been scores of them."

"How do you know that?" asked Revi.

"That's easy," interrupted Hayley, "the arrows come from many angles. They likely drove the deer into this canyon then shot from the cliffs."

"In my vision, I saw at least a hundred," Gerald added.

"Return us please, Andurak," asked Anna. "We have work to do."

Gerald felt a slight breeze brushing his face, and then he found himself back in the clearing. He glanced around to see the look of determination on everyone's face.

"We must hurry," he said. "I don't know how much time we have."

EIGHTEEN

The Battle of the Northern Wood

AUTUMN 960 MC

The village of Norwatch was little more than a small collection of buildings, reminding Gerald of Uxley in size. Its defense was an impossible task; they had very few defenders at their disposal. In addition to their own group, there were six soldiers present, along with half a dozen locals armed with makeshift weapons.

Gerald had placed Hayley atop the Fiddlers Bow, the largest structure in town. From there, her vantage point gave her a good view of the surrounding area. He had organized the townsfolk to throw up some makeshift defenses; wagons tipped on their sides, barrels roped together to provide obstacles to the attackers, and sacks and crates piled to form walls. There was no way to create a complete wall, so he settled on making a stand in the rough centre of the village where the tavern formed a 'T' inter-section along with the local church and the saddlers. He had urged the commoners to take up positions of safety, and now most huddled in the cellar of the church, praying to Malin that they be spared.

His best fighters; Jack, Beverly and Celia, he placed in the middle, making them able to respond to any location should the need arise. Alric had claimed to be quite capable with a sword, but Gerald knew he couldn't risk the life of a Prince of Weldwyn, for his death would have far-reaching consequences. He and Anna were atop the tavern, along with Revi, helping Hayley keep watch. As for himself, he stood near the town guards, behind a row of barrels, waiting for the inevitable.

It was just as well the baron wasn't present for once Alric made himself known, the locals responded to the crisis in a workmanlike manner. These were hardy people, he knew, unlikely to run and eager to defend their homes and loved ones. He prayed to Saxnor to spare them the loss that would inevitably come with a battle but felt it did little good. The affairs of men were of small consequence to the Gods. Besides, it was the clash of steel that would decide this day.

A shout of warning came from the roof of the tavern. Hayley was pointing with her bow while he readied the men in front of him. The enemy had decided on a straightforward rush, being confident in their numbers. They didn't have to take the town to accomplish their objective. In their minds, a simple attack and withdraw was all they needed to convince the locals that a Mercerian army was at their door. Gerald smiled grimly; they had no knowledge that real Mercerians were here, right now, waiting for them.

They came out of the woods in a mass, crossing the open field behind the stables, seemingly taking their time. Half of them weren't even running, merely walking toward them. There were shouts and jeers from the attackers, and then suddenly an arrow seemed to blossom from one's chest as Hayley let fly with her longbow. Her target gaped at the wound and then fell forward, breaking the shaft in his descent. Swearing erupted from the enemy troops before they then broke into a trot. Gerald wished he had more archers but there was little he could do.

The enemy was stretched out, more or less in line, and he realized that their flanks would overlap the town. He dispatched Jack and two of the local soldiers to hold the western end of his defenses while Celia and Beverly moved east. The attackers drew closer until he could just make out individual faces as they started yelling, making the final dash for the village.

In their preparations, the defenders had collected whatever tools and weapons they could find. Gerald gave the order, and the men to his front threw the hatchets and knives that they had gathered. He saw an enemy soldier take an axe to the face, screaming as he fell backwards, but his comrades surged forward.

Gerald let them come; the barricades funnelling them, making them bunch up in their eagerness to overwhelm the defenders. At the last moment, he stepped into them, slashing violently with his blade. It sliced through an invader's arm, severing the limb, which fell to the ground. The victim collapsed, screaming, but Gerald didn't pause, he jabbed forward into the belly of another man. Someone stabbed with a spear to his side, the tip glancing off his chainmail. Lacking a shield, he grabbed the haft of the spear with his left hand, pulling the weapon from his attacker's grasp. Two men tried to force their way past him, but he butted one with the newly acquired spear; not strong enough to do damage, but sufficient to make him back up in alarm.

He stomped forward, stabbing with his sword, the blade scraping across the enemy's collarbone. His foe tried to swing his axe, but Gerald followed through by smashing the man in the face with the pommel of his sword. His target fell back, blood gushing from his nose while Gerald retreated to the barricade.

A Norwatch soldier beside him took an arrow to the face while Gerald dove behind the makeshift wall. Arrows sailed over the top of the barricade as the enemy archers finally let loose. Hayley was shooting arrow after arrow, each one striking a target; the heavy draw of the longbow sufficient to make the arrows puncture the enemy's armour.

Gerald peered out from his cover, and then ducked and cursed as a hail of arrows descended on his location. He looked down the street to see Jack. He was standing on the barricade, blade dripping with blood, taunting the enemy as they withdrew from his position. The fool, thought Gerald. If they had bows to the west, he'd be a dead man.

He heard fighting to his right, the eastern flank. Beverly and Celia, both in their armour were handling the invaders without his help.

Two of the local soldiers were down. One was dead, the other bleeding from an arrow wound to the leg. Gerald reached out, grabbing the man's arm and dragging him behind the barricade. He knew the enemy couldn't continue the advance until their arrows stopped and so he bound the injured man's wound as best he could. The clatter of arrows against the barricade subsided; it would only be a matter of moments before they were on him again.

Two men in chainmail led the charge. The first was big and carried a large two-handed sword. The second had a shield and mace. Gerald silently thanked Saxnor for the enemy's stupidity. A great sword requires a lot of room to use properly, and he would use that knowledge to his advantage.

He backed up, letting the two attackers surge toward the barricade. He struck just as they drew even with the defenses to either side. The gap was sufficient to stand two abreast, but there was no room to swing the mighty sword. The large man was hefting his blade over his head, intent on bringing it down in a powerful heave, leaving him wide open. Gerald stepped forward without hesitation, stabbing the man in the groin. His target crumpled to the ground, his attack all but forgotten in his agony. As he fell his blade went wide and the second man had to raise his shield to protect himself from the wild movements of his companion. Gerald ducked, then pushed forward, using his sword like a spear, driving it into the other invader's chest. The enemy crumpled with little more than a sigh. Gerald lifted the dead man's shield, hefting it onto his arm, feeling more secure with the extra protection.

Having seen their heroes go down, the enemy balked, and Gerald ran out, past the barricade, swinging at any and all before him. Astounded by the sudden rush, they backed up then turned to run away. He knew they would be back once they reformed, so he returned to the barricade, to catch his breath. Soon, the arrows began their assault again, and he once more took refuge behind his shelter.

He heard a noise behind him and turned to see Revi crawling toward him trying to avoid the maelstrom of arrows. The mage rose to a crouch, running the last few paces, and then knelt to heal the injured guardsman.

"How many of them are out there?" he asked.

"Too many," replied Gerald. "We'll have to pull back and make a stand at the tavern."

"What about the people in the church cellar?" he called.

"They're too busy trying to kill us. When the arrows stop, get the soldiers back to the tavern."

"What about you?" the mage asked.

"I'll be fine, I've got my armour."

Revi moved the soldier to a crouching position, his wound healed. The rain of arrows ceased, and Revi stood, helping the soldier to his feet. Though healed of his wound, he had lost a lot of blood and was weak. Revi put the man's arm over his shoulder and supported him as they made their way toward safety.

Gerald watched the enemy advancing. This time, they had learned their lesson, and a mob of men, some dozen people wide, came like a great flood. They wouldn't fall for the funnel again, so he backed up slowly, hoping the mage and his patient would have time to get to safety. He heard a shout to his left and saw Jack sprinting for the final stand. His soldiers lay dead at their positions as a swarm of attackers flooded over them. Gerald turned back to face his own foes, but the distraction had been ill-timed. He was now being rushed by dozens of men with nowhere to go.

Beverly felt the weapon scrape across her chest plate, but she ignored it, swinging her blade from right to left. The tip cut through the man's arms, spraying blood in a wide arc. She struck again with a sudden jab, a kidney strike that dropped her target a moment later. The other men backed up, temporarily shocked by the ferocity of her defense. To her right stood Dame Celia, her blade and shield held in the ready position.

The small crowd in front of her parted as someone in charge stepped through. His eyes searched the defenses, as if looking for something, then locked on Dame Celia.

Beverly prepared to launch an attack. Perhaps, if they took out the leader, the others might flee. She was about to say as much when the blade struck. One moment she was watching the enemy, the next a terrible pain erupted from her leg as Celia drove a sword into her thigh. Beverly turned, looking on in horror as the blond knight stabbed at her again.

Beverly dove to the side, her leg collapsing as she tried to come upright. She cursed herself for forgetting about the traitor in their midst; the betrayer had finally revealed her true colours, and now Beverly would pay the price. The turncoat's sword came down, but Beverly managed to parry with her own, barely. It was a desperate defense while Celia's strike was swift and powerful, causing Beverly's sword to fly from her hand, coming to rest a few paces away. Now, the traitorous knight stepped forward again, rage filling her face.

"Death to Merceria!" she cried as she swung her sword overhead.

Beverly brought her shield up just in time to block, feeling the force of the enraged blow. The other attackers stood watching as if this were some form of entertainment. Again and again, the blows rained down. Beverly crouched, trying desperately to cover her body with the shield, waiting for any opportunity to counter-attack. Striking out with the edge of the shield, she heard a shriek; Celia backed up, limping slightly. Beverly forced herself to stand, hopping on her uninjured leg. She drew her dagger and held her crumpled shield, trying to maintain her balance.

Celia came forward once more, striking with her sword. The shield finally split, falling from Beverly's grip. The redheaded knight struck out with her dagger, marking Celia's face with a cut.

"It's time to die, Beverly, and put an end to the Mercerian Fitzwilliams. You've been a thorn in the side of Norland for far too long."

Beverly tried to stay upright while the wound throbbed painfully; she felt blood dripping down her leg.

"Why, Celia? Why did you betray us?"

"Why?" the blond knight responded. "Norlanders had to flee Merceria generations ago. It's time we took it back. When this battle is over, you'll all be dead, and bodies of Mercerians will be scattered about. It'll mean war, and when the dust settles, we'll move in to clean up. Bodden has been promised to me!"

The treasonous knight looked like she was about to rush forward, but a howl behind her warned of another attack. She turned, just in time to see Tempus bearing down on her. When she raised her shield to defend herself, Beverly struck, launching forward in a desperate lunge, driving the dagger into Celia's back, forcing them both to the ground, the body of the blond knight beneath her. Tempus kept moving, launching himself instead at the enemy leader, who went down in a flurry of teeth and fur.

Beverly felt a hand on her shoulder and looked up to see Alric and Anna. They were lifting her to her feet. The young prince put her arm around his shoulder and started half carrying her back to the safety of the tavern. An enemy soldier stepped forward to intervene but Anna struck with her Dwarven blade, slicing through her target like a hot knife through butter. The man fell to the ground, gripping his arm in a futile attempt to stem the flow of blood.

Anna turned and ran, catching up with them, calling to the great mastiff to follow. They rushed into the tavern, to hear a clatter of arrows striking against the doorway. Revi was there, casting as they entered and soon Beverly felt the tingle of magic knitting the flesh of her leg back into place. She grabbed a nearby sword and stood ready to guard the doorway.

Gerald was surrounded. All he could do was parry with his sword and block with the shield. He tried to back up, but there was no clear path to safety. He dropped to one knee to add force as he struck with the edge of his shield, to be rewarded with the sound of a kneecap breaking. He swung his sword upward in a wide arc, more to clear space than strike a target. The temporary respite allowed him to stand back up and he took another step backwards.

He parried a blow with his sword, only to see an arrow burrow into his opponent's eye. A second arrow impaled a man's foot and suddenly all eyes, but his, were looking up. He turned and sprinted, his feet carrying him to the tavern as quickly as they could. No sooner had he entered than Beverly closed the door, throwing her weight against it.

Gerald instantly took in his surroundings. "Where's Celia," he asked.

"She was the traitor," declared Anna. "She turned on Beverly during the battle. She's dead now."

"How did she know we'd come here?" asked Jack.

"I doubt she did," said Beverly. "It was an opportunity she couldn't pass up. If she'd managed to kill the princess, their plans would be complete. It would be war."

Alric looked confused, but Gerald saw no further time for explanations. "Jack, cover the back door, they'll try to surround us. Are there any other exits?"

"No," said Alric. "We've shuttered all the windows in here."

No sooner had he spoken than the sound of axes clattered at the door.

"They're going to hack their way in," declared Anna. "What do we do?"

"Remember when your brother visited Uxley?" Gerald asked.

"Yes," Anna responded. "Everyone up the stairs, Gerald and Beverly will hold them."

"No!" yelled Jack. "Gerald needs to protect you, Princess. I'll hold the stairs."

The rest rushed up the stairs as Beverly stood, side by side with Jack, at the bottom.

"I'm out of arrows," Hayley called from above.

The front door opened in an explosion of splinters and the enemy poured in. They swarmed across the main floor of the Tavern, rushing the stairs while someone ran to unbar the back door.

Beverly struck out as a target neared, an efficient stab to the neck. Jack parried a blow then swung with his sword. His foe tried to twist out of the way, only to lose an ear. "I hear Norlanders can't fight!" he yelled.

A spear stabbed forward but Jack twisted to the side, leaving the tip to strike at the empty space between the defenders. As the assailant pulled his weapon back, Jack ran his blade up the shaft, slicing into the man's hand.

"Let me lend you a hand!" he yelled.

Beverly worked in silence, cutting and stabbing with precision. She ignored a yell behind her, instead parrying a thrust then kicking with her leg, sending her opponent sprawling.

Anna screamed, and Gerald turned to see a man climbing in through the window. He struck with his blade, driving it into the intruder's chest. The man fell back, but it was just the beginning, for the enemy was climbing the outside walls in large numbers. Alric stepped forward, striking with his sword as two more piled through the window, but had to back up, lest he be overwhelmed.

"They're on both sides!" yelled Anna, as now even more attackers started coming through the other windows. She struck with her sword, slicing into someone's shins. Her opponent struck back with a mace, the blow glancing off her weapon, the force sending her to the ground. The enemy stood over her, preparing to smash her head in when Tempus struck, tearing into the man's neck.

"Beverly, retreat," yelled Gerald, "before the attackers swarm you from the second floor!" The thumping of their feet preceded Jack and Beverly rushing up into the room, slicing as they went.

Now the enemy charged up the stairs, and Gerald cursed at their predicament. Revi cast a spell, his target yawning before dropping from the window to smash his head below. Hayley sliced with her sword, but her armour showed multiple wounds and her blows were growing weaker, and even Revi was running low on energy, his spells becoming less effective as he did so.

The enemy pressed closer while the defenders stood, back to back, forming a defensive circle. Surely this could go on no longer.

It started as a low rumble which grew in intensity. Horns sounded in the distance and one of the attackers, who was by the window, suddenly yelled, "It's the Orcs, flee!"

The Norlanders rushed out of the room and down the stairs, while others turned to climb out the windows. Gerald, who had more than enough of these people, rushed forward, slicing a man mid-step. The rest followed his lead and exploded in a whirlwind of action, cutting down anyone they could. Soon, only the heavy breathing of the defenders filled the room. Anna made her way to the window, looking down at the scene below.

"The Orcs have saved us," she proclaimed. "It's over!"

Alric made his way to stand beside the princess. "They're broken," he exclaimed. "Their plan to blame Merceria has failed."

Beverly gazed upon the scene below. Orcs were gathering up prisoners, using their spears to herd them into groups. There would be no denying the ruse now.

They made their way down the stairs and through the carnage of the ground floor. They recognized the Shaman, Andurak, talking to another Orc, richly decorated with chainmail and bearing a great axe. As they exited the building the Shaman nodded to the axe-laiden Orc, who stepped forward, bowing his head ever so slightly.

"It is a great honour to fight with Redblade," he said. "If we had known of this, we would have been here sooner."

Beverly stood still, too shocked to speak.

"Redblade?" asked Anna.

"It's what the Orcs called Beverly," explained Hayley.

"I don't understand," said the young princess. "That was clear across the other side of Merceria. How would they know that?"

"The spirits are wise," uttered Andurak.

"Do you think," said Jack, "that we might return to Faltingham, Highness? I think we've seen enough excitement for the day."

Alric laughed, and then looked at his companion, "I think we can all agree on that, Jack."

NINETEEN

Loranguard

AUTUMN 960 MC

"You'll like Loranguard," said Alric, peering out the carriage window. "It's a port city, astride the Loran River."

"Loran was the founder of Weldwyn, wasn't he?" asked Anna.

"Yes, that's right. I'm surprised you know that. Most people don't have an interest in history."

"Her Highness is not most people," explained Gerald.

The carriage hit a rut in the road, sending it sliding. Anna was pushed up against Lady Nicole who was sitting on the other side of her.

"I wish the roads here were more like Merceria," commented Lady Nicole.

"Are the roads well-built back home?" asked Alric.

"The king's road between Kingsford and Wincaster is; it's paved, but the truth is the rest of them are just as bad as this."

"It's not so bad," mused Gerald. "At least we have a comfortable carriage to ride in." He looked out the window to see the horsemen riding in the rain.

"Wouldn't it be better to halt for the day?" asked Anna.

"When we're so close?" challenged Alric. "No, we'll be arriving soon. Up ahead is a turn in the road and then you'll see Loranguard, or at least you would if it wasn't raining. We'll be there before dinner time."

"I take it you've been there before, Highness," asked Lady Nicole.

"Yes," Alric replied, "my brother, Cuthbert, is up here. He married Lady Madeline, the earl's daughter, so he spends most of his time here."

"What's the city like, Alric?" asked Anna. "Give us some more information."

"Well," he continued, "it lies on the forks of the river Loran. There's a big castle there, we call it the Citadel. It's on the northernmost bank, with the tributary coming in from the west to join up with the river right below the castle walls."

"I would imagine," offered Gerald, "that there's quite a bit of shipping flowing through."

"Yes," agreed the young prince. "It's the northernmost port in Weldwyn, though smaller boats travel up-river to a number of settlements. You'll likely see ships from dozens of foreign lands. Do you see many in Merceria?"

"No," Gerald replied. "The sea is cut off from our ports by the Great Swamp. I'm afraid the only ships we've seen are the small river boats like the one we arrived in."

"Oh, yes, I remember Anna talking about that. We'll have to arrange a tour of the docks; I think you'd like it."

"Aren't the Twelve Clans right across the river?" asked Lady Nicole.

"Yes, on the western bank, though they don't come that close to the border. The city is quite large, some say even larger than the capital, but it's spread up and down the river so you don't notice it so much."

The carriage slewed sideways as the wheels struck a large stone in the road.

"Are there theatres in Loranguard, Highness?" enquired Lady Nicole.

"Yes, several, in fact. I'm quite a fan of them. I especially like the works of Trellian Marston. Do you have his plays in Merceria?"

"I don't think so," Nicole admitted. "Our great playwright was a man known as Califax."

"Hmm, I'm afraid I don't know the name."

"What are the plays like in Weldwyn?" asked the princess.

"They vary a lot," Alric admitted. "There are the romances, the tragedies, even comedies. My favourite, I think is 'The Dawn of Fate'. It concerns a young warrior who is raised by commoners but is secretly the bastard child of the king. It has some tremendous fight scenes. Do you like plays, Anna?"

"I think so," she answered, "though, truth be told, I've only seen one, and it was raided by the king's guard. We had to make our getaway across the rooftops of Wincaster."

"That sounds exciting," remarked Alric. "You're so full of surprises."

"How so?" asked Anna.

"Well, you seem to be a prim and proper young princess, and then you turn around and run across rooftops and fight invaders. I'm not sure I know how to take you. You remind me of my sister Althea, but she's just a pain in the arse."

"You shouldn't think that way," said Anna. "You're lucky to have a family. Imagine if you were to lose her, how would you feel about her then?"

"True," Alric admitted. "I hadn't thought about that." He flashed Anna a smile.

"Perhaps," offered Lady Nicole, "you might condescend to take the princess to a play while you're in Loranguard?"

"That's a marvellous idea!" Alric beamed. "I'll find out what's playing. You're going to love your stay here, Anna. I've so much to show you."

The constant drumming of the rain on the roof of the carriage finally ceased, so they all looked out the windows to see they were passing through the gates of the city.

"Well, that was unexpected," admitted Alric. "I suppose I've kept us talking too much."

"Don't be silly, Alric," said Anna. "It was a nice conversation. We should chat more often, you're so much more relaxed when we're alone."

"Well, hardly alone," noted Lady Nicole, "that would be most unseemly."

Gerald tried to stifle a smile. Lady Nicole wasn't much older than Beverly, but she seemed to go out of her way to act like an old matron.

"We'll be crossing the river soon," offered Alric, "and then we'll make our way to the Citadel where you'll be lodged."

"Aren't you staying there as well?" asked Anna.

"No, I'll be with the earl and his family at their mansion, but I'll check in on you during your stay."

Gerald noticed the look of disappointment written on Anna's face. The conversation died and they rode on in silence, with the young princess gazing out the window as they drove through the city.

The carriage entered the courtyard and halted. A richly dressed servant opened the door for them where they were met by Lady Madeline, who greeted the party on behalf of her husband.

"We have arranged a meal for you, Highness," she said. "If you'd like to come this way."

Alric was glancing around, "When can we expect to see Cuthbert?" he asked.

"He'll be with us shortly, Alric. He's attending to an important matter."

"We need to make arrangements for our people first," began Anna.

"I'll see to it, Highness," offered Dame Beverly. "We'll look to the horses and billeting, and then I'll find you later."

"Very well," said Anna, turning to Gerald. "Shall we?"

Gerald held out his arm for her, "Of course, Highness."

She took his arm following their host into the great hall. A few tables had been set end to end to give the appearance of a single long one. There must have been more than two dozen chairs at the table, and as Anna entered, the people rose to their feet.

Lady Madeline showed Anna to the head of the table while a servant withdrew the chair and she sat, nodding her thanks while waiting for it to be pushed in. Gerald took the seat to her right while Tempus squeezed between them to take up his customary place beneath, much to the consternation of the servants. Alric sat at Anna's left, with his sister-in-law beside him. His older brother's chair beside his wife sat empty, awaiting his arrival.

"Cuthbert insists," stated Lady Madeline, "that you don't stand on ceremony. Feel free to begin eating."

Gerald surveyed the table, his eyes coming to rest on an enormous platter of sausages. He looked to Anna, and she laughed.

"Go ahead," she said. "Dig in and toss some over to me."

Soon, the great hall echoed with the sounds of eating.

The soldiers were escorted inside for billeting while the horses were walked to the stables. Arnim had organized the watch so that Beverly could take care of Lightning. She had removed the great warhorse's tack and was just beginning to brush him down when she heard a sound at the far end of the stable; two men had just entered with their mounts.

"Damn Clansmen, I still don't trust 'em," the first man said, in a rich baritone. "After all the trouble they've caused, it's a bit strange they suddenly want to talk."

"Well, we're not at war," his companion said in a high, nasally voice.

"That's never stopped them from raiding before," the baritone reminded.

"Maybe they mean it this time," said the high voice. "After all, they sent one of their own nobles to talk to us, perhaps they're as tired of the fighting as we are."

"Hah, I'll believe it when I see it."

They walked past the stall where Beverly was grooming her horse and fell silent.

"Nice horse, miss," said the baritone. "Where'd you get it?"

"In Merceria," she offered.

"Oh yeah? Where's that?" he asked.

She was about to rebuke the man's stupidity and instead, silently rebuked herself. Merceria was over five hundred miles away, while these were simple soldiers. She thought back to Bodden Keep; half the soldiers there had no idea where Wincaster was, let alone Westland.

"It lies far to the east," she replied.

"She's a beauty," said the high pitched man.

Beverly was about to curse the man until she realized he was talking about Lightning. "Yes, he is," she said. "He's a Mercerian Charger, the largest breed in the land and a warhorse. I suggest you don't get too close."

They both nodded their heads in appreciation. "Good day to you, then," the baritone said, and they made their way down to the stalls at the end of the stables.

Later that evening, the Mercerian's found themselves in Anna's suite of rooms; the princess sitting at the head of a table with Gerald to her right, the remaining seats available for the rest to join them. Once they were seated, Gerald looked around at the faces of those present. Beverly was sitting to Gerald's right and beyond her was her cousin, Aubrey Brandon. Revi, Arnim and Hayley sat across from them with little Lily sitting at the far end.

"I have decided," started Anna, "that we shall hold regular meetings for the rest of our journey here in Weldwyn. Everyone here is now, officially, part of my council. I would like to meet every couple of days to go over anything that might be of interest."

"Sorry," said Aubrey, "but are you sure I'm meant to be here, Highness? I'm only an apprentice."

"You're here," said Anna, "because you can be trusted and your talents are valuable to this council."

"My talents?"

"Yes," continued Anna. "You are very well educated, Aubrey, and can provide insight. Beverly highly recommends you and assures me of your discretion."

"I'm flattered, Highness," the young apprentice replied.

Anna looked to Gerald, who took over. "The purpose of this council is to gather information. We want to know as much about this kingdom as we can. What do they like, what do they need? You are to keep your eyes open and your ears to the ground. Even seemingly simple matters may be of import to us. While you are here, in council, your opinions may be expressed honestly. I realize we've only arrived and so the princess thought it might be best to lay out some ground rules."

Anna stood to speak, "I have decided to officially acknowledge a chain of command. I name Gerald as my second in charge. As of now, he will be officially referred to as Commander Matheson."

"I hardly think that's necessary," Gerald protested.

"Nonsense, Gerald. You oversee the knights and the guards with Beverly and Arnim's help. That already makes you a commander. Need I remind you that you've already commanded troops in battle?"

"I suppose," he grumbled.

"Hopefully, we won't need all this going forward," she said.

"That's what we thought about Norwatch," reminded the mage.

"The point is well taken, Revi. Let's hope we have a peaceful journey from now on. If Gerald is unavailable, then Beverly will assume command, having had more battle experience, though I expect her to defer to Arnim in matters pertaining to the guard."

Beverly nodded her head in understanding.

"Under Gerald," Anna continued, "Beverly will command the knights, with Arnim commanding the foot. Revi will be in charge of anything magic related and we will call on Hayley's ranger skills as needed. Are there any questions?"

"I heard something earlier that might be important," offered Beverly.

"Tell us more," prompted Anna.

"I was in the stables when I overheard two soldiers talking. Apparently, the Twelve Clans are sending a delegation, with a noble, to negotiate. The men seemed to think it unusual."

"Perfect, this is exactly the type of thing I want to know about."

"Will we be doing anything about it?" asked Arnim

"No," replied the princess. "For now we just collect this information. I shall make a note of it in my journal for later perusal. It may be nothing, but then again it might prove valuable in the future. Anything you hear like this should be brought to my attention."

"What about the other knights," asked Beverly, "and Lady Nicole?"

Gerald spoke up, "We haven't decided if they can be trusted yet. The betrayal of Celia was a bitter lesson. For now, our discussions here shall not be shared. When the princess goes into town, the only personal bodyguards in her presence will be myself, Beverly or Hayley."

Anna laughed as a low rumbling sound interrupted the discussion, "It appears that Tempus has fallen asleep. The hour is late and we shall have much to do tomorrow if our previous visits are any indication. Does anyone have anything they'd like to add?"

"Yes," Revi spoke up. "I am pleased to announce that Aubrey here, was able to successfully cast her first spell this morning. She can now heal wounds."

"Though only small ones," admitted Aubrey. "I haven't quite mastered it."

"The rest will come with practice," encouraged Revi, "you've a natural talent."

"It wasn't that long ago that Master Bloom himself had trouble casting that spell," offered Anna.

"I remember it well," added Gerald. "Unfortunately, I was the recipient."

Everyone in the room chuckled, as they had heard the story of that fateful day back in Uxley. With the meeting now concluded they filed out, allowing Lady Nicole to enter to prepare the princess for bed. Gerald was still seated at the table and rose to follow Anna as she made her way to her bedroom.

"And what do you think you're doing?" asked Nicole, looking at the old soldier.

"I'm going to read a story to the princess," he replied.

"This is highly improper," she retorted. "She is a young lady now and needs her privacy."

Anna stepped behind the wooden dressing screen to change. "It's all right," she called out, "he usually puts me to bed."

"It's not right, Your Highness," pressed the Lady-in-Waiting. "I was sent to be your chaperone, I can't have this going on."

"Nonsense," insisted Anna. "Gerald's been reading me stories for years." She came out from behind the screen and jumped onto the bed. "If you feel so strongly about it," she said, looking at Nicole, "then go ahead and chaperone. I'll be getting a story. You never know, you might like it too!"

She climbed under the blankets, and then Gerald pulled them up for her. She patted the bed and Tempus, roused from his slumber, leaped onto the bed.

Gerald noticed Lady Nicole turn red at the sight, and she was obviously about to explode when Anna interrupted, "That will be all, Lady Nicole. You are dismissed."

Lady Nicole's mouth hung open for just a moment and then she composed herself.

"Of course, Your Highness." She bowed and left the room, closing the door behind her.

Anna waited until her footsteps had receded before speaking, "I like Sophie better. Where is she?"

"I'm afraid she's been reduced to maid," offered Gerald.

"That's not fair, she's my maid!"

"I'll make sure she's looked after," promised Gerald. "Lady Nicole was sent by the king, but I suspect Valmar's behind the appointment. We shall have to watch ourselves around her."

"Agreed," said Anna. "Now, what story have you got for me tonight?"

It didn't take long for Anna to fall asleep. Gerald looked down on her as she slumbered and observed how much older she had grown in the last few months. Soon, she would be a young woman, and he wondered how much longer he would be reading her stories. He bent over her, kissing her on the forehead and scratched the head of Tempus. The large mastiff stretched his legs as if finally relaxing, so Gerald turned, tiptoeing from the room.

TWENTY

On the Town

AUTUMN 960 MC

E arly morning saw Gerald sitting in the dining hall, eating his breakfast. He heard an approaching footfall and looked up to see Anna and Tempus enter the room.

"Good morning, Gerald," she said in greeting.

"How are you this morning, Anna?" he asked.

She sat down at the table before answering, "I was actually wondering what we have on the schedule today. Have you heard anything?"

"Yes," he replied, "Prince Alric sent a message. He wants to take you into the city and show you around."

"Aren't we already in the city?" she asked, just as he was about to take a bite of food.

He paused his action to reply, "Well, yes, but he wants to take you into the part of the city that isn't the Citadel." He finished his sentence just in time to see her laughing. "You're just jealous because I got the last sausage."

She peered around the table, "Truly?"

"No, I've hidden some over here." He moved a plate over to her seat. "I suspect young Alric wants to show you the arena, and likely the docks."

"I'll have to leave poor Tempus here," she said. "I don't want to scare the locals."

"Why don't you leave him with Sophie. He trusts her, and it'll give her something to do."

"Excellent idea, Commander Matheson," she said.

"Of course, Highness," he replied, doing his best impression of a Califax play, "I doth give it much thought."

"You're turning into quite the poet, Gerald."

"My lady," he said, placing his knuckles to his forehead.

He reached for a scone and was just breaking it open when a servant entered to announce the arrival of Alric. The young prince entered, and Gerald offered him a scone. He took one, holding it gingerly and began picking it apart to eat it.

"It seems," observed Anna, "that you and Gerald eat the same way."

Alric grinned as he stuffed a tasty morsel into his mouth. "The perks," he said, through a full mouth, "of being a prince. I don't have to follow the rules."

"Why, Prince Alric," Anna exclaimed, "you're starting to get used to us!"

The prince pulled out a chair and sat down as Gerald chuckled at the servants. They had rushed forward to settle his chair for him, and now they were returning to their positions around the room without accomplishing their mission.

"I thought I'd show you the Celestial Park this morning."

"That sounds interesting," said Anna. "Tell me more."

"It was built over two hundred years ago by the Earl of Loranguard for his wife. It's one of the great love stories of the realm."

Gerald noticed Anna watching the young prince, drinking it all in. Was he imagining it, or was there some sort of attraction he hadn't seen before.

"It sounds fascinating," she finally said.

"It gets even more interesting, though," he said, "for his wife was a commoner, and it was a scandal at the time."

"So what happened?" she asked.

"Despite objections, he married her anyway. They ended up together for many years and died within two months of each other. The nobles at the time were shocked, but the commoners loved it. They made a play about it, and it's still enacted to this day."

Anna had finished eating and set down her utensils. "Well," she announced, "we better get going. I assume we are walking?"

"We are," confirmed Alric. He rose, coming over to her side of the table. He extended his arm for her, and she stood to take hold of it. "Come along, then. Let me show you the wonders of Loranguard."

Gerald hastened to his feet to follow, pausing long enough to snag an extra sausage from Anna's plate.

Dame Beverly was waiting outside the room and quickly fell into place beside Gerald as they made their way through the Citadel. They had exited the building and were nearly at the gate when Lady Nicole put in an appearance. She hurried to catch up to them and gave Gerald a look that told him there would be no argument.

Exiting the Citadel, Alric led them along the north road toward the park. This part of the city was well groomed; it was obvious the more affluent folk lived in this region. It reminded Gerald of Wincaster, but the houses were not quite as elegant as those of the nobles of Merceria; there were, however, more of them.

Gerald turned to Beverly, "What are the others up to today?" he asked.

"Revi and Aubrey are going to browse some shops," she said, "and Hayley's taking Lily down to the water. She seems to have an affinity for it."

"How does Hayley know that?" he asked.

"She's been teaching her some hand signals. Our ranger's a clever girl."

"I could have taught her hand signals if I'd thought of it," Gerald confessed. "See?" he said, holding up his middle finger.

Beverly laughed, "I see you've learned from my father. You do him proud."

They wound their way through the wealthier section of town, finally arriving at their destination. It was a large area, with carefully trimmed trees and immaculately cut grass. Denizens of the city wandered about the meandering paths, while Gerald spied at least three fountains. They shot water into the air, and he wondered how such things were accomplished.

"I saw a fountain like that in Shrewesdale," Beverly remarked. "I think Dwarves designed it."

Anna and Alric walked at a leisurely pace. The weather seemed to be cooperating; the sun broke out from behind the clouds, and soon the grass sparkled with the morning dew, giving the entire park a dreamlike quality.

"This is amazing, Alric," she said.

"Yes, it is, isn't it. I've heard my mother talk about it before, but this is actually the first time I've seen it for myself."

She looked at him in surprise and then laughed.

Alric was grinning from ear to ear. "The park is well named. If a place could be called the Afterlife on earth, this would be it."

"The earl must have loved his wife a great deal to have this made. It would have cost a fortune."

"Oh, it did," he agreed. "Some say it took most of his wealth, though I doubt that."

"It's true," interrupted Lady Nicole. "The play explains it all."

"The play?" asked Anna.

"Yes," said Alric, "the one I told you about earlier. It's called 'The Maiden and the Earl'."

"I've arranged for tickets, Highness," added Nicole. "For this afternoon's performance. A private booth for you and His Highness."

"That's very gracious of you, Lady Nicole," said Anna. "Though I'm not sure it would be up to Prince Alric's tastes."

"Nonsense," said Alric. "I've seen it before, it's very entertaining. Lots of battles, intrigue and even a dragon."

Gerald saw Lady Nicole paling at the very thought, but the prince ended her misery quickly.

"I'm kidding, it's a romance. Though there is a little fighting in it."

"I can't wait," said Anna.

"I hope it goes better than the last play we saw," remarked Gerald.

"'We' won't be seeing it," stated the Lady-in-Waiting. "It's a private box for two, the rest of us will have to stand guard in the hallway."

Gerald looked to Beverly, who just shrugged. Lady Nicole was becoming very tiresome.

~

Revi Bloom looked through a shop window; it was a herbalist and reminded him of his parent's business back in Wincaster. He decided to enter, stepping into the small space with a quiet stride. He wandered about, looking at leaves drying on some twine and powdered plants in small containers. Many of these items he recognized but a few were unknown to him. He made a mental note to ask about them.

The proprietor finished dealing with a customer and wandered over to the mage, "Is there something I can help you with?"

"Actually," he said, "I was wondering about the price of kingsleaf."

"I'm afraid," said the shopkeeper, "that I am unfamiliar with that plant. Is it found locally?"

"It's not important," Revi replied. His eyes caught sight of a glass jar containing something strange. "What's this?"

The merchant picked up the jar, handing it to the mage. "We're not sure what it is. It was found down at the river by someone who thought it might be useful to have an expert look at it."

Revi held the jar to the light of the window, the better to see it. It looked as if someone had, perhaps, mixed paper with mud. It was clumped together, but he discerned no recognizable shape.

"Fascinating," he mused.

"It's yours if you want it," the shopkeeper said. "I can let you have it for four shillings.

"Fascinating as it is," Revi replied, "I'm afraid I can't. Were I home, with my laboratory, I'd be delighted to take it off your hands, but I'm only visiting," he said, handing the jar back to the proprietor. "I would be interested in looking at some of your herb prices, however. In Merceria we have some rare plants, but I hoped they might be more common here."

"By all means," replied the shopkeeper, "let me show you our plants."

It would be hours before they were done, but to Revi Bloom, it was like being home.

~

Dame Hayley Chambers wandered down the street, the diminutive Lily's hand in hers. People gawked, for none had seen a Saurian before, but no one interrupted their progress, so their trip to the docks was uneventful. Upon arriving, Lily started jumping up and down, a sure sign she was excited, and the ranger understood why; there were large ships here, with tall masts that towered above the buildings on the jetty.

Their interest must have been evident for all to see for they were interrupted by a voice, "I notice you like the looks of the Swift."

Hayley turned in the direction of the voice. A rather well-tanned man looked down on them from the railing of a ship, his unkempt hair tucked hastily beneath a weather-beaten cap.

"Pardon me?" responded Hayley.

"The Swift, fastest merchant on the river."

"I'm not an expert on boats, but it looks fine."

The man frowned slightly, "She's a ship, not a boat."

"What's the difference?" enquired the ranger.

"A ship sails the world's oceans," he responded. "Would you like to come up and take a look? There's a boarding ramp over yonder."

"I'd like that, thank you." She made some hand signals to Lily, who nodded her head and soon they were climbing aboard.

Their new acquaintance met them as they reached the deck.

"I'm Harnen Runell, the captain," he said, holding out his hand.

Hayley grasped it firmly, responding, "I'm Dame Hayley Chambers, Knight of the Hound."

"Strange title, that," the man replied. "I take it you're not from around here."

"No, we're visiting from Merceria. It lies many miles to the east of here. Are you from Weldwyn?"

"Me? No, I hail from a far distant land called Ilea, though I doubt you've heard of it. We sail the Sea of Storms often, it's proven to be quite profitable for us."

"My understanding is that Loranguard is a ways up river. Do you normally sail this far north?"

"No, but it's dangerous on the open sea this time of year. We've come here to refit and refurbish the ship over the winter months, and to get some rest."

They proceeded toward the bow, with Lily stopping to stare up into the rigging.

"So who's your friend, here?"

"This is Lily, she's a Saurian. Have you seen her people before?"

"No," the captain responded, "though I've seen enough races around the world that nothing much surprises me anymore. Did you say you were a knight? I didn't think this land had such things."

"They don't in Weldwyn. I'm surprised you're familiar with knights at all. I understood that only Merceria had them."

"Nonsense, lots of realms have knights, though I daresay you're the only ones in this land."

"How is that possible?"

"I imagine your ancestors came from a different continent and brought the idea with them. It's common enough. You don't have Temple Knights, do you?"

"What's that?" she asked.

"They're knights sworn to a holy order."

"I've never heard of them."

"Perhaps it's for the best, they can be a bit pretentious at times. Tell me, do knights here always carry bows?"

She laughed, "No, I used to be a King's Ranger. I'm sort of a special knight. The princess prefers me to keep my lighter armour, it's more convenient for tracking and such."

Lily, who was standing at the base of the mainmast, turned and chattered.

"I think she'd like to climb up to the top, if it's all right."

"By all means," Captain Runell replied.

Lily immediately began hauling herself up the mast, climbing it like a pole.

"There are ropes..." started the captain.

"I think she's doing fine," observed Hayley. "She has claws that make it easy. Watch carefully, she's incredibly fast."

The Saurian was already halfway up the mast and was rapidly approaching the spar that lay perpendicular to the mainmast. She sprinted across the timber with the grace of a cat and then paused. The yardarm overhung the side of the ship, and she was now staring down into the water below.

Hayley was about to call out but before she could speak Lily dove. Down she went, entering the water with little splash or noise. The ranger ran to the railing, holding her breath, only to see Lily emerge a moment later. The Saurian rolled onto her back and waved while Hayley let out a breath.

"Well, I'll be," mused the captain. "I've never seen the like before. Does she do this often?"

"I've never seen it before," Hayley replied, "but I almost entered the Afterlife when she jumped."

As they were talking, Lily swam back to the dock, and soon she was scrambling back across the boarding ramp, eager for another try.

Hayley watched her begin climbing once more, but a shout from the bow took her attention.

"Captain!" yelled a crewman. "We've got a problem."

"Excuse me a moment," he said, making his way forward.

Hayley followed a few paces behind as they approached a group of three men working on the foredeck. They had hauled up the anchor, little more than a metal claw, and placed it, still dripping, on the deck. The men were scraping it with knives in an effort to clean it of mud and dirt dragged up from the river.

"What's this?" asked the captain.

"I've never seen its like, sir," one of the men was saying. "It's some sort of pasty material."

The captain leaned in closer to examine it. "Looks like some strange sort of mud to me."

"There's something mixed in with it," the crewman added. "Some sort of plant, perhaps?"

"I don't care what it is, get it off the anchor. Does it scrape off?"

"Yes, sir."

"Then do so and toss it overboard," he said, rising from his crouch to turn and face Hayley. "Sorry about that, the men can be a little difficult sometimes."

The tiny splash as Lily once more hit the water drew his attention back to the Saurian. "You know, there's a place not too far from here where the common folk wade into the water. It's likely not busy this time of year, but I hear it's a common practice to do so in the heat of the summer. I imagine your lizard friend isn't bothered by cold water, maybe you should give it a visit?"

"Thank you, we will," she responded.

~

The window of the store looked inviting, so Lady Aubrey Brandon opened the door to hear the ring of a bell announcing her entrance. The room smelled musty, but considering the contents, that was understandable. Here was a store that offered her the most interesting of things; books, parchment, inks and all manner of quills. She browsed the shelves, stepping quietly, afraid to disturb the silence that gave this place its air of mystery.

Aubrey had always liked books. She was fascinated by magic and anything related to it. She had once spent days poring over a book about an ancient wizard, only to discover it was a work of fiction. The history of magic was her primary interest, though now that she was capable of using it herself, she wondered if her tastes might change.

"May I help you?" offered a voice.

She turned to see an elderly woman approach, her grey hair set above a friendly looking face.

"I was just looking, thank you." The woman turned to leave until Aubrey spoke again, "Actually, I was wondering if you have paper."

"We have many kinds of paper from parchment to papyrus. What, specifically, are you looking for?"

"I'm an apprentice mage," Aubrey confessed, "and I want to keep careful notes of my studies. I draw things quite often, with notations of course."

"I think I have just the thing for you," the woman offered, "follow me." She led Aubrey to the next aisle and stopped at a slim tome. "This is something we brought in from the Capital. It consists of bound pages, blank, of course, with a lockable cover for travelling. Naturally, it comes with a key."

Aubrey picked it up, feeling the weight of it. "Is this a leather cover?" she asked.

"Yes, to protect it against the weather. I can even have your name embossed if you like."

"Most impressive. How much?"

"With the embossing, I will let you have it for only five crowns."

Aubrey thought it over carefully. Her father, the baron, had provided her with a generous purse and she was usually careful with her funds, but this was a rare find.

"I'll take it," she decided.

"Excellent," replied the shopkeeper. "I will have the embossing done by tomorrow. My tradesman is free this afternoon. Will you be needing ink and quills?"

"I have some, but they're wearing out. If I have to trim them anymore, I'll be writing with my fingers."

"Ah, then I have just the quill for you. Come, take a look."

The woman moved behind the counter and opened a small wooden box, placing it in front of Aubrey. It was a feather like none she had ever seen before. It was a standard size, but the colours were breathtaking, for it contained hues of green and blue that shimmered as it was held to the light.

"This is a gryphon feather," the lady said. "As such, it is quite durable. You'll likely never need to trim it."

"Fascinating," said Aubrey. "Now, how about some ink?"

It would be late in the day by the time she was done.

～

The afternoon sun saw Beverly sitting at a table with Gerald, while nearby sat the prince and princess, with Lady Nicole watching like a hawk. The weather had remained clear, and it was proving to be an uncharacteristically warm day for the autumn. Anna had decided she was hungry and so the entourage had come here, to a tavern called the Hungry Cavalier.

To Beverly's eyes, it was very similar to her father's favourite haunt in Wincaster. She looked at Gerald, who was gazing around the place, eager to see what they had to offer.

"I swear," she said, "if they serve stinky cheese, I'm leaving."

Gerald chuckled, "Don't worry, they won't have Hawksburg Gold here. But I might try those sausages." He was looking across the room at another patron who was busy at his meal.

"I believe you could live on sausages. Don't you think about other things?"

Glancing out the window, something caught his eye. Beverly noticed his sudden shift of attention, and asked, "Something wrong?"

"Wrong? No, I was just reminded of something."

"Do tell," she pressured.

"I had meant to buy Anna a present for her birthday, but we got so caught up in Norwatch that it completely slipped my mind."

"Anything in particular?"

"No, but I've just spotted a jewellers across the way, and it's given me an idea."

"Did you want to go over there now?" Beverly asked.

"No, we're busy guarding Anna, but perhaps in a day or two I'll slip out and see what they have. I would like to order something to be made."

"That shouldn't be a problem, I can have Hayley take your place."

"Thank you. It won't take long, but don't say anything to Anna."

"Of course not, I don't want to spoil the surprise."

His gaze shifted back to the nearby table where Alric and Anna were conversing. Beverly followed suit.

"They appear to be getting along rather well," she commented.

"Yes," he agreed, "Alric seems to have grown on her."

"And her on him," she added.

"Perhaps they'll marry someday."

Beverly was shocked by the statement. "I'm surprised you would say that," she said.

"She has to marry, eventually," said Gerald. "Better to someone she gets along with than Marshal-General Valmar."

"You mean, Duke Valmar of Eastwood, now," she warned.

"You can wrap shit in a silver stocking," he spat out, "but it's still shit. He may wear the mantle of a duke, but he's definitely not noble."

"We both agree on that," she commiserated. "These two probably would make a decent match, all things considered. Are you that eager to have her marry?"

"No, I just want her to be happy, but the king is eventually going to insist on a marriage. Better a prince than a man like the duke."

Beverly shuddered at the mere thought of Valmar.

"What about you?" added Gerald. "You should be thinking about marriage, too. Your father won't live forever."

"That subject is not open for discussion," she threatened, then softened her tone. "Sorry, Gerald, I didn't mean to be so rude."

"I've known you your entire life, Beverly; no apology is necessary. I won't say any more on the subject, though I can't speak for the court."

"What do you mean?" she asked.

"You're an adult now, Beverly, a seasoned warrior. The court of Wincaster likes its nobles with heirs. The king could order you to wed."

"I know that," she responded, "but my heart's not in it. I can't wed when my heart is taken."

"I know how you feel," he sympathized. "Losing Meredith almost destroyed me, but she was dead, and there was no turning back. Aldwin will always be there, in your heart, won't he?"

"He's my foundation," she replied, "but it can never be."

"When I lost my family, I thought my life was over, and yet, fate brought me to Anna. Perhaps fate has something waiting for you. I can't believe Saxnor would deny your heart."

"That's nice of you to say, Gerald, but we make our own future. In the meantime, I would ask you not to speak of it to anyone. The only people who know about Aldwin are you and Aubrey."

"Don't worry, Beverly, your secret is safe with me."

◿

The theatre proved to be much more opulent than the one Gerald had visited in Wincaster. There were ushers here, men dressed alike, as if wearing the livery of a noble. In Wincaster, they had simply dropped coins in a box as they entered, but here the custom was different. Every patron had to have a ticket, a wooden token with the name of the theatre carved into it. Each had a number which corresponded to a seat. Lady Nicole had run ahead to finalize their seating arrangements, and as they entered they were approached by a rather richly dressed man sporting a blue velvet cap with a green plume.

"Your Highness," the man exuded, "may I say how honoured we are by your presence."

"Thank you," replied Alric. "I have the pleasure of escorting Princess Anna of Merceria."

"If you would follow me, Your Highness, I will show you to your balcony."

He led them inside with Gerald and Beverly following behind; Lady Nicole appeared from nowhere to join them. The inside of the theatre was richly decorated, reminding Gerald of the Palace back in Wincaster. The floor was covered in a thick carpet of some type, though how it was fashioned was beyond his experience. They made their way up a wide staircase where a series of doors marked the balcony seats. Their host unlocked one of these doors, opening it to reveal the comfortable chairs within.

"I do hope Your Highnesses enjoy the show," their host said.

"Thank you," said Alric, dropping a coin into the man's hand. "After you, Anna."

Anna stepped through the doorway. "It's quite a view," she said.

"We'll wait out here, Highness," added Lady Nicole. "There won't be room in the balcony for us."

Gerald was about to complain, but Alric, having already passed through, closed the door, sealing off any further conversation. Gerald stared daggers at Lady Nicole, who simply glared back, a triumphant smile on her face.

"Looks like we've got some waiting to do," commented Beverly.

She stood with her back to the door, watching the other patrons filing past. The very sight of the well-armoured knight was enough for people to keep their distance. Gerald couldn't help but notice the interest she generated.

Anna enjoyed the play immensely and couldn't stop talking about it the entire way back to the Citadel. Gerald grumbled as they walked, while Lady Nicole wore a satisfied smirk on her face. They entered the building to be greeted by Hayley and Lily, who had just returned themselves. Anna looked to her Saurian friend and uttered something which Gerald took to be unpronounceable. Lily immediately responded and he suddenly realized she was speaking Saurian fluently.

"When did Revi cast the tongues spell?" he asked.

"He didn't," offered Beverly. "She's been mastering the language for months."

"I thought she only knew a few words. When did she find time for that?" he asked.

Now it was Beverly's turn to smirk, "Every morning, while she's waiting for you to rise."

"But I'm up early every day!" he defended.

"Not so early as you used to be, Gerald. You're not as young as you once were."

Gerald couldn't decide if he'd been insulted or not. From anyone else he would have taken offense, but Beverly was close to family, so he took it in stride.

"She's full of surprises," he finally said.

Anna, meanwhile, had turned her attention to Hayley. "Lily tells me you went down to the river?"

"Yes, Highness. It appears our Saurian friend loves the water."

"What did the townsfolk think of her?" Anna asked.

"People were curious, yet respectful. We found an area where the ground slopes gently into the water. I was throwing sticks into the water for her to retrieve, but now my arm is sore. Tomorrow I'm going to take my bow. She can fetch arrows if she wants to."

"She's not a dog," admonished Gerald.

"I know that," Hayley said defensively. "It was her idea. I swear she would have stayed there all day if I'd let her. I had to promise to take her back tomorrow."

"I'm glad you two were kept entertained," said Anna. "We spent the afternoon seeing a play, well some of us anyway." She cast her eyes at Gerald and Beverly, looking apologetic.

TWENTY-ONE

The Rival

AUTUMN 960 MC

T he next morning found them all busy, for a messenger had arrived from the Earl of Loranguard himself. He had invited the princess and her entourage to a ball in their honour. Anna was excited and had Sophie combing through her wardrobe, looking for something suitable to wear. Beverly opened the door to reveal clothes strewn about the room.

"You called for me, Highness?" she asked.

The young princess looked up from the floor where she was feeling the fabric of a dress.

"Yes, Beverly, I need some help."

The redhead stepped into the room, closing the door quietly behind her.

"What precisely is it you need help with?" she asked.

"I have to pick a dress. Should I wear the blue one or the green one?"

"I wouldn't know, Highness. It's not something I've ever had to worry about."

"Come now, Beverly," Anna cajoled. "Do you mean to say you've never dressed to catch the eye of someone?"

Beverly frowned. "No, Highness. I'm not one to dress up in fancy clothes. I believe people should be judged for who they are, not how they dress."

"If only that were true," responded Anna, with all of her fourteen years of wisdom. She picked up the blue dress, holding it against her while she faced her bodyguard. "What do you think of this one?"

"It's acceptable, I suppose," Beverly replied.

"It has to be more than acceptable. Do you think Alric would like it?"

"I think Alric will like whatever you're wearing, Highness."

"You're just saying that to be nice," said Anna, though she smiled to lessen the accusation. "If you were going to wear one, which would you choose?"

Beverly walked slowly around the room, carefully eyeing the dresses which covered the chairs, the floor and even the bed. "I would pick the green one, Highness."

"Aha!" the princess cried. "Finally, an answer. Tell me, why the green one?"

"It wouldn't impede my sword arm, Highness."

Anna frowned, "Go away, Beverly, and send up your cousin, perhaps she'll be more helpful.

"Yes, Highness," she said with a smile.

Beverly made her way through the Citadel. She knew her cousin would be outside this morning; Aubrey loved to get out onto the grounds where she would while away her time making sketches. She was sitting on a small chair, an upturned tray on her lap, using it as a flat surface, sketching the scene. Beverly watched, entranced, as her cousin's skilled hand added detail after detail, filling in the blank page until the picture began to take form.

"What do you think, Cousin?" she asked, turning unexpectedly.

"It's quite nice," Beverly responded, "but how did you know I was here."

"Easy," Aubrey replied, "it's your armour. It makes noises when you walk."

"I shall have to talk to Aldwin about it when I return to Bodden. How's your morning going?"

"Very nicely, thank you. It's such a gorgeous day out today."

"Have you decided what to wear to the ball?" asked Beverly.

"That was easy," her cousin responded. "I have a nice blue dress I've been keeping for a special occasion."

"I knew you'd pick blue, you always do," accused Beverly.

"Of course, it's my favourite colour. What are you going to wear?"

"You're looking at it," said Beverly. "Of course I'll polish it up a little. I AM the Royal Bodyguard, after all!"

Aubrey laughed, "Whoever would have thought that the two of us would end up here, escorting a Princess of the Royal House."

"Yes," said Beverly, pausing for a moment. "About that. Her Highness, the princess, wants your advice."

"On what?" asked Aubrey.

"On what to wear."

"That's easy. Whenever in doubt, go with blue."

"But then YOU wouldn't be able to wear blue, Aubrey. You can't upstage the princess."

"Oh," her cousin responded, "I hadn't thought of that. This advice thing is obviously more difficult than I thought. What should I do?"

"I'd start by getting up to her room and seeing what she has to pick from."

"A very good idea," said Aubrey. "I'll drop these things off and head straight up there."

"I'll drop this stuff in your room, Cousin. You'd best get up there right away."

After Aubrey scuttled away, Beverly looked down at the discarded sketch. It showed a remarkable landscape, and even though it was rendered in shades of grey, she saw the colours in her mind. Lifting the tray, she carefully gathered up Aubrey's belongings. They shared a room, and she had to polish up her armour for the ball anyway, she might as well drop this stuff off.

Sometime later, she sat on her bed, polishing a shin guard. She could almost see her reflection and was suddenly hit by the thought that not so long ago she had thought so little of the highly polished knights in Wincaster. It made her consider her position; was she becoming a spoilt and pampered knight? It only took a moment for her to make up her mind; no, of course not, her record spoke for itself. She continued her polishing while her mind returned to more important matters; the face of the smith who had wrought such finely crafted armour.

Gerald ran the whetstone down his blade again and then held the sword up to examine its edge. Satisfied with the results so far, he continued with the exercise, each grind bringing him closer to the desired sharpness, until his concentration was disturbed by a knock on his door.

"Come in," he yelled, not bothering to look up.

When the door opened, a deep bark shook the room. He looked up to see Anna and Tempus, the mighty dog's tail wagging from side to side.

"Oh, hello, Anna, Tempus," he said casually.

"What are you doing, Gerald," the princess asked.

"I'm sharpening my sword," he said in annoyance. "What do you think I'm doing?" He glanced up again to see the look of shock on Anna's face.

"Sorry, I'm a little irritated," he said in explanation.

"So I see," said Anna, entering the room. She sat down on the bed beside him. "I'm sure that's a very fine edge you have there but shouldn't you be getting ready for the ball?"

"I don't think I should go to the ball," he suggested.

"Nonsense, you're going as my escort. You don't want me going alone, do you?"

"I'm not very good at balls," he said abashedly. "I can't dance."

"I've seen you dance at the village fair," Anna said. "Don't tell me you can't dance."

"That's different, that's just country dancing. This is a court ball. I'd look like a fool trying that kind of movement."

"You don't have to dance, Gerald, I promise, but you have to escort me. You're the only real family I've got."

"Well, it's good to know I'm being chosen because I'm the only one."

"That's not what I meant and you know it."

"I don't have anything to wear," he mumbled.

"That's where you're wrong," she said, standing in triumph. "Bring it in, Sophie," she called.

Sophie entered, carrying a green tunic. It was well made and had a collar and neck offset by yellow lace.

"It won't fit," Gerald tried again.

"That's why Sophie's here. She's going to adjust it for you. Now come along, let's get it on you."

He grumbled as he stood and Anna began pulling his old tunic over his head. He tried to resist and pretended it became stuck on his head but by the time they were done they were both laughing. Anna's enthusiasm for the ball was contagious, and soon he was wearing the new tunic comfortably.

"It seems to fit perfectly," remarked Gerald.

"That's because I had Sophie measure your old tunic."

"That was very sneaky of you, Anna."

"Of course," she returned, "I learned from you. Now, we shall be arriving in a carriage. The earl's estate is some distance away, and they'll be providing rooms for us. I've made sure you and Beverly are billeted to either side of me."

"Couldn't we just come back here?" he suggested.

"We could, but it'll likely go quite late. It'll be nice to be able to retire after the ball and not have to worry about a long ride home."

Gerald smiled at her.

"What?" she asked.

"You're happy because Alric is staying there, aren't you?"

"Of course not," she replied, but her blushing revealed the truth of it.

"What are we doing with Tempus, here?" he asked. "It's not his sort of place."

"He can stay here with me," offered Sophie. "We'll have a wonderful time without you two getting in the way.

"Thank you, Sophie," said Anna. "I know you're my servant, but you didn't have to do that."

"Nonsense, Highness," the young woman responded. "It's my pleasure, you've done so much for me."

"So," said Anna, a note of finality to her voice, "are you ready to go?"

"I thought we had more time?" protested Gerald.

"I lied. We have to leave right away."

"But what if the tunic hadn't fit?"

"There was no way that was going to happen," replied Anna, "we were very careful. I know it's not really your birthday, but happy birthday anyway." She leaned forward and planted a kiss on his cheek. "Now come along, Father dear, or we'll be late."

"But I'm not your father," he said, once again.

"Maybe not officially, but you'll always be so in my heart."

Gerald smiled, holding out his arm. "Then let us be off, Daughter dear."

She took his arm, while Tempus barked, wagging his tail again.

The hall echoed with the sound of instruments as Lady Aubrey Brandon, daughter to the Baron of Hawksburg, entered the room. Little attention was paid to her entrance, for the place was filled with the rich and powerful of the city. She spied the earl himself, seated at one end of the hall, holding court over the proceedings. He was richly adorned with jewellery, only outshone by his wife. Aubrey thought to introduce herself, for unlike the court of Merceria, the guests were not announced here. She reconsidered; the princess had sent her ahead to scope out the festivities and determine the layout of the land, and this duty she had taken to heart. She slowly scanned the area, her sharp mind absorbing it all. The more influential people were up by the earl, chatting amicably. Around the hall, guests clustered in groups. Her keen eyesight allowed her to quickly sort them; the wealthy merchants, with their gaudy jewels and wildly colourful clothes; the lesser nobles, with their formal dress and carefully manicured hands with perfect hair; the more affluent nobles, who cared little for the opinions of others and dressed for comfort.

It was strange, she thought, how easily this type of observation had come to her. She had always been inquisitive, but her studies as a mage had honed her intelligence, had helped her to strengthen her powers of observation.

A commotion erupted at the far end of the hall as the doors opened. Her view was blocked, but the guests were suddenly oohing and aahing in appreciation. Aubrey wondered if Anna had already entered but knew that could not be so; the princess would not come until Aubrey returned to make her report. Perhaps Prince Alric had arrived, or his brother, Cuthbert, for he was rumoured to be present in the city. She made her way through the crowd as politely as possible to see a small party entering. They were led by a young woman, close to Aubrey's own age. Aubrey had complimented herself on her modest choice of dress, but this new visitor clearly had no such compunctions, wearing a rather low cut yellow dress, which fell to the floor, concealing her feet. She moved with grace, veritably floating across the floor. Aubrey couldn't help but notice the great care with which the woman's sandy coloured hair had been arranged in ringlets which fell to her shoulders. Who was this person?

As if in answer to her unspoken question, a woman beside Aubrey turned to her, "Isn't she lovely? I had no idea the Clans were so fashionable."

"The Clans?" asked the young mage.

"Yes, she's the daughter of the High King of the Twelve Clans. Isn't she magnificent, full of grace and beauty?"

"So she's a princess?"

"Yes, Princess Brida," the stranger responded.

Aubrey couldn't help herself, "I thought the Clans were enemies of Weldwyn?"

"They were, but they've sent the princess to make peace. Isn't it wonderful?"

Aubrey thought the coincidence was unsettling. Having a foreign princess visit while Anna was in town seemed a little too incredulous, to her mind.

"When did she arrive?" Aubrey continued.

"They say she got here late yesterday afternoon. Prince Cuthbert himself escorted her. Oh look, she's moving toward the earl."

Aubrey was roughly jostled aside as the crowd of guests pushed forward to see the exchange. The young mage thought it best to return to Princess Anna and inform her of all that had transpired.

"So you say this Princess Brida arrived yesterday?" asked Anna.

"Yes, Your Highness," responded Aubrey.

They were in the outer courtyard, awaiting Anna's command to enter.

"It doesn't matter, Highness," said Beverly. "They're throwing this ball in your honour."

"Something smells here," commented Arnim.

"Speak, Captain," commanded Anna. "What do you mean?"

"As Lady Aubrey has indicated, her arrival here is suspicious. I think she's being used to put pressure on Merceria."

"What kind of pressure?" asked Gerald. "Of what use would this be to those in the Weldwyn court?"

Arnim turned to Aubrey, "Did you say she was brought here by Cuthbert?"

"Yes," admitted Aubrey, "at least, that's what I heard."

Arnim continued, "Prince Cuthbert has been gone for a long time. He was the only prince not present in the capital when we arrived. I think they sent him westward to seek out the possibility of an alliance. They fear us. The attack on you almost caused a war. With an alliance, or at least a lasting peace with the Clans, they could pull troops eastward, toward our border."

"I can't believe Alric would condone such a thing," defended Anna.

"With all due respect, Highness," continued Arnim, "Alric has little say in the matter."

"So how do we react to this?" asked Dame Levina. "Do you think the princess is in danger?"

"Unlikely," offered Beverly. "They don't want a war with us if they can avoid one."

"Agreed," said Anna. "So what can we expect?"

"I would suggest," Dame Levina continued, "that this new princess may have an agenda of her own."

Anna looked at the older knight carefully, trying to judge her statement, "Go on."

"When I was younger, I fell in love with a knight. He was a marvellous specimen, strong and handsome. We were introduced and found common ground on a number of things."

"Common ground?" commented Gerald. "That doesn't sound very romantic."

The knight continued her story, ignoring his jibe, "I would have sworn he felt the same way, but another woman came between us. She dazzled him with her grace and beauty, and he fell for it."

"A sad tale," offered Beverly, "but are you saying that this visitor is after Alric?"

"Of course," said Levina, "isn't it obvious? What better way to seal an alliance than with a marriage."

"But she can't!" stammered Anna.

"There's little we can do about it, Your Highness," responded Levina. "I suspect Prince Cuthbert has arranged all of this."

"We could change Cuthbert's mind," offered Gerald. "Perhaps if we broke his legs?"

"No," commanded Anna, "much as the thought pleases me, we can't jeopardize our mission here in Weldwyn. We must carry on as if it is of no concern to us. Now, let's form up and make our way inside."

Levina and Beverly took their places in front of Anna. Gerald put his arm out for Anna's hand and saw the look on her face.

"Are you all right, Anna?" he asked.

"I can do this, Gerald," she promised. "I'll make you proud of me."

"I'm always proud of you, Anna," he replied, patting her hand. "Be strong."

Beverly nodded to the servants standing by the door, who then swung the double doors open revealing the great hall before them. Like the Princess of the Clans, they entered the room, nodding to the guests as they made their way toward the earl.

Lord Mainbridge, Earl of Loranguard, rose from his chair and stepped toward Anna as Levina and Beverly moved to the side.

"I am honoured to receive you," he proclaimed, "for we have heard great things about you, Princess Anna."

"Thank you, Your Grace. I am humbled by your greeting."

The earl appeared to beam at the compliment. "May I introduce Lady Elswith..."

His wife bent low and curtsied, that strange greeting that Anna was still not used to.

"Pleased to meet you, Lady Mainbridge," Anna replied.

"To my right," offered the earl, "is our new guest. I present to you Her Highness, Princess Brida of the Twelve Clans."

The new visitor bowed slightly. "Please to meet you, Princess Anna," she said, her voice smooth and silky.

Gerald could see Anna's nervousness; she was sweating and fumbling for words. He had seen her take apart people with her commanding presence, but here, she seemed naught but a naive girl, overshadowed by this new visitor.

"Pleased to meet you, Brida," she offered.

"Your Highness," the newcomer corrected.

"I beg your pardon?" Anna stammered.

"I am a princess, like yourself. You should refer to me as 'Your Highness', or don't they have manners in Merceria?"

"Perhaps," interjected Gerald, "we should meet the others guests..."

"Yes," agreed Anna, her face red with embarrassment. "Excuse me, Your Highness."

"Of course," replied Brida.

They had only gone a few steps when Brida's words echoed behind them. "She'll get over it, she's just a child."

Anna tried to turn, but Gerald kept a firm grip on her arm. "Calm down, Anna," he whispered, "getting upset will do no good."

They nodded their way through the line of nobles and important visitors. Anna kept silent while Gerald did all the talking. Finally, they found themselves at the side of the hall.

"That was...interesting," commented Beverly.

"I'm surprised she was so rude," added Levina. "Surely the earl should have said something?"

"He won't," answered Beverly. "This is the western border of Weldwyn. The Clans are the biggest threat here. Merceria is nothing but a foreign land that has little meaning for him."

"So what do we do now?" asked Aubrey.

"We mingle," offered Gerald. "Talk to people, find out all we can about this Brida."

"Princess Brida," spat out Anna. "We must use the proper forms of address."

"Don't let her get to you, Anna," soothed Gerald. "She's trying to put you off balance."

"She's succeeding," complained Anna.

When the grand doors opened once again, they all turned to see Prince Alric and his brother, Cuthbert enter the room. They marched straight to the earl, but Alric, at least, looked over at Anna. Their eyes met and they shared a brief smile then Alric turned his attention once again to their host.

Aubrey was watching Brida and tapped Beverly on the arm, "I just saw Brida give a dirty look in this direction, Cousin. I don't think this bodes well."

Beverly sighed, "I suppose it shouldn't surprise me, nothing is ever easy around here."

The two princes were welcomed with a hearty handshake and Gerald recognized the esteem in which the earl held them. The rest of the guests continued to mingle while Gerald kept his eye on the royals. Prince Cuthbert was introducing Alric to Brida, and although he couldn't hear them over the noise of the crowd, he had a pretty good idea what was going on. Brida was smiling and looking down slightly, a sure sign that she was interested in the young prince.

"What do you see, Gerald?" asked Anna.

"Not much," he offered. "Alric is being introduced to Brida."

Even as he spoke, Brida put her hand on Alric's arm. Gerald felt sorry for Anna; the young Mercerian Princess was apparently quite fond of Alric but this upstart from the Clans was doing all the right things. The young prince appeared utterly taken in by her charms.

He turned to look at Anna, who was biting her lip. "Shall we get something to drink?" he asked.

"Yes," she murmured, "I believe we shall."

He waited until a servant was passing with wine and snagged two goblets.

"Here," he offered, "try this. I have no idea what it is but judging from the crowd around here I'd say it's expensive."

Anna took the cup and downed it in a single gulp. Gerald looked at her in surprise; was she really this upset?

"Come on, Gerald," she urged, "let's go and say hello to Alric."

"Are you sure that's wise, Anna? Brida is-"

"I don't care what Brida is. I want to greet Alric, it's the least we can do, after all, we're on a diplomatic mission, aren't we?"

Gerald sighed. He had a feeling he knew where this was going, but felt trapped. He only hoped Anna's feelings wouldn't be hurt. Anna headed off, pulling Gerald's arm by the hand. He felt like a little boy again, being led by his mother, a strange feeling considering who was leading him. They made a direct route toward Alric, who was chatting with Brida and Cuthbert.

"Hello, Alric," she said in greeting.

The young prince turned at the sound of her voice, a smile creeping out.

"Anna," he said, "so good to see you."

Anna was smiling as well and was about to speak when Brida interrupted, "Alric," she said, "I didn't know you were chaperoning children these days. Tell me, isn't the young princess here about the same age as your youngest sister?"

Anna's mouth hung open as she fought for words. Alric turned to Brida and looked as though he was about to say something but Cuthbert intervened.

"Yes," he said, "our father gave him the job. Someone has to look after our young visitor. Isn't that right Alric?"

Cuthbert looked at him, and Gerald could imagine the turmoil going through the prince's mind. He was in a difficult situation, between the proverbial rock and a hard place.

"I've had the honour to escort Princess Anna for some time now," he answered, diplomatically. "It has been my pleasure."

The smile died on Anna's face. Gerald's heart felt for her; he imagined the pain she must feel.

Cuthbert, ever the diplomat, touched his brother's shoulder. "Can I have a word in private, Brother?"

Alric stepped aside, following his brother who was heading for a side door. It left Anna and Brida facing one another. The air seemed to grow frosty.

"He's mine," stated Brida. "I've come from the Clans to marry Prince Alric. If you thought he was in love with you, you should put any such thoughts out of your head. In fact, I think you should leave the ball, perhaps retire for the evening? It would be better than causing an embarrassment; then again, you've already embarrassed yourself, and your petty little kingdom."

The venom in Brida's words stung Anna. She turned, running from the room; the little girl winning out over the stern princess that had fought and won battles. Gerald stared at Princess Brida.

"You'll come to regret that, Highness," he warned. "Your treatment of a Princess of Merceria will not be forgotten."

"And who are you to threaten me? You're nothing but a commoner. Go back where you belong, and take your stink with you."

Gerald fought hard to contain his anger. His face grew red while his hand reached for his sword, but he wasn't wearing it. He wanted to strike her down, remove the smug look off her face, not for himself, but for Anna's sake. He took a breath, bowed slightly and merely replied, "Your Highness," and then turned and strode from the room, looking for Anna.

It was getting late and Prince Alric, finally released from his burdensome duties, exited the great hall. He had wanted to find Anna, but Princess Brida had kept him busy. His brother's insistence that he accompany her was infuriating, yet he was born and bred a Prince of the Realm and must follow through with his duties, no matter how distasteful.

He stopped a servant to ask where the Mercerian delegation was roomed and was told to visit the east wing. He made his way there as quickly as he could while still maintaining his decorum. He finally found the rooms they were using; Anna had been given a suite. There was an outer visiting room that joined to a bedroom. He was surprised to see no guard in the hallway and was about to knock on the door when it opened. A young man, perhaps the same age as Alric appeared, his shirt open, exposing his chest. The lad's hair was unkempt, and he was tucking his shirt into his trousers as he opened the door.

"My lord," he said, "can I help you?"

Taken aback by the unknown visitor, Alric paused before speaking.

"Is the Princess Anna available?"

The stranger looked over his shoulder into the room behind him before looking back. "I'm afraid she is indisposed at the moment. She's dressing. Is there something I can do for you?"

Alric turned beet red, "No, I think you've done more than enough." He turned on his heels, stomping down the hallway.

The young man exited the room, closing the door behind him quietly. He travelled down the hall in the opposite direction and rounded the corner to where Brida was waiting.

"Well?" she said.

"It worked, Highness. He believes it."

"Did anyone hear you?"

"No, Highness. They were busy in the bedroom. The rest had retired for the night."

"What of the bodyguard, where was she?"

"I think she was talking to the princess."

Brida dropped a bag of coins into the young man's eager hands. "Excellent, now disappear, and if I hear of you telling anyone of this, I shall have you killed."

The youngster bowed, "Your secret is safe with me, Highness."

TWENTY-TWO

Unexpected Events

AUTUMN 960 MC

G erald was up early, determined to buy a gift for Anna. He knew she was feeling down and he thought something special might cheer her up. He ran into Dame Beverly in the dining hall as the servants set the table for Anna's morning meal.

"Did you talk to Hayley about guarding the princess?" he asked.

The look of sudden recollection was plain to see. "I forgot, sorry. Don't worry, Gerald, we've other knights I can use and anyway, Alric will have his own guards."

"I don't think Alric will be showing up, she'll likely have a quiet day. Perhaps I should leave it for tomorrow," he offered.

"No, don't do that, you wanted to get her something. She'll like that. Hopefully, it'll take her mind off things. We can cover, you head out."

He hesitated a moment, and Beverly saw the indecision on his face.

"Go," she commanded.

"All right," he caved in, "I'll go. Don't let anything happen to her."

"I won't," she promised. "Now get going before she comes down or you'll have to explain yourself."

He hurried out of the room at the warning and Beverly smiled in victory; getting Gerald to leave the princess's side was almost impossible. It would be good for him to be free of his obligation for a day.

The sound of footsteps interrupted her introspection; the heavy tread of a large dog, and the lighter patter of young feet.

"Highness," she said in greeting, wheeling about as they entered.

"Good morning, Beverly," said Anna. "Are you joining us for breakfast today?"

"I've already eaten, Highness," she offered in apology.

"Is Gerald up yet?" the young princess asked.

Beverly formed the answer in her mind before speaking, "He's on an errand, Highness. He promises to catch up to us later."

Anna looked surprised, but as she was about to open her mouth, a servant appeared, announcing the arrival of Jack Marlowe. The distraction worked to Beverly's advantage for the attention shifted to their guest, who entered, wearing an immaculate blue and white surcoat, bowing deeply.

"Good morning, Princess," he said. "Prince Alric sends his apologies, and asked me to look after you today. Might I enquire what you would like to do?"

Anna tightened her lips, and then took a deep breath.

"I thought we might go and see the tournament field I've heard so much about. Perhaps you can tell us more about such things."

"Indeed I can," said Jack. "It is a particular interest of mine for I've spent many an hour in such places perfecting my skill at arms."

Beverly rolled her eyes as the man began his infuriating description. She was sure he would drone on forever about his passion, so she excused herself by quietly exiting the room. She would wait in the hallway, free from his incessant talking, and join them when they exited.

She closed the door quietly behind her, letting out her breath, pleased at avoiding the close call. Detecting whispering coming from down the hall, she moved toward it, taking her time to avoid making any noise. Peering around the corner, she spied Lady Nicole, who was whispering something to someone, but her companion's face was blocked. The Lady-in-Waiting whispered some more, peering over her shoulder conspiratorially and Beverly was shocked at the identity of her accomplice, for it was none other than Arnim Caster.

"Why did you have Valmar send me?" Lady Nicole asked. "Surely there were others more suitable to this task?"

"You're the best at what you do, Nikki, and despite our past-"

A noise from a door opening interrupted their conversation. Arnim and Nicole separated quickly, each going in different directions. Beverly backed up slightly and then tried to act as if she was just coming down the hall. Lady Nicole passed by, paying no attention to her actions. Beverly wondered what she had stumbled across. She made a mental note to talk to Gerald about it when he returned, and then made her way back to the dining room.

The sound of Jack's voice could clearly be heard through the door, but

Beverly decided it was time to get things moving. She opened the door, interrupting the young cavalier's remarks.

"It's time to go, Your Highness. We'll want to get to the tournament field before the practice is over, or there'll be nothing left to see."

"Good point," agreed Anna. "Lead on, Jack, I'm eager to learn more about this jousting you've been on about."

They made their way out of the Citadel to the sound of Jack's eloquent descriptions. Beverly fell into step behind, the better to keep an eye on things.

The jousting field was an open area where along one side they had erected some tiered benches. Beyond that was a railing which split the field in two. It looked odd, thought Beverly, and she struggled to see the reason for it.

Anna was obviously having similar thoughts, for she asked, "What are the railings for, Jack?"

"They keep the jousters from running into each other," he offered.

"I thought," commented Beverly, "that the point of this jousting was to train you for combat?"

"It is," he confirmed.

"Then, I'm confused," the knight responded. "Do armies line up along fence posts when they fight in Weldwyn?"

"No, of course not," he objected.

"Then why the fence?" she persisted.

"It keeps the contestants from injuring the horses. They're expensive beasts, you know."

"I'm well aware of the expense of horses," she bristled. "But if you're so afraid of injuring them, why don't you fight on foot?"

"Oh, we do!" exclaimed Jack. "It's called the melee, but they don't do that here, this field is only for jousting."

"So you spend a lot of time training for a lance attack? Those are useless after the first contact. Why don't you use swords from horseback?"

"It's meant to be refined, Dame Beverly," Jack responded. "I wouldn't expect you to understand, being a foreigner and all."

Beverly's face grew red at the insult, but Anna was quick to diffuse the situation. "Perhaps you could show us the stables," she asked. "Lady Beverly is a keen horsewoman."

"I'd be delighted," he responded.

As it just so happened, there were three cavaliers tending to their horses when they entered. They bowed deferentially to their Royal Visitor, nodded politely to Beverly, but it was Jack who consumed their attention.

"Aren't you 'Mad Jack' Marlowe?" asked the tallest one.

Jack smiled, bowing slightly as he replied, "Why, yes I am."

"I heard you won the wreath at this summer's tourney," the man continued.

"It's true," offered his sandy-haired accomplice, "I saw the whole thing."

"How did you defeat Raston?" the tall man persisted.

"I went in low," explained Jack. "He has a habit of leaning back, so I ducked at the last possible moment. Completely shook him."

Once more Jack was boasting of his accomplishments. Beverly tried to ignore him by looking over the other cavaliers, trying to judge their ability, but saw little that would indicate they were battle-trained for they lacked definition. Wielding a sword and fighting developed muscles but these men clearly spent the bulk of their time on horseback. She wondered how they would fare in a real battle, but then decided it was a moot point for as far as she knew Weldwyn had been at peace for years. She allowed her gaze to wander over to Princess Anna who was absorbing everything judging by the keen look of interest on her face. If she was missing Prince Alric, she was doing a good job of hiding her emotions.

Hayley drew the bow, waiting as Lily watched her. She let loose and the arrow flew out over the water to splash in the middle of the river. Lily dove under the waves and the ranger waited patiently as her diminutive friend swam beneath the surface. A moment later she emerged, the arrow held in her hand, and then began madly swimming back toward the shore. Hayley laughed and turned to where Aubrey was sitting on the grass. The young mage had unfolded a parchment and was sketching with some charcoal.

"What are you doing, Aubrey?"

"I'm sketching," she replied.

"Sketching what?" asked Hayley. "There's nothing here."

"Nonsense, there's plenty. Take that boat over there, for example," she said, pointing with her fingers, covered as they were in the dark grey charcoal.

"The one in the middle of the river? Why would you sketch that?"

"I draw lots of things, it helps me remember them."

"Why would you want to remember that?" asked Hayley.

"As a mage's apprentice, I have to remember lots of things. Anything that can help my memory would be beneficial. I've always liked drawing, I take after my mother in that."

"Your mother's a baroness, isn't she?"

"Yes, that's right. My father is the Baron of Hawksburg."

"I've been there," the ranger remarked. "It's a nice little town."

"I'd have to agree with you there. I miss it, but visiting Weldwyn has been terribly exciting, don't you think?"

"I suppose so, although I could do without all the fighting."

"That's what we do, isn't it?" asked Aubrey. "Make the world a better place by fighting so others don't have to?"

"Good point. I suppose it's what we do, isn't it. I never thought I'd be here of all places. I was just a ranger, now I'm a Knight of the Hound in service to a princess. My father would roll over in his grave at the thought."

"Why is that?"

"He was a poacher. They hanged him for it in the end."

"What happened to you?"

"I went to live with my aunt and uncle. They have a farm outside of Wincaster."

"And so you grew up to serve the king as a ranger? That seems like an odd choice."

"Not really. My father taught me everything about hunting, what else could I do?"

"You could have worked for a noble, as a games keeper or something," Aubrey offered.

"No, that's not me. I'm not always the most sociable person. Don't get me wrong, I get along with people, but I prefer solitude. The ranger life was just the thing for me."

"So what changed your mind?" the young mage enquired.

"I recovered Prince Alfred's body from the field of battle. The king decided to knight me for it, though I never asked for it. After that, I was sought out by Beverly. She convinced me to join the princess."

"Yes, I can understand that. My cousin can be quite persuasive."

"How, exactly, are you two related?"

"My Aunt Evelyn was Beverly's mother. She was my aunt on my father's side."

"It seems the bloodline is overflowing with talent. I suppose if you decide to give up magic, you could make a living with your drawings."

"Why would I want to give up magic?" asked a confused Aubrey.

"Never mind, it was meant as a compliment."

Aubrey returned to her sketch as Lily scampered out of the water. The Saurian was moving her hand in a circular motion; the sign to repeat and so Hayley nocked another arrow and drew the bow. She aimed due south while Lily prepared to rush into the water, but at the last moment, she turned slightly, shooting an arrow further to the west. Lily chattered in delight, diving into the river again with abandon.

"There, what do you think?" asked Aubrey, holding up her parchment.

Hayley looked down at the drawing. It was very lifelike, and she stared at it for some time. Something seemed off, and then it hit her. "You haven't put any people aboard."

"There aren't any, as far as I can see," replied Aubrey.

"Are you sure? There must be someone over there."

"I've been sketching since we arrived and I haven't seen anyone. It's anchored, perhaps they're all ashore?"

"It seems odd to me, but I'm not a sailor. I would think you'd leave someone to keep watch, you wouldn't want someone stealing your ship."

"Maybe they're below decks, sleeping off a hangover?" suggested Aubrey.

"You're probably right," said Hayley. "In any event, we should head back to the Citadel, we've been here all morning, and I'm starting to get hungry."

"Good idea, just let me pack up my things."

Aubrey began returning her items to her satchel then walked down to the river's edge to wash the charcoal from her hands as best she could. Hayley waited as Lily emerged from the water. The Saurian was clutching the retrieved arrow and trotted up to her, passing a middle-aged woman who was staring out over the water. The ranger immediately felt concern for the woman and approached her.

"Excuse me, is something wrong?"

The woman turned to face her, fresh tears staining her cheeks. "It's my son," she said, through sobs, "he's gone missing."

"Have you notified anyone?"

"Aye, the watch, little good it'll do. They don't take much notice of missing children."

"Tell me more," begged Hayley, "perhaps I can help."

"I've been sick of late," the woman began explaining, "and I sent my son down to the herbalist, but he never came back. It's all my fault."

"Don't say that. You had no way of knowing. When was this?"

"Three days ago."

"And where is this herbalist?"

"Sharpe's, down on Lassiter Street. Do you know it?"

"No," Hayley replied, "but I'll see what I can find out."

"I knew it was dangerous," the woman said, "what with all the disappearances and such, but I never thought it would happen to my own blood."

"What disappearances?"

The woman stared back in shock, "Surely you've heard? It's all over town."

"I'm not from around here," offered Hayley. "Please, tell me."

"There's been people gone missing for months now. Mostly children but some adults as well."

Hayley's mind was suddenly in panic mode. Abductions were occurring while the princess wandered around town completely unaware of them! She calmed her mind. The princess was in no immediate danger, Beverly and Gerald would see to that. She resolved to bring up the topic at the next opportunity.

~

The royal party returned to the Citadel shortly before nightfall. Sophie met them at the door along with Tempus who was waving his tail happily at his mistress' return.

"Is Gerald about?" Anna asked.

"I'm afraid he hasn't returned yet, Your Highness," replied her maid.

"That's not like him," Anna said, "he's usually very punctual. What time did he say he'd be back, Beverly."

"He didn't say, but he wasn't going far, he should have been back by now."

"He's probably drunk in a whorehouse," offered Jack. "A man needs to unwind every now and again. I'm sure he'll turn up eventually."

Anna did not look amused, and Beverly saw her straining to bite back her words.

"Perhaps," offered Beverly, "Jack might be able to round up some guards and go looking for him?"

"Of course, Your Highness, I shall see to it right away." He was about to leave and then turned abruptly to face the princess, "I apologize if I have offended Your Highness."

"Thank you, Jack," she replied.

"I'll rouse the town guard and hunt him down, Highness. What will you do?"

"I'll call together my advisors; perhaps they'll have an idea. Beverly, can you gather everyone? We'll meet in the dining hall."

"Yes, Highness," the knight replied.

~

Aubrey sat in her room at a small desk making an entry in her journal, dipping her beautiful new feather into the ink as someone knocked on the door.

"Come in," she called absently, once again placing quill to parchment.

The door opened to reveal Hayley, her face framed by brown hair which was, Aubrey noted, a little out of place.

"Beverly says the princess has called a meeting, we're all to attend."

"Why?" asked Aubrey. "What's happened?"

"Gerald's gone missing," she replied.

"Missing?"

"Yes, he left this morning on an errand and should have been back by now."

"Perhaps he's just taking his time?" Aubrey offered.

"You don't know Gerald. When he runs an errand, he performs the task and returns. He's not the sort of person to dawdle."

"Should we be worried?"

"Worried? Not yet, but I am concerned, it's not like him. Beverly's known him her whole life and swears the man is never late."

"All right," said Aubrey, "I'll just clean up here and be right down."

"What are you doing?" asked Hayley, gazing down at the paper.

"I'm making entries in my journal. How do you like my new quill?"

"It's quite remarkable. What is it?"

"It's a gryphon feather," replied Aubrey.

"No, it's not."

"Yes, it is. The shopkeeper told me so," defended the young mage.

"I've seen a gryphon up close, Aubrey. Their colours are muted so they can blend into their surroundings. Their feathers are mostly brown. I'm not sure what that feather is, but it's not a gryphon."

Aubrey stared at the quill with a disappointed look. "That's annoying, I paid rather a large sum for it."

"Does it make a good quill?"

"I suppose so, why?"

"Then you've spent your coins wisely. Does it really matter what kind of feather it is?"

"No, it doesn't. I'm just disappointed I've been taken advantage of."

"Well, you best be disappointed later, we have a meeting to get to, come along."

Aubrey quickly closed up her ink pot and wiped down the tip of her quill, placing them precisely on the desktop.

"Let's go," she said, "we don't want to be late."

Princess Anna of Merceria was pacing the room. Tempus followed her, and each time she spun about, the great mastiff would run behind her to follow her steps once again. If the situation had not been so dire, Beverly would have found it quite amusing. Arnim Caster was the last to arrive, having come from the stables. He took his seat quietly, nodding to the princess in greeting.

"Gerald is missing," she started, "and we must find him. I think we can all agree that something has happened to him or else he would be here."

"What are the possibilities?" asked Aubrey.

"He might be injured somewhere," offered Arnim. "Perhaps someone tried to steal from him, and he was harmed."

"I find that hard to believe," refuted Beverly. "Gerald knows how to fight, and I don't see him giving in easily."

"I agree," confirmed Anna. "I once saw him take on three bandits with his bare hands and a cane. I can't believe a mere mugging would take him out. He's a very cautious man."

"I know where he went," said Beverly, "but I'm sworn to secrecy. I will take Hayley with me at first light, see what we can dig up?"

"Could Tempus track him?" asked Hayley. "He must know his scent."

"I'm afraid Tempus is not a great tracker, his skills lie elsewhere. The smells of the city drive him to distraction," explained Anna

"Wait a moment," said Hayley. "I just remembered something."

"What is it?" asked Anna.

"I met a woman at the waterfront today. She said her son had gone missing. Apparently, this has been happening for a while."

"Are the town watch doing anything about it?" probed Anna. "Perhaps the city guards?"

"The woman seemed to think it would do no good. I have a location where her son went missing. Somewhere near Lassiter Street. Does that name sound familiar?"

"Yes," said Beverly, "it's close to where Gerald wanted to go, not too far from the theatre."

"Arnim," said Anna, "you go to the town watch and see if they can shed any light on these disappearances, they might be related. Beverly, send the other knights out to search the streets around the area, perhaps someone's seen something."

"We need to keep a guard on you, Highness," objected Arnim. "If someone has taken Gerald, it could be an attack against you."

"Why do you say that?" the princess replied.

"It's no secret that he's your closest advisor. They might be looking for leverage."

"He has a point," agreed Beverly. "Perhaps we should keep a few guards behind to watch you."

"Organize the knights, Beverly. You and Hayley will remain behind as my bodyguards. Where was Gerald headed?"

Beverly knew she could hide the information no longer, "He was going to a jewellers, Highness. He wanted to buy you a present."

"Have the knights search the area. It'll be too dark to make much out tonight. I want you and Hayley to be there at first light to see if there's any indication of what happened."

"Yes, Your Highness," agreed the redheaded knight.

"The rest of you, help out as best you can. Aubrey, I need you with the knights. Beverly will tell you the location. I want you to oversee the search."

"Me, Your Highness?"

"Yes, Aubrey. You have a keen mind, you're likely to notice things that would escape the knight's attention. Talk to the people thereabouts. Any information, even about the other disappearances, should be considered important."

"Yes, Highness," Aubrey agreed.

"Might I suggest," said Arnim, "that Lady Aubrey accompanies me instead? I thought to talk to the town watch, and a lady of her breeding would get their attention, being a noble and all."

"Very well, then," decided Anna, "Aubrey will go with you to the town watch. Who will command the knights tonight?"

"I would suggest Dame Levina," offered Beverly, "she's the eldest, and the others respect her."

"Very well," said Anna. "Everyone on your way, you have much to do."

They all filed out of the room, save for Beverly and Anna.

"It's all my fault," lamented Anna. "If he hadn't been trying to buy me a present he'd still be safe."

"You can't blame yourself, Highness," comforted Beverly. "You had no way of knowing this was going to happen." She opened the door and called for Sophie.

Moments later, the young maid appeared, "Yes, my lady?"

"The princess is distraught, Sophie. She needs some rest, take her to her room and see if she can get a little sleep. It's likely to be a long night."

"Yes, my lady," Sophie replied. "Come along, Your Highness, you'll need your energy later, you should rest while you can."

She escorted the princess from the room, leaving Beverly pondering the situation. She tried to recall Gerald's morning words but couldn't remember any details. She was interrupted by the door opening.

Lady Nicole entered the room, "I hope I'm not intruding."

"I was just leaving," said Beverly. "What is it?"

"I was wondering if Her Highness was ready for bed."

"I'm afraid you're too late. Sophie has taken her to her room. She's rather distraught over Gerald's disappearance."

"He's probably just passed out drunk somewhere, like most men," offered Nicole.

"Gerald's not like most men," warned Beverly.

"Well," said Nicole, "I shouldn't spend too much time worrying about it. I'm sure everything will turn out fine by morning.

TWENTY-THREE

The Search

A nna paced back and forth. "Where are they?" she asked, to no one in particular. "They've been gone all night, and still we have no answers."

It was Revi Bloom who chose to respond, "Arnim and Aubrey are still at the watch-house, but they have yet to report anything of interest."

"What about Tempus?" asked Hayley. "Was he any use?"

"No," said Anna. "He follows the scent out to the road, but then he loses it. There are just too many smells for him, and he's never been a great tracker. Where are we with the shopkeeper?"

"We were just about to leave. We'll talk to the jeweller and then search the area for any signs of a mugging."

"I doubt you'll find any," responded Anna. "A mugger would take the coins and run, I don't think they'd spend time hiding the victim. It's looking more and more like a kidnapping."

"To what end, Highness?" asked Revi.

"Whoever is responsible must know how much Gerald means to me."

"That being the case," continued the mage, "wouldn't they try to contact you for a ransom or something?"

"That's true," admitted Anna, "but I don't like to think of the other possibility."

"Which is?" pressed Revi.

"That he's been murdered," the princess choked out.

Beverly noticed the princess was tearing up, "We'll find him, Highness,

I'm sure of it. Perhaps he's wandering around after being knocked on the head, he could simply be disoriented."

"Let's hope so," said Anna.

~

The sun was just rising as Aubrey paced in the front lobby of the grand building that housed the town watch. They were little more than glorified foot troops, but their presence made people more comfortable, at least the rich people. Aubrey had seen their like in Wincaster, but most of the heavy work there was done by the king's troops. In Loranguard, there was little evidence of soldiers. Those who did exist were always manning the walls, forever watching westward toward the untamed lands of the Twelve Clans.

Arnim had talked all night with the watch captain, but so far he had yielded little information. She was beginning to think her presence here was a waste of time when a voice carried across the room.

"I told you, we'll look into it," a rough looking man was saying.

Aubrey turned to see a watchman talking to a commoner, a woman very close to Aubrey's own age. The look of desperation on her face tugged at Aubrey's heart, and without even realizing it, she found herself moving toward the woman.

"Is there something I can help you with?"

The guard and the woman both looked at her in surprise. "My son's gone missing, and the watch here won't do nothing about it?"

"What would you have us do?" the man retorted. "There's no indication of what happened. You tell us your son is missing, but that happens all the time. He's probably run off."

"My son would never run off," she bit back angrily. "He's out there some-where, something's carted him away."

Aubrey seized on the words, "Something? What makes you think it's not a person responsible?"

"My boy knows everyone in the area. None of them would mean him harm. Something's carted him off, I tell you!"

The watchman turned to Aubrey, "I'm sorry, miss. We get these complaints from time to time, probably something mixed in with the gin."

The woman looked like she was about to explode and Aubrey put her hand onto her forearm to calm her.

"Let me help," she offered. "My travelling companion and I are investi-gating another disappearance, they might be connected."

"Thank you," the woman gushed. "I'd be so grateful. My Eric was taken this morning."

"Can you show us where?" she asked.

"Yes, of course, follow me."

"Arnim?" called Aubrey. "We have a recent disappearance. Come along, we must hurry!"

They followed the woman, who led them further into town. The city was a strange layout for it was built upon the side of the river. The river forked here, forming a 'Y' shape and the top of the 'Y' was the Citadel. Now they were heading south, paralleling the river as they did so.

They soon came to a rather narrow street which held a tight group of run down looking structures. They were primarily of wattle and daub construction, but most of them looked neglected and in need of repairs.

"It was right here," the woman was saying. "The last I saw him he was cutting across the back here, down this alley."

"Where does it go?" asked Arnim.

"It crosses the small back plot and then comes out on Lassiter Street."

"That's the merchant district, isn't it?" asked Aubrey.

"Aye," the woman agreed, "but that's a block north. Down here it's all houses and such."

Arnim began examining the alleyway. It was unpaved, allowing him to clearly make out numerous footprints. "How old is your son?" he asked.

"Seven," the woman answered.

"These must be his prints, then," he noted. "They're fresh, and the others are far too large."

"Can you see where they went?" asked Aubrey.

"Let's see," he muttered, beginning to move eastward, down the alley.

Aubrey followed, but they had gone only a short distance when Arnim stopped.

"What's wrong?" she asked.

"There's something strange here," he offered. "His footprints start cutting across the small open area here, but then they stop."

"Could someone have picked him up?" she asked.

"No, there's no other recent footprints at this point. I would surmise that most people cut down the alley to get to the next street, but our young friend here was likely cutting across the plot to get to a mate's house. The tracks just stop, I've never seen this sort of thing before."

Aubrey came closer to examine the ground. It was still wet from an early morning mist, a common enough occurrence by the river. Her own feet were making distinctive shapes as she moved and she could fully understand Arnim's reasoning.

"What do we do now?"

"Have you your journal with you?" he asked.

"Yes, in my pack," she answered.

"Write down what we've found," he said. "It may come in useful later."

"We should inform the princess, shouldn't we?"

"We will, but I want to check around the area some more. Something very strange is going on around here, and I want to see if anyone heard or saw anything."

~

Beverly looked in through the jeweller's window. Unlike most businesses here, it had glass windows, consisting of small panes set into a wooden structure. She marvelled at the workmanship and imagined the cost it must have entailed.

"Are we going in?" asked Hayley, already at the door.

"Of course," she agreed, "I've just never seen a shop like this before."

"They do have windows in Wincaster, you know. Haven't you ever been shopping in the capital?"

"No, I'm a knight. The only things I like to buy are for fighting."

"I'm guessing you don't socialize much," offered the ranger. "I'm a ranger, and I've still found time to wander the shops. What do you do in your downtime?"

"Downtime? I don't have 'down time'. If I'm not on campaign or patrol, I'm training."

"Doesn't that get boring?" asked Hayley.

"No, I quite like it, it keeps me strong," she said, pushing open the door.

The inside of the shop consisted of a table behind which sat an ancient bearded man. He was peering through a strange apparatus that looked like a small metal hoop, but as she got closer, Hayley saw it had glass set into the middle.

"May I help you?" he offered, though he declined to look up from his work.

"Yes," said Beverly. "We were wondering if you had seen a friend of ours. I believe he came in yesterday to see you?"

The jeweller looked up from his work at the enquiry. "Can you describe this man?" he asked.

"He's an older gentleman. He has a short beard with rather a lot of grey in it."

"Oh yes, I remember him. He's a visitor to these parts. I'm guessing you two are as well."

"Yes," agreed Beverly. "We're from the Kingdom of Merceria, to the east."

"Yes, I remember now," said the man, starting to rise. He hopped from his stool only to reveal his short stature for he was a member of the Dwarven race. "He quite surprised me," he continued, "even knew a few words of my native tongue. What would you like to know?"

Beverly continued, "Can you tell us what time he left here?"

"It was just before noon," the Dwarf answered. "I remember it very well. We chatted for quite a while, he's an interesting chap. We would have continued, but my noon meal was brought in by my son and interrupted us. Your friend said he didn't want to take up my time and so he left."

"Have you any idea which way he might have gone?" Hayley prompted.

"Well, I sold him a nice necklace. He said it was for a young girl, I assumed his daughter."

"Can you describe this necklace?" asked Beverly. "We fear he might have been robbed and we should like to recognize it when we find the culprits."

"Oh dear," the Dwarf muttered, "I hope he's all right. It was about the size and shape of a shilling, though it was on a silver chain. It had an etching of a dog on it. I had made it years ago for a client, but they passed away before they could pick it up."

"That sounds like just the sort of thing Gerald would look for," confirmed Beverly. "If he had what he came for he'd head back to the Citadel."

"What if he decided to go somewhere to eat?" asked Hayley.

"I've known Gerald a long time," the knight replied. "I doubt he'd pay for food when he can get free meals at the Citadel. No, he would have headed straight home. Let's get outside and take our bearings."

The exited the building and looked up and down the street.

"The Citadel lies to the north," commented Beverly.

"North and west actually," corrected Hayley. "Two bridges cross the river to the Citadel, both of which lie to the north. Of course, he could have hired a boat to ferry him."

"No," said Beverly, "Gerald doesn't like deep water. I think we can safely assume he'd head for the bridge. What's the most likely way for him to go?"

"The nearest bridge is about five blocks away, but the road there curves to the east. He'd have to cut across a side street somewhere."

"Or an alley," said Beverly. "I doubt he'd go missing if he was on the main street. I should think whoever attacked him either lured him into an alley or took advantage as he was taking a shortcut."

"Seems a reasonable assumption. Let's head north and look for shortcuts along the way."

They began moving north, and had only gone two blocks when the road curved eastward where they noticed a small alleyway which cut west.

"That should lead to Lassiter Street, if I'm not mistaken," offered Hayley.

"That name's familiar. Didn't you say that woman lost her son near Lassiter Street?"

"She did," admitted the ranger. "We must be on the right track."

It was Hayley who spotted it first. They were halfway down the alleyway when something shiny caught her eye.

"Over here," she said, squatting down. She moved some leaves to reveal a silver chain on which a circular coin dangled. "This might be the one Gerald bought. See? There's an engraving of a dog on it."

Beverly crouched down beside her. "You're right. He must have been attacked and lost it in the struggle. Do you see any footprints?"

"Yes," confirmed Hayley. "The ground here has been soaked by runoff from the roofs, it's still quite damp. Was Gerald wearing his chainmail when he left?"

"Yes, he doesn't go anywhere without it, why?"

"Chainmail has weight, meaning the deeper prints here are likely his."

"Could they belong to someone else?"

"Unlikely. There's only one set of deeper prints that are fresh. They lead westward, toward the river."

"Then lead on, ranger," urged Beverly.

"I'd love to," said Hayley, "but the prints stop here."

"How is that even possible?"

Hayley cast her eyes to the sky. "I think something attacked from above."

"Like bandits coming from the rooftops? That seems a little unlikely."

"No, I think something took him and flew off."

"He was a grown man in armour, Hayley. He'd be far too heavy for someone to carry in flight."

"You'd be surprised," commented Hayley. "Gryphons can carry very heavy weights for short distances."

"Are you suggesting a gryphon is on the loose in Loranguard?"

"A gryphon? No, you're not likely to find one of those in a city. It must be something else."

"What else would be big enough to carry away a full grown man?"

"I don't know, it's only a working theory right now."

"So how do we confirm it?" asked the knight.

"If I had to guess, I'd say it would lie in wait. It was probably an attack of opportunity. Nobody has reported seeing large creatures circling around, so it must be perched somewhere, waiting for food."

"Like a bat?"

"Perhaps," she cast her eyes about. "I want to get up there," she said, indicating the roof to their north.

"Why there?" asked Beverly.

"It looks like a good vantage point. The roof is also made of clay tiles, more likely to take my weight. The one to the south is thatched. I haven't had good luck with those."

"What's that mean?"

Hayley blushed, "I was visiting the town of Stilldale once, and I might have had to vacate the building quickly. I climbed out onto the roof, but I fell through."

Beverly was intrigued, "You must tell me more about it sometime when we haven't more important things to do. If you climbed onto my shoulders you'd likely be able to reach the roof; shall we give it a try?"

Hayley agreed, and so they went about their task. Beverly put her back to the wall with her hands cupped in front of her. The ranger stepped into her hands while Beverly raised her into the air.

"I thought I was going to stand on your shoulders," Hayley protested.

"It's easier this way," Beverly said through clenched teeth. "You're lighter than I expected. Can you grab the edge of the roof?"

"I've got it," she confirmed.

Beverly felt the weight lift as Hayley pulled herself onto the roof. "Can you see anything?"

"Hold on a moment," said Hayley, "there's some damage over here."

Beverly stood away from the wall, looking upward to where she could just see the top of Hayley's head. "What is it?"

Hayley disappeared from view to reappear a moment later. "There's been damage to some tiles up here," she said. "It looks like something heavy was perched here."

"Can you estimate how large it was?"

"Not precisely, but it appears to have had talons of some sort. They're spread apart from each other. I'd have to guess this thing was big, certainly bigger than a Human."

"And likely big enough to carry away Gerald?" asked Beverly.

"Yes, but I've no idea what it might be."

"Surely something that big must have been seen!" pondered Beverly.

"I would certainly think so, but we've heard no reports of large flying creatures in the area. What do we do now?"

Beverly thought about the issue for a moment before responding, "We need to talk to Revi, perhaps he'd have some idea of what we're facing."

Beverly and Hayley returned to the Citadel to find the rest of the party gathered in the dining room, Princess Anna nervously pacing back and forth, her face wrinkled in worry. Not wanting to disturb her, Beverly walked over to her cousin to find out what had transpired in her absence.

"Aubrey, what's happened since this morning?"

"Arnim and I found out about another kidnapping. We discovered tracks that just stopped. Arnim's not sure what to make of it."

"Is the prince about?"

"No," Aubrey replied. "We were told he went to the earl's residence this morning and we haven't heard anything since."

Anna stopped her pacing and took a seat at the head of the table.

"Sit, everyone," she commanded. "Let us put our heads together and sift through our information carefully, perhaps we can make some headway. Beverly, did you and Hayley discover anything useful?"

"Yes, Your Highness, though we still don't know the full story. It appears Gerald was making his way back to the Citadel and cut down an alleyway as a shortcut."

"That seems to fit with the other disappearances," offered Arnim. "The Captain of the Watch indicated there's been more than a dozen people disappear over the last month or so."

"Well," continued Beverly, pausing to word their suspicions carefully, "Hayley and I think that something flew off with him."

"Preposterous," exclaimed Arnim. "A creature large enough to do that would be obvious to everyone. Did you check for sewer entrances?"

"What's a sewer?" asked Aubrey.

"It's an underground waterway," offered Revi. "They're used to channel water back to the river after a rain, along with more undesirable liquids."

"Undesirable liquids?" repeated Aubrey.

"Yes, primarily urine, but any liquid that is dumped will run down the sewers."

"Exactly," added Arnim. "I think it likely that thieves waylaid him and then made off to the sewers."

"That wouldn't work," commented Revi. "The sewers in that part of the city would be too small, the city uses children to clean them out, and even they find it a tight fit."

"How on earth would you know that?" asked Arnim.

"The knowledge of a mage is infinite," remarked Revi.

"With all due respect, Master Revi, that sounds like a steaming pile of dragon shit," said Hayley. "How do you really know?"

Revi smiled, "It just so happens that today I obtained a map of the city which shows the sewer lines. Sophie, would you be kind enough to retrieve my satchel from the hallway?"

Anna's maid left the room, returning with a carefully rolled square of paper, "Is this it?"

"Yes, thank you," he said, accepting the package with care. "Let me spread it out here, and we can examine it together. I know the princess loves maps, so I thought this might be of some use."

"An excellent idea, Master Revi," complimented Anna. "Arnim, show us where the missing people were last seen."

"I have a list here," interrupted Aubrey. "Captain Caster had me write everything down."

"Have you your charcoal, Lady Aubrey?" asked the princess.

"Yes, Your Highness."

"Good, then mark each location on the map with a cross. Beverly, you show us where you think Gerald was taken."

"Right here," Beverly replied, stabbing her finger down. "There's an alley between two buildings, though it's not marked on the map."

"What would be big enough to carry Gerald away?" asked Anna, looking to Hayley.

"I don't know," responded the ranger. "It would have to be large. We found crushed tiles on the roof of one of the buildings. It looked like feet of some sort, possibly talons, had crushed some of the clay tiles. I would say they were a good two feet or so apart. It couldn't be too large, or it would likely have crashed through the roof."

"So what would be the upper limit, do you think?" asked the princess.

"Perhaps slightly larger than a man," Hayley offered.

"If it was flying," said Revi, "and it was that large, its wingspan would have to be immense."

"Could it be using magic to fly?" asked Arnim.

"No," said Revi with some finality, "it's impossible to fly with magic."

"Can you say that with absolute conviction?" asked the princess.

"Your Highness," he responded, "it has been the dream of mages for centuries to be able to fly. Certainly, a creature could bear a mage into the sky, a dragon perhaps, but there has been no written record of a mage ever developing a spell of flying."

"So," mused Anna, "we have a large creature flying, possibly carrying a full grown Human. Why has no one seen it?"

"No one is watching the sky," offered Arnim. "And why would they? People go about their business. They don't look for what they don't expect."

"I don't agree with that," countered Beverly. "People don't walk around all day staring at the ground. If there were a large creature like this flying around, someone would see it, or at the very least, hear it."

"What if," offered Aubrey, "the creature has some way of disguising itself?"

"Intriguing," said Anna, "go on."

"Well, what about the blend spell, Master Revi?"

"What's that?" asked Arnim.

"It's an enchantment," replied Revi, "so it's a little out of my domain, but essentially when cast, it allows the recipient to blend in with the surroundings."

"You mean it looks like a person?" clarified Hayley.

"No, not exactly. Imagine you and I are walking down the street. I'm wearing my robes and people look at me and think 'look, a mage', or they might see your bow and think 'look, a ranger'. With a blend spell, they would see us as we are, but they would take no notice of us. To the viewer, we would just seem like we belong."

"So our mysterious attacker is an enchanter?" asked Arnim.

"I doubt that," offered Aubrey, "but spells are often recreations of effects held by magical creatures."

"Fairy Tales!" uttered Arnim.

"No," contradicted Revi, "creatures with magical abilities are well documented, though we don't see them these days in Merceria."

"Are there any creatures that you know of that would have this 'blend' ability?" asked Anna.

"No, Highness," confessed Revi, "and in any event, the effect of a blend would be cancelled as soon as aggressive action was taken. I feel confident when I say that attacking and carrying off a victim would render the creature visible."

"What if it was invisible?" blurted out Sophie.

Anna turned to her maid in surprise, "An excellent question, Sophie. Do you think that's possible, Master Bloom?"

Revi Bloom pursed his lips as he thought. His eyes scanned the ceiling as he tried to recall anything he might have read on the subject.

"As far as I know, no one has been able to master invisibility, but they have managed to distort the image of a target to make it harder to see."

"What does that mean?" asked Beverly.

"I know," said Hayley. "There are lizards in the Forest of Mist that disguise themselves by changing their colour. Is that what you mean?"

"Similar to that, yes," confirmed Revi, "though the magic is a bit harder to describe. Think of someone you know that is very old. Their eyesight begins to go, and then they have difficulty recognizing faces. The spell is similar to that. It 'fuzzes' the outline, makes it less distinct. If it was powerful enough, people might only see a slight distortion. They might not even notice it."

"Especially if it were airborne," commented the princess, "but do we know of any such creature?"

"No," admitted the mage, "I'm afraid not. My notes only extend so far, and my library is back in Wincaster, at least the part I have access to."

Aubrey was startled, "The part you have access to? What do you mean?"

"I must confess," said Revi, "that when Andronicus died, he hadn't completed my training. He told me he had a tower which contained a wealth of knowledge, but he went to the Afterlife before he revealed its location to me."

"So we'll have to go on gut instincts," said Anna. "Hayley, you're the ranger here. Tell me, if there were such a creature, what do you think it would do?"

Hayley gazed at the map. Aubrey had been marking X's all over it, and now it was evident to all that they covered a relatively small area of the town.

"I should think it has a lair somewhere," she offered. "No one's found any bodies, so it must be taking them home to eat. Sorry, Your Highness."

Anna had paled at the comment. "No," she stated, "I refuse to believe that Gerald is dead. I just know that he's still alive. What kind of place would work as a lair?"

"If it's taking people, it would need some space. If we assume it's flying, then it must have wings. It would need an open area where it could fit into, and yet be far enough away from people that it wouldn't be seen. I suspect there must be an abandoned building of some type, maybe an old warehouse?"

"The map only shows the streets and sewers," commented Arnim. "We'll have to search the area for likely candidates."

"How big an area are we talking about?" asked the princess.

"Based on the marks on the map we're talking about a significant area, almost a tenth of the city."

"Then that's what we'll do, starting immediately. Beverly, organize the knights. Arnim, call out the entire bodyguard, we're heading into the streets of Loranguard."

"Is that wise, Highness," protested Arnim. "Someone must protect you."

"And so you will, I'm going with you," said Anna, and the look on her face told everyone there would be no arguing.

TWENTY-FOUR

The Nest

AUTUMN 960 MC

A nna rose from her bed, unable to sleep. She paced the room, talking to Tempus who wagged his tail in appreciation of the attention. She was near the door, turning to repeat her steps when Tempus growled, running to the window. He placed his paws on the sill and Anna moved beside him to see what had alarmed him.

Outside, it was quite dark, and she cursed the candlelight that obscured her night vision. She quickly retraced her steps to her bed to blow out the candle which sat beside her headboard. Returning to the window, she gazed down on the yard below. She could make out what looked like a wolf. It was all one shade of grey and seemed to be staring at her window. She opened the shutters and felt the need to call out.

"Gerald!" she yelled. Tempus barked, his tail wagging, and she called out again, "Gerald."

Lights began appearing in nearby windows as servants were awoken by the noise. The wolf howled once; a long, forlorn sound, and then started heading south. Anna rushed to the door, Tempus following. She ran down the hallway calling Gerald's name, but servants came forth, blocking her way.

They tried to calm her, told her she was imagining things, but she wouldn't listen. She attempted to push past them, but they weren't her own people, they served the earl, and they feared she might be out of her mind.

She finally called out for Beverly who must have already been on her way, for she rounded the corner almost immediately. The red-haired knight ordered the servants to release her, and Anna ran for the stairs. Down she flew, rushing out the *front door in a vain attempt to see the strange figure once more, but it was too late. The wolf had disappeared into the darkness.*

It was early morning when Anna called everyone together. They were assembled, once again, in the dining hall for it was one of the few rooms that had the capacity, for not only were her advisors present but all of the Knights of the Hound, as well.

"We're running out of time," she started.

"We are doing all we can, Highness," offered Sir Arnim. "We've narrowed down the possible home of this creature to a considerable degree, but much of the city still remains unknown to us."

"We should be engaging the townsfolk," offered Hayley. "They know the city better than anyone in charge."

"An excellent idea," added Beverly. "That would save a lot of time."

"What are we looking for?" asked Dame Aelwyth. "Can you be more specific?"

"We're looking for an abandoned building," Hayley replied. "It will have to have a roof that would support a fairly large creature, so no steep slopes. We think it takes its victims there to eat so it would have to be able to hide them."

"Wouldn't dead bodies smell?" offered Sir Barnsley. "Surely someone would smell something?"

"A good point," commented Anna. "I hadn't thought of that."

It was the mage, Revi Bloom that spoke next, "There might be a reason why no smell is reported."

"What's that?" asked Anna.

"I propose that the creature might be using venom to paralyze its victims."

"What makes you think that?" asked Sir Howard.

"There was no sign of blood at Gerald's last location. If he was carried away, he was likely still alive. Even an injured man can cry out if needed."

"Couldn't he have been unconscious?" asked Aubrey.

"Certainly, but the attack would have had to be perfectly timed to take him down without a struggle, and what of all the other disappearances. Could no single person find the strength to cry out? No, I believe it's using some sort of venom to do its dirty work, and that means some of them may still be alive. Remember, we still have yet to find any bodies."

"I find the whole idea revolting," offered Sir Barnsley. "The very idea that it's keeping its victims alive is exceedingly grotesque."

"It's imperative," said Beverly, "that we act as quickly as we can. I suggest breaking into four groups. We'll approach the area within this circle from north, south, east and west."

"Well said, Beverly," added Anna, "we'll do precisely that. Arnim, you will enter from the north, along with Sir Barnsley and Sir Howard. Revi, you'll take Aelwyth and Dame Juliet in from the east. Hayley, you, Dame Levina, and Dame Abigail will enter from the west. That leaves Beverly, Aubrey and myself to enter from the south."

"I must object, Highness," said Arnim. "That would leave you dangerously exposed."

"Beverly is more than capable of guarding me, and Aubrey is a healer. Besides, we'll have Tempus with us. Now let me make something perfectly clear: I'm going!" She looked around the table, daring anyone to speak, but they all wisely remained silent.

The door opened, as if on cue, and Sophie entered. She was carrying a tray with something heaped on it. "Perfect timing, Sophie," said Anna. "I had Sophie carry a message to the soldiers stationed here. They've given us some horns to use as a signal. I want every group to make sure they've got at least one person who knows how to use them. Nothing fancy, just blow the horn if you find the lair. If anyone hears one of these go off, you head toward it as quickly as possible. Any questions?"

"Where, precisely, do we enter the area?" asked Revi.

"I've already marked the entry points on the map," the princess said. "In addition, Sophie has directions for each of you."

Beverly looked up in surprise, "You've been quite busy, Your Highness."

"I wasn't in the mood for sleep," Anna retorted. "This gave me something to do."

Alric had risen early and was heading toward the Citadel, Jack in tow. He noticed the Mercerian group heading out of the mighty fortress and rode to intercept them.

"What's happening, Highness?" he asked.

Anna gave him a stare that warned him to back off. It was Lady Aubrey who rode over to explain. "We're off to locate Commander Matheson," she said.

"You know where he is?" asked Alric.

"Not precisely, no," admitted the new mage, "but we will soon." She looked over Alric's shoulder, past Jack. "It appears you have other, more pressing matters to attend to, if I'm not mistaken."

Alric turned, trying to see what she was looking at. Off in the distance, he saw Brida riding toward him. He cursed at his bad luck and turned back to talk to Aubrey, but she had spurred her horse to join the princess's entourage. He was tempted to run after her, but the Clan Princess was now calling his name.

"Alric, I'm so glad I found you." She rode over to him, pulling her horse close so that they were almost leg to leg. "I do hope I'm not interrupting anything?"

"Actually..." said Alric.

"I'm sure it's nothing important," she continued. "Your brother wants us to get to know each other. I can't have you riding off with other people when I'm trying to learn more about you, can I? We must find something to keep us busy today."

Alric stumbled for words. A fragrance in the air intoxicated him, and he found himself bereft of objection. "What would you like to do?"

"I don't know, I was hoping you might suggest something? Didn't you say you liked tournaments?"

"I did, yes," he fumbled.

"Excellent, then it's decided. Come along then, Your Highness, we have things to see and people to meet."

Alric was led away in confusion.

~

Hayley, Levina and Abigail had entered the search area and were keeping their eyes out for any indication of a nest of some sort. The shopkeepers were just setting up in the early morning sun, and Hayley looked at a vendor with a vegetable cart who was stocking his wares.

"Might I have a word, sir?"

The man looked startled, "I beg your pardon?"

Hayley dropped a coin onto his cart. "I was wondering if you might help me, I need some information."

He lifted the strange coin to his eyes, examining the image of the warrior's crown of Merceria that was emblazoned on it. Satisfied that it was valuable, he tucked it into his pouch.

"What type of information are you looking for?"

"We've been investigating some disappearances in these parts. Perhaps you've heard of them?"

"I have indeed," he admitted. "Terrible they are, but I don't see how I can help you."

"We think the perpetrator is holed up somewhere in an abandoned building. He'd likely have a vantage point where he can see the whole area. Do you know of any building like that?"

"Let me think now," the man said, scratching his head. "There's an old temple a couple of blocks away."

"A temple? Tell me more," she urged.

"It's been abandoned for years. They say it was founded by a holy man who arrived from across the sea and preached about five holy saints. I don't know much about it, but in my grandfather's day, it was quite popular. They used to peal the bell to call the worshipers to Morning Prayer. When the priest died, there was no one else to carry on, so the temple fell into disuse."

"How long ago was this?" Hayley asked.

"I reckon the bells haven't been rung for nigh on fifty years."

"Can you tell me where I would find it?"

"Well, you can't see it from here because the streets are too narrow and the houses block your line of sight. But if you go down two blocks and turn south, it should be visible, it'll be on your left-hand side."

"Thank you," said the ranger, "you've been most helpful."

They made their way down the street, keeping their eyes open. No sooner had they turned south than the ranger's keen eyes spotted their target.

"There it is," she said.

"Not very grandiose, for a temple," retorted Dame Abigail.

"The merchant said it was built by a foreigner, he likely didn't have a rich purse," suggested Hayley.

"It's big enough for worship," said Levina, "and the old bell tower offers a commanding view. I suspect we've found our target. Shall we call the others?"

Hayley thought it over a moment before responding, "I suppose so, but let's not get too close yet. If it is inside, I don't want to scare it away, we want to get in there and deal with it once and for all."

Abigail lifted the horn and gave the signal; three short notes. A moment later the response came; two longer notes. It was repeated two more times, telling them that help was on the way. They waited, two blocks from their target, repeating the call after a suitable time. Once more the replies came, this time getting much closer.

It was Tempus who came into view first. He was galloping down the street, Anna in hot pursuit. Beverly trotted along behind while Lady Aubrey struggled to keep up in her dress. It was a comical sight, for Aubrey was clutching her dress and holding it above her knees to avoid tripping herself.

Anna had already spotted the temple. "You've found it!" she exclaimed.

"We think so, Highness. A vendor told us it's been abandoned for years.

It meets all the criteria. We chose not to advance until everyone was present."

"A wise move," Anna agreed. "We want to stop this creature before it can move along. You and Beverly move closer and take a look around, but under no circumstance do you enter yet. Understood?"

"Yes, Highness," Hayley responded.

"We'll join you as soon as the others arrive. We need to know all the doors and windows that might be used before we make a move, so see what you can ascertain."

Beverly and Hayley moved south, toward the temple, while the rest waited. Revi's group arrived shortly thereafter. They had already encountered Arnim's group, and now the six of them were marching up the street, right past the very building that was their target.

"I take it you found something?" asked the mage.

Aubrey stared at her mentor in disbelief, "Didn't you notice the building you just walked past, Master Revi?"

The mage stopped suddenly and looked back the way he came. "Oh, I suppose I didn't. Is that our target?"

"None other," replied Aubrey, shaking her head. He could be oblivious to his surroundings at times, and she hoped this wasn't a by-product of magic, for she would hate to find herself in a similar situation.

"What are we waiting for?" asked Arnim.

"Hayley and Beverly are taking a quick look before we enter. They should be back shortly," offered the princess.

It didn't take long for her prediction to come true for Beverly and Hayley were soon trotting back up the street.

"It's a simple structure," remarked Hayley, "with only two doors. The main double door is facing the street, and there's a door at the back, likely leading into the priest's office, beneath the bell tower. I suspect they're both locked."

"What of the windows?" asked Arnim. "Any sign we could get in that way?"

"I'm afraid not," replied Beverly. "They're high up and covered with stained glass. I don't think they're made to open. The only other entrance would be the bell tower."

"Precisely as we thought," said Revi.

"How shall we proceed?" asked Dame Juliet.

"We'll split into two groups. Beverly, you pick three people and try getting in the back door. The rest of us will go in through the front."

"I'll take Hayley, Aubrey and Levina," the redhead stated.

"Very well, let's get going, we don't want to waste any more time,' said Anna.

They were soon in position. Beverly grasped the handle to the priest's door, but to no one's surprise, it was locked.

"What do we do now?" she asked.

"Let me have a look," offered Hayley. She knelt while she examined the lock. "It looks to be a fairly standard lock, if only we had a key. Aubrey, do you have a spell we could use?"

"Only if you want me to put the door to sleep," she countered, "even magic has its limits. We'll have to force it."

"There's some timber over here," observed Levina. "They must have stacked it years ago to cut up for firewood. We could use a larger piece as a sort of battering ram."

They looked over the woodpile, and then Levina and Beverly pulled forth a likely candidate.

"Try to strike the lock as best you can," suggested Aubrey. "It's likely the weakest part."

The two knights stood to either side of the log and hefted it forward. It struck the lock solidly, bending the handle and providing a satisfying noise as the metal started to give way. They hefted the wood once more and were rewarded with the snap of metal. The door swung inward, revealing a narrow corridor leading to the main hall of worship. To the left was a small room, though sparsely furnished, it had obviously been the priest's office while to the right was the stairwell leading to the bell tower.

Levina poked her head into the stairwell. "It appears to be blocked by debris," she said, "though it looks a decent size up there, from what I can see."

"It would make sense," said Hayley, "the bell's quite large. It would take a strong structure to hold it in place."

Without warning, the door from the nave opened, and in walked Arnim.

"Arnim!" said Beverly. "We didn't hear you breaking in."

"That's because we didn't," he replied, "I managed to pick the lock."

Beverly wore a look of surprise, "I thought you used to be a member of the town watch?"

"I was," he confirmed.

"So when did you learn to pick locks?"

"It's surprising the things you pick up over the years," he replied cryptically. "What have you found?"

"There's an empty office and a stairwell leading up to the tower, but it's blocked by debris."

Arnim pushed past to have a look for himself. Revi wandered into the priest's office, fascinated by its contents.

"It must be up there somewhere," offered Hayley, "unless it's out hunting."

"We'll need to clear away this debris," stated Arnim. "I think if we move a timber or two, we'll be able to get past."

"Where did all this come from?" asked the ranger.

"Some of it is from the stairs, but I think our visitor might have brought some from elsewhere. One or two of the timbers look like they're driftwood."

"Are you saying it came from the river?" asked Aubrey.

"It's merely speculation at this point," replied Arnim. "Now let's see about clearing a path."

They examined the blockage carefully before beginning. They didn't want to cause a collapse that would bury themselves in the stairwell. With the help of the knights, they managed to pull forth two large timbers and an assortment of odds and ends, enough that the blockage was navigable.

"I'll go first," said Beverly, pushing forward. She squeezed past an old table to find herself standing on a broken step. "Watch your feet," she said, "some of the treads are missing."

She placed her feet carefully, avoiding the damaged sections and slowly made her way upward. There had been railings at some point, but these had now joined the debris in the bottom of the tower. Revi looked up at her progress and then started an incantation. Moments later a small sphere of light manoeuvred through the wreckage to illuminate the way. Once past the debris, Beverly's progress was swift.

She soon called down to the others, "There's a hatch here, in the ceiling."

"It likely leads to the bell pull," offered Aubrey. "Then there'll be another hatch leading to the top of the tower itself. If the creature is here, it'll likely be in that room. Be careful, Cousin."

"Wait until everyone is in position," yelled Anna. "We want Revi up there, along with at least one other knight."

"I'll go," offered Levina. "No offense Hayley, but we need someone with real armour up there, not your ranger leathers."

"No offense taken, Levina," replied Hayley. "I'd much rather be some-where I can use my bow."

"Get outside, Hayley," commanded Anna, "in case it tries to fly away. Maybe you can pick it off with an arrow. Take Aubrey with you as an extra set of eyes."

The pair headed out while Levina and Revi navigated the jumble of wreckage on the stairs. Beverly stood ready to open the hatch while Revi concentrated on keeping the orb of light floating nearby.

"As soon as you open the door," said the mage, "I'll move the globe into the room; it should provide you with enough light to see what's going on. Levina will follow you, and then I'll climb up. If you see anything dangerous, act decisively. Remember, this creature has carried away a grown adult, we can't take chances."

Beverly took a breath and drew her sword. It would be confined quarters, far too cramped for a shield, and so she leaned hers on the wall at the base of the small ladder. Grasping the handle of the hatch, she paused, holding her sword in her right hand where she saw the rose that Aldwin had so lovingly embossed onto the cross guard. It made her smile, and then she looked down at Revi and nodded.

She heaved against the hatch, and it flew open with little resistance. This was the moment of greatest peril, entering the breach; if the creature was waiting, she would be helpless, unable to swing her sword as she climbed.

Through the hatch she went and soon found herself in a small chamber, its beams thick with cobwebs. The room, illuminated by the orb of light, was filled with strange mounds of some sort which she couldn't explain. They reminded her of a wasp's nest they had cleared out of the Keep long ago, but there appeared to be no openings through which an insect could crawl. It was as if a large pile of dried mud had been erected to form a cocoon of some sort. It was almost as tall as Beverly and wide enough to hold a fully grown adult.

She heard a movement and turned toward it, but couldn't make out anything save for more of the mysterious mounds of mud. Levina came up behind her, sword in hand and Beverly pointed with her own weapon toward where she had heard the sound. Her companion came to stand beside her, blocking the creature's escape route, if it was indeed here. The room was small with little space for anyone else in their two-person line. Revi came up behind them and was immediately struck by the strange constructions.

"What is this?" he murmured. "Fascinating!"

Again there was a scraping noise, and both knights narrowed their gaze. "Did you hear that?" asked Levina.

"Yes," replied Beverly, "but I can't see anything, can you?"

An indistinct blur passed in front of Beverly, and then suddenly Levina was knocked backwards with such great force that she hit the far wall. Beverly struck back by instinct, feeling her sword scrape across something hard. Sparks flew from the tip, and for a moment she had a flash of an immense shape. In bulk, it reminded her of an Orc, but she had only a glimpse. It struck her with something, perhaps an arm or a wing, she couldn't be sure. She was knocked to the floor by the force of it and instantly rolled. The floorboards beside her shook with the impact, dust flying up.

She struck again, guessing where the creature might be. Her blade hit true, encountering resistance as her sword dug in. The thing issued a hissing noise, and then it backed up, threatening to take her sword with it. She yanked back on the blade in desperation.

Whatever it was, it had had enough. The upper hatch suddenly flew open, and she thought she saw a strange distortion around the egress. Leaping to her feet, she slashed once more with her sword, but the blade scrapped across the creature's hide, like a knife across stone. A moment later, a flapping sound broke the quiet, and then silence. She poked her head through the upper hatch, but all was quiet. She climbed through, swinging her sword about experimentally, but the creature had fled.

Leaning out over the top of the bell tower, she called down to Hayley, "Did you see anything?"

"No," replied the ranger. "Why? What happened?"

"We found it," Beverly replied, "but it managed to get away."

"What about Gerald?"

"I don't know yet, we're still looking, you might as well come back inside." She climbed back down into the room. Levina was lying on the floor, unmoving, while Revi cast a spell.

"How is she?" asked Dame Beverly.

"She's had the wind knocked out her," replied the mage. "She'll be bruised, but should make a full recovery."

"What was that thing?" she asked.

"I don't know," confessed Revi, "but of more import to us at the moment is what these things are." He indicated the mounds of mud.

Arnim poked his head through the lower hatch, "Is it safe? The princess wants to come up."

"The creature's gone," said Revi, rising from his place beside Levina. "I think it's safe to say there's no danger up here."

"What are those," asked Arnim, pointing to the mounds.

"I have no idea," the mage replied. "They appear to be made of mud, though now that I can see them clearer, they seem to have fibres in them, much like paper. I've seen this somewhere before."

Soon, Anna was staring at the mounds, trying to make sense of them. "Get Hayley," she said, "perhaps she knows of a creature that might make something like this."

Revi had withdrawn a dagger and was scraping a small piece of the mud away from a mound. "It's a strange composition," he observed. "I suspect the creature excreted this material."

"Are you saying we're looking at shit?" asked Arnim.

"No, I'm suggesting it excretes this material from a gland, possibly from its mouth. It likely regurgitates it. My guess is there's something inside this."

"Could it be Gerald?" asked Anna. "We have to get him out!"

"We can't just carve into it, Highness," offered the mage. "We have no idea what kind of condition he might be in. We might injure or even kill him if we're not careful."

"Do what you must, Mage," said Anna, "but be quick about it."

Revi poked the dried mud and walked around it, using his globe of light to illuminate his examination.

Aubrey and Hayley arrived, and now the small room was feeling positively claustrophobic. "We should get Levina downstairs," suggested Aubrey.

"Yes, yes," agreed Revi. "See to it Aubrey, I've much to examine here."

Aubrey went about her task. Luckily, Levina had regained consciousness and was able to facilitate her exit. The other knights below helped her down.

Revi had completed his examination. "These mounds are one of two things," he stated. "Either the creature uses them to keep his victims imprisoned, much like a spider, or they're cocoons, holding the creature's young."

Beverly was looking about the room, "I think they're more likely to be victims," she stated.

"What makes you say that?" the mage testily replied.

"There's no sign of bones here. If it lairs here, wouldn't it likely eat here as well?" She looked to Hayley for confirmation.

"I agree," offered Hayley, "the creature must eat something. I suggest these cocoons are its victims."

"Are they still alive?" asked Anna.

"I wish I knew, Highness. Had my training been complete, I'd be able to tell you."

"What does that mean?" asked Beverly.

"It means that Andronicus would have taught me how to detect life, a most useful skill for a healer. As it is, I have no idea how to incant that spell."

"Then how do we proceed," asked Anna.

"We cut into one of the mounds very carefully," suggested Beverly. "We'll start at the top and try shaving off layers until we find something."

"Do it now," commanded the princess.

Revi stepped back while Hayley and Beverly began using their daggers to dig through the mud and fibres. Aubrey watched with great interest as they made slow but deliberate progress. Finally, as Hayley drew her knife across the top, a portion of the structure collapsed, revealing a hollow interior. Revi immediately took notice, floating the ball of light over the opening.

Hayley peered into the dark cavity. "It appears to be a body," she stated, "a child, by the looks of it. It's collapsed to the bottom."

"Let's cut away to the top half," said Beverly, "and we can get a better view."

She drove her sword into the cocoon and began sawing away with it. Soon, they had the top removed and were looking at the exposed body.

"It's terribly shrivelled," offered Hayley, "as if all the moisture's been drained."

"It's called mummification," explained Revi, "though I've never heard of a creature doing this sort of thing. I would suspect it lives off the moisture, or at least the life force."

"How long would it take to make a body like this?" asked Anna.

"I would suspect some time," replied Revi. "I would suggest this body was desiccated over a period of a week or more."

"Open up the rest of these husks," ordered the princess. "If Gerald's here, he's likely still alive."

They began their work, but it soon became apparent that their friend's body was not among those they found.

TWENTY-FIVE

Chaperone

AUTUMN 960 MC

P rince Alric sat in the foyer, waiting for his brother. He had been summoned here, to the earl's estate, and now he wondered what was of such urgency. The cavalier, Jack Marlow, sat opposite him, glancing up and down the hallway as if expecting some great revelation.

"How did your day go yesterday, Highness?" he asked.

"It was fine, Jack. I took Brida to the tournament field. She was most impressed."

"I was there two days ago with Princess Anna," offered Jack, "it was most entertaining. Naturally, I regaled them with my past accomplishments."

Alric smiled, "Oh yes? And how did the princess find that?"

"She loved it," said Jack. "Though I daresay she was a little upset with you."

The young prince sat forward, "Did she say why?"

"She seemed to think you were snubbing her."

"That's a little rich," Alric observed. "She's the one who was entertaining in her rooms."

Jack stared back at him in disbelief, "Are you sure, Highness? I find that hard to believe. She's still a young innocent."

"I saw it with my own eyes, Jack. A young man answered her door. He was...partially undressed. He said she was indisposed."

Jack shook his head, "And you believed it?"

"Of course, I saw it with my own eyes."

"Your Highness, we've travelled with these Mercerians for some time now. Do you think that the old man would allow that?"

"You mean Commander Matheson? I very much doubt it."

"There has to be more to it, Highness. Think for a moment, if she was looking for a sexual escapade, wouldn't she pick me? After all, I am very good looking."

Alric laughed at the jest, "You have a point, Jack, but where does that leave me?"

"You never actually saw the princess or her maid, did you?"

"No," Alric admitted.

"I suggest someone took advantage of you, Highness."

"I would rather it was so," Alric said, "but who would do such a thing?" As soon as the words came out of his mouth, he knew the answer. "It has to be my brother, or Brida herself. Cuthbert's made no secret of the fact that he wants me married to the Clan Chief's daughter."

"There, you see? You've figured it out, but what will you do now?"

"I shall have a rather frank discussion with Cuthbert. It's a dangerous game he's playing, interfering with the Mercerian delegation."

"How so?" asked Jack.

"Who do you think poses a bigger threat, Jack? Militarily, I mean."

"I should think the army of Merceria is much more dangerous than the raiders from the Clans."

Their discussion was interrupted by a door opening. Cuthbert stood looking at his younger brother, "Come along, Alric, let's get this over with."

Alric entered the room, but Jack was stalled by a hand from Cuthbert. "You wait out here," he simply said.

The elder prince pointed to a chair and then fetched a bottle from the table, talking as he poured its contents into glasses.

"Tell me, Brother, how has the Princess Brida been doing?"

"She's been fine," said Alric, on the alert for his brother's trap.

"I will tell you why you're here, Alric, but please bear me out. I have much to explain before we get to any grievances you may have."

"Very well, Cuthbert, pray continue."

"As you know, there was panic in the court when we learned that an army had crossed from our border into Merceria. It set into motion a whole host of actions. Father was concerned that we might face an unbeatable war."

"We've faced that before," objected Alric, "why is now any different?"

"The difference is that this time most of our troops were tied up along our western frontier because of the Clans. If we were to have any hope against a Mercerian invasion, we would need to free them up. Father sent me to the west to secure a peace treaty with the Clans. Now I've returned with a solution, provided you marry Princess Brida."

"Isn't it equally important that we make peace with Merceria? Surely they are the greater threat?"

"You forget, Brother, Merceria recently had an uprising. They are in no position to invade us."

"Which leaves me wondering why this western alliance is so important?"

"The Clans are powerful, Alric. Imagine what we might do with them as our allies. There wouldn't be an army in the land that could stand against us."

"You want to invade Merceria?" Alric was stunned by the revelation.

"Oh, come now, Alric. They've threatened our borders for almost a thousand years. Do you really believe they mean peace?"

"But they sent us the princess," objected Alric.

"Who is illegitimate, Brother. Do you think King Andred gives two shits about her? She's nothing but a pawn."

"She saved their kingdom, even helped fight off a raid in the north."

"A ruse, Alric, meant to gain favour with us."

"You forget, Cuthbert, I was with her at Norwatch! I can't believe we're even having this discussion."

"Grow up, Brother. You're not a child anymore. This alliance is going to happen, whether you like it or not. Father has given me free rein on this. You'll marry Brida, whether you want to or not."

"I won't," declared Alric.

"Listen, you little shit," yelled Cuthbert. "You'll do your duty, and you won't complain about it."

Alric smiled. This was the second time he'd been called a little shit in the last year. The first time, Gerald had been concerned about Anna dying from her wound. He knew the old man had meant well, he had even apologized for it afterwards, but now, as he stared back at his brother, he saw no regret and no concern for his welfare. Cuthbert had always been the headstrong one, but since the fight in Norwatch, Alric had matured significantly. Perhaps it was the influence of the Mercerians, but his mind was made up. He was about to object, but knowing his brother would protest, he changed his tactics.

"Very well," he said, in a polite tone.

Cuthbert was taken aback by the sudden switch in his brother's demeanour. He took a deep breath, letting it out slowly. "Glad to see you've come to your senses."

"Oh, I have, Brother, I have indeed. Shall I be on my way? I'm supposed to take Brida around the town today."

"Yes, of course," Cuthbert agreed, "and thank you, Alric."

"Whatever for, Brother?"

"For seeing the wisdom in this. I know it's not something you wanted."

"You might be surprised at what I want, Cuthbert, but likely you'll never know."

"What's that supposed to mean?"

"Nothing," mused Alric, "nothing at all. I shall be on my way."

Alric returned to the hallway to find Jack waiting for him.

"My prince," commented the cavalier, "that went well."

Alric spoke as they left, "How much did you hear?"

"Pretty much everything, Highness. Is your brother serious?"

"I'm afraid so. Tell me, what do you think, Jack? Is marriage a good thing?" He could almost see Jack cringe at the question.

"Well, I can't say I would be happy at the idea of marriage myself, after all, I'd be depriving all those women of my comfort. Then again, you're in a different position. Purely from a political point of view, it makes perfect sense. What do you think?"

"I don't want to get married," said Alric. "And if I did it wouldn't be to a woman I hardly know. What do we have in common? What is there to keep me interested in her?"

"Her body," replied Jack. "That's the most comforting thing about them."

"What about her mind?" asked Alric. "I'd at least like to be able to carry out a decent conversation with my wife."

"You don't know much about her," the cavalier responded.

"Exactly my point, the woman keeps the conversation about me. I can't recall learning anything about her or her home."

"Give it some time, Your Highness. Get to know her a little better, and then make a decision. It's not as if the entire fate of the kingdom was in the balance. Oh, hold on a moment, it is, isn't it."

Jack's advice was causing Alric more than a fair share of anxiety. "No more, Jack. I can't deal with this right now. Let's just get going on this tour."

"Tour?" said Jack.

"Yes, we're taking her around the city."

"We?"

"Yes, Jack. You're my bodyguard now. It's only proper you accompany me."

Jack smiled, "'Mad Jack' Marlowe, prince's bodyguard. I could get used to that. Do we have a particular destination in mind?"

"I thought we might start with the gardens," said Alric.

"Didn't we just go there?" Jack complained.

"That was with Anna," the prince retorted.

"This'll be easy," offered the cavalier.

"Why do you say that?"

"Simple," said Jack. "You've been showing Princess Anna all over town. All we have to do is repeat the process with Princess what's her name."

"Brida," Alric said.

Jack, ignoring the correction, continued, "What do we do about Princess Anna?"

Alric fought with his conscience. He liked Anna, but knew his duty was to the crown. Would she understand that his royal duty came first? "I'll write her a letter explaining everything and have it delivered."

"I see," said Jack, "so you're taking the coward's way out."

Alric bristled, "What's that supposed to mean?"

"You're not telling her face to face."

He had to admit the cavalier was right, but Alric couldn't stand to see the look of disappointment on her face when he told her. Alric suddenly realized he had grown fond of Anna and looked on her as a friend. He owed it to her to speak to her in person. He resolved to do so immediately and set off for the Citadel.

Prince Alric rode over to the Citadel only to be told by Lady Nicole that Anna was going into town. He wanted to find out more, but Brida had appeared as if by magic. He was beginning to wonder if she didn't have agents watching his every move. She was accompanied by her bodyguard. The man was a head taller than Alric, one of the tallest men he could recall. He was wearing a chain shirt, but his arms were bare, revealing huge muscles that could easily wield the broad-bladed sword which hung from his belt.

Brida was wearing a low cut, pale blue dress which threatened to expose her assets if she bowed too low. Alric dismounted to greet her, but it was Jack who saved the day. As she began to bow, he grasped her hand, holding it high enough that she couldn't lower her height.

"Pleased to see you again, Highness," he said, in a silky smooth tone.

"Yes," agreed Alric. "Shall we proceed?" He held out his arm, and she walked forward, grasping it in her own. Once again the strange scent wafted over him, and he struggled to keep his head clear.

"I thought we might take a stroll," he said at last.

"A wonderful idea, my prince," she replied, and then she smiled coyly at him.

Being raised in the court, he was quite used to this behaviour, but something was different about Brida. He struggled to explain it and then it came to him; she was a woman. He realized with a start that he was no longer the lost young prince. She was the same age as him, and she was a fully developed young woman. He felt the need to protect her, and he stood up a little straighter as he took her arm.

"Come along, Brida," he said, "and I shall show you the Celestial Park."

As they wandered through the park, Alric found the Clanswoman to be cultured and refined. They strolled and talked about all sorts of things. Life at the Weldwyn court, tournaments, the cavaliers, all topics that Alric found fascinating. They left the park, continuing through town and Alric was watching the people as they strode by. He was reminded of his visit to town with Anna, and he wondered how the search for Gerald was going.

"Are you good with that thing?" she asked.

Alric felt guilty for having let his thoughts wander; now he faced the embarrassment of acknowledging it. He tried to bluff it out, "I think I do all right with it," he replied, not sure what she was talking about.

"He fought with it at Norwatch," offered Jack. "It was quite a fight."

Alric pushed down his panic. "Yes," he added picking up on the conversation, "this sword's been most useful to me."

Brida gripped his arm tightly, "You have marvellous definition in your arm, Highness, you must practice constantly."

"Not as often as I'd like, Brida. Now please stop calling me Highness. We're both nobles, just call me Alric."

Somehow she managed to blush, "Very well, Alric." She bit her lip slightly, overwhelming Alric with unbridled emotions. "Oh dear," she said suddenly. "My necklace seems to be caught in my hair. Would you help, please?"

She turned her back to him, pulling up her braid to reveal her slender neck. He fumbled with the chain but saw no sign of impediment. She wheeled about quite unexpectedly to come face to face with Alric, their noses almost touching. He looked directly into her eyes, a conflict of sensations coursing through him. There was no denying that she was a beautiful woman and yet something was 'wrong' about her, though he couldn't put his finger on it.

She turned her head to the side. "Oh look," she cried, "swans. Can we go over and watch them?"

He nodded his agreement, too afraid to speak lest he reveal his inner turmoil. She grabbed him by the hand, dragging him towards the river, where Alric saw ugly white birds. He had never had an interest in animals outside of horses. Birds were game creatures in his mind, suitable only for hunting. Brida had released his hand to kneel at the water's edge. She cast her eyes over her shoulder at him and smiled. He saw the barest flash of her teeth and knew she was attractive, but now, with some distance between them, he felt different. Without her heavy, intoxicating scent, he could look at her dispassionately. She was still an attractive young woman, but he saw her actions as manipulative and highly calculated. He played along, smiling back, but inside his head, he was determined to test his theory.

They found a tavern that catered to the upper classes and sat outside eating a pleasant meal. Brida ate sparingly and drank little. She asked Alric all about the capital, so he indulged her with tales from court. He tried to find out more about the Clans and her life there, but every time he brought the subject up, she would carefully manoeuvre the conversation to a different topic. By the time the meal was done, he concluded that she merely agreed with everything he said. No matter what the topic she responded with words like 'fascinating' and 'it must be wonderful, tell me more.' He longed to have a real conversation like he did with Anna.

They went riding in the afternoon, to the east of the city. She proved to be an exceptional horsewoman as they raced across the fields.

"I envy you," she said, pulling back on the reins.

"How's that?" he asked, now on the alert for her tactics.

"You have a lot of freedom for a prince. Everything I do is carefully orchestrated and controlled. You have two older brothers; the throne is not your concern."

"I've never seen it that way," he conceded. "I've always struggled to find my place at court. I used to try to keep busy, to find something to occupy my time."

"I feel the same way, sometimes," she commiserated. "Perhaps we could go riding again tomorrow?"

"Of course," he promised. "I'd be delighted. Shall I meet you at the manor at noon?"

"Or earlier, if you like," she gushed.

Alric caught her inflection, but declined to take the bait. "I'm afraid I have some pressing details to see to. I am, after all, a Prince of the Realm, I wouldn't want to ignore my official duties."

"Of course not," she said, smiling once again.

They rode back to the city, but each time she tried to engage him in conversation, he would race forward, daring her to catch him. By the time they arrived back at the manor house, the horses were heavily lathered, and the stable master gave Alric a look of silent reprimand over the condition of their mounts. The young prince ignored the man. Ordinarily, he would show concern, but now other things weighed heavily on his mind.

His duty to Princess Brida complete, he called for a carriage and climbed inside, accompanied by Jack. "The Citadel," he called to the driver, and the carriage rolled forward.

"The Citadel?" said Jack. "Why there? Isn't it time to get some sleep?"

"I want to talk to the princess," said Alric. "I need to see how she's getting along."

"I hear," offered Jack, "that the old man is still missing."

"Gerald? How do you know that?"

"A maid told me," offered the cavalier. "He's probably lying in an alley somewhere or floating in the river. He was an interesting chap, but old. He's likely not in his full wits."

"I have to disagree, Jack. Gerald Matheson is old, it's true, but I've found him to be very clear headed."

"It makes no difference to me, Highness. But I still say he's blind drunk somewhere."

They rode in silence for a while. The Citadel, with its great towers, loomed closer.

"What do you make of the princess?" asked Jack.

"She's nice," replied Alric, "for a Clanswoman."

"That's not the princess I was referring to," said Jack.

"You mean Anna?"

"Of course I mean Anna. What do you think of her?"

"She's entertaining," he admitted. "She challenges me, and I find that quite pleasant. I've come to know her quite well over the last few months."

"Yes," said Jack, "and..."

"And what? What is it your trying to say, Jack?"

"Do you like her?"

"I do, Jack, but what does that have to do with anything? I'm only looking out for her because that's my duty."

"Mmm," muttered Jack.

Alric was turning red in the face. He tapped the side of the carriage. "Driver? Never mind the Citadel, get me back to the mansion." He looked back across at Jack, but all the cavalier was doing was smiling at him. "You can be infuriating at times, Jack."

"Yes, Your Highness," he admitted, "that's what I'm here for."

TWENTY-SIX

The Ship

AUTUMN 960 MC

"There must be more somewhere," said Anna.
"There is," said Revi, pointing towards the bar. "There's a whole lot more ale over there."

"That's not what I meant, Master Mage," she retorted. They were sitting at a tavern, partaking of a meal. They made a large group, including the knights. The lot of them were tightly packed into the relatively small confines of the place.

"I mean I still think there's more victims, somewhere," the princess repeated.

"But where?" pondered Aubrey.

"I saw something like this mud in a shop," offered Revi. "It was in a jar, floating in some water."

"Water," remembered Hayley. "I saw something similar. Lily and I went aboard a ship called the Swift. They were cleaning something like that off of the anchor. Do you think they're connected?"

"Yes," said Revi, "something brought this creature here, perhaps by accident. I suspect it was a boat."

"But the city lines the river," complained Arnim, "it could be anywhere."

Anna suddenly spoke, "It's south of the Citadel."

"How do you know that?" asked Arnim.

"Something tried to tell me, a wolf," she commented.

"With all due respect, Highness, you're imagining things. No one else saw this wolf you speak of."

"Tempus did, he barked and wagged his tail. It was Gerald, I know it was."

"Why would Gerald look like a wolf?" asked Revi.

"Remember the Greatwood?" asked Anna. "The Orcs took us on a spirit journey. Gerald collapsed when we were sitting around the fire. He told me he was in the body of a wolf."

"I've never heard of such a thing," said Arnim.

"I have," said Revi. "It's a common belief amongst some races. Both the Orcs and Elves are said to believe in such things."

"South of the Citadel still means a lot of water to search," complained Arnim.

"There was an abandoned ship in that area," offered Aubrey. "Don't you remember, Hayley? I was drawing a picture of it."

"Yes," agreed the ranger. "We even commented on it, at the time. We thought it strange there were no people aboard."

"That must be it," exclaimed Anna. "We must get to the river!"

Everyone stood in a rush of activity, buckling on swords and gauntlets. Lady Aubrey had been put in charge of the Royal Purse and paid out the grateful tavern keeper while the rest made their way outside.

"Where do we begin?" asked Beverly. "It's starting to get dark. If we don't find it soon, we'll have to put it off till morning."

"We're close," offered Anna, "I can feel it. We'll head to the docks directly. Aubrey, do you remember the name of the ship you sketched?"

"Yes," the young mage replied, "it was the 'Sentinel'. I remember thinking it was a strange name at the time."

"And you say it was just south of the Citadel?"

"Yes, that's right. It was anchored in the confluence, where the two rivers meet."

"We'll need to get across to the north shore, then," offered Arnim.

"No," refuted Hayley, "it would be quicker to head directly to the river's edge. We'll hire a boat to take us out, that should save us some time."

"Lead on, ranger," commanded Anna, and they headed west.

The docks on this side of the river were rather convoluted. The piers crisscrossed each other and the Mercerians, not used to the ways of boats, found it to be very confusing. It was starting to get dark, and their group was spread out along the shoreline, searching the river for the boat in question.

Anna heard a noise, as did Tempus, whose ears immediately picked up. "Did you hear that?" she asked.

"Hear what?" asked Hayley.

"It sounded like a baying," she replied.

"Didn't hear a thing," grumbled Arnim.

"There it is again, it's coming from that dock," she was pointing toward a ramshackle wooden structure that looked like it might collapse at any moment.

Tempus barked and suddenly Anna sprang into action, "I see the wolf!" she exclaimed.

Arnim strained his eyes but saw naught of what she spoke. Anna was running down the pier, shouting for the others. She came up short at the end, staring out into the river.

Beverly ran up beside her only to see, revealed by the setting sun, the abandoned ship for which they searched.

"We need a boat," she called.

It was Hayley who surprised them all. She strung her bow and let an arrow fly. It sailed over the water, to strike a ship lying at anchor nearby, eliciting a cry of alarm. Shortly after, a man appeared at the railing.

Hayley waved her hand in the air, "We need a boat," she called, "and we have coin!"

The man at the railing waved back, and soon there was a flurry of activity aboard the vessel.

"What are you doing, Hayley?" asked Beverly.

"It's the Swift. The captain there's a decent enough fellow. I'm sure he'll have a boat for us to use."

"How much is that going to cost us?" asked Arnim.

"It doesn't matter," said Anna, "no cost is too high."

A rowboat was soon seen moving around the end of the Swift. It had been tied up on the opposite side to them and now came into view, its captain urging on the oarsmen.

"We need to organize who's going," suggested Arnim. "We won't all fit in the longboat."

Anna nodded, "Tempus will obviously have to stay here, he won't be able to climb up the side of the ship. We'll take Beverly, Hayley, Arnim..." she was looking around the group as she spoke, "Revi and myself. That's about all that'll fit into the boat."

"You have to stay here, Princess," said Arnim. "It's too dangerous."

"If you think I'm staying here, you've got the wrong idea," she bristled.

The boat was soon alongside the dock, so they climbed aboard.

"We need to get to that derelict out there," Hayley said to Captain Runell. "Can you get us there?"

"Of course," he replied, "but we're not armed."

"The fighting you can leave to us," confirmed Beverly. "We've tracked down a creature that's been preying on people."

"Then let's get you there as quickly as possible," the captain said.

The rowing seemed to take forever, and for quite some time it appeared as if the derelict wasn't getting any closer. With the setting of the sun, the whole river took on an eerie glow, illuminated as it was by only the lights of the city.

Revi cast a spell; his globe of light sailing across the water, guiding them. Suddenly, they were closer than expected and the target loomed out of the darkness. The rowers used their oars to prevent the tiny boat from hitting the derelict, and then came the difficult task of boarding the vessel.

"Wait here," said Hayley, grasping the anchor line. "I'll climb up and find some rope."

The ranger ascended quickly, disappearing over the railing. A moment later came some noise from above, and then a rope splashed down beside them. Beverly went first. The small rowboat was bouncing around in the waves and made for an unsteady footing. She jumped slightly, grasping the line higher up, and then swung onto the side of the ship, her feet finding purchase, and she hauled herself, hand over hand, up the hull. Soon, she was over the railing, standing on the deck, the ranger beside her. She called down to the rowboat for Arnim to began the trip. Revi came next, and then Beverly had Anna tie the rope around her waist, pulling her up with minimal effort. They were soon all aboard, save for the rowboat's crew. The captain tied off the rowboat, waiting for the adventurous party's return.

The deck spread out before them, with a hatch amidships and a raised cabin at the aft end, but the foredeck was flush and offered no entrance. Starting at the bow, they spread out and began moving toward the stern, walking in a line running perpendicular to the beam, their weapons drawn. Knowing the creature was almost impossible to see, they swung their swords in front of them, hoping to hit the unseen target, but there were no signs of life.

Soon, they were over the hatch in the centre of the deck and stopped while Arnim took a look. The grating was of a heavy wooden construction, yet they could see no way to lift it.

"It must be hoisted off with a block and tackle," offered Revi. "I saw the masons using something similar when they rebuilt the north gate in Wincaster."

Hayley looked up, "There's plenty of places they could run the rope, the whole ships a mass of the stuff."

"Do you think the creature would be able to escape through this hatch?" asked Anna.

"Unlikely, I should think," offered Revi, "this grate looks exceedingly heavy. It would have to be, or it would come loose at the first sign of a heavy wave."

"Head for the back," said Anna, "that should lead us below."

The back of the ship was raised and housed what looked like a small cabin. The door was easy enough to open and looked into a short corridor, barely long enough for a tall man to lie down in, and ended in a door. To either side was an alcove, each with a hatch in the floor. Beverly lifted one to peer into the darkness.

"Bring your light over here, Revi. Let's see what's below."

The mage did as he was bidden and the small globe descended into the blackness. Beverly saw sacks stacked along the side of the hull along with wooden crates.

"What do you see?" asked Arnim.

"There's a ladder here," the knight responded, "but I don't see any sign of the creature. I'm going down." She scabbarded her sword and began the descent. "It's a low ceiling," she commented as her head disappeared below the level of the main deck.

Reaching the bottom of the deck, she drew her sword, "It's wet down here, there's a finger's length of water loose on the bottom."

Hayley followed, "Keep your eye's peeled, Bev, I wouldn't like to be surprised by that creature."

Beverly poked a sack with the tip of her sword. "Looks like these sacks are filled with flour. It stinks down here, I suspect something is rotting."

Arnim was next to lower himself down the ladder. "I know that smell, it's rotting grain."

"So we have sacks of grain and flour?" queried Hayley. "It doesn't seem very scary so far."

They began moving forward slowly, examining the area as carefully as they could in the gloom.

"Can you cast more of those orbs?" asked Anna, who had been the last to descend.

"I'm afraid not, Highness," he replied. "I can only control one at a time, but I shall move it forward to illuminate the way."

The shadows stretched as the tiny globe moved ahead. They all saw more crates; some broken open while small urns and shards of clay lay littering the deck.

"There are more of those cocoons," observed the mage. "About half a dozen or so of them, from what I can see."

The crates appeared to be stacked in the middle haphazardly, but there were two clear paths, one to either side of them. On the outside, the paths were lined with sacks, though as they drew closer, they spotted some more smaller cocoons mixed in among them.

"The children!" exclaimed Anna. "What a terrible fate."

Hayley began moving down the left-hand pathway while Beverly took the right. The rest were strung out along behind them, moving slowly, lest they slip in the water. A sudden commotion to the left had the ranger crying out as she was smashed into some crates. For just a moment Beverly feared the whole centre mass might collapse, burying them all.

"It's here," cried Arnim, quite unnecessarily. He jabbed into the darkness, the sound of steel hitting stone ringing out.

Beverly ran forward, trying to move closer to the action, her combat senses alert. Finding a gap in the centre of the crates, she moved through, coming out, she hoped, behind the creature. She saw Arnim backing up, but his image was twisted and distorted. It was then she realized she must be seeing through the creature. She thrust her sword forward, feeling a jarring impact, but it merely scraped across the creature's skin and then struck a wooden crate.

She stepped back slightly, striking with an overhead blow, but it stopped mid-swing, hitting a hard surface; the creature had blocked her attack. She had no choice but to back up, giving her the space she needed to use her weapon effectively.

"Where's Hayley?" she yelled.

"I'm fine," the ranger called back, "just trying to extricate myself from these crates. Give me a hand, Revi."

Arnim struck out again, to hear the sound of his sword contacting stone.

"For Saxnor's sake, we might have a chance if we could only see the thing," he griped.

Hayley pulled herself back into the tiny aisle. "If only Tempus were here," she said, "he'd at least be able to smell the thing."

"He'd never be able to climb aboard." Anna called out,"Prepare to duck."

"What?" replied Hayley?

"I said duck!"

The ranger dropped to the floor, as did Arnim while something sailed overhead and struck the creature, creating an explosion of sorts; suddenly the air was thick with flour. Beverly closed her eyes at the impact, averting her gaze. The flour soon sank to the deck, and as she turned back to face her foe, she spotted the outline of a leg.

"I can see it," she cried out as she slashed forward. This time she was rewarded with a solid hit. Her blade struck true, but the creature's flesh was hard, and only the tip of her blade made any mark. "A minor wound," she cried out. "It'll take forever to kill this thing."

She concentrated all her effort on the leg, but the creature struck out, and Beverly's shin took the brunt of the force. Staggering back, thankful for her shin guards, she swung again, but met nothing but air.

"Here comes another one," yelled Anna.

Beverly watched the second urn fly through the air. It struck the creature squarely this time, and she watched in amazement as it took shape before her.

It was massively tall, having to stoop while it was below the decks, and she estimated it to be seven feet or more in height. Its enormous folded wings were bat-like, while its head was horse-like, long and angular. As it turned to confront her, she saw the horror that was its face, for it had no mouth, only a small opening surrounded by strange tentacles that waved about menacingly, reminding her of lampreys or leeches.

The creature, now fully exposed, took an arrow to the back and turned away from Beverly to face this new threat. It struck out at Arnim trying to get to the ranger behind him, but the warrior ducked low, striking for the creature's injured leg.

Beverly reversed her sword and drove it, two-handed, into the back of the creature, between its folded wings. It turned back to face her, letting out a defiant roar that shook the very hull of the ship. Its claws were a blur of motion. Beverly strained to defend herself, but she was driven to the floor by the fury of the attack. It stood over her, ready to end her once and for all, until Arnim drove his blade into the creature's calf.

It wheeled about, striking at nothing, for the captain had backed up. Revi gesticulated, and suddenly the globe of light went out, leaving everyone in darkness. It soon erupted again, directly in the face of the creature. It tried to cover its eyes, and, in that moment, Anna darted forward. Beverly cried out in alarm, but could not stop the princess as she drove her Dwarf blade forward, slicing easily through the creature's thick skin. The look of shock on the girl's face revealed her surprise, and then she backed up, trying desperately to get away from it.

"Let it come after me," yelled Beverly, getting to her feet. "I'll draw it into the open where we can all get at it."

She struck again, and then stepped backwards, repeating the action as the creature pursued her. It was thrashing about wildly now, its eyes still blinded by the bright light. Soon, they had it in an open area, no longer confined by the crates, and they all gathered around it. In they darted, striking with precision, but the thick skin of the creature prevented them from doing significant harm.

"We need to bring it down," yelled Beverly. "Strike at the legs."

Arnim sliced forward, opening a small gash in the creature's left thigh, and as he backed up an arrow struck the same wound, burying itself into the soft flesh beneath the hard exterior.

The creature bellowed, falling to one knee and then Beverly yelled, "Highness, toss me your sword!"

She had dropped her own weapon, and using a crate to launch herself into the air, she reached out with her hands, and to Hayley's eyes, it appeared she was flailing wildly, but Anna had understood. The small Dwarf blade tumbled through the air toward the knight. Beverly, grasping the handle as she came down, drove the blade through the back of the creature's head. There was the briefest of movement, and then the monster was dead.

They all stood around, catching their breath, overcome with the exertion.

"Beverly," exclaimed Revi, "that was amazing!"

"It was lucky," the redhead replied.

"Let's find Gerald," yelled Anna. "Open up all the husks, but be careful, there may be people alive in some of them."

They moved toward the husks, pulling them apart with daggers and even bare hands, desperately seeking their friend. It was Hayley who found the first survivor

"Revi," she called, "over here."

The healer rushed over. The ranger had pulled the top off of a husk, and now a young woman was exposed, gasping for breath. Revi immediately began an incantation.

Anna was clawing at the largest of the cocoons. Soon, her small hands revealed chainmail.

"It's Gerald," she called out. "It must be him!"

Beverly was there in an instant, and together, they pulled the muddy casing from the old warrior. His face was grey, and as they dug him loose, they noticed he had lost a great deal of weight, but at least he was breathing. As they ripped away more mud, he collapsed to the floor.

Revi was soon there, casting a spell, but he looked up to Anna with a solemn expression. "I'm afraid there's little I can do, Highness. The flesh is intact. I suspect he's had most of the fluid drained from his body. I can stabilize him, but only time will tell if he'll survive."

"Let's get him up to the main deck," Anna commanded, "perhaps the fresh air will help. Arnim, go and tell the captain to get help. We'll need more hands to clean up this mess, and let's see if there are any other survivors."

It was early morning by the time help arrived. A larger ship was brought alongside, with a boarding ramp laid between the two vessels. There were only two survivors of the creature's attacks, but the bodies of at least a dozen more, many of them children, had been recovered.

The mood was sombre as they carried Gerald across, and laid him out on the deck; a rolled up cloak for a pillow. He was breathing easier now, but his colour had not improved.

"It's been suggested we take him to the Temple of Malin, Highness," offered Revi. "I'll have to examine both our survivors in more detail. I'm afraid there's a possibility that they might have been poisoned or injected with spores or even eggs; we know so little about this creature."

"What are they doing with the body?" she asked.

"They're taking it to the local chapter of the mages council. I'll examine it later to see what I can learn."

He was called away to see to his other patient while Anna sat on the deck, holding Gerald's hand. A shadow fell over her, and she looked up to see Dame Beverly.

"Do you think he'll survive?" asked Anna.

The knight looked down at the old warrior, "He's a fighter, Highness, and I'm sure he'll do all he can to return to us."

"He lost his family, twice," she proclaimed. "It's not fair that he should die now, of all times."

"He won't die," Beverly said, calmly. "He has too much to live for. You're his family now, Highness, he won't leave you. You saw the grey wolf when no one else did, you have a connection."

"I hope you're right, Beverly. I pray that Saxnor will return him to me."

TWENTY-SEVEN

The Recovery

AUTUMN 960 MC

S ophie pulled the cords tight and tied them off in a bow. "Are you sure about this, Your Highness?" she asked. "This corset looks so uncomfortable."

Anna smiled, "It's the custom here in Weldwyn, Sophie, though I hope it doesn't catch on in Merceria." She turned slightly to look in the mirror. "Is that me?"

"It is, Highness," answered Sophie. "You're a young woman now."

Anna smiled at the compliment and twirled around. "What do you think, Beverly?"

"I think you look more elegant than all the ladies of the Wincaster court, Highness."

Anna blushed, "Thank you, Beverly, for everything. If it hadn't been for you, we never would have killed that creature."

"It was you that made it possible, Highness. If you hadn't had that Dwarven blade, we never would have been able to defeat it. Where ever did you get such a weapon?"

"It was a gift from a Dwarven smith, a friend of Gerald's. He thought I was his daughter."

Beverly smiled, "And so you are, Highness, at least in all things that matter. Nothing will ever change that."

"Shall we proceed?" the princess asked.

"Yes, Highness, Gerald is waiting in the anteroom."

Beverly opened the door, and Anna glided out, followed by her servants.

Gerald was sitting in a rather narrow armchair. To Beverly's mind, it looked more like a dining room chair. She wondered why this strange piece of furniture would be here, of all places.

"I still think you should have stayed at the temple," said Anna.

"Nonsense," Gerald slurred, "I'll recover faster here. All I need do is rest and relax.

Anna looked to Revi, who was standing behind the chair.

"He is still drained of energy, Highness, but will make a full recovery, I promise you. He will slur his words for a while and must refrain from any strenuous activity for perhaps a week or so, but should be in fine form after that."

"And the creature?" she asked.

"Arnim has named it a soul eater, a fitting name, considering the manner of its attacks. It fed off the essence of life. Draining it, if you will, to sustain itself. I have examined both survivors in detail and can assure you there is no sign of toxins or spores. Gerald's wounds are clean, he merely needs time to build up his energy."

Anna moved closer to Gerald and hugged him, then kissed him on the cheek. "I'm so glad we found you, Gerald," she said, tears forming in her eyes. She straightened herself and shook her arms to release tension. "Shall we continue?" she nodded to Sophie, who called in two male servants. They entered carrying poles and these they carefully threaded through small rings set into the chair. Then they took up position in front and behind Gerald, lifting the poles, and the chair, into the air.

"Where on earth did you get this mad idea from, Anna?" objected Gerald. "Surely it would be better if I walked."

"Where do I get all my ideas, Gerald? From a book, of course. It's called a sedan chair, at least my version of one. I had them make it up yesterday. Now you just relax while we go downstairs. We've arranged a little party to welcome you back."

"Wait," objected Gerald, "shouldn't we wait for Lady Nicole? She's your Lady-in-Waiting, after all."

"Not anymore," replied Anna. "I've dismissed her. Almost losing you made me realize I want my friends close, that includes Sophie; she's been with me for years. I don't need a Lady-in-Waiting, particularly one sent by Valmar."

"Valmar? How do you know he sent her?"

"I don't," Anna admitted, "but I always felt she was watching me. From now on I'll make the decision about who accompanies me."

Gerald smiled, "Very well, Highness, after you."

The procession left the anteroom and made their way through the hallways of the Citadel. They paused at the door to the dining hall while Anna turned to face the group.

"I had them clear out the dining hall, it's the largest room in the Citadel. Tonight it is to be the great hall, and there shall be dancing and merriment, except for you, Gerald. You can be merry, but no dancing."

"Lucky you, Gerald," Beverly said under her breath.

"What was that, Dame Beverly?" enquired the princess.

"Nothing, Highness. Shall we proceed?"

Anna turned again and composed herself while a servant grasped the door handle. She nodded, and the door swung open, revealing a room packed with visitors. She stepped forward and paused, bowing to her guests. There were murmurs of approval at her stylish dress and then she turned, beckoning the rest to enter.

Gerald was carried into much applause, and the old man blushed. Beverly was pleased to see the colour in his face again. Anna introduced them all, including Sophie and then she bid her guests to enjoy themselves.

Her maid turned to leave, but Anna halted her, "I want you to stay, Sophie, and enjoy yourself. You're not a servant tonight, you're my friend. Dance, drink, eat, do what you like, I want you to have fun."

Beverly was smiling, seeing the princess happy for the first time in days. Anna cast her eyes around the assembled crowd and rested them on Prince Alric, who was standing beside Princess Brida. Beverly could well imagine the feelings going through Anna's mind. It took her back years. She remembered visiting the smithy and seeing Aldwin surrounded by a bevy of young girls and how it made her feel. She knew she should say something to help diffuse the situation, but she was caught up in the moment and couldn't help but watch, mesmerized as the scene unfolded before her.

Anna strode directly toward Alric, ignoring the greetings of those she passed. She stopped immediately in front of the young prince who was too dumbstruck to speak. She looked at Brida and then back to Alric.

"You look very nice tonight, Highness," offered the Clanswoman. "Perhaps one day you'll be old enough to wear a grown-up dress."

Anna ignored the princess, staring into Alric's eyes. The music began, and Brida tried to interrupt the moment by uttering, "Shall we dance, Alric?"

Anna leaned forward, kissing Alric on the lips. Beverly stood silently, witness to the shock that reverberated around the room as the kiss lingered.

"I believe this dance is mine," Anna finally said, taking the hapless youth by the hand.

A voice interrupted Beverly's observations. Jack Marlowe was standing beside her, holding out his hand. "Shall we dance?" he offered.

"No, we shall not," she replied.

The look on the cavalier's face was priceless. For once, the young man was struck dumb, and Beverly revelled in the quiet moment. He soon recovered, however, spotting a black-haired beauty across the room, moving quickly to intercept her. Beverly chuckled, some people never changed. She wandered over to Gerald who sat in his chair, the poles now removed.

"How are you feeling?" she asked.

"Much better, Beverly, thank you. It does me good to be here, seeing her have fun like this."

Beverly reached toward her sword.

"Are you expecting trouble?" he asked in concern.

"No," she responded, "just getting this." She dangled a necklace in front of him. "We found it when we went looking for you. I thought you might like to give it to the princess."

"Thank you," he said, deeply touched. "It cost a lot."

"It certainly did," she agreed. "Perhaps next time you go out to buy a present you can NOT get kidnapped by a strange creature?"

He chuckled, "I shall do my best!"

Lady Aubrey wandered over. "The princess seems to be enjoying herself," she commented.

"She's growing up," said Gerald.

"Was I like that?" Beverly asked.

"No," said Gerald, "you were worse."

"Worse?" she objected. "How was I worse?"

"Oh come on, Beverly. You were sneaking off to the smithy all the time."

Beverly blushed, while Aubrey smiled, "That sounds more like the Beverly I know.

A well-dressed young man approached them, bowing deeply at the waist. "Might I beg the honour of a dance, Dame Beverly?" he asked.

It was Aubrey who answered the question, "She won't dance, but I'd love to."

The man smiled, extending his hand to Lady Aubrey, and guided her onto the dance floor.

"Do you miss Bodden?" asked Gerald.

"I do," Beverly responded, "though I know one day I'll return there to settle down."

"Will that include marriage, do you think?"

Beverly turned to him, her face turning red.

Gerald was holding up his hand to ward off her anger, "I only ask out of curiosity. One day Bodden will need an heir."

"I will never marry," Beverly stated, calming her voice. "You, of all people, should know that."

"Never is long time," he said. "It can be quite lonely. Believe me, I've trod that path."

"You don't have to be married to have a family," she said. "You and the princess are proof of that."

"Fair enough," he replied.

They lapsed into a companionable silence while they watched the dancers perform their graceful moves.

"What do you think the princess will have us do next?" asked Beverly. "It's nearly winter."

Gerald watched the princess as she gazed into Alric's eyes. "I suspect we'll winter here and then move south in the spring. I think we'll be seeing much more of the young prince in our future."

"What lies to the south?" she asked.

"The Great Sea of Storms. She's always wanted to visit the ocean."

"It would be nice to relax by the sea," Beverly said.

"Relax? I doubt we'll relax. Life with this Princess of Merceria is anything but relaxing."

"You sound disappointed."

"Nonsense, I thrive on it. It keeps me young."

"You know, Gerald, it's a pity you have to stay in that chair, else I'd ask you to dance."

Gerald tore his eyes off the princess to look in horror at Beverly, "Are you serious?"

"No, Gerald, I know how much you hate dancing. But perhaps one day, when the princess weds, you'll have to make an exception."

"I would gladly do that," he replied.

A small commotion at the door captured Beverly's attention, and she spotted Dame Hayley entering, still wearing her armour. As soon as the ranger spotted the two of them, she made her way toward them.

"Where's the princess?" she asked, a flushed look to her face.

"She's dancing with the prince," said Gerald. "Why, whatever's the matter?"

"We've received news from Merceria. The princess needs to hear it."

"Let them finish their dance," said Gerald. "She deserves to enjoy this moment."

They waited in silence, though Hayley kept shifting her feet in agitation.

The music ended, and Alric gallantly escorted Anna back to where the rest were waiting.

"I return her to you, Commander Matheson," he said, bowing.

Anna smiled at the compliment, and then noticed the ranger, "Hayley? Is something wrong? I thought you were on duty?"

"I was, Highness, but we've received news from Merceria."

"Speak freely, Hayley. We have no secrets from Prince Alric."

"I'm afraid your mother, the queen, is dead."

If Anna was upset, she didn't show it. "Do we know how she died?"

"The letter said she had a very short illness and then passed away in her sleep. We've only just received the news. I'm afraid it took weeks just to get here."

"What will you do, Anna?" asked Alric. "Will you return to Merceria?"

Anna looked around at the small group before answering, "No, I shall remain. She's been dead to me for years. These people are my family now, and this is where I need to be."

TWENTY-EIGHT

Tivilton

SPRING 961 MC

W inter was mild that year, and soon the cold weather made way for the warmer days of spring. They had wintered in Loranguard, much as Gerald had predicted, and now they were travelling south toward Riversend and the sea.

Alric rode with Anna in the carriage while the Royal Train, which had grown significantly since their last trip, was trailing along behind. Anna had placed Gerald in charge of the entourage, and he had, at the prince's suggestion, coordinated the efforts with the cavalier, Jack Marlowe. It had been quite the job, but Anna had seen little of the details for she had spent most her time with Prince Alric.

"Isn't it glorious?" she mused, looking out the window.

Alric was sitting across from her and smiled. "It's a lovely part of the country," he agreed.

"I'm so glad you came with us," she said. "I've grown very accustomed to your presence."

"And I with yours," he agreed, "though it took some doing to arrange this."

"Whatever happened to Brida?" she asked.

Alric looked a trifle uncomfortable. He shifted in his seat before answering, "She went back home, to the Clans."

"She didn't stay? I thought she wanted to marry you?"

"She did, but I refused. It was all part of Cuthbert's plan, you see, and I didn't want any part of it."

"What plan?" she asked, growing concerned.

"I suppose it doesn't matter if I tell you now. My brother wanted an alliance with the Clans."

"That doesn't sound so bad," she remarked. "Wouldn't that bring peace to the border?"

"Oh, there's a lot more," he warned. "He wanted them to help invade Merceria."

"Surely not! Doesn't he realize how powerful we are?"

"He was convinced that you were weak from the uprising. Thought it would just be a matter of marching. He had information that your father is not a popular ruler; perhaps they would incite another uprising."

"I'm sure that wouldn't work, not after what happened to the last rebels."

"He said he had the blessings of my father, but I didn't believe him. My father would never support someone usurping a rightful king. He said as much when we were approached by the Earl of Eastwood's man."

"They came to you for help?"

"Yes, but he was thrown out of court for it."

"So what did you do about your brother?"

"I wrote to the one person who could sort out this whole mess," he replied.

"Your father?"

"No, my mother. She's the sensible one and the king's closest advisor, if the truth be known."

"What did you tell her, exactly?"

"I suggested that the future of Weldwyn lay with Merceria, not the Clans."

"Was that because of me, Alric?"

"Partially," he replied, and then smiled. "The Clans often fight amongst themselves, there's no guarantee an alliance or treaty would be honoured by all."

"What makes you think it would work with Merceria?" she asked, a look of mischief in her eyes.

"You do delight in challenging me, Anna," he replied. "I thought perhaps a Royal Marriage would cement an alliance. What do you think?"

"Are you proposing, Alric?"

"I'm afraid it's not up to me, Anna, or you, for that matter. We are both bound by our duty to our respective kingdoms. These things take time, but they're not beyond the realm of possibility. It would be years before a decision were made, and you're still young."

"I would be happy to wait for such a thing if it were to happen," she said.

"You say that now," observed Alric, "but when you've returned to the

Mercerian court, and young nobles are fawning all over you, you might change your mind. You'll probably forget all about me."

"I will never forget about you, Alric. You're a true friend."

They sat quietly for a while, watching the green fields as they passed. It was Alric who finally broke the silence, "I think you'll like the sea."

"I hear it's quite fascinating," she said. "How much further have we to go?"

Alric chuckled, "Quite a while yet. We've passed Walverton but we still have to go through Tivilton, and that's just over half way."

"Tivilton," mused Anna, "that's an interesting name. Who rules there?"

"A baron by the name of Lord Parvan Luminor."

"It sounds Elvish," she said.

"He is. He's been the baron for hundreds of years."

"Is the entire town full of elves?"

"No," Alric replied, "but there's a lot of them there. Centuries ago the elves lived in the Draenor Wood. During the founding, they helped King Loran, and as a reward, the elves were given a seat on the council."

"So the elves live in the woods?"

"No, they moved into a town when Humans began showing up. It's quite remarkable, really, Elves and Humans working together. I wish other races could get along so easily."

"They can," Anna remarked. "We worked with Elves and Dwarves during the uprising. It's not their races that are problematic, it's people's attitudes."

"I suppose you're right," he agreed.

"Will we see the baron do you think?"

"I see no reason why we might not visit him, although we might want to send a rider ahead to warn him we're coming."

Anna perked up, "Let's do so, immediately. I'd love a chance to use some of my Elvish."

"You speak Elvish?" he asked, a look of incredulity on his face.

"As a matter of fact, I do. It's one of several languages I've managed to pick up."

"What other languages do you speak?" he asked.

"I'm now fluent in Saurian," she replied, "and I know quite a bit of Elvish and a smattering of Dwarf. I'd love to learn Orcish someday."

"You astound me, Anna, how do you find time for such things?"

"I have an active mind," she replied. "I'm always thinking about things, and I love planning. Gerald says it's my gift."

As the wagon began to slow, Anna sat forward, peering out the windows. "It looks like they're preparing to water the horses. I suppose it would be a good time to send a rider ahead.

Alric made an exaggerated bow, "I shall do as Your Highness requests."

It took a further two days to reach Tivilton, but by the time the carriage arrived the baron was prepared for them. They pulled up in front of a keep located at one end of the town. It reminded Anna of Bodden, but on a much larger scale. The baron greeted them with a deep bow as they exited their carriage.

"Greetings, Lord Prince, Your Highness," he said.

"*It is a great honour to meet you, most noble Elf,*" Anna said in Elvish.

The look of surprise on Lord Parvan's face told Alric all he needed to know. He might not understand the Elven tongue, but he saw the effect the compliment had on the Elf.

"You honour me, Highness," the baron responded. "It is a great honour to host you as our guest. Shall we proceed to the hall? I have gathered the notables to welcome you."

"Notables?" whispered Anna to Alric.

The young prince leaned toward her to whisper, "Yes, people who have proved their worth. More than just nobles or rich people. It's an Elven tradition, I hear."

"It's true," offered the baron, his keen hearing picking up on their conversation. "We Elves do not have the same class structure you have in Human society."

"And yet," observed Anna, "you are still called baron?"

"I am," he acknowledged, "though it is more of a Human affectation. I prefer to be called simply Lord Parvan."

"Tell me, Lord Parvan, do you know Lord Arandil Stormcloak?" asked Anna.

The Elf stopped to look her in the face. "I do, though I haven't seen him for centuries. I'm surprised you know his name."

"He helped us stop an invasion," she replied. "He was of great assistance to us."

"Indeed?" replied the baron, resuming his walk. "You are full of surprises for one so young. You must tell me more of this, later."

"I would be delighted," she replied. She looked at Alric whose face wore a smile. "Shall we proceed, Your Highness?"

Just then the second carriage pulled up. Out climbed Revi, Lady Aubrey, and Lily. The Saurian was chattering on in her own language when the baron suddenly wheeled upon hearing the noise.

"What is this?" he enquired.

"This is Lily," offered Anna, "she's a Saurian. We found her in Merceria."

"It cannot be," observed the baron, "for the Saurians are extinct."

"Apparently not," volunteered Alric. "What do you know of them?"

The baron composed himself, resuming his earlier state of calmness, "They died off long before I was born."

"As you can see," corrected Anna, "they still exist."

"That much is readily apparent," said the baron, "however, it matters not. We have made preparations for your arrival, Highness, shall we proceed?"

Alric nodded, "By all means, Baron."

They were led into the great hall where tables had been set in anticipation of their arrival. The servants came in to usher people to their assigned seats. Anna was placed to Lord Parvan's left, with Gerald beside her, while Alric sat to the baron's right-hand side. Anna was surprised to see a small mat beside her chair and realized it was for Tempus. The great dog trotted in with Sophie and then lay down, dwarfing the tiny mat with his bulk while Sophie was shown to a chair further down the table.

Once they were seated, the baron rose to his feet, holding his goblet before him. "It is with great honour that I welcome his most Royal Highness, Prince Alric to our fair city of Tivilton," he announced, "and that of his guest, Princess Anna of Merceria. May they live long and healthy lives."

There were cheers all around and then the baron sat, waving his hand in a circle above his head. Anna was about to ask the purpose for such behaviour when some music started. It was played on a harp, the sound echoing in the great hall, lending an other-worldly beauty to the place.

"Such a haunting refrain," commented Gerald "Tell me, Lord Baron, what is this tune?"

"It is an Elven lament, called the Lost. If you prefer, I can have them play something more cheerful? We normally play this first to remember our brethren."

"Why is it called the Lost?" asked Anna.

"Many centuries ago, before the coming of man, a great fleet set forth on a voyage of discovery. What became of them is unknown to us, but it is said that even today, when Elves scan the seas, they are looking for the return of their lost cousins."

"I had no idea Elves went to sea," commented Anna.

"Oh yes," said the baron, "the sea Elves of Telethor are the stuff of legend."

"Were you around when this happened?" asked Anna.

"No, I was not," the baron replied, "even Elves don't live forever."

"I thought Elves were immortal," said Gerald.

"Immortal? No, but we live a very long time compared to Humans. I, myself, have lived over a thousand years, though I am considered old by my race."

"Well," commented Gerald, "you don't look a day over five hundred." He raised his cup in salute, touching goblets with the baron, who laughed at the compliment. Gerald gaped at the meal placed before him, for it was rich with succulent meats and heaps of vegetables. The baron ate sparingly, but his guests dug in with gusto.

Gerald was beginning to feel the effects of the food, for his belt had tightened significantly. He was about to say as much to Anna, but when he turned to speak to her, he saw an Elf in fine clothes approach the baron. The messenger stooped to whisper in the baron's ear while Lord Parvan nodded his head.

"Is something wrong, Baron?" asked Alric.

"Nothing that need concern Your Highness," the baron replied. "Let us continue this feast."

The room fell silent for a moment, and then individual conversations arose, once more. Gerald whispered to Anna, "The baron doesn't look happy."

"I suspect," she replied, "that he received some bad news."

"You'd think if it was that bad, he'd be running off to see to it," said Gerald.

"He's an Elf," she said. "They have a much longer view of things. I've read that they'll sometimes take years to make a decision."

"That's probably why Humans were able to drive them back into the woods."

"That may be true, Gerald, but let's not forget they smashed the cities of the Orcs into the ground, forcing them to take refuge in the far reaches of the land."

"I suppose that's true," he confessed. "I'm glad they're on our side."

The meal seemed to carry on forever, and it was well past midnight by the time it started to break up. Gerald was now recovered from his overindulgence of food and escorted Anna to her room.

"The baron has asked for a meeting tomorrow," she said, "so try to get some sleep."

"I think I had plenty of that after the meal. I slept through most of the speeches. Did I miss anything important?"

"Only the part where they complained about your snoring," she replied.

"What?" he said, his face growing red in embarrassment.

"I'm kidding, Gerald, no one saw you sleeping, except me. I thought you needed the rest."

"I'm fully recovered from Loranguard, Anna," he said defensively.

"I know, Gerald. You just looked so peaceful after the heavy meal; I didn't have the heart to wake you."

"That's nice of you," he relented, "but now I'm wide awake."

"You could take Tempus for a stroll; he's a little restless. He hasn't had much exercise today."

"I'll take you up on that offer," he replied. "A nice walk in the cool evening air would do wonders for me. I'll bring him back in the morning, I wouldn't want him to wake you up."

"An excellent idea," she replied, "and that way I'll know you have someone to look after you while you're walking around."

The grounds of the baron's estate were quite elaborate. It was decorated in an Elven style, with high, slender columns covered with vines and other plants. The entire area looked almost like a forest glade, save for the spots where the great stone of the house was exposed. Wonderful as the estate was, Gerald found it stuffy and unearthly. He wandered across the grounds heading in the direction of the town, intent on seeing more common architecture. They had been told that Humans came to the city after the baron was appointed and he was glad to see the buildings in town looked more like what he was accustomed to. Being late at night, the streets were mostly empty, but as he walked Tempus, he heard the sounds of voices and altered course. In due time he came across the source; an old tavern that was packed with locals. When he drew closer, the voices grew more distinct, and he soon heard an argument.

"The baron will do nothing, I tell you," a man was yelling.

"Then we must talk to the prince, surely he'll help," a woman's voice replied.

"Lord Parvan won't permit it, you know it's illegal to enter the wood," the first voice stated.

Gerald moved closer and opened the door to the tavern, eliciting a loud squeak from the hinges. The warmth of the room washed over him as he stood in the doorway, surveying his surroundings.

"Good evening," he said to the suddenly quiet room. "I couldn't help but overhear your conversation. Is there something I can help you with?"

A rather large man in a dirty brown tunic stepped forward, "Be welcome, stranger," he called out. "Can I get you a drink?"

As Gerald stepped forward, the eyes of the crowd went wide when

Tempus followed behind him. "Don't mind him," Gerald offered, "his name's Tempus. He's friendly, more or less."

A dark-haired woman spoke up, "Are you here with the prince?" she asked.

"I am," he confirmed. "I'm actually here with Princess Anna of Merceria. Our party is the guest of His Highness, and we are travelling through here on our way south."

"Perhaps," she rasped, "you may be able to help us."

"I would certainly like to try," he replied. "What seems to be the trouble?"

Emboldened by the response, the woman stepped forward. "Something in the Draenor Wood has been killing our livestock and needs to be tracked down."

"Surely," said Gerald, "that's something better brought to your baron's attention, isn't it?"

"The baron won't listen," she said, "and it's forbidden to enter the woods. Only the baron and his guards go there."

"Why is that? Surely you hunt?"

"He won't allow it, it carries the penalty of death."

"Doesn't that seem a tad extreme for going into the woods?"

"Now you see our dilemma," the woman complained. "We're not allowed in the woods, and yet the creature that kills our animals wanders free."

"Perhaps," offered Gerald, "there is a reasonable explanation. He might be concerned for your welfare? How long has the woods been off limits?"

The woman gazed at him as if dumbstruck. "It has always been so, but I forget, you're not from these parts. Perhaps you hold some sway over the prince?"

"I think it's safe to say I know him, aye."

"Would you bring our concerns to him? Perhaps he could persuade the baron to stop this creature, whatever it is."

"I shall bring it to his attention immediately," Gerald promised, "though I cannot guarantee his actions."

"That is all we can ask," she replied.

The walk back to the hall found Gerald deep in thought. Why would the baron forbid his people to go into the woods? Didn't they come from the woods in the first place? He thought back to the tavern and tried to recall their faces. They had all been Human; was that the crux of the matter? Was there something in the woods that the baron didn't want Humans to see? It was a far-fetched idea, but he was unable to come up with anything else.

It was the middle of the night by the time he returned. Making his way to his room, he resolved to talk it over with Prince Alric at the first opportunity. He climbed into bed and prepared to close his eyes only to have the feeling he was being watched. Opening his eyes, he saw Tempus staring at him.

"Lie down, Tempus," he commanded. "It's time to go to sleep."

The dog sat, staring at him in mute reply.

"There's no room for you on my bed, Tempus, you'll have to make do with the floor."

The great beast lay down on the floor and let out a large yawn. Gerald smiled and closed his eyes once more.

Early in the morning Gerald made his way to the princess's room. Sophie was already up and carrying a tray of food as Gerald found her.

"Let me get the door for you, Sophie," he said.

"Thank you, Gerald," she replied.

The door opened to reveal the princess, sitting up in her bed. She was poring over some letters, which were scattered all over her sheets.

Tempus bounded through the doorway, eliciting a cry of joy from Anna. He jumped up on the bed, and she pat his head, shoving the letters aside.

"What's all this?" asked Gerald, his eyes taking in the mass of paper.

"Letters from my couriers," she replied. "Most of them have only just caught up to me."

"Anything of interest?"

"Quite a lot, actually. You remember Edgar Greenfield?"

"Yes, of course. He was the first courier you hired. I haven't seen him in years."

"He's been corresponding regularly. He has provided more details on the death of the queen."

"Your mother? I thought she died after an illness?"

"So did everyone else, but it looks more like she was poisoned. She did grow sick, but less than a day later she was dead. The talk in the town is that she was poisoned and rumours are it was done by Lady Penelope."

"Rumours will say all kinds of things," offered Gerald. "What makes you think these are any different?"

"He describes the symptoms of her illness. I should like to confer with Revi, but I suspect they are caused by warriors bane. You once said to me that there were plants similar to warriors moss, do you remember?"

"Aye, you have to look for the flecks of blue to identify it."

"That's true, but after you were injured, I had to prepare the moss to help you. I found a book describing warriors bane, it's very similar but without the blue specks."

"I'm glad you did so, or I'd likely not be here today. So you think warriors bane was used on the queen?"

"Yes, the symptoms are similar. The skin takes on an almost waxy look, with a darkening around the eyes. Edgar talked to some of the queen's servants. He remarks that they mentioned another curious side effect, a darkening of the roots of the fingernails."

"But she'd have to have it applied to her, wouldn't she?"

"That's what I thought at first, but then I remembered that it can be boiled into a tea, I suspect that's how it was done."

"So it looks like the king's mistress killed the queen? I suppose it makes sense, she wants her out of the way. What do you think will happen now?"

"I suspect she'll convince the king to marry her, after a suitable mourning period, of course."

"You don't seem overly upset," he observed.

"I'm not," she replied. "I know at one time I would have been devastated, but my mother abandoned me many years ago. I feel no sympathy for her."

"Remind me never to get on your bad side," he commented.

"You could never do that, Gerald. I value your opinion, even if we don't always agree. You shall always be able to speak your mind."

"Yes, well, on that matter, there's something I need to bring to Prince Alric's attention."

"What is it?" she responded.

"When I was out walking Tempus last night we found ourselves at a tavern."

Anna laughed, "That's just like you, Gerald. Going out in the middle of the night and finding a place to drink."

He couldn't help but grin, "Yes, well, anyway, we ran across a group of locals. They were friendly enough, but they claim to have a big problem."

"What's that?"

"Something's been killing off their livestock, and the baron won't do anything about it."

"That seems surprising," countered Anna. "Are you sure? He didn't strike me as that type of person."

"Whatever is doing it lives in the woods, but the townsfolk are forbidden to enter it."

"What do you mean, forbidden?"

"Precisely what I said. The Draenor Wood has always been forbidden to enter."

"That seems strange," said Anna, "perhaps there's something dangerous in there."

"Of course there is, and it's killing their livelihood. Something needs to be done!"

"Should we take this to the baron?" she asked.

"I suspect he'll just stonewall us. It was suggested we might talk to Alric directly. Wouldn't he be able to overrule the baron?"

"Difficult to say," said Anna. "The rules are different here than in Merceria. Were I at home I would say definitely, but here in Weldwyn there are limits to the power of the Royal House."

"So what do we do?" he asked.

"We'll talk to Alric," she replied. "He'll hopefully have a better idea of what's possible."

"Do you think he'll help?"

Anna smiled before replying, "I'm sure he will, now let me have my breakfast, and then we'll go find him." She looked down at the plate Sophie had set on the side table. "You better have the sausages, Gerald, they look a bit over-cooked to me."

"With pleasure, Your Highness," he said, filching a link.

Alric, standing in front of a fire as he read a letter, heard a knock. He turned to see Jack opening the door.

"The princess and Commander Matheson are here to see you, Highness," the caviler announced.

"Show them in, Jack," he replied.

"News from home?" asked Anna, as she spied the paper.

"Yes, from my brother, Alstan. It seems the queen has agreed with my decision regarding the Clan alliance."

"I'm happy for you, Alric," she said, "but I need to bring some disturbing facts to your attention."

"This sounds serious," he responded. "Shall we sit?"

"Of course," she agreed, taking a seat.

Alric sat down in the chair facing her while Gerald moved toward the fireplace to warm his hands. "There's quite a chill in the hall this morning," he commented.

"And likely to grow even chillier with the news I bring," added Anna.

"Now that sounds truly ominous," Alric responded. "You have me intrigued."

"It seems the baron is keeping secrets from you, Alric."

"We all have secrets, Anna. What specific secrets are you talking about?"

"Gerald was out walking last night and came across some locals, Humans that is."

"I see," the young prince responded. "And?"

"I'll let Gerald explain," said Anna. "He was there."

Alric turned his attention to the old commander who was briskly rubbing his hands. "It looks like something's been killing livestock."

"I assume, when you say 'something', you mean an animal of some sort?"

"Aye, that's the impression I got."

"Why don't they hunt it down?" Alric asked.

"The creature is coming from the Draenor Wood, a place that is forbidden to enter."

"Forbidden? Under whose authority?"

"The baron's."

"Has the baron sent anyone into the woods?"

"He has gone there on occasion over the years, along with his personal guard, but no one's been dispatched to deal with this problem."

"Has he said anything to them?"

"He appears to be unresponsive to their requests," said Gerald.

"We thought," added Anna, "that you might have some sway over the baron. Perhaps you might recommend a course of action?"

"I doubt he'd listen to me," said Alric.

"But you're the prince," exclaimed Anna. "Surely you have authority over him?"

"This isn't Merceria, Anna," Alric explained. "There are limits to what I can do. The baron would surely take offense at any attempt to overrule him, and I daresay my father would agree. The Elves of Tivilton have always been allies of the crown."

"So what are we to do," asked Gerald, "let them suffer?"

"No," replied Alric, "I won't do that. I shall speak to the baron, perhaps if I reason with him, he'll do something."

"Thank you, Alric," said Anna. "I know it puts you in a difficult situation."

"I'm beginning to see there's a lot more to being a prince than carousing all the time," Alric responded. "I shall visit the baron this afternoon, it'll give me some time to go over my arguments. Would you care to join me?"

"I'd be delighted," said Anna. "I've a few ideas of my own."

"It's settled, then. Jack, if you'd be so kind, I think we'll need to make some notes."

"Yes, Highness, I'll fetch quill and ink."

TWENTY-NINE

Baron Parvan

SPRING 961 MC

B aron Parvan Luminor waited in the great hall. He had been told the prince wanted to see him and so stood, dressed in his most exquisite robes. He was an imposing Elf, fully six feet tall with long, black hair and a fair complexion. He was old, by Elven standards, and yet appeared as youthful as anyone else in the court, save for the young prince himself.

When the visitors were announced, he turned from his thoughts to see Prince Alric and his entourage arrive. He was accompanied by his body-guard, the cavalier Jack Marlowe, but the baron was surprised to see the Mercerian visitor, Princess Anna and her advisor.

"Greetings, Lord Prince," said the baron, with ever so slight a nod of his head.

"Lord Parvan," said Alric, "I'm happy we have this opportunity to speak, I understand you are a very busy man."

"I am always at your disposal, Highness," the baron soothed. "Please tell me what is so vexing that such an assembly must be required in so short a time?"

"I understand that there have been animal attacks of late?" Alric queried.

The baron narrowed his eyes, "Yes, there have, though it is no concern of yours, Highness. I have taken steps to rectify the situation."

"Might I enquire what those steps are?" asked Anna.

"Those are the concerns of Weldwyn," said Lord Parvan with a frosty stare, "and are not to be discussed with outsiders."

"And if I ask the same question?" queried Alric.

Lord Parvan bowed slightly, "Then I might be willing to discuss such matters, but, I fear, the present company precludes such possibilities."

"I must insist," pressed Alric. "Princess Anna here is an ally and a friend."

"Still," the baron persisted, "there are certain aspects which are not open for discussion."

"And if I command you?" pressed Alric, growing red in the face.

The baron sighed, "Very well, Highness, ask your questions, and I shall endeavour to answer them."

"What steps are you taking to protect your people?" asked the young prince.

"I have stepped up the patrols," Lord Parvan responded. "Though I doubt many have noticed, the Elven Guard are good at concealing their presence."

"The Elven Guard?" said Gerald.

Lord Parvan looked at Gerald with a look of contempt, "My own personal guard. You see, Lord Prince, I take this situation very seriously."

"Have you tried to track down this creature?" asked Anna.

"It is forbidden to enter the Draenor Wood," he replied.

"Forbidden by who?" asked Gerald.

"By ancient law," burst out Lord Parvan. "A fact which should even penetrate that thick skull of yours."

Alric was surprised by the sudden outburst, "I know of no such law."

The baron smiled, but looked insincere, "It is an ancient law, Your Highness, handed down through the generations. It is forbidden to enter the Draenor Wood."

"Why?" pressed Gerald, his anger increasing. "What's there?"

"Nothing that would interest you, Human!" burst out the baron.

Alric was incensed, "Answer the question, Baron. What is in the woods?"

The baron turned his attention back to the young prince. He was fighting to calm himself until a strange sense of serenity seemed to descend on him. "It is a dangerous place, Highness, full of all sorts of creatures. It was thought that the safest approach was to leave the woods to look after itself."

"But it doesn't," said Anna, "as evidenced by the attacks."

"Yes," agreed Alric, "how long have these attacks been going on?"

"It has been on and off for years, Highness. It lapses in the winter and returns in the spring. The deaths are manageable."

"Manageable? We're talking about peoples livelihoods here!" exclaimed Gerald.

"I must agree with Commander Matheson," said Alric. "These attacks must be stopped."

"And what would you have me do?" said the baron. "It is forbidden to enter the woods."

"And yet," said Alric, "I have word that you have done so with your guards on several occasions over the years."

The baron looked speechless.

"I propose a hunting expedition," offered Alric.

"My men will not enter the wood," stated Lord Parvan.

"Mine will," said Alric.

"You have no hunters," commented the baron. "They would be useless."

"Not so," offered Anna, "we have a ranger, and my people are not intimidated by your laws."

The baron's firm resolve began to weaken, "Very well, Highness. If you are determined to continue this quest, there is little I can do to stop you."

"Thank you," said Alric. "We shall make plans to leave tomorrow; it's far too late in the day to organize a hunt of this size."

"As you see fit," surrendered Lord Parvan, "but I warn you, you will not like what you discover and once you witness it, there is no going back."

"What's that supposed to mean?" asked Alric. "Is that meant as a threat?"

The baron sighed, "No, Highness, merely a warning. I will stand in your way no longer."

Alric felt out of his depth. Something strange was happening here, but he couldn't quite fathom it. He turned to Anna, "We have preparations to make," he said.

"Of course, Highness," she responded.

They swept from the room leaving Lord Parvan wandering back and forth, deep in thought.

"What do you think has him so riled up?" asked Alric.

"I think," said Anna, "that Gerald managed to hit a soft spot. His true colours are coming out. He's hiding something."

"Yes," agreed Alric, "but what? I don't want to lead us into unnecessary danger."

"We have your guards and the Knights of the Hound," offered Gerald. "We can take care of ourselves."

"What's our next move?" asked Alric.

"Gerald will see to organizing the hunt. I'll send Hayley out to discover what information she can gather about the attacks."

"Don't send her out alone, Anna," said Alric. "I wouldn't put it past the baron to throw up barriers."

"Well said," replied Anna. "I'll send two knights with her. Right now she's the only tracker we have."

"Actually," offered Gerald, "I've done some tracking in my time."

"You're just full of surprises, Commander," commented Alric. "I'm glad you're on our side."

Gerald smiled at the compliment.

"All right, you two," said Anna, "if you're finished with this bonding moment, we have work to do."

～

The edge of the woods was clearly defined. Hayley looked up from the carcass toward the heavily forested tree line. Two Elven guards watched them from a distance, but neither interfered as she traced the prints across the ground.

"They look to head straight into the woods," she remarked.

"Can you tell what it is?" asked Sir Barnsley.

"Something large," the ranger countered, "but definitely not a wolf or cat. Whatever it is has claws and teeth."

"So it's not a gryphon?"

"No," replied Hayley. "Why is everyone so quick to complain about gryphons? They have beaks; this creature definitely had teeth, rather large ones actually."

"So, not a gryphon, then," said Dame Abigail. "Perhaps a dragon?"

Hayley had to think that one over carefully before answering, "I hadn't thought of that, but I would say it's unlikely. A dragon has wings; this creature ran across the ground back to the woods."

"That still doesn't preclude a dragon," Abigail insisted.

"Dragons are said to be quite large, I think it's unlikely."

"How about a wyvern?" Dame Abigail persisted.

"They're smaller, but they still fly. No, I think this is something else."

"I've never understood the difference between a dragon and a wyvern," remarked Abigail. "Aren't they really the same thing?"

"No," commented Hayley, "dragons are large and intelligent. Some say they even have their own language. They fly using wings that grow from their back. Wyverns, on the other hand, have wings instead of arms, more like a bird I suppose. They also have a stinger in their tail."

"What about a flightless dragon?" offered Sir Barnsley. "Do such things actually exist?"

"They're called drakes," replied Hayley. "I've never seen one, but they do exist."

"And what are those, exactly," asked Abigail.

"They're related to dragons but without wings. They're said to be less intelligent, more like wild animals." She stared at the tracks before her. "I think you've got it, Abby. These tracks would be consistent with a drake."

"Glad I could help," the knight replied.

"Somehow," said Sir Barnsley, "I felt safer when I didn't know. Are you sure it's a drake?"

"Unless it's something else we don't know about, sure."

"So you're positive?" he asked.

"More or less," admitted Hayley.

"And how do we fight a drake?"

"I have no idea," said Hayley, "I've never had to fight one. We'll have to speak to Master Bloom, he's the expert in such things."

"How much further will we follow the trail?" asked Dame Abigail.

"This is as far as we go," stated Hayley. "We'll wait for the full expedition to be assembled. We don't want to encounter this thing by ourselves."

"What do we do now?" asked Sir Barnsley.

"We return to the hall and report our findings. We'll start pushing into the woods at first light tomorrow, the tracks are relatively easy to follow."

Anna and Gerald rode over to where Alric was astride his horse.

"Is everything ready?" asked Anna.

"I have my guards formed up and ready to go. What's the order of march?"

"Hayley and her escort will lead," offered Gerald, "followed by the Knights of the Hound and your men. Once the tracks get fresher, we'll spread out into a line."

"How do we kill this thing?" asked the prince.

"That's for Revi to explain," said Anna. "Here he comes now."

Revi Bloom rode beside his apprentice, Aubrey. "We're here," called out the mage. "I hope we didn't keep you waiting."

"What took you so long?" asked Gerald, slightly annoyed. "We've been waiting all morning."

"Never mind him, Master Bloom," said Anna, "we've only just arrived. What can you tell us about this creature?"

"If what Dame Hayley has told us is true, it appears likely to be a drake."

"Can we kill a drake?" asked Alric.

"Certainly, Your Highness, but it will be difficult."

"Care to elaborate?" asked Anna.

"I mean to say it will not be easy," countered the mage.

"Details?" pressed Gerald.

"Well, it's likely to be tough," replied Revi with a smirk.

"What he means to say," offered Lady Aubrey, "is that the skin of a drake is quite tough. Our weapons are likely to bounce off of it."

"Then how do we injure it," asked Gerald.

"It has a soft underbelly," explained Aubrey. "We'll have to get in what hits we can."

"Doesn't this thing walk on all fours?" asked Alric.

"Yes," agreed Revi, "making it all the more difficult."

"So you're saying what, exactly? We're supposed to have it roll over on its back so we can kill it?" the confused young price asked.

"However unlikely that is, yes, that would be the preferred method of doing it in," agreed Revi.

"Anything else we should know about, Master Mage?" asked Gerald. "Does it breathe fire, for example?"

"No," the mage replied, "though it will have very sharp claws. Its tail is likely not prehensile, so I doubt it will use it as a weapon."

"We disagree on that point," offered Aubrey.

"You're not exactly making me feel better about this expedition," complained Alric. "Is there any good news?"

"Look on the bright side of things," Revi offered. "Dame Hayley will have no problem following the trail!"

"What about magic?" asked Anna.

"Drakes are not known to use magic," offered the mage.

"Not known? How much about drakes do you truly know?" asked the princess.

"Very little, actually," confessed Aubrey. "It would be different if we were back in Wincaster with a library full of books, but we're going on memory alone here. We never expected to come across a drake in Weldwyn."

"Then we shall have to improvise," suggested Gerald.

"I don't like the sound of that," complained Alric.

"Gerald and Beverly are great at improvising," stated Anna. "Don't worry, Alric, things will turn out fine. Will your men stand against such a creature?"

Alric turned in the saddle to look at his guard. Their swords were scabbarded, but each carried a long spear and shield. "I believe they will, yes. They're loyal and brave, but all the same, I'd hate to lose any of them."

"Then we shall do our best to ensure that doesn't happen," said Anna, turning to Gerald. "Where's Beverly?"

"She's up front with Hayley, along with Arnim. Where's Tempus?"

"I had him stay behind with Sophie and Lady Nicole. He can be overly protective sometimes, and I don't want him getting killed by a drake."

"We will move out on your command, Highness," Gerald said, looking to Alric.

"Very well," he declared, "let's begin."

The host began moving forward, Hayley out in front. Her bow was strung, but she carried it parallel to the ground as she cast about for tracks. Beverly and Arnim stood nearby, their swords in hand, watching to either side, alert to any possible danger. The ranger cast her eyes about, waving the group forward a hundred paces or so and then signalled a stop while she once more looked over the ground in front of her.

The pace was leisurely, but all were on alert, for a creature such as this could spring upon them on a moment's notice. Anna rode at the back of the line, along with Alric and his men, while her knights followed the ranger's small group. Revi and Aubrey rode just between the knights and Alric's guard.

The morning seemed to drag on with the trek through the woods soon becoming monotonous. The woods were thick with underbrush, while the canopy of the leaves blocked the direct sunlight, lending an eerie gloom to the proceedings.

Beverly, astride her great warhorse, galloped down the line. "We are getting close, Highness," she reported. "Dame Hayley says we should ready our weapons. She suspects a lair will be about here somewhere."

"Is it likely to attack us from hiding?" asked Gerald.

"Hayley thinks it unlikely," replied the redheaded knight. "The creature attacks at night and appears to be nocturnal."

"So it may be sleeping?" asked Alric.

"Hayley suspects it will have a keen sense of smell," Beverly continued. "It'll likely smell us coming, or perhaps hear us. We should be ready to fight as soon as it's visible. It'll know the terrain in these parts, so under no circumstances should anyone run after it."

"Understood," replied Anna. "We'll heed the ranger's advice. Shall we begin to spread out?"

"Yes," agreed Beverly. "The soldiers should disperse to either side and try to keep some semblance of a line. They should be within arms reach of each other, it'll slow the pace, but if anyone sees anything, they must sing out. I'm going to send knights to either side of the line to cover the flanks."

Alric turned to Jack who barked out the commands to the troops. The line began to form while Beverly turned her mighty steed around, making her way back to the front of the column.

The troops took up their position and then began inching forward. The woods fell silent; everyone was holding their breath. Gerald could just make out Beverly on the left side of the line, anchoring the end. He glanced in the opposite direction to see Dame Levina holding her position with two other knights, but the foliage obstructed his view.

He caught sight of Hayley, moving down the line toward them.

"News?" he enquired.

"I think we've found the lair," she said. "It appears to be some old ruins of some sort."

"Ruins?" piped up Revi.

"Yes, overgrown stones, quite a lot of them, actually."

"What do you think, Aubrey?" the mage asked.

"That's likely the lair," she offered. "There are probably not very many caves in terrain like this."

"Agreed," said Revi. "The ruins will have some sort of cover, perhaps a partially built wall or floor that's still intact. Did you say it was made of stone?"

"Yes," confirmed Hayley, "though I don't recognize the style. It's like no stonework I've ever seen before."

"I should like to get a closer look," said Revi, "with Your Highness's permission?"

Anna nodded her approval, "All right, Master Bloom, but be careful. Hayley, take him down there."

"Yes, Highness," replied the ranger. "You'll have to leave your horse here, Master Bloom."

Gerald began to dismount.

"What do you think you're doing?" asked Anna.

"Going with them, Highness. Someone has to look after the healer."

"Good point," she agreed. "Gerald, be careful."

"I shall," he promised.

"I suppose," said Aubrey, "that means I have to stay here?"

"Precisely," said Anna. "You're a healer as well, we can't go risking the both of you."

"And I'm perfectly fine with that decision," Aubrey replied. "I'll happily let the others do all the work today."

"Come along then, Commander," said Hayley, "we have ruins to look at."

They advanced down the line until they were back out front. It was, to Gerald's eyes, a comical sight, for as he and Hayley crept forward, Revi insisted on hiking up his robes to free up his movement.

"You know," commented Hayley, "you don't have to wear robes all the time, Master Mage."

"I like the freedom it gives me," responded the mage, "and stop calling me Master Mage, you make me sound like an old man."

"But you are a Master Mage," she argued.

"Yes, but I'm not old like Gerald, here."

"Let's get on with this," interrupted Gerald, "and stop calling me old. Where are the stones, Hayley?"

"Just up there, you can see the first one on the right, covered in moss."

Gerald glanced ahead, spying his target. It was a large stone, easily two feet in height and equally as thick. There was something about it that didn't look right, but he was at a loss to recognize what it was. They moved forward until they could touch it.

"It's massive," commented Gerald. "How on earth would they get it here?"

"Magic," offered Revi. "They likely brought smaller stones and then merged them."

"You can do that with magic?" asked Hayley.

"I can't, but Earth Mages are known to be able to manipulate stone. It's said the Dwarven mages of the east build their city walls out of a single piece of stone."

"How would they do that?" asked Gerald.

"They would merge smaller stones together, much like melding two pieces of clay. Of course, it would take years for a wall of that size, but then Dwarves live a very long time compared to us."

"So why is the top of this stone so uneven?" asked Hayley.

"It's been blasted off, likely by magic," answered the mage.

"What kind of magic would do that?" asked Gerald. "Are we in danger?"

"Only from the drake. This likely happened hundreds of years ago, the rough stone surface has been smoothed a little with time and then overgrown with moss. I think it's safe to say whatever did this is long since gone."

"I can see another stone up ahead," pointed Gerald.

"Yes, there are all kinds around if you look carefully," added Hayley.

"It looks like a structure of some sort, though it's hard to say how big it was," offered Revi. "Let's move closer to get a better look."

"All right," agreed the ranger, "but remember, there's still a drake that hasn't been accounted for."

Further forward they ventured, and soon there were stones all around them. Out of nowhere came a rumbling, and they all crouched, expectantly.

"It sounds like it's coming from below us," said Hayley.

"It likely is," confirmed the mage. "Look!" He scuffed some dirt to reveal a stone beneath them. "It appears we are on a floor of some type. This whole area is just overgrown."

"I suggest we move back to safety," declared Hayley. "Whatever is below us could burst through at any time."

"Nonsense," argued the mage. "We have made a discovery of monumental importance!"

"What makes you say that?" asked Gerald.

"I believe we've found the ruins of a Saurian Temple," he declared.

"Seriously?" asked Gerald. "For Saxnor's sake, why would there be one here?"

"We're on the confluence of two Ley Lines," said Revi.

"What does that mean?" asked Hayley.

"For years mages have known about the Ley Lines; vertical lines that run roughly north and south. I have formed an opinion that there are also cross-cutting lines of force, roughly east-west if you like. The intersection of these lines unleashes all sorts of possibilities."

"Like what?" challenged Gerald. "Are we to have genies popping up in front of us?"

"No, but a mage could tap into this and unleash powerful magic," warned the mage.

Gerald glanced about the ruins, "Do think that's what happened here? That some powerful magic was unleashed?"

"Perhaps," said Revi, "but I sense something darker. Great magic was used here, that much is clear, it lingers even to this day."

"You can sense that?" asked Hayley.

"No, not really, but look all around you. What could possibly account for all this mayhem? Something powerful definitely finished this place off. Those stones have been blasted by something."

"Shall we retire?" asked Gerald, sensing another rumbling.

"What's that?" snapped Revi, turning to his right. He was looking at something through the undergrowth and moved quickly, crossing a small clearing.

Gerald cursed and ran after him, "Saxnor's balls, Revi, we're in danger here. You're putting all of us at risk."

The mage was examining a stone, scraping the plants away from it. "There's some writing here it-"

His voice was cut off by a scraping sound when the stone beneath him gave way, swallowing him up in the darkness.

"Revi!" called out Gerald, skidding to a stop.

"It's all right," a voice called from below. "I've fallen into some sort of chamber. I'm just going to conjure some light."

Gerald heard the mage muttering below as Hayley came up beside him.

"What happened?" she asked.

"Our blessed mage seems to have found a loose stone and decided to fall in."

"That's one way to get to the Underworld," she quipped.

"He's fine, he's casting a spell."

A moment later a bright light appeared below and then suddenly winked out of existence.

"What happened," called out Gerald.

"I cancelled the spell," spoke Revi in a hushed voice. "There's something down here. Something big."

"We need to get you out," called out Gerald. "Can you see the opening?"

"Yes," replied the mage, "but I can't get to it."

"Are you injured?" called out Hayley.

"Of course not," replied the indignant mage, "and even if I was, I'm a Life Mage, I'd simply heal myself."

Gerald looked to the ranger, "I knew this was going to be a bad idea."

"We need rope," said Hayley.

"We're going to need a lot more than rope," he replied.

"What do you mean?" she said.

"If we try getting him out, it'll attract the attention of the creature."

"So what do we do?" she asked.

"We get the others ready to fight. There has to be another entrance to that underground chamber. The drake had to get down there somehow."

"I'll start looking," she decided.

"No, get the others up here first. We'll have to draw it out and keep it busy while we pull out the mage."

"Are all mages like this?" she queried.

"For Saxnor's sake, I hope not," he exclaimed.

THIRTY

Trapped

SPRING 961 MC

"I thought Life Mages were supposed to heal us, not lead us into danger," quipped Arnim.

"So did I," remarked Beverly, "but it seems we have little choice. We can't just leave him here."

"Can't we?" Arnim replied. "It would make life so much easier."

"Has Hayley found anything?" interrupted Anna.

"Yes, Highness, some distance up ahead there's a larger collapsed floor panel. It appears to open into a lower chamber of some sort."

"Do we go in after it?" asked Arnim.

"That would be suicidal," answered Beverly. "We need to draw it out in the open where we can take advantage of our superior numbers."

"We'll form a line back from the entrance," offered Alric. "The men will present spears, but we'll need to flush it out."

"I can do that," offered Beverly.

"Not alone, you won't," warned Gerald. "If it's as large as Hayley says, you'll need help."

"I'll go," offered Jack. "I can't sit back and be outshone by Dame Beverly."

"This is no laughing matter, Jack," warned Gerald.

"I never said it was," he turned to Alric. "What say you, Highness?"

"I agree with Jack," the prince returned.

"Then it's settled," said Beverly, "Gerald, Jack and I will enter the chamber. All we have to do is get its attention and then run out again."

"How fast does this thing move?" asked Jack.

Gerald shrugged his shoulders, so they all turned to Hayley.

"I have no idea," stated the ranger. "I'm sure Revi would know, though. Shall we go and ask him?"

"No," objected Alric, "we need to get moving quickly."

"All right, then," said Anna. "Take up your stations. We'll signal when everyone's in position, then you move. Aubrey and Arnim will stand by to lower a rope and lift Revi out."

"Shouldn't we do that first?" asked Jack.

"They need light to see what they're working with, but a light would attract the attention of the beast."

"Fair enough," said the cavalier. "Let us prepare to meet death."

Alric's guard formed a line in front of the opening, setting their spears as if to repel cavalry. Gerald, Beverly and Jack stood to the side, ready to make their way forward once signalled.

Jack looked at Beverly, and their eyes met for an instant. "If we're going to die today," he said in all earnestness, "then I think you should at least kiss me."

Beverly frowned, "That's not going to happen, Jack."

Gerald glanced over, "Don't look at me, Jack, I'm not your type."

The cavalier shrugged his shoulders, "Oh well, you can't blame me for trying."

"Yes, I can," remarked Beverly. "Keep your thoughts to yourself, and your eyes forward."

Alric waved his sword in the air; the signal to move forward and the trio began their advance. The ground was smooth for the first few feet, then broken stone was revealed. Dirt and greenery had created a ramp of sorts which they slowly descended, taking their time to let their eyes adjust to the darkness. They took slow, deliberate steps, their weapons and shields extended in front of them.

Gerald felt perspiration on his neck. He had stood in the line of battle, had fought Saxnor knew how many times and yet this task was more unnerving than anything he had ever done before. They walked into the darkness from which the creature might attack at any moment. He nearly jumped when a scraping noise echoed through the chamber as if a great bulk was rubbing against stone. Gerald turned slightly, raised his shield and peeked over its rim to see the first signs of movement, the barest glimmer of reflected light from the creature's tail.

"Here," he whispered, "on my left, against the wall."

Beverly moved up beside him, their shields almost touching. The air was fetid with the smell of rotting flesh. Jack, still behind them, watching their backs, muttered over his shoulder, "I just had a thought."

"What?" whispered Gerald in reply.

"What if there's more than one of them?"

Gerald silently cursed himself, he should have thought of that. The distant sound of muttering broke his musings, then suddenly a light sprang to life. Revi, from his vantage point, had cast a globe of light into the chamber and now it hung, casting an eerie glow over the area.

Gerald saw the massive creature in front of him, its eyes reflecting the light like a cat. The drake snaked out a tongue and hissed. A moment later a similar sound erupted in front of Jack.

"We have a large one, Jack," said Beverly. "What do you see?"

"Another one here," he replied, "but only the size of a horse."

"What kind of horse?" she asked.

"What?"

"Big, like mine, or smaller like yours?" she replied.

"Is this really the time to compare sizes?" he complained.

"We still carry out the plan," interjected Gerald. "All we need to do is draw them out. Are we ready?"

"Yes," replied Beverly.

"As ready as I'll ever be," confirmed Jack.

"Start backing up towards the entrance," said Gerald, "but keep your eyes peeled. If it looks like it's going to lunge, use your sword."

"How do we hurt it?" asked Jack. "The things covered in scales."

"Think of it like a giant dog," said Gerald, "and smack it on the snout."

"Will that kill it," the cavalier asked.

"No, but it'll likely enrage it."

"Is it wise to anger it?" asked Jack.

"Yes," Beverly reminded, "we're trying to get it to charge out, remember?"

They started backing up slowly, keeping their faces to the enemy. It was difficult, for they had to turn slightly and walk up the slope of debris. One issued a roar of challenge, then suddenly the largest creature snapped forward. Gerald raised his shield, feeling the impact while Beverly struck with her sword, hitting the creature's mouth. It withdrew its snakelike neck and raised its head for a strike from above.

"Run!" yelled Beverly, and as a trio, they turned and fled, their feet carrying them as fast as they could.

The drake followed them, emerging into the dimly lit glade, slowly revealing its immense size. The head appeared first; an extended face attached to a long, serpentine neck, swaying about looking for its first victim. In the ruins, it had seemed to be large, but now, as its body cleared the cover, it was easily twice the length of a horse and cart with a tail that was nearly the same length, whipping about before curling around its body.

"Loose arrows," Alric commanded. Arrows flew forward, only to bounce harmlessly off the tough scales of the beast. It roared a challenge, shattering the air with its bellow, then surged ahead, plunging into the line of spearmen, snapping spears and knocking soldiers from their feet. Preparing to strike again, it raised its head, chose its next target and then lanced down to pluck a man from those assembled before it, biting the unfortunate soul in two. The remaining soldiers surrounded the drake, jabbing out with their spears, but the weapons barely scratched the thing's scales.

~

The second creature, about half the size the first, suddenly darted out, barrelling into the back of the spearmen who had surrounded the first, knocking them over with its mass. Gerald pushed forward, through the fallen men to strike at the smaller one, hoping to draw its attention away from the exposed spearman. It drew back its head to dodge the blow and then paused for only a moment before lunging back at Gerald, who dove to the side just in time to avoid the jaws of death that descended toward him.

Again, it snapped at Gerald, and he ducked, barely having time to hold his shield above him. It tried to bite him, but its mouth was not wide enough; its teeth merely scraping across the shield's surface. Gerald struck with his sword, its tip sinking in deep enough to draw blood, but the creature shifted, pulling out of range.

~

"Attack!" Anna's command rang through the air; the Knights of the Hound rushing forward, intent on finishing these creatures off before they were able to do any more damage. Sir Barnsley struck at the hindquarters of the larger drake; his sword finding a gap in the scales and drawing blood. A thick black ichor issued forth as the drake rotated, lashing out with its tail to knock the knight from his feet. Almost immediately, the creature's foot came down, its claws scraping the knight's armour as he rolled to avoid being crushed. It roared in frustration, raising its head in preparation to snap up another victim, but instead, it leaped forward, crushing a spearman beneath its massive body.

Beverly, seeing an opportunity while the drake was occupied with its latest prey, strode forward, driving her sword into creature's chest, only to have the sword held fast between two scales. The beast, enraged by the pain, thrashed about, its neck sweeping the redheaded knight from her feet.

Jack, realizing Beverly's dire predicament, dashed into the fray to protect her, but his sword merely bounced off of the creature's head, while the gallant cavalier growled in rage at his failure.

The drake crawled forward, its claws scratching the ground at Beverly's feet, ready to pounce on the thing that had hurt it. Beverly rolled to the side and then jumped up, now weaponless, her sword still lodged in the creature's hide. A spearman ran forward, trying to stab at the existing wound, but the creature's long, sinewy neck twisted, and the jaws came down, lifting the man into the air by the leg. With a shake of its head, the man flew into the trees, his limb still gripped in the maw of the beast.

Sir Barnsley struck again, and then Dame Levina was there, lending her blade, slicing down at the creature's hind foot, severing a claw, covering them both in the black ichor that coursed through the creature's veins. Dame Abigail stepped up to take advantage of the wound, but she slipped on the blood, sending her crashing to the ground. The beast twisted, biting down at the fallen knight, but Dame Juliet came to the rescue, standing over her comrade, her shield absorbing the impact.

"Form a line," Alric yelled at his men, trying to keep some sort of order. The larger beast lashed out with its tail, sending half a dozen more soldiers to the ground, then turned on one of the fallen, ripping open the man's chest with its claws. The prince stepped forward and attacked, his blade coming down on the creature's flank, glancing off the tough scales, doing little damage, but enough to draw the creature's attention. It had turned in anger, snapping its jaws toward Alric, when a soldier pushed him out of the way. The hapless individual's head popped like a melon as it was crushed in the drake's mouth.

All about was chaos, their weapons unable to inflict more than minor wounds. The ground was slick with the blood of those who had tried and failed. Gerald slipped on someone's entrails, sending him crashing to the ground. He crawled from the fray to regain his feet and cast about, trying to take in the battle. He spotted Beverly, mounting Lightning, and he understood what was coming.

"Back up," he commanded. "Get out of range!"

The soldiers backed up, giving the smaller creature some space. Gerald struck out, getting the beast's attention then turned and ran back toward the woods, his heart pounding.

Beverly watched the creature following Gerald and then urged Lightning forward. She held her hand out, and a spearmen gave her his weapon. Now, she couched the weapon as her mighty Mercerian Charger surged ahead. Straight at the beast she rode, its flank exposed as it chased after Gerald. Channelling all the strength she could muster, she drove the spear deep into the creature's flesh, releasing her grip after impact to avoid crashing into the drake.

Raising its head in one final scream of agony, the drake fell to the ground, lifeless. The larger drake, hearing the death howl of its companion, roared out, then whipped its head around, knocking a pair of spearmen across the clearing.

Gerald was catching his breath, watching as the Knights of the Hound moved back in, still struggling to defeat the remaining vile creature. Beverly rode over to him, dismounting, drawing her hammer from the saddle.

"What do we do now?" she asked. "I can't spear that one, it has a longer reach; I'd never get close enough."

"It's a lot bigger than the one you just killed," he said, "but perhaps we can use that against it."

"What's that mean?"

Gerald looked at his shield, seeing the teeth marks where the smaller beast had struck. "I have an idea, but we have to get in close."

He jogged forward, with Beverly following. The Hounds were there; Dame Aelwyth struck down with her axe and severed another claw, sending black blood flying into the air. The ichor splashed her face, temporarily blinding her, and when the drake shifted, she was knocked back by its tail. It advanced, intent on crushing her with its weight, but Sir Howard grabbed her arm, dragging her from danger.

"Get ready!" called out Gerald, rushing forward.

The creature swivelled its head, looking down on the lone swordsman rushing towards it. It snaked its head back, and then struck, its jaws open wide, but its victim held a shield in front of him, and then pushed it forward, wedging it into the creature's mouth, preventing it from closing its jaws. Even so, it had struck him with the full force of the attack, sending him sprawling.

It raised its head, desperate to get the obstruction from its mouth, flailing about in an unsuccessful bid to remove the obstacle.

Beverly waited, her hammer held ready, the roar of the vile beast spraying her with spittle. The head came back down, and the knight struck, a two-handed blow, driving the hammer down onto the creature's head. It felt like she was hitting a stone, the vibration travelling up her arm, but the deed was done. The creature stopped flailing about, stunned by the blow, and then an arrow flew through the air, sinking deep into the drake's eye. It roared again, falling to the ground, its body now twisting about, trying to avoid the blows of the knights who had moved in on it. A claw struck out, scraping across Beverly's chest plate, and she struck again, bringing the hammer down onto the creature's foot.

Jack rushed past and slipped on the wet ground, causing him to slide forward, face up. He kept his wits about him, striking up with his sword, sinking the blade into the creature's soft underbelly and then rolling out of the way.

There was one final bellow, and then the creature collapsed to the ground, convulsed, and then went still. For a moment, all was quiet, and then a spontaneous cheer erupted from the soldiers.

Aubrey was already running toward the injured while Revi had just climbed out of the hole with Arnim's help.

"It worked," an elated Jack exclaimed. He calmed himself before continuing, "As I knew it would. We make a good team, Dame Beverly."

"You're wasting your energy," said Gerald, "her heart's spoken for."

Jack looked at the old man, "By you? You're far too old for her!"

"No, you imbecile. Someone back in Merceria."

"He's not here, is he," the cavalier countered. "That makes her fair game."

"I'm no one's game," countered Beverly, "and if you persist in this behaviour, I shall have to silence you, permanently."

Jack took a deep breath, "I apologize, Dame Beverly, if I have overstepped the rules of etiquette."

"Apology accepted," said Beverly, "now shut up and help out here, we've got injured."

The toll had been high. The spearmen had suffered the most, with eight deaths and twelve more wounded. Even the Knights of the Hound had not come out of it unscathed, and Gerald watched as Aubrey and Revi cast spells of healing to those they could help.

"Fascinating," mused Anna, looking over the bodies of the drakes.

"Yes," agreed Aubrey. "I've never seen their likes before."

"Arnim," yelled Anna, "what are you doing?"

He was beneath the body of the great drake, hacking away with a sharp knife. "The hide on this thing is very strong, Highness, I thought it might be made into armour."

Gerald shook his head, "What armourer would have such skill?" he asked.

"I never said it would be easy," replied the captain, "but there's no hurry. The hide should last."

Revi, finished with his last spell of healing, hustled the group back down the ramp.

"You must come with me," he gushed. "There's something quite interesting down here."

They followed him down into the lair, his globe of light guiding the way. They came across a wall of stone and Gerald instantly recognized the writing carved into it.

"It's Saurian," he said.

"Yes," said Revi, casting a spell, the familiar buzzing filling the air, and then the mage stood before the wall.

"What's happening?" asked Alric.

"He's cast a spell of tongues," replied Anna, "so he can read the ancient words."

"What do they say?" asked Alric.

"It tells of a great battle," recounted Revi as he made his way across the wall, following the writing. "No, I stand corrected, it was a great war, and it lasted for years."

"Who were they fighting?" asked Anna.

Revi stopped suddenly, his mind grappling with what he had read.

"Well?" prompted Gerald.

"What is it, Revi?" prompted the princess.

He turned to look at them, his face pale, "I'm afraid it was the Elves."

"The Elves? Why would they fight the Saurians?" asked Anna.

"These writings talk of dark magic, of the undead," explained the mage.

"You mean the Saurians were necromancers?" asked Anna in disbelief.

"No, the Elves were." Revi let the words sink in.

"Surely there's a mistake," offered Alric. "The Elves have been our allies for years."

"There's no mistaking these runes, Highness," Revi replied. "It is laid here for all to see."

"Maybe there were other Elves. Not all of them can be masters of the undead?" offered Alric.

"Likely not," replied Revi, "but the baron didn't want us to find it. If it wasn't the baron's Elves, he certainly knew of it."

"What are you saying?" asked Gerald, fearful of the answer.

"I'm saying that the Elves likely eradicated the entire Saurian race," said Revi.

"They tried to do the same to the Orcs," said Anna.

"The Orcs?" asked Alric.

"Yes, they destroyed the ancient cities of the Orcs, completely wiped them out. The Orcs who live in the area now are poor descendants of a once mighty people."

"That would explain the enmity between them," said Aubrey.

"What do we do about this?" asked Alric. "I'm at a loss, here."

"We tell them nothing," said Anna. "Swear your men to secrecy, Alric. The less said about this, the better. We shall keep it to ourselves, for now."

"Is that wise, Anna?" Alric asked.

"Do you want to sacrifice the alliance with the Elves?" she asked.

"No," he admitted. "I see your reasoning. We shall take the bodies and say nothing of the ruins. As far as the baron is concerned, we found the creatures in amongst the trees."

"Yes, Highness," said Jack. "I'll see to it."

"I should like to examine the ruins a bit closer before we leave, Your Highness," remarked Revi. "There is much to learn from this place."

"By all means, Master Bloom, as long as we are out of here by nightfall," replied Anna.

It was quite dark by the time they returned to the hall. The group was hauling the heads of the two drakes, suspended from poles with two soldiers carrying each end. Even so, the beasts were so heavy that they had to frequently stop to change bearers.

"It would have been a good idea to bring a wagon," commented Gerald.

"A wagon would never have made it through the woods," said Hayley. "Besides, they'll be bragging about this tomorrow. It isn't every day that a drake gets slain, let alone two."

"What is that smell?" Gerald said, turning in his saddle.

"That's Arnim's pelt; it's slung over his horse," the ranger explained.

"I feel sorry for the poor beast, it stinks."

"He's going to drop it off at the tanner; I suspect it will take a few days to get the smell out."

"Why on earth would he want the skin? Surely chainmail would give him more protection," said Gerald.

"Drake skin is rare; perhaps he thinks it might hold an enchantment. Magic armour is hard to come by."

"And who, precisely, would enchant it? I haven't heard of any mages of that ilk in Merceria."

"True," admitted the ranger, "but we're in Weldwyn now. Even if he can't get it enchanted, its pelt will still likely fetch a high price."

"Waste of time, if you ask me," grumbled the old warrior.

"Why is that?"

"Coins don't buy happiness."

"So, you're a philosopher now, Gerald?" teased Hayley.

"No," he admitted, "but chasing down wealth has been the ruin of many. Better to enjoy the simple pleasures of life."

"Which are?"

"Friendship and family," Gerald affirmed. "That's all we really need."

"What about sausages?" the ranger remarked.

"Yes, those too, along with an occasional scone," he said, his face breaking into a grin.

The hall was now in sight, and the townsfolk had gathered to gape at the trophies of their encounter. Alric watched their faces, saw the happiness and relief and felt at peace. He had been hesitant to act contrary to the baron's desires, but now that it was done, he knew, deep inside, that they had done the right thing. All that remained was to return to Lord Parvan and show him their prizes.

If he was expecting a warm welcome, he was sorely disappointed. As the procession arrived, Lord Parvan was not there to greet them, neither was there any of his advisors to thank them for their success. Alric dismissed the men, leaving the mage, Revi Bloom, to look after the heads. He asked Anna to join him, and together they made their way to Lord Parvan's audience chamber.

Jack and Gerald dutifully fell in behind them as they walked through the high ceilinged halls. Their boots echoed in the silence and Alric was struck by the idea that they were about to face some sort of judgement. He hadn't felt this way in years, not since he was a little boy, brought before his father for destroying his mother's flower garden.

Anna, as if sensing his unease, grasped his hand and squeezed it. He turned his head slightly to look at her, but her gaze remained fixed firmly ahead of her. He took comfort in the feeling and squeezed back as the doors to the audience chamber opened before them.

The Elven Guard stood to either side, lining the hall like a processional. The small party had paused as the doors swung open, but now they stepped forward in unison, to make their way down the marble-floored room. The guards snapped to attention, holding their spears vertically by their sides. The discipline of Elven warriors was legendary, but Alric began to wonder if they had walked into a death trap.

Lord Parvan Luminor sat upon an elegant chair. He rose as the party drew near, bowing respectfully as they came to a halt before him.

"Greetings, Highnesses," he said.

His face was unreadable; the Elven features locked into a rigid stare.

Alric found it intimidating at first, but the more he stared, the more he became annoyed by it.

"Lord Parvan," he finally spoke in greeting, "we return bearing great news. We have slain the drakes that have troubled your barony these last few years."

"So I have heard," the baron replied neutrally.

"We found them nested in the wood," Alric continued, "and at great risk, battled them. I lost eight good men today, and it would have been worse had it not been for the efforts of the two Life Mages."

The mention of the Life Mages seemed to catch the baron off guard. Alric saw him flinch and wondered why it might upset him so.

"I see," said the baron. "And what are your intentions now, Lord Prince?"

"With your permission, we will continue on our way," Alric announced, "for we are travelling to Riversend."

"It seems my permission was not required to enter the wood," commented the baron, "and yet now you seek it?"

Alric, annoyed by the baron's attitude, spoke freely, "I am being polite, Lord Parvan. It is quite clear that you didn't want us here and yet it is my sworn duty, as a prince, to protect my people. That protection includes all who swear fealty to the crown, including your own barony, whether you like it or not."

"And so the young prince grows a spine," the baron returned. "How interesting. Pray, tell me, Lord Prince, what did you find in the wood, aside from the drakes?"

Alric was taken aback. Did the baron know? Perhaps Lord Parvan knew of the drakes home for some time?

"What did you expect me to find?" he countered.

If the baron was surprised by his answer, he didn't seem to show it. Alric had heard that Elves were notoriously difficult to read.

"I know exactly what you discovered," said Lord Parvan. "Did you think that anything could happen in my wood without my knowledge?"

"And yet you did nothing to protect your people. Our people!"

"There are more important things in life that need protection, Lord Prince," he countered.

"So you would sacrifice the safety of your people to hide a ruin?"

"You know it's much more than a ruin. Imagine the power if it fell into the wrong hands."

Alric was confused by his words and looked to Anna, but she, too, looked startled by the Elf's declaration.

"You lied," accused Anna.

"I have told the truth," defended the baron.

"That's not entirely true," she accused. "You told us you were a thousand years old."

"And what of it?" Lord Parvan enquired.

"You're actually older, far older in fact."

Alric looked at her in amazement, "What are you saying, Anna?"

"You forget, Lord Parvan," said Anna, "we Mercerians worked with Lord Greycloak. We travelled with him for months, got to know him quite well. He told us Elves are immortal. They live forever."

"Forever?" said Alric in disbelief.

"Oh, they can still die due to disease or war, but their natural lifespan is endless."

Lord Parvan, for once, looked surprised, "What is it you are accusing me of?"

"It's an interesting ring you wear, my Lord Baron," she continued. "If I'm not mistaken, that's a Saurian rune emblazoned on the top."

The baron's sudden attempt to hide the ring beneath his other hand was all the proof she needed.

"You were there, weren't you? You were present when the temple was destroyed."

"I said nothing about a temple!" he exclaimed.

"No, you called them ruins, but what you don't know, is that we've found proof of other Saurian Temples. I've actually been inside one. The secret you speak of, the power you're so afraid of is the eternal flame, isn't it?"

Lord Parvan paled, "How can you possibly know of such things; you're just a child?"

"I'm not a child anymore," Anna responded, "and I have surrounded myself with friends. Friends who have all sorts of knowledge and abilities. You destroyed the Saurians because you feared them, didn't you?"

"You understand nothing of the past," the baron accused. "Your pathetic race is too young to grasp such things."

"Is that why the Elves broke the Orc cities? Were they getting close to the secret of the flames?"

Alric was stunned. Where had this come from? How had Anna put this together?

She turned to face the Weldwyn prince. "I only just realized this, Alric, sorry for not informing you sooner. We found an ancient temple back in Merceria. Lily helped us understand it. I'm sure Revi could tell you more if you were to ask him. Lord Greycloak was a trusted ally, but this baron of yours puts the Elves in a bad light. I rather suspect that he has witnessed dark magic first hand, though I doubt he's used it himself."

"That's quite the accusation, Anna," Alric replied. "How can you be so sure?"

"I don't forget things, Alric. I remember almost everything; I've been this way all my life. I have devoured every book I can find. You'd be surprised what you can put together from scattered information."

"She's making the whole thing up," accused the baron, "and I find it most insulting."

"Isn't' it a bit late to play the insulted card, Baron?" accused Anna. "I should think righteous indignation would fit you better. Your very behaviour confirms what I've said. Unlike Prince Alric, I don't have to sneak around the subject. I'm a Mercerian, we value strength above all, and you lack strength of character. You can't hide from your past, Lord Parvan, it will always catch up with you. The truth always wins out in the end; I truly believe that. It's not my place to judge you, but I can make sure that your story is told. What you do after that is beyond my control. I will pass to the Afterlife knowing that Saxnor will welcome me for doing what is right."

"I don't have to stand here and listen to this," the baron spat out.

"No, you don't," agreed Alric. "You are free to leave, but if you value your position within the kingdom, you will report to the king at court and lay all in front of him, before I do."

Lord Parvan sat down in his chair, too stunned to speak any further.

"We are done, Baron," said Alric, "and so we take our leave of you. I look forward to hearing my father's view on all this. I truly wonder what he will make of it all."

Alric bowed slightly, then Anna mimicked his actions.

"Come, Anna," he said. "It's time we were away from this place."

THIRTY-ONE

Riversend

Anna looked out the window as the fields passed by, absently petting Tempus' ears as she did so, and the great dog let out a gigantic yawn.

"Tempus is tired," said Gerald, sitting beside her.

"Yes," she agreed, "he's getting old, he likes his comforts."

"He's not the only one," commented Revi. "I saw Gerald nod off earlier."

"I was thinking," the old warrior defended himself.

"Stop it you two," said Aubrey. "Honestly, Master Revi, sometimes you can be really cruel."

"I'm only pulling his leg, Lady Aubrey," the mage confessed. "I meant no offense."

"Let's get onto other matters, shall we?" said Anna. "I didn't invite you into the carriage to pick on Gerald."

"Of course, Highness," said Revi. "What is it you wish to speak of?"

"I told you what happened in Lord Parvan's hall. I wanted your opinions."

"Where do I start?" asked Revi.

"Master Revi can get off track," explained Aubrey. "Perhaps if you were more specific?"

"Yes," agreed Anna, "let's start off with the Saurians. What do we really know about them?"

"Well," mused Revi, "we know they had a huge trading empire, although they were never a numerous people."

"What does that mean, exactly?" asked Gerald. "It's well and fine to say they have an empire, but how can they do that if there's not a lot of them?"

"I see your point," responded the mage. "We know they traded with all the races, except for Humans, of course."

"Why not Humans?" asked Gerald.

"They weren't around in this part of the world at the time. The first Humans didn't come into the land until centuries later. We don't know exact dates, of course."

"Yes," agreed Aubrey, "the land was isolated from the rest of the world through geography. The great Sea of Storms blocked approach by sea and the mountains by land. The first Humans came through the passes to find an untamed wilderness."

"Untamed, yes," agreed Revi, "though not uninhabited. The ruins of ancient Orc cities were still around, but the Saurians had long since left. We didn't know anything about them until centuries later. We've likely discovered more about them in the past few years than for generations before. Lily is the only living Saurian that we know of."

"And yet," observed Gerald, "if she lives, there may be more."

"Yes," Revi agreed. "I suspect there are many more. A whole city full, in fact."

"All right, Revi," prompted Anna, "spit it out. What is it you're hiding?"

"Me? Hiding something? What makes you say that?"

"The grin on your face. You always do that when you know something that we don't," said the princess.

"The ruins in the Draenor Wood revealed many things to me. I still have yet to fully comprehend the details, but I believe I have found the secret of their trading empire."

"Which is?" prompted Gerald.

"I think they discovered the secret of disapparation," he smiled, waiting for his announcement to have an effect.

"They learned what?" asked Gerald.

"He means they could teleport," explained Aubrey. "That is to say, travel large distances by use of magic."

"Isn't that impossible?" asked Anna.

"It was always thought so," confessed Revi. "Mages have been trying to perfect that type of magic since the beginning of time, but have never succeeded. I suspect Andronicus was working on such a spell just before he died."

"Did he succeed?" asked Anna.

"I believe it drove him mad," confessed Revi. "He was never fully aware in his final days."

"We know the Saurians were masters of magic," explained Aubrey, "and we think they used portals to send their goods to distant lands. There's certainly no indication they used ships or trade caravans, and yet somehow they traded goods."

"It makes sense from a certain point of view," said Gerald, "but how do we know they didn't have caravans?"

"There are no mentions of them," confessed Aubrey, "and they would have been ripe for plunder by bandits and such."

"Would that explain why the Elves destroyed them?" asked Gerald.

"Knowledge of teleportation would change the balance of power," said Revi. "That's why it's been so sought after. Perhaps the Elves thought they could seize the magic for themselves?"

"I remember reading something about the temples being great sources of information. Could that be related?" enquired the princess.

"Yes," agreed Revi, "though I suspect the word power would be more appropriate."

"Whatever do you mean?" asked Anna.

"Our knowledge of magic comes primarily from the Elves," admitted Revi. "Over the years Humans have built on that knowledge and explored the boundaries of our abilities. Some of the wisest minds in the three kingdoms agree that the power of magic flows from within. Based on that, there is a finite amount of power that can be called upon."

"What does that mean?" asked Gerald. "I don't understand."

It was Aubrey that offered an explanation, "Our bodies contain the fuel that powers magic. Much like wood is needed for a fire, except that this magical energy replenishes itself over time. If you've only got two logs for your fire, you can only build a flame of a certain size."

"So you're saying that even a powerful mage has limitations?" asked Gerald.

"Precisely," agreed Revi, "but here's where it gets interesting. What do you remember about Ley Lines?"

Anna spoke before anyone else could, "They're magical lines of force that cross the land."

"Yes," Revi responded, "precisely. I suspect that the Saurians found some way to tap into the magical potential of them. With that type of power at their disposal, they would be capable of all sorts of things."

"Like teleportation?" said Gerald.

"Precisely!"

"But how does that lead you to believe there's a city somewhere?" asked Gerald.

"Let me put it this way; if you could teleport and your city was attacked, what would you do?"

"Teleport to safety?" interjected Anna.

"Exactly!"

"So where is this city you speculate about?" asked Anna.

Revi sat back in his chair, "I'm afraid I don't know."

"Well, that's a bit of a disappointment," said Gerald. "I thought you knew everything."

"I know a lot," the mage admitted, "but I never said I know everything."

"Agreed," offered Aubrey. "He doesn't even know how to cook."

"I know how to cook," he defended, "I just choose not to."

"So where does that leave us?" interrupted Anna.

"I'm sure I can crack this once we return to Merceria. I have books that might shed some light on it."

"You shouldn't have long to wait," offered Gerald. "Summer's just around the corner, and then we're on our way home."

Anna fell silent while Gerald looked at her, understanding her mood. "Perhaps the prince might come and visit us in Merceria?" he offered.

She smiled before answering, "That would be nice," she confessed, "but I don't think it will happen. King Leofric will want to keep him close; he knows a lot about us, and therefore he'll be a valuable source of information to the court."

"Still," he persisted, "he's developed a mind of his own. He may decide to visit anyway?"

"Perhaps," she mused. "We can only hope."

The city of Riversend was located at the mouth of the Loran River, the same river that hosted Loranguard further to the north. Unlike that city, however, Riversend was situated on the western bank, for the eastern side was occupied by an enormous cliff which overlooked the city for miles. The road ran along the base of these cliffs, turning abruptly to meet with a stone causeway that led across the river into the city. It wasn't until she was halfway across that Beverly realized it was a draw-bridge that allowed the river traffic through.

She rode across the bridge to come up to the far side, where a trio of soldiers stood, watching her approach. Two of them had been sitting at a small table, tossing dice but their companion alerted them, and now they all stood, intent on their new visitor. Beverly halted her mount, waiting for the inevitable challenge.

"Who are you?" asked the tallest man.

"I am Dame Beverly Fitzwilliam," she answered, "Knight of the Hound. I am here to announce the arrival of Princess Anna of Merceria and Prince Alric of Weldwyn."

Anna's name had carried no weight here, but the mere mention of Alric girded them into action. The tall man's eyes appeared to bulge slightly as he stammered out a reply, "We had no word of the prince's coming. We shall send word to the earl immediately."

The tall guard turned to talk to his companions, and one was soon racing into town while the remaining two stood to attention and tried to look official.

"They shall be here shortly," Beverly warned, "with a large entourage."

"It won't take long to get word to the earl," the tall guard replied, "there's horses billeted close by. I suspect the earl himself will be back here shortly, this time of day he's drilling the troops."

"The earl trains his own troops?" said Beverly. "Does he not have a Sergeant-at-Arms?"

"Not sure what that is," the man confessed, "but the earl likes to do things himself."

"His Grace sounds like a most interesting man. Has he always been so dedicated to his men?"

"Riversend has been attacked twice in recent memory. He takes his responsibilities quite seriously."

"Glad to hear it," said Beverly. "I wish more nobles were as dedicated."

"Would you care to rest your horse?" the guard asked. "We have water troughs just the other side of the gate."

"No, thank you," she replied. "I shall ride back to find the column. I'll return shortly with the rest."

The column had halted on the road to await Beverly's return. Anna stretched her legs while Tempus bounded across the field.

"He's still got lots of energy for his age," commented Gerald.

"Yes," she agreed. "I don't know where he gets it from. He can be dead tired one moment and then tearing across a field the next."

"Would that we were all that energetic in old age."

"You're not that old yet, Gerald. I know we like to tease you, but you'll be around for years."

A hail from the front of the column brought their attention to Alric, who was approaching them.

278 • HEART OF THE CROWN

"How much further?" asked Anna, turning to the prince.

"Not long, now," Alric promised. "The road up ahead bends around that group of trees, and then you can see the city itself."

"Couldn't we have just ridden on, then?" asked Anna.

"I shouldn't like to upset the earl," Alric admitted. "It's not very polite to drop in without a welcoming committee."

"Didn't you inform him we were coming, Alric?"

"I did," he admitted, "though that was weeks ago. We didn't know the exact day we would arrive and as it turns out we ended up having that stop off in Tivilton, so everything worked out. We just need to give the earl some time to put everything together."

"What does that mean?" asked Gerald, though he had a suspicion he already knew.

Alric smiled, "I thought it would be fitting to have a proper escort for a visiting princess."

"Which means?" prompted Anna.

"An honour guard, of course. The earl takes pride in his soldiers; he'll want to put on a show."

"I see," said Anna, "and what do we need to do to make this show worthy of the great earl?"

"I'll move my men to the front," Alric said, warming to the task. "It's only proper that the men of Weldwyn escort your party. I might suggest you split the knights, half in front and half behind, but I'll leave that to your discretion."

"How thoughtful of you," Anna bristled. "Anything else? Is my dress suitable? Should I fawn on you at the appropriate time?"

Alric blushed, "I'm sorry if I've offended you, Anna. It's just that the earl is a very accomplished General. I've always looked up to him, and I wanted to make a good impression.

Anna's expression softened, "Very well, Alric. We shall do as you wish." She made an exaggerated bow and then gracefully turned back to the open field. Alric was about to speak when Anna placed two fingers to her mouth and let out a piercing whistle. Tempus bounded across the field to halt in front of her, his mouth open and dog slobber dripping to the ground.

Anna laughed and turned back to Alric, "I think Tempus wants to kiss you, Alric."

Alric backed up, "I can't get that mess on my tunic, Anna. What would the earl think?"

She laughed again and the young prince, caught up in the fun, soon joined her.

"I'll see to Tempus," offered Gerald, "but we should get the column organized. It'll take some time to rearrange, and Beverly will be back here shortly, ready to move."

"Agreed," said Alric. "I'll have Jack take his cue from you, Gerald, if that's all right."

"Yes, Highness," the old warrior agreed.

The troops began to move, and by the time Beverly returned, all was in order. Alric suggested that he and Anna ride in front of the column, preceded by Jack, who would announce them, but Anna had insisted she have her own herald, and so Beverly joined the cavalier at the head of the procession.

As Alric had predicted, when they rounded the clump of trees the city of Riversend came into view; it's grey walls standing in stark contrast to the chalk cliffs of the eastern bank.

Gerald, who was riding just behind the prince and princess, could clearly see the earl on the eastern bank, waiting before the bridge to welcome his visitors. He had his men in line with the bottom of their kite shields resting on the ground, their hands steadying the top. They each held a spear, and Gerald wondered how well they could use them.

As the riders grew near, the earl gave a shout of command, and the shields were lifted in unison, to be held in combat position. The soldiers dipped their spears in respect and Gerald couldn't help but admire their discipline, for they all moved in one swift motion, perfectly synchronized.

He watched Jack ride forward with Beverly. They exchanged words with the earl, but the wind had picked up, leaving Gerald unable make out the details. Jack and Beverly turned their horses and escorted the earl back to Alric and Anna.

"Greetings, Your Highnesses," the earl said, nodding his head in acknowledgement.

"Well met, Lord Warford," said Alric. "It has been far too long since we have seen you at court."

"Your Highness is most gracious," the earl replied.

"May I introduce Her Highness, Princess Anna of Merceria?" said Alric.

The earl nodded his head again, "I am pleased to make your acquaintance, Your Highness. I trust our young prince has kept you entertained during your visit?"

Anna nodded her head in reply, "He has indeed, Your Grace. Prince Alric tells us that you have had quite the military career. You must swap stories with my military advisor, Commander Gerald Matheson," she said, waving Gerald forward.

Gerald moved his mount closer but felt humbled by this man's reputation. "Your Grace," he stumbled out.

"He is a man of few words," said Alric, "but his modesty hides an accomplished career."

"Indeed?" noted the earl. "Then I look forward to chatting in more depth. If Your Highnesses would follow me, I've arranged a little welcome for you. My captain will see to your troops and servants, if you will permit."

"Of course," replied Anna. "He can coordinate with Dame Beverly."

"Excellent!" the earl exclaimed. "Now let me show you our city."

Alric and Anna followed the earl, with Gerald trailing behind. Beverly wheeled her horse about, riding toward the earl's captain for instructions while Hayley took up her place in the reduced entourage. The ranger rode beside Jack, who followed the royals.

They entered the city through the massive gates, and Gerald marvelled at their size. They were both open, to allow the free flow of goods and people, but could be closed and barricaded in a siege. He looked up at the massive structures, but what he saw was unexpected, for the doors themselves were thinner than he would have thought for such defenses and he estimated it would not take much to batter them down. The gates of Wincaster, though smaller in scale, could withstand the most powerful of battering rams.

Onward they rode through the cobbled city streets. People watched as they travelled past, but there was no spectacle here. Onlookers paused only to take in the scene and then returned to their daily lives, dismissing the event as an unnecessary distraction.

They passed an open field on the north where Gerald saw troops drilling. They were lined up, three deep and he watched with interest as they lowered their spears, forming a wall of spear tips. The idea was old, of course, but it took well-trained troops to carry out the manoeuvre in such a style, quickly and efficiently. He wondered what the knights might make of such a tactic and decided he was glad the Norlanders had never adopted the trick.

Soon, they rode up to a large stone building; the earl's residence. It was a fortified manor house, complete with crenellations, which backed on to the northern city wall. It was a towering structure that must give the earl a great view of the city. He thought of the map room back in Bodden and wondered what Baron Fitzwilliam might make of this place.

They dismounted in the courtyard and servants rushed forward to take the horses. The earl led them into the manor, where other guests were waiting. Gerald had been expecting a large extravaganza, perhaps even a banquet, but the earl had kept it small. He introduced less than a dozen people, and then led them into a sitting room; a far more comfortable atmosphere.

"I hope you don't mind, Your Highness," said the earl, "but I prefer less formal occasions. I know that a long carriage ride can prove strenuous, even at the best of times, and so I thought it might be more comfortable to have a more informal gathering."

"An excellent idea," offered Alric in response. "What do you think, Anna?"

"I would agree," she said, choosing a seat. "This is a very nice room, Your Grace. My compliments."

"Thank you," he replied, "but it is all thanks to my dear, late wife. It was her hand that guided its decoration."

Servants entered and began distributing drinks. Alric grabbed a goblet and took a sip, "I notice most of your people here are soldiers, Your Grace."

"Yes," he admitted, "though I mean no disrespect. Since the loss of my wife, I find little time to socialize. Most of my associates happen to be soldiers. Captain Fraser here has served me for...how long has it been, Jeremy?"

"A little less than nine years, Your Grace," the captain replied.

"Nine years? Has it been so long?"

"Ever since the last siege, my lord."

"Yes, that's right. I'd forgotten."

"You forgot the siege?" asked Alric.

"No, Your Highness, I could never forget that. I had forgotten that's where I came across Captain Fraser."

"This sounds like an interesting tale," prompted Anna.

"Yes," agreed Alric, "and the princess does so love stories. Perhaps you might tell it to us?"

"Of course," said the earl. "I shall be delighted."

"Just what we needed," groaned the captain, "an excuse for a story. You'll never hear the end of it now."

There was good-natured chuckling from the crowd while the earl waited patiently for it to die down.

"There have been two sieges of Riversend in recent history," he began. "The first such attack was nigh on twenty years ago, but that was relatively minor. It was eight years ago that they put in their best effort."

"When you say 'they', who are you referring to?" asked Anna.

"Oh, my apologies, I forgot you're not from around here. By 'they', I mean the Kurathians."

"I should have thought the Clans a bigger threat," commented Anna.

The earl snorted in derision, "The Clans could never organize a siege. No, our threat has always been from the sea. What do you know of the Kurathians?"

"They're from a group of islands, aren't they? I believe they're a collection of principalities, very independent of each other. My understanding is they raid, plunder and occasionally hire out as mercenaries."

The earl looked stunned, "You surprise me with your knowledge, Your Highness. How is it that you know so much about them?"

Anna smiled at the compliment and took a sip of the wine, looking to Gerald.

"Her Highness has always had an interest in them," Gerald said, "largely because of Tempus."

"Tempus?" said the earl. "What's that?"

"Not what," offered Alric, "more like who. He's her dog."

"Yes," agreed Gerald, "a Kurathian Mastiff."

"Indeed? Their reputation on the battlefield is legendary, but I've never heard of one being a pet before. Can we meet this Tempus of yours? I'd love to see one up close."

"Of course," uttered Anna. "Gerald, would you go and fetch him? There's only a handful of people he'll listen to."

"Certainly, Highness," the old warrior said, standing. "I shall be back shortly."

"Please, Your Grace," Anna requested, "continue your story, I'm afraid we have ridden off course."

"Where was I?" the earl mused. "Oh yes, the siege, eight years ago. They came across the Sea of Storms, in large numbers. They like to use catapult ships, throwing fire bundles onto the docks. We pulled everyone back to the walls and settled in for the long haul."

"Is this a common occurrence?" asked Anna.

"Yes," said Alric. "Kurathians have raided our shores since...well since we've had shores for them to raid."

"His Highness speaks the truth," agreed the earl, "though their attacks in the past were seldom more than a few ships. The attack back in '53 was quite different; they arrived with a massive armada to take the city."

"How did they navigate the Sea of Storms?" asked Anna. "I hear it's very difficult to sail."

"Water Mages," supplied Captain Fraser.

"I shall have to ask my mage about them," replied Anna. "Do they control the waves?"

"Not exactly," offered the earl, "but they can help with wind and currents. The Kurathian ships are very robust, but we still occasionally see one wrecked on the beach. I suspect that's how your dog came to be here, I doubt very much they'd be willing to sell or trade one."

"How did the siege progress?" prompted Alric.

"Much as you might surmise, Highness. They battered the wall quite a bit and destroyed the Traders Gate. Some of them made it into the city, but we pushed back, hard, driving them back to the sea. There was a frightful loss of life on their side, they're very lightly armoured, you see."

"Did they try taking the bluff?" asked Anna."I would think it would provide the perfect overview of the city."

"No," he responded, "the cliffs are too steep to climb, and even if they did, there is a watchtower up there just for that possibility. They sailed right into the docks and unloaded with everything they had."

"And where, if I might ask," said Alric, "does the captain fit into this? You said you met him during the siege."

"I did," exclaimed the earl. "He was a soldier in the third company. They had suffered great losses, and when I needed the troops to lead the counter-attack, he rallied the men for me. I was so impressed by his bravery that I promoted him. He's been my aide ever since. That's the short version, anyway."

"You mentioned the Traders Gate? What's that?" asked Anna.

"That's the largest gate leading to the docks. There are three gates all told; the Traders Gate, the Centre Gate and the Fishermans Gate."

"Strange names," observed Alric.

"Indeed," agreed the earl. "The Traders Gate is so called because it's the largest, allowing large wagons and such to make their way through to load and unload ships. The Centre Gate is in the middle of the south wall, beyond which lies, naturally, the docks. The Fishermans Gate is a much smaller gate right at the southeastern tip of the wall. It's the gate the fishermen used, historically, to get to their boats in the early morning hours. Of course, they weren't originally called this, they have far more grandiose names, but I'm not picky about titles, save for Your Highnesses, of course."

"Fascinating," mused Anna, "and an interesting tale. You must tell us more about this siege when we have time, Your Grace. Military history is something I am enthralled with."

The earl smiled but then made a grimace. Anna looked at him in alarm but he held up a hand, "Pardon me, Highness, I am merely suffering from a bout of indigestion."

"Is there anything we can do?" offered Alric.

"I'm afraid not, Your Highness," he replied. "It shall pass soon, it usually does."

"We have a Life Mage with us, Your Grace," offered Anna. "Perhaps he should examine you?"

"I would look upon it as a kindness," he said, "but for now I must excuse myself, these attacks can be quite uncomfortable."

"We should leave you, Your Grace," said Alric. "I would hate to impose."

"Nonsense," the earl replied, "stay and enjoy yourselves. There is much wine to drink, and I shall have my kitchen feed you. I'll return once I've had a chance to rest."

Alric and Anna both rose to their feet. "We look forward to it," said Anna.

The earl was escorted from the room, leaving the visitors to their own devices.

"What do you make of that?" asked Alric.

"I'm not sure," replied Anna, "but I'm not taking chances. Let's get Revi to take a look at him."

"Agreed," said Alric. "You see to the mage, and I'll clear it with the earl's people."

"I suppose we'll have to introduce Tempus another time," she mused.

"Don't worry," said Alric, "I'm sure this is just an inconvenience. The earl will be back up and among us in no time."

"I hope you're right," said Anna. "I'd hate to see him take a turn for the worse."

THIRTY-TWO

A Strange Malady

SPRING 961 MC

G erald stood on the city walls, looking south, across the surface of the Sea of Storms. The brisk wind here threatened to blow his cape back into the city.

"Magnificent, isn't it," said Anna, peering over the parapet.

"You always wanted to see the ocean," he said. "Well, there it is."

"You don't seem overly impressed," she commented.

"It's just water. I'll keep my feet on dry land, if it's all right with you."

"I've never seen so many boats before," she said. "I thought Loranguard had a lot, but this place has even more."

"Yes," agreed Gerald, "and these ships are larger."

"They're seagoing vessels, not just riverboats. They say the Sea of Storms is well named."

"Prince Alric mentioned that this was normal weather for around here, and yet the wind is quite strong."

"Yes," agreed Anna, "it allows traders to get here. It's said it makes it difficult to sail down the coast."

"Why would someone want to sail down the coast?" asked Gerald. "It's nothing but swamp."

"That's only Merceria's coast. There's another Weldwyn city to the east of here called Southport, though it's hundreds of miles away."

"It's a pity that ships can't make Colbridge anymore," mused Gerald. "I've heard it used to be a great port. I imagine it must have been something like this." He watched as a smaller vessel turned, edging further away. "That fellow looks like he's in trouble," he noted.

"No," disagreed Anna, "he's tacking."

"Tacking?"

"Yes, he needs to sail against the wind; he has to keep turning so he's not facing the wind straight on. He's basically zig-zagging."

"When did you become a ship expert?" he asked.

"Alric told me all about it," she answered.

They stood in silence, watching the tiny ship trying to make progress. Their solitude was interrupted by a yell off to the side, and they turned to see Revi Bloom approaching. He was saying something, but the wind ripped the words away.

"What was that?" called Gerald, as the mage drew closer.

"I was saying I've just been to the manor."

"How's the earl?" asked Anna.

"He's doing well. He had another bout of indigestion this morning but seems to be making a full recovery. He's quite active for such an old man."

"You'd be surprised what an 'old man' can do," complained Gerald.

The mage ignored his comment, "I've used some healing magic on him, just in case, but there doesn't seem to be anything wrong with him. I suspect he's just been overwhelmed with all the festivities being planned."

"I'd still feel better if you kept an eye on him," said Anna. "There doesn't seem to be a healer in these parts."

"I noticed that," replied the mage. "I thought there'd be more of them around. There's certainly quite a few in the capital."

"They're likely training," offered Gerald. "Much like a soldier seeks out a mentor to train, a mage would likely seek out a more powerful magician to learn their art."

"It's a silly way to do things," offered the mage.

"Silly?" countered Anna. "You, yourself are using the same technique with Lady Aubrey."

"Yes," he agreed, "but it's very inefficient. It takes years to train an apprentice and then they have to take on an apprentice of their own. If one person down the line dies, it messes with the whole system. It's one of the reasons there are so few mages in Merceria."

"What are you suggesting as an alternative?" asked Gerald.

"I'm not sure," he responded, "but there must be something better."

"We used to train soldiers in groups," said Gerald.

"You need an academy," realized Anna.

"What's that?" asked Revi.

"A school where you can teach more than one person at a time."

"How would I do that?" he asked. "I have little enough time to train Aubrey."

"You would need help," she said, "perhaps a group of mages might band together to share their knowledge."

"An interesting concept," Revi mused. "I shall have to give it some thought."

"Other than telling us about the earl," said Gerald, "was there something else you came here for?"

"What? Oh, yes, I almost forgot. The earl has decided to put together a little party tonight. Not a formal affair, I'm told, but some dancing and such. He said it was more of a friendly visit with some entertainment."

"Is the earl up to it?" asked Anna.

"I'm sure he will be," proclaimed Revi. "He was in fine form when I left him."

"Then please tell him we gratefully accept," she said.

Revi looked back at her as if he'd been slapped, "Can't you send a messenger?"

"Do you see a messenger up here on the wall, Master Bloom?" she said.

"Well, no, but I'm far too busy to carry a message all the way back to the manor."

"But you were going there anyway," accused Gerald.

"I was?" said Revi. "What for?"

"You're the Royal Mage, Master Bloom, we can't have just anyone delivering our acceptance. What else have you got to do?"

"I'm quite busy," Revi responded.

"Doing what, exactly?" asked the princess.

The mage looked confused and slightly panicked. Gerald saw him struggling to make sense of the conversation. Finally, he slumped his shoulders, "Very well," he acquiesced, "I shall deliver your message."

He turned and trotted off down the ramparts, clutching his robes to stop them from blowing about.

"I never know what to make of our mage," commented Gerald.

"I know what you mean," said Anna. "He's a good man, but he tends to be a trifle confusing at times."

"Yes," agreed Gerald, "but you can count on him when you need to. You're lucky in that respect."

"I prefer to think it's more planning than luck," she said. "I've gathered friends about me, that's not luck."

"True, I suppose," he returned, "but what brought these people all together at this point in time?"

Anna smiled at the thought, "You're getting quite philosophical, Gerald. Perhaps you should become a mage."

"And give up the sword? No thank you, I'll stick with what I know."

"Have it your way," she said, "but regardless, we need to get back. Revi didn't tell us what time this little get together is, and we'll likely have to change."

"He did mention it's tonight," offered Gerald.

"Yes, but what time? Did it include food, or are we to eat before we go? Who, precisely is invited? There are many questions that need to be answered."

"Very well, Your Highness," he said, bowing low, "let us unravel this mysterious invitation in a less...windy place."

The music swelled as the dancers performed their delicate moves. Each pair perfectly in step with the steady strum of the instruments as they built to a crescendo, and when the music stopped, the dancers bowed deeply to each other.

The audience clapped in appreciation as the entertainers exited the room.

"Quite the show," exclaimed Revi, "though I'm surprised people would learn such moves."

"Why do you say that?" asked Beverly.

"I see no purpose to it," he countered.

"The purpose," said Hayley, "is to entertain people. Were you not entertained?"

"I suppose," he admitted, "but surely there are more important things for them to do?"

"Careful, Master Mage, you're beginning to sound like Beverly," warned the ranger.

"Hey!" exclaimed Beverly. "I know how to have fun on occasion, you know."

"You do, do you?" mused Hayley. "Give me an example?"

Beverly was at a loss for words, but as luck would have it, the earl was approaching. "Your Grace," she said, bowing.

"Dame Beverly," said the earl, "I've been told that in your hometown they have a rather unique dance."

"The Bodden Jig?" she asked. "It's not really a dance, just people swinging around moving on the dance floor."

"I thought you might demonstrate it for us?" he pressed.

"Yes, go ahead, Beverly," goaded Hayley. "You should demonstrate it for us."

Beverly wanted to object but knew she couldn't back down now. "Very well, Your Grace, I shall be honoured to demonstrate. Can your musicians play something with a lively step?"

"Of course," he replied.

She looked to Hayley. "Wish me luck," she said, and walked across the dance floor toward the opposite side of the room. Jack saw her coming and moved to intercept, but she ignored his offered hand, instead making her way toward a rather surprised Gerald.

"It seems," she stated, "that for the honour of Bodden we must dance the jig. Would you condescend to be my partner?"

Gerald smiled and was about to laugh but saw the look of seriousness on her face. He looked at Anna, but all she did was smile back and nod.

"Very well, Lady Beverly," he replied, "I shall be honoured."

They walked out to the middle of the room which had now been cleared of dancers. He stood facing her, holding her hands as they waited for the music to start. "Are you sure about this?" he asked.

"I have to, Gerald. I've been dared. Why? Is there a reason you don't want to dance with me?"

"I haven't seen you dance for years, Beverly. Not since we left Bodden. I thought you only danced with your father?"

"I did, but he's not here. Surely you remember the jig?"

"Of course, not that there's much to it."

The music started, and they began moving sideways, bouncing along as they did so, taking about a dozen steps. Repeating the same technique, they returned to where they started, then began haphazardly wheeling around the room to the muted sound of applause. Dame Levina then grabbed Sir Barnsley and joined them on the dance floor. Once the audience realized there were no rules to this dance, they flooded the area in pairs. People were bumping into one another, laughing as they did so. The nobles here were so enthralled by the experience that by the time the song was done they were shouting for more.

Gerald bowed before Beverly, who smiled back.

"Thank you, Gerald, you've been a most pleasant companion."

"My pleasure, Beverly," he replied. "Now I must get back to the princess."

"Why, is something wrong?"

"No, but there's a chair over there with my name on it. I'm afraid you've worn me out."

Beverly returned to Hayley who had been watching intently. "There," said the ranger, "that wasn't so bad, was it?"

"It's been years since I've done that," she confessed.

"Lady Beverly," interrupted a voice, "may I have the honour?" Jack was standing beside her, holding out his hand.

"No, Jack, you may not. My dancing is done for the day, but I thank you for the offer."

The cavalier bowed gracefully, "As you wish," he said with a twinkle in his eye, "though I daresay you do not know what you're missing."

"Oh, I'm pretty sure I do," she said, under her breath.

"Pardon?" he asked.

"Nothing, Jack. Enjoy yourself, I wouldn't want to deprive the other ladies of your company."

Jack made his way back onto the crowded floor.

"That was interesting," commented Hayley.

"He never gives up," said Beverly.

"That's not what I meant," the ranger returned.

"Then what's so interesting?"

"You didn't bite his head off," mused Hayley. "You're actually becoming diplomatic. There's hope for you yet."

"I didn't see you dancing," said Beverly, "Why don't you go and give it a try?"

Hayley peered through the crowd as if searching for someone. "I think I shall," she commented. "Wish me luck," she said as she disappeared into the crowd.

Beverly edged around the room, avoiding the centre mass of dancers. She noticed the princess was deep in conversation with the earl, who was petting Tempus' head. His Grace appeared enamoured of the great dog, and the animation on their faces told her they'd been talking at some length.

She spied Aubrey, watching the dancers, and edged her way toward her.

"Cousin!" called Aubrey. "That was quite the performance."

"Thank you," replied Beverly. "I would have danced longer, but I didn't know if Gerald could take it."

They both chuckled at the warrior's expense. "It's good to see you relaxing," observed Aubrey. "The last few months have been quite taxing."

"They have, haven't they," replied Beverly. "It seems like ever since we started this trip, trouble's followed us."

"I don't know about that," offered Aubrey. "That creature in Loranguard was there long before us, and the drake in Tivilton had been giving them trouble for years."

"So you're saying it's fate?" asked Beverly. "I didn't think you believed in that."

"I don't think it's fate. I think we're the type of people who like to investigate problems. As a group, we don't like things remaining the way they've always been. We strive to make change."

"I think the princess is rubbing off on you," said Beverly, "or maybe it's Revi's influence. I hope he's not making improper suggestions."

"Who, Revi? Don't be absurd, he's been the perfect gentleman in that regard."

"Where is he? I thought he'd be over here with you."

"He's on the dance floor," she said, pointing.

Beverly followed her finger to spy him across the room, dancing and twirling with a brunette. The view was blocked for a moment and then she saw his partner; it was Hayley!

"Well, I never..." she lost her train of thought.

"Who would have thought," added Aubrey.

"Certainly not me," said Beverly.

"I bet Aldwin would be able to dance like this," said Aubrey, a wisp of a smile escaping her lips.

"Yes," agreed Beverly, "he definitely would. Wait a moment, whose guarding the princess?" She was looking around, counting her knights, but they all appeared to be on the dance floor. "I better get over there."

"I'm sure she's fine," added Aubrey, as her cousin disappeared through the crowd.

~

The earl held out his goblet while a servant refilled it. "Such a magnificent beast," he said. "I've never seen one up close."

"Didn't the Kurathians use them when they attacked the city?" Anna asked.

"No, they're primarily used against cavalry. Not much good in the city streets. They need space to bring their prey down. I've never seen them in action myself, but I've read about their use; terrifying on the battlefield."

"And they can actually bring down a horse?" she asked.

"Oh yes, they go for the legs, you see. Their powerful jaws clamp down on them, breaking bones and rending flesh. They're trained to bring down a horse and then go for the next one. Usually, the Kurathians bring in foot troops to finish off the riders."

"That sounds grim," she observed.

"Oh, it is," he replied. He opened his mouth to say more and then clutched his stomach letting out a moan of pain.

"Are you all right, Your Grace?" Anna asked.

He doubled over, falling from his chair while shouts of alarm erupted nearby.

Revi had seen him fall and was soon there, beside him. "Let's get him to somewhere he can lie down," he ordered the servants.

The room erupted into confusion. Soon, Aubrey was there as well, and the two mages followed the servants as the earl was carried away.

Beverly and Gerald both arrived at Anna's side. "We should get you to safety," urged Beverly.

"The earl has had an attack," said Anna. "We must do something."

"The mages have it in hand," coaxed Gerald, "but we can't rule out poison. We need to get you to safety."

"Where's Alric?" asked the princess, looking around. "Is he all right?"

"He's fine," soothed Beverly. "Jack has him. He'll meet us upstairs in the visitors wing."

"Very well," she acquiesced, "lead on."

Troops had entered the room, likely to keep order and for a moment Gerald wondered if it was a plot to seize power, but Captain Fraser addressed the assembled guests, assuring them that all was well, asking everyone to take their leave.

They made their way to their rooms, to find Hayley had already set Knights of the Hound to watch the hallways. Things calmed down quickly, and Anna sent word for her advisors to gather in her room. Soon, they were all assembled, save for the two mages. They stood around while Anna related all that had transpired.

"Isn't this a little bit of an overreaction for indigestion?" asked Arnim.

"There's something else going on around here," explained Anna. "This is too much of a coincidence."

"Meaning?" asked Hayley.

"We arrive in Riversend, and barely two days later the earl has collapsed? That strikes me as odd."

"Hasn't he had this problem for a while?" asked Beverly.

"He has," agreed Anna, "but Revi used magic on him. He should have gotten better. If it was simple indigestion, wouldn't he have had to have eaten something? They hadn't served the food yet!"

"It was likely his lunch," offered Arnim. "We don't know what the earl eats. Perhaps he's had some bad fish."

"Possibly," admitted Anna, "but I have a feeling something is happening here. I just can't put my finger on it."

A knock on the door was dutifully answered by Sophie who opened it to reveal Aubrey. The young woman looked fretful, and upon entering the room, the light revealed tears in her eyes.

"The earl is dead," she announced.

THIRTY-THREE

Mourning

SPRING 961 MC

I t was a sombre morning. The flags had been lowered to half-mast in mourning for the earl while the whole manor had taken on an air of gloominess. Alric knocked on Anna's door, and Sophie opened it to bow deeply.

"Is the princess available?" he asked.

"Yes, Highness," replied Sophie. "She's just finished dressing. Would you like to come in?"

"Thank you," he replied, entering the room.

Anna stepped through the bedroom door to join him. "Alric," she said, "I assume you're heading down to pay your respects?"

"Yes," he admitted, "though I wondered if you would accompany me."

"I should love to," she said, "but I'm not clear on your customs in this regard."

"The earl's body will be laid out on a table so that people can pass him and say a prayer."

"Isn't that a bit ghastly?" she asked. "He's only been dead for a few hours."

"His body is set to be interred later today. We don't keep bodies around for long in Weldwyn. We believe that once their soul has left, the body is just a vessel."

"Then why display the body?" she asked.

"It's an old tradition. Originally, it was to prove the death so that people could accept it. They dress the body in fine clothes and make it look as presentable as possible."

"What if they met a grisly end?" she asked.

"If the body were un-viewable, they would pass by one of his treasured possessions, or possibly his widow, if he had one. Have you no such traditions in Merceria?"

"No," she admitted. "However, bodies are examined to make sure they're dead before cremation or burial. There's no public display, though."

"What if a king dies? Or an earl?"

"That's a little different. They'll take the body in a coffin to the cathedral for interment, but the body isn't on display. Only the coffin is visible."

"Perhaps you should stay here," he suggested, "I wouldn't like to make you feel uncomfortable."

"Nonsense," she replied. "I've seen my share of dead bodies in the past, I'm not squeamish."

"Very well," said Alric, "shall we?" He held out his arm for her to hold.

"Sophie," she said, taking the arm, "would you look after Tempus for me? And please send word to have Gerald meet us downstairs?"

"Certainly, Highness."

They made their way down the corridor to the great staircase and paused to look upon on the long line of visitors waiting to see the body.

"I've never seen a line up this long before," remarked Anna. "How long is it?"

"Let's go and have a look, shall we?" he replied.

They descended the stairs and then exited the building. People in the line bowed and nodded their heads as they passed, though Alric paid them little attention. The line seemed to go on forever, and it wasn't until they turned a corner, two blocks away, that they saw the end.

"There must be several thousand people here," noted Anna. "And most of them are commoners. Is that the custom here?"

"Is what the custom here?" asked Alric. "That there's a long line of commoners?"

"That people would line up like this for a noble?"

"He was well-loved," explained the prince. "Surely you have such men in Merceria."

"Very few," she admitted, "though I daresay Lord Fitzwilliam might command such loyalty."

"Dame Beverly's father?"

"Yes, he's much beloved by his people, though I don't think he would approve of people lining up to view his body. He's actually quite a private man."

"Perhaps someday I'll meet him," offered Alric. "He sounds quite fascinating. How do you know him, if I might ask?"

Conover, Richard Craig
65713
Unclaim : 8/20/2019

Held date   : 8/12/2019
Pickup location : Central Branch

Title   : Mercerian tales : storie
s of the past
Call number   : F BEN
Item barcode   : 31267507363354
Assigned branch : Miller Branch

Notification   : Email Address

Notes:
A+ (only Howard County): (none)
Staff Initials: hla updated
Receive Library News By Email:

"He was Gerald's mentor, so I knew about him long before I met him. He came to Uxley, the Hall where I was raised. He was concerned for my welfare."

"We have people like that in Weldwyn," he said. "They're usually working to their own advantage. He likely thought he could manipulate you. My father warned me about such men."

"No," she objected, "he's not like that. He was only concerned for my safety. He's never asked me to do anything. He even sent his own daughter to keep me safe, and she's proven to be a loyal companion and friend."

"You seem to collect those," he observed.

"Yes, I'm fortunate in my companions. I wouldn't like to think how I'd have turned out if Gerald hadn't found me."

They started walking back to the manor. "I'm glad he did," Alric admitted. "I didn't like him at first, but he's grown on me in the time I've known him. I shall sleep better at night knowing that when you return to Merceria, he'll be watching out for you."

"Me too," she admitted, and then changed the subject. "Will we stand in line to see the earl?"

"No," he said, "I'm a Prince of the Realm. We'll get to see him before they open the doors."

"And when will that be?"

"Shortly, I expect. They've been preparing the body all morning."

"Preparing?"

"Yes, they'll wash it and dress it in fine clothes for its display."

"You keep calling him 'it'."

"Yes, it's his body, but he no longer resides in it. Malin has taken his spirit to the Afterlife. What do you believe in Merceria?"

"We must make our own way to the Afterlife where Saxnor will judge our strength. If we are deemed worthy, he will welcome us into his halls."

"And if you are unworthy?"

"Then it's to the Underworld with you," she replied.

"But surely not everyone can be strong?" he noted.

"Strength isn't just about physical power. A person can be strong of character or strong of heart and still be welcomed."

"It still sounds like a very exclusive place."

"I suppose it is," she admitted, "but it gives people something to strive for in their lives. A code of conduct, if you will."

Alric mulled this over, and Anna let him take his time. They were soon before the manor and servants conducted them inside. Gerald was waiting for them, dressed in his armour, complete with helm and sword.

"What's this?" asked Alric.

"It is our custom," said Gerald, "that we say goodbye to our fallen warriors with honour."

"He would be pleased," remarked Alric. "Shall we enter?"

Gerald fell in behind the two royals as they strode through the door into the great hall. The body had been laid out on a marble-topped table which had been draped with the flag of the earl's house. His body rested upon it, wearing his chainmail and clutching his sword between his hands, its tip resting near his feet. His head was bare of helmet, but his hair and beard had been carefully combed. He had a look of peace to him as if he was sleeping.

The royal party stepped up, standing before the body, gazing down upon it. Gerald watched Anna lean forward slightly as if something had grabbed her attention. She said nothing as Alric went to his knees to say a silent prayer. He rose and then moved off to the left side of the room, Anna following.

Gerald stepped forward and gazed down at the earl. At first glance, the man looked like he was sleeping and Gerald marvelled at the skill with which he had been laid out. Knowing that Anna had seen something, he leaned forward slightly, examining things in more detail. He noticed the pale skin, understandable in a dead body. The earl's face looked painted, and he realized that the body had been coloured to give it the appearance of life. The eyes, however, had not been sufficiently covered and he spotted dark rings around the sockets. He looked down to the body's hands and discovered what had drawn Anna's attention; the roots of the fingernails were darkened.

He stood up straight. There could be only one conclusion; the earl had been poisoned. For a moment he wanted to yell out, to tell everyone of the crime, but then he remembered where he was and looked to his left. Anna and Alric were waiting for him, but as his eyes met those of the princess, she nodded her head; she knew what he had seen. Once he made his way over to them, they exited the room. The doors shut behind them and Gerald made to speak, but Anna shook her head slightly to stop him.

"Thank you, Anna," said Alric. "It has been a great comfort to me to have you here."

"It was my pleasure," she said, "to be able to assist in this time of great loss. If there is anything I, or my people can do for you, please don't hesitate to ask."

"I will," he promised. "Now I'm afraid I must leave you for I have much to do. The earl left no one in charge, so it has fallen to me to arrange things."

"Has he no family?" Anna asked.

"A son. He's all grown up now, but he's in the capital. Word has been sent, but it'll be weeks before he can return."

"What about the funeral?" Gerald asked. "Is there anything we can do to help?"

"He will be interred in the crypt once the viewing is over," Alric responded. "It is our way." He was about to leave but turned, unexpectedly, "Actually, there is something you can do for me, Gerald."

"Certainly, Highness," Gerald responded.

"I should like you to contact Captain Fraser. I'd like to address the soldiers later this afternoon. Can you tell him to assemble them? I'll leave the details up to you."

"Of course, Highness," he responded.

Alric nodded, then turned, striding away with purpose.

"What was that all about?" asked Gerald.

"He trusts you. He's known you for months. He's unsure how to address the men, he's never had to do this type of thing before."

"He was there when we fought the drake," offered Gerald.

"That was different," she replied, "those were his men. He's here now, having to follow in some very big footsteps."

"Then I'll make sure he doesn't trip, Anna."

"Thank you, Gerald. I knew you could be counted on."

"What of the earl and his death?"

"I'd like to discuss this with Revi. Can you find him and bring him to my room?"

"Of course, Anna. What about the rest of them."

"We'll fill them in later. I'd like to confirm a few things first, make sure our suspicions are correct before proceeding."

"Very well, I'll hunt down the mage."

Anna sat at a table, quill in hand, writing out notes, as Gerald entered with Revi. Tempus, in his usual position beneath the desk, opened his eyes to view the new visitors then promptly went back to sleep when it was evident there was no threat.

"Master Revi," Anna began, "please have a seat. I know you did all you could for the earl, but I wanted to hear from you what happened. Do you have a cause of death?"

The mage sat, unsure of where to start, "He was perfectly fine when I saw him this morning," he protested.

"No one is arguing your effectiveness, Master Bloom," she said. "What can you tell us about his sudden turn for the worse?"

"The servants took him to his room and laid him on the bed. He was very pale, his skin almost waxy looking. I've never seen its like before."

"I see," observed Anna. "Anything else? Any unusual symptoms?"

"His eyes appeared sunken, with dark marks under them but other than that, I would say no."

"Your parents are herbalists, are they not?" asked Gerald.

"Yes, why?" responded the mage.

"We were wondering how much you remember about herbs," said Anna.

"Why? Is this an inquisition? I had nothing to do with the earl's death."

"We know that," said Gerald, trying to soothe him. "We just need to confirm something. Ever heard of Warriors Bane?"

Revi leaned back in his chair, stroking his chin absently. "It's a type of moss, isn't it?"

"How common is it?" asked Anna.

"Not common at all," replied the mage. "In fact, it's very rare indeed. Why do you ask?"

"It's poisonous. We think the earl was murdered," the princess continued.

"How can you be so sure?" asked the mage.

"The queen died with the same symptoms."

"I thought the queen died of a sudden illness," said Revi.

"That's what they want people to think," said Anna.

"Who are 'they'?" asked the mage.

"That part we don't know yet," commented Gerald, "though we had some suspicions it might be the king's mistress, but that seems unlikely now."

"Might it be simple coincidence?" Revi enquired.

Anna pondered the concept for a moment. "I think it unlikely that two high ranking people died within a year of the exact same rare poison, don't you?"

"Yes," admitted the mage, "but what does that leave us with? Who would benefit from these two deaths? How can they possibly be related?"

"I was wondering the same thing," admitted Anna.

Gerald intervened, "Didn't Albreda warn about a dark shadow?"

"Yes," confirmed Anna, "she said 'a dark shadow grips the land', but I can't figure out what that means."

"I'm beginning to suspect," offered Revi, "that what we found in Tivilton may have something to do with it."

"What do you mean?" asked Gerald.

"Well, what do you think of when I say a dark shadow?" asked Revi.

"Someone creeping around in the background?" said Gerald.

"Yes. I think that someone, or some group, is trying to orchestrate something," said the mage.

"To what end?" asked Anna.

"Of that, I'm not sure," Revi responded, "but because of Tivilton we now know that Elves had dark magic. Could one of their necromancers be behind these acts?"

"Isn't it a bit of stretch," asked Gerald, "to go from two deaths to Death Mages?"

"But you admit," defended Revi, "that it's likely these two deaths were related. That being the case, we must find out how. What do these deaths have in common?"

"We don't know," observed Anna, "but we shall investigate further."

"What do we do now?" asked Gerald. "We seem to be at a dead end."

"Not really," Anna said. "Whoever killed the earl wanted him out of the way for some reason. I'm confident that in the next few days we shall find out why. In the meantime, we must keep this to ourselves."

"When you say 'ourselves,'" asked Revi, "who precisely does that mean?"

"My council," she responded, "that includes Gerald, yourself, Beverly, Hayley, Arnim and Aubrey."

"What about Sophie and Lady Nicole?" asked Gerald.

"Sophie, yes," the princess affirmed, "but let's not inform Lady Nicole, I'm still not entirely sure I can trust her."

"Are you going to inform Prince Alric?" asked the mage.

"No, I think it best we keep this to ourselves for now. The fewer people who know about it, the better."

"What do I tell them, Gerald?" asked Alric.

They were standing at the side of the practice field, watching as the troops lined up. The garrison of Riversend was larger than the small army that had defeated the invaders in Merceria, though perhaps not quite as large as the group that had marched on Eastwood.

"Tell them what they want to hear," offered Gerald, "that usually works."

"What do they want to hear?"

"That they must carry on. The earl would want them to do their duty."

"Is that all?" asked Alric.

"Soldiers are simple men," Gerald explained. "They like to know they're doing their job, that they'll be paid and looked after. You look after the men, and they'll look after you."

"Is that true?"

"It always worked for Baron Fitzwilliam. I've seen troops that didn't respect their officers, it doesn't usually end well."

"When was this?" Alric asked.

"Last year, when we marched on Eastwood. We were crushing a rebellion. The Earl of Shrewesdale abused his troops, and they didn't take kindly to it."

"How so?" the young prince enquired.

"He didn't feed them properly. They rose up in anger, threatened to mutiny."

"What did the earl do?" Alric asked, enthralled by the story.

"The earl didn't do anything; it was the princess that solved the problem. She raided the earl's personal baggage and handed out food to the starving men. When the earl complained, she said he could take it up with her father, the king."

"I should have liked to have seen that," said Alric.

"Remember, keep the men fed and paid, and you'll keep them happy."

"Anything else I should do?" he asked. "This is all so overwhelming."

"Yes, talk to them."

"I'm just about to," objected Alric, "that's why we're here, isn't it?"

"No, Highness. I mean talk to them, individually. Not every one of them, mind you. Walk the lines, chat with a soldier every so often, you'll be amazed at the loyalty you'll gain."

"And when do I do this?" he asked.

"Right after you give them an amazing speech."

"That's the part I'm afraid of. What if I say the wrong thing?"

Gerald looked the young prince straight in the eyes. "You're a Prince of the Realm. You won't say the wrong thing. Soldiers aren't generally well bred. They're commoners, just talk to them like regular people, they'll appreciate it."

"You're full of wisdom, Gerald," said Alric. "Thank you for helping."

"My pleasure, Highness. Now let's go out and give them a show, shall we? Captain Fraser is coming over now, and I've got a standard bearer to carry your pennant as we walk. I assume they'll recognize your Royal Flag?"

"Yes," admitted Alric, "all the companies of Weldwyn have one for occasions like this, though I suspect it's been dusty for some time."

"Then it's time," Gerald announced.

Captain Fraser halted in front of the prince. "Your Highness," he said, bowing.

"Captain," Alric nodded his head, "shall we begin?"

"Whenever you're ready, Highness," confirmed Fraser.

Alric strode forward with great determination, followed by Captain

Fraser and Gerald. He hoped the old warrior would lend an air of respectability to his presence. Gerald had cleaned his mail, sharpened and polished his sword, and now presented an imposing sight; a seasoned warrior.

Alric stopped in front of the men. Five hundred strong, they raised their voices in a cheer for the young royal. He held up his hands and paused, waiting for quiet to descend upon the field.

"Men of Weldwyn," he announced, "I have come here today to bring you sad tidings, for your beloved earl no longer treads upon this mortal earth."

There were some grumblings among the men, and Alric let them continue for a moment before raising his hands once more. "Though we mourn his loss, he would have wished us to carry on. To once more shoulder the burden of protecting this great city from those who would seek to do it harm."

He took a breath. They were staring back at him in great anticipation. He felt the sweat running down his back and was suddenly speechless.

"You're doing fine, Highness," muttered Gerald, "keep talking, it'll get easier."

"The kingdom thanks you for your valiant service..." his voice trailed off. "I'm losing them, Gerald," he murmured.

Gerald looked over to his right; barrels sat by the side of the field, a gift from Anna. "Almost done, Highness," he coaxed. "Just one more thing. See those barrels to the right?"

Alric quickly glanced over and nodded.

"They're full of ale for the men. Tell them to have a drink in the earl's name. They'll remember that for the rest of their lives."

Alric nodded, and then continued his speech, "In gratitude, and in memory of the earl, we have arranged for you to drink to his honour."

It was working. Suddenly, he had their undivided attention.

"When your captain dismisses you," announced Alric, "you will exit to the right side of the field where ale has been provided for you."

The troops broke out in spontaneous applause and Alric couldn't help but smile. "Captain Fraser?" he called.

"Highness?"

"You may dismiss the men." Alric turned to his left and strode toward the waiting barrels.

Gerald followed behind dutifully while the captain called the men to attention and then dismissed them. There was another cheer as the men rushed to the barrels, filling the air with their exuberance.

"I thought you were going to talk to them?" Gerald asked. "One on one, I mean."

"And so I shall," promised Alric, "but I thought it better to do that while sharing a drink with them."

"A nice touch, Highness," Gerald admitted. "You learn fast."

Alric turned to offer his hand, "You're an excellent teacher, Gerald. I'm glad you're here."

Gerald shook the prince's hand, "So am I, Highness, so am I."

As the last rays of the setting sun disappeared over the horizon, lights began appearing in the city. The noise of the evening drifted up to the wall, the sounds echoing through the air. The city was in mourning and Gerald watched from the walls as people staggered to and from the taverns and pubs.

"It's a cool evening," interrupted a voice, and Gerald turned to see Beverly approaching.

"What are you doing up here?" asked Gerald.

"I could ask you the same question," retorted the knight. "Had enough of the celebrations?"

"It's a strange custom," he replied, "celebrating a man's life when he's dead."

"It's what they do," she exclaimed. "They don't mourn the same as us. Perhaps it's better this way, remembering people the way they were, not the way they died."

"They'll regret it in the morning," he predicted.

"The princess told me you'd be up here. Do you come up here a lot?"

"Lately, I do. It's quiet up here. I can organize my thoughts."

"Which are?" she pressed.

"Something's wrong here. I can feel it. Something big's about to happen, but I can't tell you what that is."

"Are you sure? Perhaps someone just had it out for the earl, a rival perhaps?"

"We only just met the earl, but he seemed like a nice enough person. Perhaps that's the problem. There are far too few people like him in the world; we can't afford to lose even one. It irks me."

"It irks you? You're beginning to sound like my father."

"I'll take that as a compliment," he said.

In the distance there was a call, and they turned their attention to the bluff that overlooked the city from the east bank of the river.

"Something's going on," observed Beverly.

"That's just the changing of the guard at the watchtower," explained Gerald. "You can make out the soldiers chatting."

"Why do they use spears up there?" Beverly asked. "I would have thought a sword easier to carry."

"If an enemy soldier is climbing a cliff, it's the perfect weapon; easier to stab down with a spear than a sword."

"I hadn't thought of that," she mused.

"See? I can still teach you a thing or two about fighting."

"I never doubted it, Gerald."

"Do you miss Bodden?" he asked.

"I miss my father, and Aldwin, but no. I've come to see this group as my family. I've found my purpose in life, and I'm quite happy."

"I'm glad to hear you say so," said Gerald. "I feel the same way, but if you tell anyone, I'll deny it."

Beverly laughed, "So be it, Gerald. You shall retain your reputation as the grumpy old man. Now, it's getting late, you should be to bed.

Gerald touched her forearm as she was about to leave. "Look," he said, pointing north.

All across the northern part of the city, tiny lights appeared, flickering, and then began rising into the air.

"They're little paper lanterns," explained Gerald. "I saw them preparing some earlier today. They put a candle in the bottom, and then float them up into the sky."

"It's breathtaking," observed Beverly. "What's their purpose?"

"To guide the spirit of a loved one to the Afterlife," he explained.

They watched the lights as they rose higher and began making their way inland. One by one the tiny flames flickered and died as they burned out or were snuffed out by the wind. The sky finally returned to its raven hue.

"It's a bad portend," said Gerald.

"How so?"

"Not one candle stayed lit. Something is coming, something that will snuff the life out of this city, I can smell it in the air."

"That's just the smell of the sea, Gerald."

"It smells different tonight, I can't explain it."

"Is there something we should do to prepare?"

"Like what? We can't prepare when we don't know what's coming. Perhaps in the morning I'll have a better idea."

They left the wall, but Beverly took precautions before turning in for the night, posting extra guards on the princess.

THIRTY-FOUR

Trouble

SPRING 961 MC

The early morning sun broke through the clouds, sending streaks of light down as if the Gods were watching them. Gerald was up early, Tempus in tow, walking the wall to give the great beast's legs a stretch. He noticed the morning guard on the bluffs, looking down over the city, their swords gleaming in the early morning light. He nodded to a garrison soldier as he passed, the man giving the mastiff a wide berth. Gerald leaned against the parapet, gazing over the sea. Tempus, intrigued by this action, rose up on his rear legs to join him.

"That's the sea, Tempus," he explained. "That's where you come from, across the water."

As if in agreement, Tempus barked.

Gerald laughed, patting the dog's head. It was beautiful up here, so peaceful; he was sad to think that they would have to leave. They must return to Merceria soon, he knew, for the princess was due back in Wincaster by the end of summer and there were many miles to traverse to get there.

Tempus barked again, and this time he heard a warning tone.

"What is it, boy? What is it you see?"

Gerald gazed over the water, cursing his eyes for not being as perceptive as they once were. "You there!" he yelled at a soldier.

The man turned at the shout.

"Come here, quickly," he called.

The soldier ran over, eager to please. "Yes, sir?"

"Look out there," he commanded. "What do you see?"

The soldier looked over the parapet, shading his eyes from the morning sun. "Sails!" he cried in surprise. "So many sails!"

"Sound the alarm," ordered Gerald. "We're under attack."

The soldier ran down the wall toward the nearest tower. It would likely be noon by the time the ships were in range, but Gerald wanted to make sure everything was in place. He was suddenly struck by his earlier observance of the guards on the bluff, and berated himself for not investigating further; they should have had spears not swords.

He looked to the cliff to see a streak of flame shoot through the sky, landing in the city. The soldiers were still there, watching the city, but someone had wheeled up catapults to the edge of the bluff and now missile after missile began to rain down on Riversend.

"I should have known," he cursed out loud. "We have to get to the manor, they need to know."

He ran toward the tower, Tempus in hot pursuit.

The manor was a beehive of activity by the time Gerald arrived. He found Anna in the great hall, along with Alric and his advisors. They had a map spread out on a table and were making defensive plans.

"They've taken the bluffs," announced Gerald as he entered.

"So we've gathered," said Alric. "They've set fire to a good portion of the city."

Gerald made a quick scan of the map. "What's been done so far?" he asked.

"We've ordered the evacuation of the docks," said Alric. "Once everyone is through, we'll close the gates."

"Then what?" asked Gerald.

Alric looked at the seasoned veteran, "We were just discussing that. I was hoping you might have some suggestions."

Gerald looked to Anna, who nodded.

"Let me see," he muttered, more to himself. "Those catapults will cause havoc. Any idea how they got there?"

"They must have climbed the cliffs," suggested Anna.

"Impossible," exclaimed Alric. "The guards would have seen them."

"Not if the guards were in on it," said Anna.

Alric looked at her with a stunned expression.

"It only makes sense, Alric. And the timing is too coincidental. The earl dies, and one day later a fleet arrives? They've caught you at your most vulnerable."

"The walls should hold them," he announced.

"They won't," said Gerald. "If they were smart enough to take the bluffs, they'll have a plan to get in."

"I've sent Hayley to spy out the fleet," added Anna. "Perhaps she can provide more information."

"You've been in a siege before, Gerald," said Alric. "What can we expect."

"Nothing nice, Your Highness. The bombardment alone will play havoc with the city. It'll also make it tough to move troops around."

"But we don't know who we can trust!" exclaimed Alric. "If treachery was involved, we could be putting ourselves further at risk."

"We can't let that paralyze us, Alric," said Anna. "You must use the people you trust."

Alric looked around the room, taking the measure of those assembled.

"What shall we do, Highness?" asked a noble.

Alric stared at the map for a moment before answering. "Gerald, I'm putting you in charge of the defenses. You've seen this type of thing before, I trust your judgement."

"Yes, Highness," he agreed.

"Anna, I need a word in private." The prince continued, "Please come with me."

They stepped into the hallway and Alric looked around to make sure they were alone.

"Someone here has betrayed the crown," he said at last, "but I still need somebody to look into it. You have people you can trust to carry this out?"

"Of course, Alric. What shall I do if I find them?"

"Do whatever you feel is best, I'll support your decision. This is war, we have no time for courts."

"Understood," she acknowledged. "I'll get people on it right away. What will you do?"

"I'll see what Gerald thinks is best. If nothing else, I can command my own guard."

"Be careful, Alric, your life is important to me."

"As yours is to me," he said.

Gerald was pointing at the map. "The trouble is here," he said, pointing to the cliffs. "If we can't dislodge them from the bluffs, they'll burn this city to the ground."

"I can take the knights and sweep them clear," offered Beverly. "We will exit by the north gate and climb the slope from across the river."

"I like the idea," confirmed Gerald, "but I'm going to need you here, Beverly, there'll be lots of work once they break the gate."

"What makes you think they'll break the gate?" asked Captain Fraser.

"They wouldn't have sailed all this way without a plan, Captain. I don't know how they'll do it, but they'll break the gate and then flood into the city."

He turned his attention back to the redheaded knight. "Who's best qualified to lead the knights, after you, Beverly?"

"Dame Hayley," she responded.

"Send her with the rest of the knights."

"So few?" said Arnim.

"They've likely never faced heavily armoured riders before," explained Gerald. "The knights should have a tremendous advantage."

"I'll go with them," offered Revi, "I might be of some use?"

"Very well," ordered Gerald, "but Aubrey stays here, we'll need to set up a place for wounded."

"Yes, Commander," responded the young apprentice.

"The main roads all run from the three gates toward the manor. Beverly, I want you to gather the troops. You'll build barricades here, here and here." He stabbed down with his finger to indicate their positions.

"You can't do that," complained Captain Fraser. "We need the men for the wall. How else will we repel invaders?"

"The invaders are coming in ships," Gerald said. "It would require very tall ladders to scale those walls. I doubt such things would be easy to carry aboard ship."

"Then we can use the walls to fire down on them," the captain declared.

"Unfortunately, that won't work. Whoever designed this city did a bad job of building these gates. The walls don't provide flanking fire, they're too straight, so it leaves the gates vulnerable. They'd also be easy to pick off from the bluffs, or had you forgotten they're in the hands of the enemy?"

The captain fell silent.

"Beverly, as soon as Hayley gets back from the wall have her gather the knights and get to the cliffs, we must stop those catapults."

"What can I do?" asked Alric.

"I need you to assemble whatever cavalry you have here. We'll hold them in reserve, they'll form the counter-attack."

"When will that be?" he asked.

"We won't know for sure until we see the attacking force in more detail."

"Captain Fraser, I want you down at the Traders Gate. Hold it for as long as you can, but pull back at the first indication of a breach. I don't want you being swamped. You'll pull back to this barricade."

"I must object," said the captain, turning to Prince Alric.

"You have your orders, Captain. I placed Commander Matheson in charge, I expect you to follow his orders as if I gave them myself."

The captain closed his mouth, stunned by the response.

"Be about your business, Captain," said Alric. "We all have our parts to play."

Captain Fraser stormed from the room.

Gerald spotted Anna; she had called over Arnim and was talking to him in hushed tones. He waited until the guard captain left, and then wandered over while others examined the map in more detail.

"Where's Lily?" he asked.

"She's in her room," said Anna. "Do you think you'll need her?"

"Not yet, but she may prove useful. Do you remember the battle at Colbridge?"

"Of course, I remember everything."

"If things get desperate, we might need her ability to mask our retreat."

"Are things that bad?" she asked, worry lines furrowing her brow.

"No, not yet, but I suspect the invaders will have a trick or two up their sleeves. We must plan for all eventualities. I'm afraid we're going to need your household guard to man the barricades."

"I'll order them to report to Beverly, but I've got Arnim busy with something else."

"I noticed," he confirmed. "I assume he's looking into the betrayal?"

"He is, though I'd rather not go into details here, there are too many people present."

"Fair enough," he responded, "but let me know if you find anything."

"What can I do, Gerald? I feel so useless right now."

He put his hands on her shoulders, "I need you to help Aubrey. No one here really knows her, and we need a station for the wounded. You're a royal, people will listen to you. Take Tempus with you and pick a spot out of the reach of those catapults, if you can."

"Aye, Commander," she replied.

Gerald returned to the map, wondering if he was doing all he could?

Arnim quietly closed the door behind him, leaving the rest to plot the defense of the city. To him had fallen the task of identifying the traitor who had allowed this invasion plan to proceed. But where to begin?

"Arnim?"

Recognizing the voice, he turned to see Lady Nicole.

"What is it?" he asked in irritation.

"Where are you going?" she queried.

"I don't have time to explain, I've important work to do."

"Let me come with you," she begged. "You know I can be useful."

He paused for a moment, trying to read her face.

"Come on, Arnim, let me help. The princess has no use for me anymore. I don't fit in with the servants, and I'm not trusted by the rest of her party. You know I have skills you can use."

"Very well," he said at last. "Come with me."

Turning, he set off at a fast pace, Lady Nicole struggling to catch up.

"Where are we going?" she asked.

"Someone around here is working against the Weldwyn Crown. It's time we had a look at them in more detail."

"How do we do that?"

"We're going to look in their quarters, wherever those may be."

"Isn't that dangerous?" she asked.

"Not at the moment, they're all busy with the siege, but we have to investigate as quickly as possible.

∼

Dame Hayley Chambers looked out from the tower atop of the Traders Gate. The enemy fleet was much clearer now, and she estimated over one hundred ships would soon be within range. She looked on in fascination as one of the largest ships came into view; it was a gigantic barge pulled by the largest creature the ranger had ever seen. Its long neck extended out of the water far higher than the ship's deck. There were chains fashioned to a ring about its neck which ran back to the barge where a man in coloured robes stood upon the forecastle, gesticulating, no doubt controlling the beast.

Behind him, Hayley saw the flat deck holding a number of large catapults. Even as she watched, the barge surged forward, only to begin a wide turn, presenting its side to the city. Without warning, flames erupted from torches evenly spaced along the vessel, and then the missiles in the catapults were lit on fire. Even from this distance she could hear the sound as the catapults fired, the fiery globes hurtling toward the shore, leaving a sooty trail of smoke as they crashed against the wall, shaking it down to the foundations. She knew it would take a few ranging shots to get their aim adjusted, and so she waited, taking in as much detail as she could in the time she had.

Another barge appeared, following the path of the first and once again a strange massive creature towed the payload. She watched as a plethora of smaller vessels, shallow draft boats with ranks of oars and their decks packed with men, rowed forward, quickly outdistancing their slower cousins.

One more shot hit the wall, and then Hayley was gone, rushing down the tower to make her way back to the command centre.

◆

Hayley rode up to the manor, pushing her mount as much as she could. She recognized Dame Beverly out front along with half a dozen knights formed up. She pulled up short, halting just before the redheaded knight.

"They've brought siege weapons. I have a full listing here," she said, pulling forth a folded paper.

"You're to take the knights out the north gate," said Beverly, taking the note from her hand, "and push the enemy from the bluffs, they're doing a tremendous amount of damage to the city."

"Shouldn't you be doing that?" she asked.

"I have other pressing business to attend to," Beverly replied. "Gerald is in charge, and he wants you to go. Also, Revi will be joining you."

"Revi?" questioned Hayley. "What's he going to do? He's a healer."

"You might be surprised," responded Beverly. "Now get going, you've a long ride ahead of you, and we need that cliff cleared as soon as possible."

Hayley turned to look at the assembled knights; six of them, all there was, save for herself, Beverly and Arnim. She wondered how many of them would be left at the end of this day. Hearing the sounds of horseshoes, she turned to see Revi Bloom coming down the road.

"Let's go," she shouted. "The mage will catch up, he's not slowed by armour."

She moved out, the group falling into pairs behind their leader. Revi soon caught up and took his position beside the ranger.

He grinned at her, "Lovely day for a ride."

"Are you insane?" she reacted. "We're going into battle."

"Oh, I know," he retorted, "but still, it's nice weather. I like to look on the bright side of things."

Hayley shook her head; she didn't know what would happen on the bluff, but Revi Bloom certainly made things interesting.

◆

"The assault has begun," announced Beverly, "and I have Hayley's report."

"What do they have?" asked Gerald.

"She estimates a hundred or so ships. They have two large barges with siege engines being pulled by some sort of large creatures. They appear to be controlled by mages."

"How are the barricades?" he asked.

"They're almost ready," she returned. "Hayley has set off for the bluff."

"Are the ships landing troops?"

"They're sending forward multiple ships jammed with men. They seem to know exactly what they're doing."

"I would expect no less," he groused. "They've already demonstrated their abilities by claiming the bluffs. How long do you think the gates will last?"

"She says the catapults are quite large. Once they get the range, the gates won't last long."

As if to emphasize the fact, a large rumble ran underneath their feet.

"Get to the barricades, Beverly, they'll need you there. Hold back far enough to see them all, then rush to whichever one needs help the most. See if Prince Alric can spare some horsemen, you'll need a quick reaction force."

Beverly rushed out of the room while Gerald looked down at his map with all its annotations. "I should be out there," he said, through gritted teeth.

"You're needed here," chided Anna. "You're far more important to the defense where you can control things."

～

Arnim looked down the corridor in frustration. "Five rooms so far and nothing. Perhaps we're on a fool's errand."

"Are you sure there IS a traitor?" asked Lady Nicole.

"There had to be collusion to get the siege engines to the bluff without sounding the alarm. Someone has to be responsible."

"How many more rooms are there?"

"From my conversation with the princess, there are only a half dozen or so people with the authority to pull this off, and there's only two rooms left."

He grasped the door handle to find it wouldn't budge. "This one's locked."

"That's surprising," commented Nicole. "None of the others were."

Arnim knelt by the door, examining the keyhole, "This is no ordinary lock."

"Meaning?"

"Meaning, someone has something important to keep safe."

"Whose room is it?"

Arnim consulted a folded piece of paper, "Captain Fraser."

He returned his attention to the lock, withdrawing some small metal tools from his belt pouch. Lady Nicole kept her eyes on the corridor while he worked until she heard the knight curse.

Turning her head, she asked, "What is it?"

"Saxnor's balls, this lock's too hard," he exclaimed.

"Shall I have a go?" she volunteered.

He moved to the side to allow her room, "Do you still have your tools?"

In answer, she lifted her skirt to reveal a small folded pouch tucked into her garter belt.

"I see you're still prepared," he commented.

"Some things never change," she returned, removing the tool she needed and deftly inserting it into the lock. A moment later there was a clicking sound, and the door swung inward.

"It seems you have been successful," Arnim glumly observed.

"Let's see what's here," she suggested.

They stepped inside to a rather nondescript room. Save for a wooden bed and a chest, there was little to offer in the way of adornments. Arnim bent to open the chest, the lid springing open easily. Nicole began patting down the bed, but it didn't take long to realize there was nothing of interest here. Arnim stood, pondering the situation while Nicole threw her arms up in resignation.

"What now?" she asked.

"You don't put that type of lock on a door for no reason," he commented. "We must have missed something."

"Like what? There isn't exactly a bounty of furniture here."

Arnim cast his eyes about, taking in every detail. Nicole waited patiently, but the silence began to wear on her. She was about to speak when he held up his hand, forestalling her.

"The floor is discoloured there," he said, pointing.

She came over to examine the indicated boards. "A hidden stash, perchance?" she asked.

"Let's find out," he replied, pulling out his knife and digging the tip in between the floorboards. One of the planks popped up. "It seems the captain has a few secrets," he remarked.

As he withdrew the board, the small space beneath revealed a pouch, which he removed, spilling its contents onto the floor.

"Very interesting," said Nicole as the gold coins poured forth.

"Indeed," agreed Arnim. "What do you make of it?"

"It seems a large amount of gold for a captain."

"I would have to agree. If I made this much, I could retire."

Nicole crouched beside him, reaching forward to take a coin, examining it in the light that streamed through the windows.

"What can you tell from the coins?" asked Arnim.

"It's definitely foreign," she observed. "It's nothing like the coins they have here in Weldwyn."

"Could it be Mercerian? Or maybe from the Clans?"

"No," offered Nicole, "or at least I don't think so. The Clans speak the same language as us, don't they?"

"I believe so, why?"

"These have different symbols on them. It's not a language I recognize." She held the coin in the palm of her hand, testing its weight. "It's about the same size as one of our crowns, though. Any merchant worth his salt would take this in payment."

Arnim started gathering up the coins, returning them to the pouch. "It seems we have found our traitor."

~

The Knights of the Hound galloped across the causeway, taking the road north until they found the path they were looking for. It ran east for a short space, then turned south, where the ground sloped up gradually towards the top of the cliffs. Hayley slowed them to a trot to conserve their strength, while further up the hill, a group of soldiers was forming a thin defense. Beyond them, the catapults rained down their fire on the defenseless city.

They spread out, with Hayley and Revi in the middle. "Hold the line," she yelled, above the beating of the horse's hooves. Slowly, but surely, they climbed, a constant formation moving against a rail-thin defense. A few arrows whizzed by, one even striking Dame Levina, but the armour protected them, and the knight simply snapped off the shaft that jutted from her cape.

Revi sat low in the saddle, using his horse's head for cover, for he alone did not wear armour. Hayley cast him a glance as they pushed forward. "Are you still thinking this is a nice day?" she called.

The mage didn't answer, merely kept his head down as they rode. The enemy line grew closer, and Hayley knew this was the moment of truth. She drew her sword and raised it over her head, then pointed it forward, the signal to begin their charge. Onward the mounts surged, bringing them inexorably closer to their prey. One more flurry of arrows, and then the knights were among their enemies.

Hayley struck out with her sword, and then pushed her mount forward. The nimble beast sidestepped a soldier as she struck again, driving the blade into an enemy. She felt an arrow hit her shoulder; deflected by her armour it bounced harmlessly off into the distance. The other knights were attacking all around her. Dame Abigail struck with her mace, an underhand swing that came up into a raider's face, exploding blood and bone in a wide arc. She kept riding, her massive mount trampling the body as she advanced.

They all knew the target, the catapults, and so they rushed past most of the defenders, not bothering to destroy every soldier, only doing enough damage to push through, to make it to the siege engines that were destroying the city below. The catapults grew close, and Hayley watched in amazement as an enemy soldier, intent on loading a catapult, suddenly twitched and collapsed. She cast her eyes about to see Revi finishing a spell.

Dame Levina was struggling with a group of three men. Sir Barnsley rode to her rescue, cutting down a man as he went, and trampling another.

Chaos reigned, and before she realized it, Hayley was among the catapults, slicing down anyone who was within range. The crews started running while the knights chased after them. Suddenly, a series of sharp twangs emanated from the watchtower, and she realized that crossbows had been fired. She saw one dig into Sir Howard's arm, causing him to drop his sword. He clutched the wound but still managed to keep control of his mount. Another shot narrowly missed Hayley, sinking instead into a nearby catapult. Dame Juliet rode past, her sandy hair flowing behind her, an arrow protruding from her back. All around her, Hayley saw the effect the bolts were having.

"Back! Back!" she shouted, turning her mount and driving her horse down the hill, all the while hearing bolts fly past her. The knights followed her until they were finally out of range and came to a rest, their mounts breathing heavily. Revi, riding over to Sir Howard, cast the spell of healing. Hayley, looking around, was thankful there had been no loss to her group.

"Well, that didn't go as expected," yelled Dame Levina.

Revi, finished with Sir Howard, now rode over to Dame Juliet to examine her wound. "You're lucky," he said. "The wound missed vital organs. Hold still while I pull it out and then I'll heal you. This will hurt...a lot."

As he tugged at the bolt the Dame let out a scream of agony.

"Pulling it out like that will cause more damage," offered Dame Levina.

"It doesn't matter," said Revi, "I'm healing it anyway. This is faster." Once he removed the bolt, he began gesticulating with his hands, reciting the magic words while the wound closed up.

"What do we do now?" asked Dame Abigail.

"We stopped them for a moment," replied Hayley, "but they're already returning to the catapults; we need to take out that tower. As soon as we were among them, they started firing, and unfortunately, our armour doesn't protect us from bolts."

∼

Wounded soldiers and scared citizens were streaming past, clogging the road and making progress difficult.

"We'll never get to the Traders Gate at this rate," grumbled Arnim.

"Thank Saxnor, I thought we were headed for the docks."

"Still afraid to get wet, Nicole?"

"Don't be an arse, Arnim, you know I can't swim. Do you think this Captain Fraser will be at the gate?"

"That's what I was told. He's a seasoned warrior so when we find him, be careful, he's likely going to put up a fight."

"It's just like old times, Arnim," she responded with a smile.

He stopped short, turning on her, his face a mask of rage, "Like when you betrayed me? I think the past is best buried!" He turned his attention back to the gate and continued his progress.

Nicole fell silent, a tear running down her cheek. She struggled to find the words, to explain, but thoughts flew from her mind as they approached the gate and saw the scene that was before them.

The Traders Gate was an immense double door, held in place by a large bar dropped across it. A tremendous sound of thunder erupted as a great ram struck the door, splintering the drop bar at its centre. The defenders moved back, behind a secondary barricade, their spears and swords ready to repel the attackers, should the gate fall.

Arnim spied Captain Fraser; he was behind the barricade, holding his men in place. They all had their attention riveted on the door in front of them that shook each time the ram struck. The sounds of the attack suddenly went quiet, the enemy no longer battering the gate.

It was an intense moment of silence that Arnim broke, calling out, "Captain Fraser!"

Fraser turned to see Arnim, advancing with drawn sword, but at that precise moment the next phase of the attack began as a giant ball of flame struck the door. Another battered the guard tower on the west side of the gate, sending fragments of stone flying. Men abandoned their barricade rushing to the door, desperate to keep it closed, but whatever they had used to light their missile was burning through the wood with alarming speed.

"Hold the door at all costs," Captain Fraser yelled, then he turned and fled.

A final giant crash and the door flew into pieces, shards going everywhere. There was a lull in the fighting while the defenders looked to the opening, waiting for the enemy to come. It didn't take long until a swarm of men came forward, their weapons drawn.

Arnim was closing the distance, but when the gate fell, he dove to the ground, burning chunks of wood passing overhead. Glancing over to his left, he spotted Nicole crouching behind an upturned cart.

In mere moments, the defenders were overwhelmed and cut down, the surge of invaders rushing past him into the city. Arnim rose, trying desperately to spot Captain Fraser, but he was nowhere to be seen.

Beverly moved cautiously down the street toward the gatehouse, followed by a dozen mounted men. The base of the gate couldn't be seen from her position, but a lull in the fighting was evident from the sounds around her. She drew her sword, her men doing likewise, and waited. The rush came soon after, a veritable wave of Kurathians pouring up the street.

"We must buy the barricade some time," she yelled. "Follow me!"

They charged forth, their horses rushing into the mad mob. Lightning knocked men aside with his mass while Beverly struck left and right, her sword biting deep as she swung; the light armour of the raiders unable to stop the fury of her steel.

A sword stabbed at her from the left, while to the right a spear bounced harmlessly off of her shin guard. She smashed her sword down, using the hilt to break the haft, and then stabbed with the tip, feeling the blade pierce flesh.

The riders of Weldwyn slashed and hacked away, the sound of the conflict ringing in her ears. Lightning rose up to come crashing down in a flurry of hooves, pulverizing an attacker into a red mess. The masses continued to flow in from the gate, and she quickly cast a glance over her shoulder to see her own men struggling to stay in their saddles.

"Back," she yelled, "back to the barricades!"

Lightning whipped around, sideswiping another attacker while she struck out again with her sword. She urged him forward, coming to the rescue of a soldier fighting the invaders. Looking down from her mount, she recognized Sir Arnim Caster, and she held out her hand for him. Instead of taking it, he pushed a woman forward, and Beverly was stunned to see Lady Nicole Arendale. She grabbed the woman's hand, pulling the maid up behind her. Arnim had already begun sprinting north, helped by the gap in the assault caused by the horsemen. Someone tried to grab Lightning's reins, but the great beast bit down, tearing into the man's forearm. They wheeled around, and Beverly struck out once more, a wide sweep of her sword to keep the attackers at bay.

Back up the street they rushed, the others quickly joining, to the barricade where the defenders were set to stop the flood of raiders who approached. The riders cleared a small gap in the defenses, and then men rushed to move a wagon into the empty space.

"What happened?" asked an officer. "Where are the soldiers from the gate? They were supposed to fall back when the gate fell."

"This is it," she responded. "This is all we've got."

"Then Malin have mercy on us," the man prayed aloud.

All morning the reports came into the manor. Gerald had been marking the progress of the enemy in red paint, but now, as he looked down at the map, all he saw was crimson.

A warrior stumbled in, his armour covered in blood. "The Fishermans Gate holds, Commander."

"Get this man to the healer," he commanded.

"They're getting close," observed a sergeant.

"Order the men at the Fishermans Gate to fall back, or they'll be cut off from the rear. Form them here," he stabbed down with his hand. "See to it personally."

"Aye, sir," the man responded, rushing from the room.

Sophie had come to help, and now she stood, looking incomprehensibly at the marks littering the map.

"How is it going?" she innocently asked.

"They've broken two of the gates, and we'll soon have to abandon the third. We've formed up on the barricades, but the western one is weak. Beverly reports there were no survivors from the Traders Gate."

"Will they hold do you think?"

"I honestly don't know, Sophie. I think you should get Lily and prepare to escape. It won't be a pretty sight once the city's fallen."

"We'll stay," replied the maid, "to the bitter end, if necessary. What can we do to help? Both Lily and I can fight, if need be."

"No," said Gerald, "I can't ask that of you. But I will send you to Alric. Tell him to bring his men here, to the western barricade. He must charge

with his horse and drive the enemy back. If we can get the enemy to hesitate, even for a moment, then they'll lose the momentum."

"Any news from the bluff?"

"No, we've heard nothing, and the catapults are still firing. I pray to
Saxnor that Hayley hasn't failed."

~

"You all know what you have to do," said Hayley. "If we don't do it right,
there won't be another chance."

They all nodded their heads.

"Keep in formation," she continued. "We need to keep the mage covered."

"Are you sure this is going to work?" asked Abigail. "It's very dangerous."

Hayley grinned, "I've done dangerous things before. I once climbed
down into a gryphon's lair."

"Impressive," commented Sir Barnsley.

"Not as impressive as you might think," she retorted, "it wasn't home. Of
course, I didn't know that at the time."

"I find that bravery and stupidity rank equally in the annals of history,"
observed Revi.

"And which of those is this, Master Mage?" enquired Hayley.

"I'm inclined to believe the bravery side, though I suppose ultimately it
depends on if we're successful or not. The brave survive, the stupid usually
die."

"All right people," called out Hayley, "you know what to do. The objective is the tower, nothing else matters. Don't let anything get in our way and
keep the formation."

They moved out at a trot, careful to maintain a constant speed. Slowly
they climbed the hill, gradually speeding up but still holding their positions.
Revi had the hardest time, for not being a knight, he was unused to
matching someone else's pace.

Another thin line of foot soldiers stood in their way, but this time they
wisely ran at the approach of the knights.

The Knights of the Hound ignored the catapults, making a direct path
for the tower.

"Shields up!" yelled Hayley and the riders to either side raised their
shields over their heads, the better to protect them from the coming storm
of bolts.

Sure enough, as the tower grew closer, the shots began. Hayley heard
them striking the metal shields reminding her of hail hitting a clay roof. A
bolt pierced her shield, pointing menacingly at her, but luckily missing the

hand that held her defense in place. The shots grew more frequent, and she heard Dame Aelwyth groan as a bolt tore into her shoulder.

"Almost there," Hayley shouted while the knights made their last dash to the base of the tower.

Bolts came crashing down on the knights from above, with Dame Abigail taking one to the leg. Levina's horse went down, so she grabbed Sir Howard's arm as he rode past. The knights fled back down the hill, bolts chasing them the entire way.

～

Sir Arnim Caster parried a blow and struck back at a Kurathian who had reached the top of the barricade. As the blade bit deep into his stomach, the raider toppled, falling back amongst his own men. The fighting had grown ever more desperate as the enemy tried to overwhelm the defenses. The valiant captain glanced around to see reinforcements returning from the north. Beverly was holding the gap, her great horse keeping the enemy at bay, for now. The raiders were trying to wear them down by attrition; the only thing saving them was the trickle of lightly wounded defenders returning from the north. Aubrey was healing them as fast as she could, but many were too injured, and so the replacements were growing sparse.

A sudden cry of alarm to Armin's left had him turning just in time to see the makeshift wall collapse. It was as if the sea had found a hole in the breakwater; the raiders surging through. Arnim yelled for support and moved down the line in a futile attempt to stem the flood of attackers. Swords and spears jabbed at him from everywhere. He felt a weapon glide across this hip, scraping along his chainmail shirt. He swung to the side, his left-handedness taking his closest foe by surprise, ripping the man's chest, turning the ground crimson.

Armin pushed into the fray, heedless of danger. He took a stab to the leg but willed himself to ignore the pain. The attackers, sensing his fury, gave way to him, surging past to overwhelm the defenses.

～

Prince Alric sat on his horse, surveying the cavalry before him. They were a ragtag group, cobbled together from whatever people they could find. A handful were experienced horsemen, part of the garrison of this city, but many more were pulled from the militia; inexperienced and hastily equipped. He knew he must lead them into the fray, but he saw the looks of fear and dismay on their faces.

"They are a miserable looking bunch, Highness," commented Jack.

"They are more than that, Jack," he responded. "They are the last hope. We must win through today, or the city will fall."

"That would open up all of Weldwyn," acknowledged Jack. "We can't allow that to happen."

"These are desperate times, calling for desperate acts."

"What are you suggesting, my prince?" asked the cavalier.

In response, Alric drew his sword, holding it above his head, drawing everyone's attention. "Men of Weldwyn!" He stood in his stirrups as he called out. "We stand, this day, on the precipice. The entire kingdom is in peril, and only you can save it."

He looked at his men, saw determination set on their faces. "We must push the enemy back. Drive them into the sea. Let us show our Mercerian friends that the men of Weldwyn fear no foe!"

He wheeled his horse about as the troops cheered, pointing his sword toward the south. "Advance!" Alric yelled and began trotting. Jack was there, beside him, and soon he heard the echoing sounds of horses' hooves behind him. He risked a backward glance to see them, following along in one large mass. So be it, he thought; this will not be some orderly march, but a storm of revenge on those who would do his kingdom harm.

Down the avenue they continued, until the westernmost barricade came into view. He spotted where the line had broken, and he angled toward it, yelling as he did so, "For Weldwyn!"

Arnim took a spear to the right arm, grunting in pain. The attacker, his weapon now caught, collapsed as the knight's steel pierced his chest. Arnim withdrew the blade just as another raider slashed at him. It struck the cross-guard of his sword, sending a tremendous vibration up his left arm. A spear appeared out of nowhere, thrusting into the attacker's side. The final defenders had gathered to form a small knot of defiance amid the swirling chaos of the fight.

The sound of a horn rent the air moments before the fury of the cavalry descended into the melee at the barricade. Arnim was pushed aside as a horse rushed past, the rider flailing his sword about in an attempt to drive back the invaders. The horsemen flowed past Arnim like a river un-dammed, and all before them were cut down.

Jack struck left, his sword cutting into the haft of a spear, easily knocking it aside. He hit again, this time the milder resistance of flesh was his reward. His attacker shrunk back, dropping his weapon, but the cavalier pushed forward. He saw Alric, deep among the enemy, rising in his stirrups to bring his blade down onto a Kurathian's head. There were far too many invaders here, he thought, and though the small group of horsemen had pushed them back, he noticed a larger group, just beyond the barricade, forming up to rush forward.

"My prince!" he yelled, but his voice was carried away in the maelstrom of battle. He spurred his horse forward, using it as a wedge to push through the melee. Something grazed his leg, and he instinctively released his stirrups and kicked out; a grunt of pain the result as his boot met a face, and then he urged his horse forward yet again. A spear clattered against his shield, then fell to the ground. He struck to the right, forcing an opponent to give way. Alric was just before him now, but the young prince was surrounded by the enemy; attracted by his rich looking armour, no doubt.

The cavalier saw the weapon before it struck, unable to help. A raider had managed to work his way in behind Alric's horse. Now his spear tip came forward, sinking deep into the prince's side. Alric went stiff in the saddle and then toppled, falling to the right. His horse, taken aback by the change in weight, scrambled forward, confused by his rider's commands, clearing a path through the opposition. Jack rushed into the gap, intent on saving his master.

He halted, staring down at Alric as other horsemen surged past him, clearing the enemy from the area. Jack dismounted, ignoring the commotion around him, his eyes locked on the inert form of the young prince that had so changed his life.

"Your Highness," he cried out.

Alric lay on his side, a growing pool of blood staining the ground. Jack heard him groaning in pain and ran to his side. "We must get you away from here, my Lord Prince," he said.

In short order, others gathered around the fallen prince. "We can't move him," someone said, "it'll kill him."

Jack looked around, hoping beyond all hope, for some miracle.

"We must get him to the healer," said a familiar voice and Jack looked up to see one of the Mercerian Knights.

"Sir Arnim?" said the cavalier.

"Lady Aubrey can save him," said the knight, "but we must buy him some time. Can someone bind his wound?"

"I can!" offered one of the defenders, grabbing a cloak from a body and ripping it into strips.

"We'll need to fashion a stretcher of some sort to carry him," said Arnim.
"Like we use at the tournaments," offered Jack.
"If you say so, but we must hurry if he's not to bleed to death."
"Can we save him?" asked Jack.

Arnim looked directly into the cavalier's eyes, "I won't lie to you Jack, this is very serious. I don't know if Lady Aubrey has the skill, she's only an apprentice. I'm sure Revi could do it, but I don't know what's happened to him."

All throughout Riversend, people were panicking, a constant flood heading toward the northeastern gate in a bid to escape the doomed city.

Lady Nicole was trying to push her way through to Arnim when she spotted the fugitive. His head was down, his helmet discarded, but there was no mistaking the man's identity.

"Captain Fraser!" she called out.

The traitor's eyes swivelled in her direction, and then he ran, pushing through the crowd in a bid to escape.

"Arnim!" she shouted, rushing to follow, "He's over here, Fraser is over here!"

Fraser rushed into the river of people, pushing them aside in his mad dash for freedom.

Nicole turned briefly to call out Arnim's name once more, then plunged in after the captain, hot on his trail.

THIRTY-FIVE

Counter Attack

SPRING 961 MC

R evi Bloom pushed his back against the wall. The cliff was before them, looking down onto the sea, the rocks below smashed by waves. "Are you sure this is going to work?" he whispered.

Hayley put her finger to her lips and turned to the task at hand. It had been a reckless plan, to charge the tower, but somehow it had worked, or at least, part of it had worked. She and the mage were now behind the tower, looking south, out to sea while the knights retreated to the north. They had gambled that the defenders would be occupied by the activities of the knights, buying them the time they needed to complete their task. The ranger turned her attention back to the tower. It was an old structure, built of irregular stone blocks. It had built for a purpose, to watch over the coast and to that end its defenses were minimal. If not for the crossbowmen, it would scarcely offer a threat.

The mage stared intently out to sea, watching the vast armada that had been assembled. She tugged his sleeve and pointed upward; now was the time to start climbing. She gripped the coarse irregular stones with her fingers, easily finding purchase and was soon halfway up the tower. Surprised by the sound of her scabbard clattering on the stone, she froze, afraid of alerting the defenders above. Glancing down, she spotted the mage, following her. Despite his attire, he appeared equal to the task, so she turned her concentration back to the rest of her climb.

Soon, the battlements were close at hand and, perhaps, the most dangerous part of their plan. The top of the tower was flush with the wall, encircled with crenellations. She must finish the climb and get to the flat roof before being spotted, or she would face a cruel death. She paused to steel herself for the final assault.

A noise from above captured her attention, and as she looked up, a figure appeared at the wall. He was leaning in the crenel, the gap between two merlons, looking out to sea. Hayley shifted slightly to get a better grip and the tip of her bow, which was slung over her shoulder, struck the wall to her side, causing a sound.

The guard looked down, his eyes widening in surprise. He opened his mouth, but all that came forth was a yawn, and then he collapsed, disappearing from sight. She looked down at the mage, who was gripping the stone wall with his left hand and somehow gesticulating with his right.

She resumed her climb, throwing caution to the wind, for if there was anyone else on the roof, she was doomed. Her hands gripped the stone embrasure, and she hauled herself upward, squeezing between the merlons and crouching, her hand instinctively reaching for her sword. The guard lay snoring on the rooftop, and she let out a sigh of relief. She turned back to the embrasure to offer her hand to Revi and soon they were both on the roof.

"That wasn't so bad," noted the mage.

"We still have to keep them busy," she commented in return, "or did you forget that part?"

The mage grinned back, "I take it we're ready for the next step, then?"

Hayley nodded, and the mage began another spell.

"Are you sure that'll work?" she asked. "It's only a small light, will the knights be able to see it?"

When he finished his incantation, the globe of light appeared. He floated it above the tower and then began to increase its intensity. Soon, a bright light flooded the area, forcing Hayley to avert her eyes.

"How long can you keep that up?" she asked.

"As long as I need to," he smirked, "providing I can remain concentrating on it."

Revi moved to the northern face and looked out upon the top of the bluff. "I can see the knights off in the distance, they've seen the signal and are forming up now."

"Good," said Hayley. "It takes time to close the distance, they'll start sending up the crossbowmen just before they get within range." She scabbarded her blade and prepared her bow.

"Wouldn't you be better with the sword in these confines?" he asked.

"I don't intend on letting them up here at all. As soon as they poke their heads through the hatch, I'm firing."

"Let the first one through," he said. "I have an idea."

"Care to share?" she asked.

"We can't just pin them down, they'll still fire out the arrow slits in the tower. We have to get into the tower itself."

"We're only two people, I thought we were a diversion."

"We are," he replied, "but what if we could open the front door?"

"They wouldn't stand a chance against the knights," she replied. "I like your thinking. But how do we do that?"

"One step at a time," he said.

Just as they were about to open the hatch, they heard the sounds of footsteps on stone coming from below. Revi stood back, indicating that the ranger should move back further. The hatch lifted and an archer climbed out. He was dressed in light leather armour and carrying a crossbow, which he laid on the floor as he exited the hatch.

"Hello," said Revi.

The man merely blinked in surprise while Revi wiggled his fingers. The bowman knelt to pick up his crossbow and just collapsed. His companion, still on the ladder, let out a cry. He was halfway out of the hatch as an arrow took him in the back. He disappeared from view, tumbling down the ladder, hitting others as he fell.

Hayley rushed to the ladder, pointing down through the hatch with her bow, only to see a body lying at the bottom, its legs twisted in a macabre manner, while two other men nursed wounds. The ranger sent an arrow flying down the ladder, felling a man, the shaft hitting him squarely in the chest. Hayley discarded the bow and grabbed her knife, placing it between her teeth. Dropping through the hatch, she grasped the side of the ladder with both hands, her feet gripped the rails. She slid down rapidly, landing with a soft thud, then wheeled on the last man, pulling her dagger from her mouth and thrusting forward. The raider died with a complete look of confusion on his face as the blade penetrated his throat.

She was in a circular room and to her left, she saw six men. Two were occupied by events to the north, peering out of arrow slits while the rest were busy loading their crossbows using a cranking mechanism. Hayley threw her dagger, taking one unawares. He clutched his face, crying out in pain and collapsed to the floor. One of his companions dropped his crossbow and fumbled to withdraw his belt knife, but Hayley was quicker. She closed the distance, drawing her sword as she did so and stuck him in the chest.

A quarrel whisked past her as she kicked out, knocking another to the ground. She looked to her right to see one of the men turning from the arrow slit, his crossbow ready to fire, but Revi cast his light spell, the bright ball appearing directly in front of his target, filling the room with its brilliance.

Hayley struck again, slicing through a man's leg, and then backhanded another with the hilt of her sword. As both opponents fell, she looked around to see Revi gesticulating again. The remaining men dropped their weapons and raised their hands in surrender. Hayley briefly pondered what to do with them, but then Revi's casting took effect, and they were soon fast asleep.

"Should we finish them off?" she asked.

"No," he insisted, "it'll all be over by the time they wake up. We have more important things to do. The knights will be here soon, we must open the door. How high up would you say we are?"

"There's two more levels beneath us, plus the ground floor. The tower widens as we descend, there's likely a lot more men below."

"I have an idea," said Revi. "Help me get this man out of his clothes."

They began stripping off the man's armour. "Are you sure this is going to work?" asked Hayley.

"Confusion is our ally," he said, handing her a leather jerkin. "At a quick glance, they'll likely take no notice."

"What if they heard the fighting," she protested.

"Then they'd already be up here. I think they have more important things to occupy their minds."

Within a few moments, they were armoured in the rough leather of their enemy. "Come," said Revi. "We must make haste."

They slowly descended the circular staircase in the centre of the tower. The next floor opened into a similar scene while Hayley watched in fascination as the dozen or more men, who were so intent on the approaching horsemen, ignored their presence entirely. Soon, they were on the ground floor where supplies were piled up to either side of the stairwell, but the door to the tower, complete with a drop bar, stood revealed, along with a bored looking guard.

The guard had been peering through a small slit in the door, but at the sound of their approaching footsteps he turned, opening his eyes wide as they drew closer. Revi quickly gesticulated, inducing the man to yawn, but still, he drew his sword. Hayley stepped forward and slashed, then watched as he collapsed to the floor.

"What happened?" she asked. "He didn't succumb to your spell."

"No," he uttered. "I've almost exhausted my energy. Quick, move the body and remove the drop bar while I gather some things together."

Hayley did as she was bid. The bar lifted easily, and the door swung open to reveal the field beyond with the knights approaching, but she still heard the familiar sound of crossbows being fired.

"We must do something," she urged, turning her attention inward.

Revi had found some sacks that he was now pouring oil over. "Get that lantern over there lit," he said, pointing. "This won't take much to burn."

She grabbed the lantern and crouched in the doorway, pulling forth a flint and steel from her belt pouch. In no time at all she had it lit and lifted it up to observe the room in more detail.

Revi rushed toward her, running for the open door. "Don't just stand there," he shouted, "toss the damned thing and then run."

She threw the lantern toward the pile he had made and watched as it slowly burned to life. Revi grabbed her arm, pulling her outside and then dove for the ground, still grasping her. They rolled and then Revi sat up, straddling her.

"What was that for?" she asked.

Revi blushed. "I thought it was going to explode," he confessed. "I was afraid we'd be caught in the blast."

"It's just a fire, Revi," she reassured him. "We had plenty of time."

They looked back at the tower to see thick black smoke beginning to spread.

"Looks like it worked," said Hayley.

"Sorry," said Revi. "I should let you get up."

"It's all right," offered the ranger. "I kind of like the view from down here. Tell me Master Mage, is this how all mages court?"

Revi blushed again, rising to his feet. "I hardly think..." his voice trailed off.

"I'm just teasing you, Revi."

The crossbowmen were calling out in alarm as the smoke made its way up the tower. The knights, no longer molested by flying bolts, rode up and made short work of the catapults, then advanced on the tower.

"The defenders should be coming out shortly," Revi informed them.

A tremendous explosion from within the tower blew bits of debris through the doorway, creating a deadly cone of shrapnel that barely missed the mage as he bent over to help the ranger up.

"Or not," continued the mage. He turned back to the ranger, "I thought you said it's just a fire."

"Hey, now," said Hayley, "don't look at me. I'm not the expert."

Arnim, hearing Nicole's voice, had struck out after them, but the press of people slowed his progress. Now he found himself exiting the city through the northeast gate, across the drawbridge and onto the causeway. He pushed his way to the side and stood on the lip of the causeway, desperate to catch sight of his target. Peering through the throngs of people he spied Nicole first, pushing her way past carts and animals, hot on the trail of Captain Fraser. Just in front of her was the fugitive, and as Arnim watched, she called out to him. The man wheeled on her, drawing a dagger, but Nicole was just as quick. She hefted her skirt and produced her own weapon from the garter on her left leg. Now they faced each other; the crowd backing up to give them room.

Arnim jumped down from his perch, making his way toward them as quickly as he could.

Nicole struck with the blade, drawing first blood as it sliced across the back of his hand. Fraser cursed and stabbed forward, but the maid was fleet of foot, and his weapon met empty air. Again she sliced forward, this time a feint and he moved to block the blow. Her leg came up, and she kicked him in the stomach, winding him as she drove him back.

He circled his blade, daring her to come forward once more, but she held her distance, weighing her options. He was wearing chainmail, and she knew her dagger could do little to penetrate the well-made links. She would have to get in close, where she could use her mass to push the blade through the armour. She stabbed forward, driving him back and then rushed him suddenly, her dagger held before her.

Her attack was quick, but his response was faster. He parried with his own weapon, and the blade flew from her hand, to land amongst the crowd. She had only a moment to register the attack and then there was a dagger at her throat; she immediately ceased her movement.

"Go ahead," she said through gritted teeth, "get it over with."

"Oh no," he gloated, "I'm not going to kill you yet. You're going to help me get away."

"Never!" she said.

"Turn around," he commanded.

She wanted to fight, to die with the knowledge that she could defeat his purpose, but couldn't do it. She turned her back to him, and a moment later his arm was around her, the knife held at her throat. His other hand was holding her by the waist, to use as a hostage as he began backing up. From her vantage point, she could clearly see the look of horror on the crowd's faces as they watched the scene unfold before them.

The bystanders parted, and suddenly Arnim was there; his sword drawn, ready for action.

~

Arnim stepped forward, "Surrender, Fraser, it's all over."

"Not for me," the traitor responded. "You seem to forget, I have your friend here."

"You won't get away," said Arnim. "You've nowhere to run."

"I'll take my chances," he announced, his eyes casting around desperately. He took a step backwards, closer to the edge of the causeway and Arnim took a step forward to follow.

"Stay where you are," commanded Fraser, "or I'll kill her right now."

"Kill her," growled Arnim, "and your hostage is gone, and I'll cut you to ribbons."

Captain Fraser seemed to relax, a strange sense of calm coming over him. "Perhaps you're right," he said, his voice no longer strained. "I should have realized that a hostage wouldn't have worked with Mercerians, you're barbarians after all."

Arnim saw the trap, but it was too late. Captain Fraser lowered the dagger from Nicole's throat, but before Arnim could react, he pushed her to the side, sending her tumbling into the water.

"Goodbye, Sir Arnim," the man gloated, "may we never meet again." He turned, running eastward across the causeway.

Arnim saw him run, started to go after him, but then the panicked sounds of Nicole in the water pulled his attention to her plight. Her head disappeared beneath the surface, and she re-emerged only to be carried downstream. She was clearly struggling, and then her head submerged once more, her hands flailing about uselessly.

Arnim cursed, dropping his weapon. He began unbuckling his sword belt and called to the crowd, "Someone help me out of this mail."

Freed of the weight of the chainmail, he stood a moment on the low wall and then dove into the water, disappearing beneath its surface. He emerged a moment later, trying to get his bearings. The people watching from the causeway pointed downstream, and he struck out with his arms and legs, swimming toward the indicated area.

~

Nicole felt her strength failing, felt the cold of the water seeping into her bones. Her dress, now a great weight, sucked her into the depths of the river. She struggled to battle the rising panic, to surrender to the sweet bliss of death, but she couldn't fight her nature. All her life she had fought to survive; she would not submit to this fate!

Somehow she managed to break the surface, taking a ragged breath of air, but then a wave caught her, splashing into her mouth, sending sea water down her throat. She tried to call out, but her head sank beneath the waves again, the water surrounding her.

Something grabbed her, pulling her to the surface until she was floating on her back as someone dragged her toward the bank.

"I've got you, Nikki," came Sir Arnim's reassuring voice, and she thought she was in the past. Was this the Underworld, she pondered, to be forced to relive your memories?

Her foot hit bottom, and suddenly she was hauled to her feet.

A gentle hand brushed her hair from her eyes. "You're safe now," came Arnim's voice again.

Nicole blinked, her saviour's face coming into focus just before she collapsed into his arms.

~

Lady Aubrey Brandon knelt, examining a wound. The soldier was clutching his arm, his shoulder a mess of blood. She laid her blood-soaked hands on him and murmured an incantation. Flesh and bone knitted itself together while her patient's breathing grew normal once again, a sure sign that the pain had been removed.

"Get this man out of here," she called, "he's needed back at the barricade."

She saw Princess Anna moving between the patients who were laid out on the cathedral floor. She was giving them hope, holding the hands of the ones who were dying and comforting those she could.

A yell from the doorway, caused Aubrey to rise to her feet. She spotted the cavalier, Jack Marlowe, leading a procession of men who were bearing a stretcher. She rushed over, her own eyes confirming her suspicions; Prince Alric laying deathly pale between them.

"Put him down at once," she commanded as she began to examine him for wounds.

"He took one from the back, into his side," said Jack. "He's lost a lot of blood."

They lowered him carefully, stepping back to allow her access. His breathing was shallow, his skin pale and she thought at first she might be too late. She lowered her ear to his chest to hear a slight fluttering of his heart.

She began the spell, trying to pull forth all the power she could muster. Surface wounds were easy to heal, but this was something altogether different. She was still only an apprentice, and she worried it might be too much for her. The familiar tingling was in her fingers, and soon a warmth spread over her as the energy began to flow. She closed her eyes, tried to concentrate on the task at hand. The wound manifested itself in her mind; she imagined the flesh and bone knitting itself back together. She opened her eyes to see her hands, glowing brightly, infusing Alric with her magic. His body appeared to illuminate and then it slowly dissipated.

"Will he live?" came a voice.

Aubrey turned her head, too exhausted by her spell to talk. Beside her, Princess Anna knelt, holding the young prince's hand.

"I'm not sure," she stammered out, wiping a trickle of blood from her nose. "I've done all I can, but I've been healing people all day, I have no energy left. If Revi were here..."

"Revi will be here shortly," said Anna, her voice breaking.

"How can you be so sure?" asked Jack.

"The catapults have stopped," the princess replied. "The bluff has been retaken."

Jack looked down on his prince, tears running down his face, "You would have been proud of him, Princess. He led the cavalry, retook the barricade-"

Anna wheeled on him, fury in her eyes, "He's not dead, Jack. Don't talk of him as if he is!"

"Sorry, Highness," Jack said, falling silent.

"Let's get him somewhere more comfortable," said Anna, casting her eyes about for an orderly.

"No," muttered Alric. "I shall stay here, with the men."

Anna teared up, gripping his hand even tighter, "Alric, I thought I'd lost you."

"I'll be fine," the prince bravely responded. "Your healer has seen to that. What news? Have we retaken the city?"

"I'm afraid not," offered Anna. "The catapults on the bluff are silent, but the fleet is still bombarding the walls. They've broken through the Traders Gate, but we've managed to contain them."

"It's not enough," stated Alric. "They'll just keep landing more men."

"Rest, Highness," said Aubrey. "You've lost a lot of blood. Others must take up the mantle, now."

"We must destroy the fleet," declared Alric. "It's the only way to beat them."

"It's getting dark, my prince," said Jack. "The catapults will have to cease, or they risk hitting their own men. Perhaps morning will bring better news."

Anna stood. She was gazing off to the distance, deep in thought.

A holy mother was chiding a helper, "Don't put the candle there, girl, you'll set fire to the whole cathedral."

Anna stood, "Look after him, Aubrey. I have an idea." She rushed from the room, her loyal dog following behind.

The small boat rocked with the incoming tide, all but enveloped by the darkness of night.

"Hold the boat steady, Beverly," said Hayley, "or we'll hit the riverbank."

"Easier said than done," she responded. "How are you holding up, Arnim?"

The captain gave another broad stroke of his oar, "I'm keeping up with you if that's what you mean. Remind me again, whose idea this was?"

Hayley was perched at the front of the vessel, "The princess came up with it."

"And you're how comfortable with it?" asked Arnim.

Lily chattered from the back seat, and Hayley, who was the only one the mage had cast tongues on, chuckled. "Lily is ready as soon as we clear the mouth of the river, so we'll have to get our bearings quickly. As soon as the mist rises, we won't be able to see anything."

"Steer straight," complained Arnim.

"I'm trying," said Beverly, "but the current is taking us."

The boat wobbled as it hit some waves and then they saw, off in the distance, the dim light of ships' lanterns.

"Can you see the barges?" asked Beverly.

"Yes," replied Hayley. "Swing the boat a little to the right."

As the vessel turned ever so slightly, Hayley raised her hand. She sliced it down through the air, and then Lily summoned a thick mist that surrounded them, dampening even the sound of water against their hull.

"Keep rowing," said Beverly, though her voice was now little more than a whisper.

They kept rowing while Hayley peered through the gloom. It was a risky gamble, for any alarm on the side of the Kurathian fleet would spell disaster for the tiny group.

"How did we get picked again?" whispered Arnim.

"We're the only ones who know how to swim," replied Beverly, beside him. "Anyway, you've got nothing to complain about, you volunteered."

"Don't remind me," the dour captain replied.

They rowed on in silence.

With the mist enveloping them, it felt as if time stood still, for they could see no landmarks, nor any nearby ships to mark their progress. Soon, however, lanterns began to penetrate the gloom, while voices echoed through the night, though, as yet, no sound of alarm.

Onward they rowed, their arms aching with the strain. A very low groaning noise up ahead alerted them to possible danger, so they stopped rowing, merely drifting forward until the side of one of the barges floated into view. Its deck was flush, the massive catapults doubtless just above them, though from their current viewpoint, none could be seen. The hull towered above them and they held their breath.

Hayley pointed to her left, and the tiny boat turned, making its way toward the front of the barge. She picked up her bow, notching an arrow. Beverly and Arnim stopped rowing and waited, the water slapping against the hull the only sound penetrating the darkness.

Hayley noticed the massive chain fastened to the side of the vessel. It seemed to disappear into the darkness, but the ranger knew better, for the other end was attached to a collar around the great beast which pulled this siege vessel. Peering into the darkness, she waved her hand down low. The Saurian dropped the mist. It clung for only a moment, and then floated away as the prevailing wind pushed it toward shore.

On the deck above they saw the raised platform near the bow of the ship. A man was standing there, his thick woollen coat keeping him warm against the night's chill.

Hayley drew an arrow and waited. Behind her, Arnim did likewise while Beverly took both oar handles. The twang of the bow was nearly silent as an arrow sunk into the man's side. He turned in surprise but before he could raise the alarm, a second arrow flew into his chest. He staggered forward, falling from his raised perch and tumbled to the deck below. Almost instantly, the chain grew taut, followed by a low, deep-throated groan directly in front of them.

"Back up," sang out Hayley, "quickly!"

Arnim fell back into his seat, grabbing the second oar from Beverly. It was difficult to row the boat backward, for they were facing the wrong way, so they rowed in opposite directions, turning the tiny vessel in place. As soon as they had done so, they began sinking their backs into it. The mist reappeared, engulfing them in its protective fold, allowing them only to hear what was happening; the sound of water splashing as the great beast thrashed about.

They rowed their way down the length of the barge as voices yelled in alarm above them. Another roar punctured the mist, and then a splintering of wood just before the barge shuddered and violently shifted, pushing against the tiny boat.

They rowed like mad, desperate to escape the clutches of the doomed ship. They cleared the aft section of the barge just in time to see it reach high into the air. Something had split the vessel arching the bow and stern up high as the midships shattered beneath the tremendous weight of the creature. A giant wave threatened to tip their tiny vessel, sending them spinning and then a large dark mass moved past them, just barely below the surface of the water.

Shortly thereafter, a pair of moans echoed across the water.

"Head for the noise," whispered Hayley. "The other barge must be close."

Onward they travelled, still protected by the night and the mist, and when the sounds drew closer, Hayley bid them bear right. The water here was more turbulent, tossing them about unexpectedly. She gave the signal and once again Lily dropped the mist. It drifted slowly away, revealing the long neck of an immense creature only a stone's throw from their position. It struggled against the iron collar which bound it to its burden, while beyond it, the second creature bellowed, somewhere closer into shore.

The sound of chanting came from the deck above. Hayley looked up to see a woman dressed in an exquisitely embroidered gown, waving her hands in the middle of a spell. While the chained creature began to calm Hayley grabbed her bow. The arrow was no sooner knocked than she let it fly. It struck the mage in the shoulder, doing little damage, but the spell was broken. A long neck appeared out of the darkness, the creature plucking the woman from her perch. A scream pierced the night as she was pulled out over the water, and then the second creature used its mouth to grab hold of her flailing legs. There was a sickening noise, like the snapping of a twig as the body was pulled in half.

The harnessed creature began thrashing about in an attempt to break the chains. Hayley quickly took her bearings and guided the boat onward. They had been lucky in the first part of the plan, but now came the more dangerous element.

Without the siege engines, the invaders had little chance of doing more damage to the city, but the gates had already been breached. They knew that, come morning, the rest of the soldiers would disembark, and then the final onslaught would begin. The barges had been anchored within range of the gates, but the reinforcements consisted of a large host of sailing ships, lay at anchor just beyond the barges. They rowed toward them, closing the distance as quickly as possible.

"Get the fire going," called Beverly.

Hayley crouched in the bow, trying to shelter herself against the wind. Steel struck flint, a tiny spark falling to the deck, but it was quickly blown away by the southerly wind. People yelled in the distance, drawn to the rails by the sound of the barge splintering beneath its onslaught.

"Almost there," cried Beverly.

"It won't catch," complained Hayley.

A tiny spark appeared once more and this time, thank Saxnor, the fire took hold. The ranger lifted the burning fuse, ready to start the process.

"Wait a little further," suggested Beverly. "We have to get as close as we can. Get ready to go overboard."

The boat rolled as a wave hit it and the ranger struggled to hold onto the fuse. It fell to the deck, to ignite the oil-soaked cloth that had been prepared.

"Go!" yelled Hayley.

They carefully lowered themselves into the water, for they surely didn't want to upset the boat and extinguish the flame.

Beverly felt the water engulf her as the current tried to pull her beneath the waves to an eternal slumber. Kicking out with her legs, she struggled back to the surface, thankful for once that she did not have her armour on. As she flipped her head to clear the hair from her face, she saw the flames climbing higher as the little boat floated inexorably toward its target. Arrows were loosed from above to thud into the rowboat, but, as if in answer, the flames simply grew higher.

Sailors and warriors alike were yelling and screaming on deck as their panic grew. She watched the men jump from the ship as the rowboat passed beneath the bow. The sail mounted on the bowsprit was furled, but that failed to protect it from the flames that began to engulf it. The fire roared to life, spreading down the bowsprit to reach the tarred rigging.

Beverly looked about, trying to get her bearings. A brilliant flash drew her gaze back to the ill-fated ship. The fire had rushed to the other masts; the entire vessel was now ablaze.

"I knew Revi could do it!" cried a voice.

She turned to see Hayley swimming toward her.

"Revi?"

"Yes," replied the ranger, spitting out some water, "he packed the boat."

"Where's Arnim?" she called back.

"Just behind me," the ranger replied.

The ships were panicking now, and even over the roar of the fire, they heard the sounds of confusion as Kurathians desperately struggled to distance themselves from the flames. Beverly couldn't see through the darkness, but a horrific grinding noise informed her that at least two ships had collided in their haste to escape a fiery doom.

THIRTY-SIX

Aftermath

SPRING 961 MC

G erald stood on the wall, looking out to sea. The wreckage of the
barges had washed ashore, though there was no sign of the great
beasts that had pulled them. Six ships had burnt, but many more had been
damaged in their rush to escape. Even now they were sailing south, away
from this land and the fearsome defenders of Weldwyn.

"It worked," he said out loud.

"Of course it worked," remarked Anna. She was feeding the birds that
had gathered on the wall. "Why wouldn't it have worked?"

"It was a gamble," he said.

"There was nothing else we could do," she replied, tossing some seeds
across the walkway. The gulls descended on their new food supply with
gusto, but a lone blackbird watched intensely from the parapet.

"What are you doing?" asked Gerald, turning at the sound of the birds.

"Enjoying nature," she responded. "It has been rather hectic of late."

"How is Prince Alric?" he asked.

"Revi says he'll make a full recovery."

"I thought you'd be with him."

"I was, but he's sleeping."

"I thought his wounds were grievous. How did he last long enough for
Master Bloom? He was on the bluff."

"Lady Aubrey used the very last of her energy to slow the bleeding," she
explained. "I sense a great career ahead for her, though I doubt Revi would
admit it."

Gerald lapsed into silence and returned his gaze to the sea.

"Do you think they'll return?" Anna asked.

"I doubt it. They'll never be able to surprise us again. I'd love to know how they got onto the bluffs."

"They had an inside man," she said.

"Yes," he agreed, "but who?"

"It was Captain Fraser," she replied.

"How do you know it was him?"

"There was only a few men who it could have been so I sent Arnim to check out their rooms. Care to guess what he found?"

"I'm guessing no Captain Fraser," supplied Gerald.

"No, but he did find a rather large sum of foreign coins. I'm guessing he never had a chance to recover his bounty before he fled."

"So he got away?"

"Yes, unfortunately. His description will be sent all across the kingdom. He's a wanted man now."

"A shame," said Gerald, "I would have loved to know who was behind this. It seems unlikely for the Kurathians to attack the city like this all on their own."

"I agree," she said. "It would have cost a fortune to mount an expedition like this. Whoever hired them must have large reserves of gold."

"That rules out the Norlanders, they're pretty much broke as far as kingdoms go."

"Yes," she agreed, "and the Clans are no better off. Someone else is pulling the strings."

"So there's another player," he mused, "someone we haven't encountered yet."

"It would appear so," she said, then lapsed into silence.

The wind picked up slightly, driving the gulls away temporarily. The large blackbird kept his perch, eyeing Anna.

"What have we here?" called out Revi.

They both turned to see the mage approaching, clutching the edge of his robes to stop them from blowing up.

"Just feeding the birds," said Anna.

"You seem to have found a rather unusual one there," noted the mage.

Anna looked at the blackbird. "I named him Jamie," she said. "It seems to suit him. He doesn't eat much, but he seems to like watching me. Perhaps he wants to eat me?"

"He's a fine specimen," continued Revi.

"What's that supposed to mean?" asked Gerald. "Are you becoming an expert on birds now, Master Bloom?"

"It means," continued the mage, "that he'd likely make a good familiar."

"Familiar?" said Anna.

"Yes, an animal companion," added Revi.

"Albreda has those," she said, "like her wolves."

"More than that," the mage retorted. "A mage can see through the familiar's eyes and can communicate through him."

"More like Albreda's hawk, then," said Anna.

"Precisely," he agreed.

"Fascinating. How, exactly, does he become a familiar?

"I cast a spell," said Revi. "If he's exceptional enough, we would be bonded."

"Does every mage have a familiar?" asked Gerald.

"No," explained Revi, "it's actually quite rare."

"Why is that?" asked the old warrior.

"Although a familiar grants some abilities to the caster, it comes with a price. If the familiar should die, part of the mage would die with him, leaving him weaker. Few choose that option."

"So will you try to take Jamie, here, as your familiar?" she asked.

"Jamie?" Revi enquired.

"That's what I named him," she reminded him.

"Well, with your permission, I shall try," he replied.

"Go ahead, Revi," she said. "I'm eager to see what happens."

Revi Bloom closed his eyes, holding his arms out to his sides. He began murmuring the words of magic while his hands started to move, tracing intricate movements through the air. Small lights appeared to emanate from his fingertips, leaving the air swirling with hues of blue and amber.

Gerald and Anna watched, enthralled by the process. The spell appeared to go on forever, and they wondered if perhaps the young mage had fallen into a trance, but then he snapped open his eyes and ceased his murmuring.

"It worked," said Revi.

"Nothing seems to have changed," remarked Gerald. "Are you sure?"

"Everything has changed," said Revi.

The bird flew into the air, flying in a circle and then headed out to sea. Revi closed his eyes and gasped. "I can see through his eyes," he said. "It's like I'm flying over the sea myself."

"Where did Jamie go?" asked Anna, caught up in the mage's excitement.

"His name's Shellbreaker," he replied, "and he's flying south, across the water. I can see the fleeing ships in the distance; I can even make out faces. His eyesight is incredible!"

"So you can follow him forever?" she asked.

"No, there's a range limit, but as I grow in power, so, too, will my range."

They stood, watching the young mage with interest. It was evident when the bird was swooping, for Revi would crouch as if expecting to land somewhere.

"Hello," called out a voice.

The mage turned, his concentration interrupted. He looked unhappy at first, but when he saw it was Hayley, his face split into a smile.

"It seems we've finally found something that can distract Revi, other than magic," observed Gerald.

"So it would seem," agreed Anna. "What brings you to the wall, Hayley?"

The ranger reached into her tunic, "We've received news from Merceria," she said, handing over a folded note.

Gerald took the note, unfolding it with great care. It bore the seal of the Royal House, and he showed it to Anna before reading its contents.

"What does it say?" asked Anna.

Gerald lowered the note. "We've been summoned home. King Andred has died," he announced. "Your brother, Henry, is to be crowned king."

"I don't want to go," she said. "I'm enjoying it here."

"It's a Royal Summons, Anna, even you can't refuse that. We must prepare for the return journey."

"Very well," Anna said, turning to look out to sea. "Just let me have one last look at the water."

Gerald watched Anna as she gazed to the south. A tear had formed and now ran down her face. He turned away from her.

"You'd best get back, Hayley, there'll be arrangements to be made."

"Of course, Gerald. I'll see to it myself. Will the princess be all right?"

"She'll be fine," he responded, though in truth he knew she would deeply miss this foreign land and the people that lived here.

THIRTY-SEVEN

Farewell

The return journey from Riversend had been broken only by a brief stay in Summersgate. They left the Weldwyn capital on their way eastward, but instead of returning through Falford, they chose to head directly east, toward Kingsford. Now they waited, while a Mercerian barge poled across the river to take them back to their home.

"It's hard to believe we're leaving," commented Gerald. "We've been here so long."

"A lot has happened," said Anna. "It seems like a lifetime ago when we left Merceria."

Gerald looked to the barge; it drew near the bank, and people were scrambling with ropes to tie it off. He turned his gaze back to Anna to see her smiling as Alric and Jack approached.

"Anna, Gerald," said the prince, nodding his head in greeting.

"Have you come to say goodbye?" asked Anna.

"Yes," he admitted, "though I wish it were not so. I will miss you terribly, Anna."

"And I, you," she confessed.

"Shall I give you two some privacy?" asked Gerald.

"No, Gerald," replied Alric, "not yet, there's something I want to talk about with Anna, and I know how much she values your counsel."

"What is it, Alric?" asked the princess.

In answer, Alric held out his right hand, palm upward and waited. Jack dutifully placed a scroll case in his hand, its surface richly decorated with gold. Alric took it, cradling it in both hands for a moment as he struggled to find the words. A calmness fell over his face, and he smiled, handing the item to Anna.

"I spoke with my father, and he thinks it a sound idea," he mysteriously explained.

Gerald could almost see Anna's pulse quicken, but she put on a calm demeanour. "What idea might that be?" she asked.

Alric continued his speech, "It's a message from my father to King Henry, proposing a union through marriage. If your brother agrees, we would be wed. I will leave it up to you if you wish to deliver this missive. If you should choose to decline, toss it in the river and we shall speak of it no more."

"Were it my choice," she revealed, "there would be no doubt, but only my brother, King Henry can make that decision. I shall deliver it to him and pray to Saxnor that he sees the wisdom in it."

"Is he likely to agree?" asked Alric.

"He'd be a fool not to," interrupted Gerald, who then blushed at his intrusion. "Sorry," he added, "ignore me."

Anna, who had smiled at Gerald's outburst, continued, "Were it my father, I would have had no doubt he would have refused, but I've always gotten along well with Henry. I have hope he'll be amenable to the proposal."

The two royals stared longingly into each other's eyes. Gerald turned, to face those assembled nearby. "Lady Beverly," he called out, "would you please give the order to give these two some privacy?"

Dame Beverly complied, and everyone turned away from the young couple. Only Tempus refused, barking at the command and wagging his tail.

Anna leaned forward and kissed Alric, the gentle touch of their lips lingering for just a moment.

"It's time for me to leave," announced Anna. "Know that, regardless of what happens in the future, I shall never forget you."

She withdrew and tapped Gerald on the shoulder. Her dearest friend turned back around.

"It's time to go, Gerald."

Alric watched them walk down to the waiting barge.

"And I shall never forget you, Anna," he said softly.

He watched her as she was helped aboard the waiting vessel.

Jack came up to stand beside him, "Do you think King Henry will approve the marriage?"

"I pray so," answered Alric. "All my life I've wondered about my place at court, but all that changed when Anna came to Weldwyn. I have a hard time believing the Gods would let me find her only to take her from me."

"You must have faith," replied Jack.

~

The barge pulled away from the river bank, toward Kingsford, and Gerald watched as Prince Alric and his retinue remained on the shore. They had spent more than a year in Weldwyn, but now he wondered what the future might bring. Beverly came up to stand beside him.

"You seem rather at ease for someone who hates water?"

"Being stuck in a cocoon aboard a ship for days on end seems to have cured me of that, although I don't recommend it as a way to get over your fears," he chuckled.

"I'll keep that in mind for the future," quipped Beverly.

"Perhaps now that we're heading home, things will quiet down."

"Agreed. I'm going to miss Weldwyn," she said, "but it'll be nice to be back on friendly soil."

"Yes," he agreed, "though I must say I was impressed with the food. They did feed us exceptionally well."

"I daresay too much," she teased. "Your armour's gotten a little tight of late."

Gerald laughed. It was good to finally be able to relax.

"I wonder what they made of us?" he mused.

"I suspect they were surprised to find we weren't all monsters with horns."

"Why would you say that?"

"They've made us into villains for centuries. When we arrived, they were fearful of war, but we really aren't so different after all."

"True," Gerald admitted, "any one of them could pass for a Mercerian."

"Except, perhaps, for Jack," offered Beverly.

"Oh, I don't know. There are lots of knights in Merceria who are just like him."

"True enough," Beverly admitted, "but at least Jack shut up when he was told."

"You liked him, didn't you?" asked Gerald.

"I respected him, but I'll be glad to get home."

"We're going to Wincaster, not Bodden," he warned.

"True, but we'll get there eventually," she said with a faraway look to her eyes.

They fell into a companionable silence, both staring over the rail. The barge moved slowly, and Gerald could still make out Alric on the far shore.

"It feels like we're all going our separate ways," Beverly mused out loud.

"How so?"

"Well, Aubrey's going back to Hawksburg and Hayley has asked to visit her uncle. Even Lily is leaving us."

"Lily? Where's she going?"

"Revi's asked her to return to Uxley to examine the underground temple again. He thinks he's close to making a big discovery."

"He always thinks he's about to make a big discovery. He needs to discover what's under his very nose."

Gerald turned around to look behind him. The mage was holding his arm out, waiting for Shellbreaker to land, while he was chatting with Hayley, who stood beside him, watching the bird as it circled the barge.

"It seems he has," added Beverly.

"So Aubrey and Hayley are both leaving us. How long will they be gone for, do you suppose?"

"We likely won't see Aubrey for some time. She'll be working on perfecting her spells. Hayley will only be gone for a few days, her uncle lives on a farm just outside of Wincaster. It feels like all my friends are leaving me."

"Not all of us, Beverly. There are still some of us here."

The redheaded knight smiled, "Yes, you're right. Thank you for reminding me, Gerald."

"That's what I'm here for," he responded.

"Do you think it was worth it?" she asked.

"Worth it?"

"Yes, all the effort. Do you think it will have any long-lasting effects?"

Gerald thought it over before replying. The prince was just one of many in the distance now, but still, the royal eyes watched them.

"I think," he finally said, "that both sides have gained in this exchange. We've learned more about their culture and they, ours. Had we not undertaken this journey, it might well have been war. As it is, both realms came away with a newfound respect for each other."

"I never thought of it that way," Beverly admitted. "What do you think was our greatest gift to them?"

Gerald glanced about the barge, his eyes finally settling on Anna. She had grown so much in the last year, and now he saw a young woman where the young girl had been such a short time ago. She was staring back at the western bank where Alric sat on his horse, returning her gaze.

"Prince Alric has received the greatest gift of all," he said.
"What's that?" asked Beverly.
"The rarest of treasures; the heart of the crown."

Epilogue

SUMMER 961 MC

The Royal Procession was welcomed back to Wincaster with an escort of fifty knights leading them through the streets to the Palace, where they were met by King Henry, himself. They entered the great hall to find it packed with guests for a joyous celebration. Many speeches were made as the food was served; even Henry stood to propose a toast.

"Lords and ladies," he began, "my loyal subjects, we have gathered here this day to welcome the return of my dear sister, Anna, on the triumphant conclusion of her diplomatic visit to Westland."

Gerald raised his goblet. It was funny how easily they slipped back into calling it 'Westland'.

"I propose a toast," the king continued, "to Princess Anna and her companions."

Everybody rose, with Gerald scrambling to his feet to join them, cheering as they knocked their cups together, then sat, waiting while the food was brought out. Wild boar, deer and beef crowded the table, along with other, stranger meats. Gerald filled his plate to overflowing and dug in. The succulent juices dripped down his chin, and he absently wiped it on his sleeve. He watched Anna chatting to her brother while she dug into the roast fowl. Even Tempus was happy, having been tossed a shank of beef.

All around him were the Knights of the Hound, enjoying their reward for a job well done. Even the mage, Revi Bloom, joined in. Only Lady Nicole declined the offer, for she had come down with a cold. She sat, nursing her nose with a kerchief, while those around her indulged. She did not seem to be enjoying herself at all, and when a plate was offered to her, she turned her head, her stomach obviously protesting at the smell.

Gerald finished chewing and grabbed his cup, intending to make a toast. He tried to stand, but his legs were numb. Casting his eyes about the room, he caught sight of Beverly, her head falling to the table. From the sides of the room, he saw soldiers moving, their weapons drawn. He tried to make out what was happening, but his mind was foggy. He watched, helplessly, as one by one the Knights of the Hound were mysteriously felled. His eyes slowly turned to Anna, to see her in a similar state. Standing just behind Anna and Henry was a woman; her hand resting on the king's shoulder. His vision began to blur, but just before the haze completely overwhelmed his sight, he made out her face; Lady Penelope, the old king's mistress. King Henry laughed as guards grasped his arms, and then everything turned black.

Share your thoughts!

If you enjoyed this book, share your favourite part! These positive reviews encourage other potential readers to give the series a try and help the book to populate when people are searching for a new fantasy series. And the best part is, each review I receive inspires me to write more in the land of Merceria and beyond.

Thank you!

How to get Battle at the River for free

Paul J Bennett's newsletter members are the first to hear about upcoming books, along with receiving exclusive content and Work In Progress updates.

Join the newsletter and receive *Battle at the River*, a Mercerian Short Story for free: PaulJBennettAuthor.com/newsletter

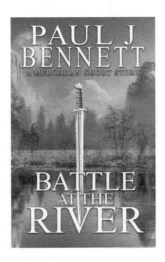

An enemy commander. A skilled tactician. Only one can be victorious.

The Norland raiders are at it again. When the Baron of Bodden splits their defensive forces, Sergeant Gerald Matheson thinks that today is a day like any other, but then something is different. At the last moment, Gerald recognizes the warning signs, but they are outnumbered, outmaneuvered, and out of luck. How can they win this unbeatable battle?

If you like intense battle scenes and unexpected plot twists, then you will love Paul J Bennett's tale of a soldier who thinks outside the box.

A few words from Paul

When I first started thinking about Heart of the Crown, I knew I needed to introduce Alric; a young man who, like many, doesn't know his place in the world. As the book unfolds he learns more about himself as he struggles with his role in society and his obligations to the throne of Weldwyn.

The relationship between Alric and Anna develops in a way that is not the main focus of the story, but is woven seamlessly throughout. While they come from completely different backgrounds; Alric from a life of privilege, whereas Anna has lived in isolation, they soon find common ground and, like many people, grow to respect each other.

This tale is much more than that of a prince and princess, however, for the dark forces that have remained hidden for so long are now emerging to threaten the fabric of their lives.

The story will continue in Shadow of the Crown.

Many people helped mold this tale, allowing it to grow from its original form, to a fully developed novel. Once again I must thank Christie Kramburger for the wonderful cover. I would also like to thank our Alpha reader, Brad Aitken, who kept reminding us when we forgot about Revi Bloom (the character he played in the original RPG) and Jeffrey Parker and Stephen Brown for their inspiration into the characters of Armin Caster and Jack Marlowe.

I owe a debt of gratitude to my Beta readers who were instrumental in bringing more depth to this story and characters. Thank you to: Stuart Rae, Rigel Chiokis, Tim James, Paul Castellano, Mark Tracy, Jim Burk, Marie Aitken, Laurie Bratscher, Amanda Benentt, and Stephanie Sandrock.

As ever, I must thank my wife, Carol Bennett, for her unending support and exuberance for this series and her excellent work as editor, marketer, social media expert and a host of other roles that she has performed, allowing me to concentrate on writing.

Last, but certainly not least, I must thank you, the reader of this book. We have been pleasantly surprised by the popularity of the series, and Carol and I enjoy reading each review that you post.

About the Author

Paul Bennett emerged into this world in Maidstone, Kent, England at the beginning of the 60's, then immigrated to Southwestern Ontario with his family six years later. In his teen years, Paul discovered military models, leading him to serve in the Canadian Armed Forces. Around the same time, he was introduced to role-playing games in the form of Dungeons & Dragons (D & D). What attracted him to this new hobby was the creativity it required; the need to create realms, worlds and adventures that pull the gamers into his stories.

In his 30's, Paul started to dabble in creating his own role-playing system, using the Peninsular War in Portugal as his backdrop. His regular gaming group were willing victims, er, participants in helping to play test the new system. A few years later he took his role-playing system and added additional settings; including Science Fiction, Post-Apocalyptic, World War II, and the all-important Fantasy Realm.

The beginnings of Servant to the Crown originated three years ago when he began a new fantasy campaign. For the world of Merceria, he ran his adventures like a TV show; with seasons that each had twelve episodes, and an overarching plot. After the campaign ended, he was inspired to sit down to write his first novel. He knew all the characters, what they had to accomplish, what needed to happen to move the plot along. 124,000 words later, Servant of the Crown was written!

Paul has mapped out a whole series of books in the land of Merceria and is looking forward to sharing them all with his readers over the next few years.

CPSIA information can be obtained
at www.ICGtesting.com
Printed in the USA
LVHW040826070719
623349LV00004B/486